In for
a Dime

In for a Dime

A Novel

Book 2 of The Tildon Chronicles

JOHN JANTUNEN

ECW PRESS

Published by ECW Press
665 Gerrard Street East
Toronto, Ontario, Canada M4M 1Y2
416-694-3348 / info@ecwpress.com

Cover design: Michel Vrana

LIBRARY AND ARCHIVES CANADA CATALOGUING
IN PUBLICATION

Title: In for a dime : a novel / John Jantunen.

Names: Jantunen, John, 1971- author.

Identifiers: Canadiana (print) 20220131201 |
Canadiana (ebook) 2022013121X

ISBN 978-1-77041-615-4 (softcover)
ISBN 978-1-77305-916-7 (ePub)
ISBN 978-1-77305-917-4 (PDF)
ISBN 978-1-77305-918-1 (Kindle)

Classification: LCC PS8619.A6783 I5 2022 |
DDC C813/.6—dc23

This book is funded in part by the Government of Canada. *Ce livre est financé en partie par le gouvernement du
Canada.* We acknowledge the support of the Canada Council for the Arts. *Nous remercions le Conseil des arts
du Canada de son soutien.* We acknowledge the support of the Ontario Arts Council (OAC), an agency of the
Government of Ontario, which last year funded 1,965 individual artists and 1,152 organizations in 197 communities
across Ontario for a total of $51.9 million. We also acknowledge the support of the Government of Ontario through
the Ontario Book Publishing Tax Credit, and through Ontario Creates.

PRINTED AND BOUND IN CANADA   PRINTING: MARQUIS   5 4 3 2 1

To Jack

Dear camerado! I confess I have urged you onward with me,
and still urge you, without the least idea what is our destination,
Or whether we shall be victorious, or utterly quell'd and defeated.

Walt Whitman

1

They'd been following the flashing blue light atop a snow-plough driving north on Highway 60 for over an hour. The signs passing by at intervals placed the speed limit at *90 kph*, though the plough had rarely topped sixty. The highway's two lanes had just opened up into a third to allow for passing and the incessant fidget of Crystal's fingers on the steering wheel was giving Deacon every indication that she was at least considering making a move but was deterred from this by the three-foot-tall windrow churned up in the plough's wake. A billowy mist all but engulfed the truck and whorls of spiralling white battered the Land Rover's windshield, resembling not so much snowflakes as an endless barrage of powdered sugar.

For most of the drive Deacon had been inching his way through the film script Crystal had thrust into his lap just after they'd passed the *We Already Miss You!* billboard Tildon's Chamber of Commerce had erected on the side of the road to complement the *Your Gateway To Summer* sign they'd placed ten kilometres to the south. It was a film adaptation of *A Precious Few*, the ninth of George Cleary's fictions and a book that Crystal and her husband, Ward Swanson, had been trying to bring to life on the silver screen practically since the day they'd met, some eight years earlier. Reading in the car always made Deacon queasy and the blue light strobing across the page wasn't much helping matters. Nor, for that matter, was the script itself. He'd only managed to get to page 36 but that was enough for him to glean that the only similarity between it and the novel was the title, the setting and a few of the characters' names. All in all it was reading like some cheap horror flick, heavy on the cheese, and from what Deacon had read thus far it was making the film based on George's *A Bad Man's Son* look like a cinematic masterpiece, though *Der Wüstling* was anything but.

There was no doubt in Deacon's mind that if George knew what his granddaughter and her husband were up to, he'd be rolling over in his proverbial grave. That thought as much as the motion sickness was making Deacon feel like he was going to hurl at any moment and so when he felt his Samsung S10 vibrating in his jacket pocket he took that as a more than welcome excuse to take a break.

The text on the phone's screen read: *It has begun again. D.*

The caller was *Unknown* but the *D.* left little doubt in Deacon's mind that Dylan had sent it and he was overcome with the same creeping dread as he'd had sitting in the church's front pew before George's funeral, some ten years previous. He'd only been staring at the text for a moment before Crystal asked, "What's the matter, Deacon?"

He looked up from his phone, expecting to hear sirens. But the only sounds were the seesaw squeak of windshield wipers and the musical saw, like something out of an old horror movie, warbling out of the SUV's speakers — the latest track on a playlist of demos Ward had sent her from a half-dozen composers he was considering for the film.

It was three hours past sunset and the sky, darkened by clouds, resided above them as a fathomless expanse of charcoal black. Aside from the intermittent spot of flashing blue, Deacon couldn't see anything beyond the glare refracting from the Land Rover's headlights. In its fluorescent sheen, Crystal's expression betrayed a tremulous concern in perfect sync with Deacon's mood and the music, though from the way her right hand kept wandering to the bump pressing out from within the folds of her unzipped parka, Deacon supposed she was more concerned for the safety of her unborn child than with anything he'd just read.

"You okay?" Crystal prodded when he hadn't answered within a couple of breaths. "You look like you've seen a ghost."

It was a question begging for an answer, but he hadn't the faintest idea of how to explain why it seemed like maybe he had, so instead he answered, "It's nothing. Just work."

"Work? But it's New Year's Eve."

Plenty of answers to that sprung to mind. The foremost among them was, "The truth never takes a night off," a line from a movie he'd once seen, said by some hotshot investigative journalist to his girlfriend when he'd begged off dinner with her parents. The journalist was on the trail of a corrupt cop, or maybe it was a serial killer, Deacon couldn't remember which. Both could have equally applied to the text but hardly to Deacon's position as the lead reporter, and owner, at a small-town newspaper and he held his tongue, instead looking back at the screen.

There were thirty-two unanswered messages below Dylan's. The second-to-most-recent was from Gabe, the *Chronicle*'s newly appointed Managing Editor, and simply asked, *Deacon?* It was from 7:52 — an hour and a half ago. Deacon had ignored it at the time because he hadn't been able to summon the will to explain why he'd just up and disappeared in the middle of snow-blowing the driveway of George's old house on Baker Street, which Gabe and his wife, Cheryl, rented from Deacon. He thumbed the snapshot of Gabe's cherubic face beside the message, as much to distract himself from Dylan's text as it was so that he could assure Gabe he was all right.

While he was waiting out four rings, Crystal was back to casting him fleeting glances, less skittish now than slightly amused, as if this was yet another ruse to get out of going with her, the subtle implication being that nothing short of an avalanche could possibly warrant their turning back now.

"There you are," Gabe answered in lieu of his usual "What's up, boss?" (itself a refinement of "What's up, chief?"; a habit Cheryl had cured him of within a few short weeks of his taking over the paper, chastising him for cultural insensitivity though it was clear he'd only ever meant it in the journalistic sense). "I was about to send out a search party."

"I'm with Crystal," Deacon answered.

"Crystal?" Gabe asked, momentarily confused. Then: "You're actually going to that thing?"

"It's not like I had much of a choice."

He threw a scornful glance Crystal's way but she was bent forward, straining for any sign of the blue light, which had since vanished into the billowing haze, and didn't notice.

There was a pause on the other end of the line, Gabe considering that, and then:

"Well, you did say you always wanted to see the place." That much was true, since George had used the Swanson family's northern retreat as the setting for *A Precious Few*, though that seemed of little consolation to Deacon now. "And who knows, you might actually have fun."

"Stranger things have happened, for sure."

"It'll be good for you to get out of town for a few days, anyway."

It was exactly what Crystal herself had said when she'd shown up at the house, enticing him to come along after he'd used every excuse he could think of not to, all sweet and cajoling, smiling and batting her eyes in playful self-mockery of the way she used to act whenever she invited him to a party back in high school: "It'll be good for you to get out of town for a few days. It'll be fun, I promise."

He'd answered, "Really, I can't," firmly enough that he hoped it would put an end to the matter.

"You say so."

In hindsight it was hard not to hear in that an inflection of her brother, who'd often said the same thing when Deacon had been on the wrong side of a losing argument with him. And there she was, wearing a carbon copy of Dylan's shit-eating grin as she lashed out her hand, snatching at the drape of his hair, grabbing a fistful and winding two fingers' worth around her knuckles almost to his scalp, dragging him wincing and cursing towards the Land Rover parked on the road.

It might make a funny story someday but he wasn't quite ready to laugh at it yet and, by way of changing the subject, asked, "How's things on your end?"

"Well, the town's still buried under ten feet of snow . . ." Gabe answered.

"Nothing odd just happen?"

"Odd?"

"I don't know. Out of place."

"Aside from you up and vanishing . . ."

Deacon could hardly argue with that.

"What about the power?" he asked, sidestepping. "Has it come back on yet?"

5

"Nope. And that is a little odd. They always make sure we get back on right quick, since we're on the same grid as the hospital. Storm of the Century, we sure got that right, huh?"

It had been the headline on the front page of last week's paper, what the Environment Canada meteorologist Deacon had spoken to called the confluence of weather fronts tracking in from the north, east and west, dumping snow at a rate of almost two feet a day for six days straight and spreading its reach as far as the Texas panhandle. The meteorologist, as he often did whenever Deacon spoke to him, had then gone into his prophet-of-doom routine, warning that they could expect the frequency of these kinds of "weather events" to increase exponentially over the next few decades and since it was already too late to do anything about that, then maybe it was best we accepted the fact and started preparing for the worst. He was never specific about what that might entail and he'd sign off with a bombastic, "But then nobody ever listens to me. I don't even know why I bother talking anymore!" Click.

In the article, Deacon had omitted any mention of the meteorologist's dire prognostications, instead advising his readers what precautions they might take to make sure they were still around to dig themselves out on the other side, the foremost being, *Whatever you do, stay off the highways!* It was a warning well reflected in the vehicle's dashboard monitor — the line designating Highway 60 on the GPS was flashing crimson on either side of the Rover's slowly creeping green arrow.

On the other end of the phone line, a storm of no less furious intent was rising towards a crescendo — a wailing cry of such piercing volume that it made Deacon ease the phone a notch away from his ear. A voice he recognized as Cheryl's then pierced the din.

"I'm done," she said perfunctorily and the wailing increased a notch, her and Gabe's infant daughter, Adele, crying out with renewed vigour, watching her mother, no doubt, walking away.

"Sounds like you got your hands full," Deacon said.

"Damned diaper rash. It's like we've been wiping her ass with sandpaper."

"I'll leave you to it, then. Give my best to Cheryl."

"Will do."

He pressed *End* and thought about calling Grover Parks, who'd retired as the *Chronicle*'s Managing Editor six months ago, then remembered he was visiting his daughter in Vancouver. He scrolled down his list of contacts until he'd reached Tawyne, who, the one time he'd called him that, had rebuffed him, grim-faced, with "Only my dad calls me that," using the present tense though his father, René, had been dead for three years by then. Deacon had called him Kiefer or Keef ever since but for reasons of his own always thought of him as Tawyne and had entered it as such in his contacts. He stared at the name for a moment, knowing the boy was staying with his aunt Jean up on the reserve over the holidays and thus wouldn't be in any better position than Gabe to tell him if anything strange had just happened in Tildon.

The memory of Dylan at George's funeral saying, "Buck up son, we ain't even hardly yet just begun," rebounded in his thoughts as clear as if he'd delivered his cryptic warning yesterday and not a decade ago. In the interval, Deacon had left Mesaquakee only a half-dozen times, the last when he'd driven out to the Calgary Stampede with an ex-girlfriend, Laney, because she'd always wanted to do so. That was three years ago and it seemed no mere coincidence that Dylan would have sent him the text on the very night Crystal had disrupted his self-imposed exile.

Just as likely though, he told himself, it was simply Dylan yanking his chain, as he had at irregular intervals, feeding him signs that the day when "it" would begin again was ever close at hand. All of those had amounted to nothing more than an impending sense of doom risen to a fever pitch since he'd read the text and now given perfect expression by the sudden staccato screech of a violin's bow being slapped against its strings — a track that conjured a knife slashing downwards and the stifled scream of some unsuspecting victim who'd made the mistake of taking a shower with a crazed killer on the loose.

"Jesus!"

Crystal was shaking her head and scowling as she hammered at the phone secured to the dash, skipping to the next track. The violins were replaced by a few notes of *Deliverance*-style hillbilly twang plucked out on a banjo, and she hammered at the screen again, this time bringing the music to a stop altogether.

"It's all so fucking derivative! He really is trying to turn it into a goddamned —"

Unwilling for whatever reason to complete the thought, she bit her lip. Shaking her head again, her knuckles blanched white under their grip on the wheel and the Land Rover raged forward as if she meant to swerve into the passing lane, three-foot windrow be damned. If it wasn't for her third-trimester pregnancy bump, Deacon would have sworn she'd lost weight since he'd last seen her. Her cheekbones stood out as sharp as her mom's had during the third round of chemo that had again saved her life at the cost of reducing her to a near skeleton. It was a pallor Crystal seemed to have adopted as her own through less invasive means — a stealthy application of makeup that had made Deacon think she'd had her freckles surgically removed, or had simply eradicated them through sheer force of will. A certain mania had crept into her eyes, and between her devilish fray of orange curls and the caustic determination pursing her lips, she called to Deacon's mind some old-time Disney cartoon villain — Anne of Green Gables become Madame Medusa. It was an impression no doubt exacerbated by the current state of his high, reupped from the roach he'd smoked in the parking lot of the mall where Highway 11

8

intersected with the 60 while Crystal was getting herself a decaf mocha and him a double Americano at the Starbucks.

But that impression only lasted for a moment.

The reflective warning sticker on the back of the plough shimmered through the powdery mist — *Stay Back 30 Metres*. She was well within that when better sense seemed to prevail. Her expression softened and she eased her foot off the gas, the plough once again reduced to a beacon flashing blue through the white haze.

"You'll back me up, right?" she said as he was reaching for his takeout cup in the holder below the monitor. There was a time, not so long ago, when the delicate plead in her voice and more so the crimp to her lips would have stirred thoughts of a most unsavoury kind. But the juvenile crush he'd had on her all through high school had long diminished into a more brotherly sort of affection and the way she was looking at him now only served to rekindle his mounting dread.

"Back you up? I don't —"

"The script, goddammit! Haven't you been listening to a word I said?"

That she'd been carrying on a conversation entirely with herself was plenty clear to Deacon but how to respond to it not so much. She was looking at him like he was just another idiot male and her life already full to the brim. He'd forgotten about the script ever since he'd received the text from Dylan. It was still sitting in his lap and he scanned over the open page now, seeking some sort of clue as to how he might respond.

This is what it read at the top:

DOUG
(eyes wide in disbelief)
Split up? Are you fucking crazy? Haven't
any of you ever seen a horror movie?

A rather glib bit of self-reference that had stopped him short when he'd read it the first time, the same thought bubbling to the surface of his mind then that emerged from his lips now.

"Ward's turned it into a cheap slasher flick."

Crystal laughed derisively. "It's not going to be cheap, I can promise you that."

She would know, having produced all three of her husband's previous films.

For lack of anything to add, Deacon's eyes drifted down the page.

> WILT
>
> You worry too much, Doug. If this was a movie, wouldn't it be more of an apocalyptic thriller than a horror?

> POLLY
>
> Why couldn't it be a miraculous tale of survival?

> WILT
>
> That's the spirit!

> POLLY
>
> At least then we'd have a chance for a happy ending.

> BRAD
>
> As long as we don't start eating each other.

"George'd be rolling over in his grave," Crystal was saying. "You've got to talk some sense into Ward."

That snapped Deacon back from the page.

"Me?!"

"Unless you want him to turn it into another *Bad Man's Son*."

He opened his mouth about to say, "You mean *Der Wüstling*," but the way Crystal was scowling gave him every reason to reconsider.

"We're not going to let him get away with this," she fumed. "No fucking way!"

She'd gone all Madame Medusa again at the wheel and Deacon began to suspect that getting him out of town for a few fun-fuelled days was the least of her intent, that really she was bent on using him as a prop in some rapidly escalating domestic drama.

"I'm sure it's not all that bad," he offered, trying to set a conciliatory tone.

"Not all that bad? Have you got to page 60 yet?"

"No. I'm, uh —" Glancing down and finding the number etched in the top right. "I'm only on page 36. Why, what happens on page 60?"

She let out another derisive laugh, short and sharp, almost a snort. "I wouldn't want to spoil it for you."

Her sardonic tone and crooked smile told him that she well remembered he'd once answered her with the same line when she'd asked him about *The Stray*, George's last published novel and one that was inspired by the time Deacon was attacked by his neighbour's three Rottweilers when he was all of two years old.

"Well, what are you waiting for?" Crystal said after he'd spent a moment too long reflecting on that. "Go on, read."

2

By the time he'd reached *FADE OUT*, the highway's four lanes had been replaced by a thin slice of snow-packed road tenuously carved into the boreal that stretched from Tildon all the way to the tundra some two thousand klicks north. An unbroken wall of pines crowded either side, their boughs sagging under the weight of the snow clinging in precarious drifts atop their branches so that they more resembled an endless diorama of mountaintops than trees. The snowplough's swirling blue cast an otherworldly glow over their staggered slopes and also over the dedication centred on the script's last page, open in Deacon's lap.

```
In memory of George Cleary
Who Brought Us Together
```

A peace offering perhaps, for Ward must have known how Crystal would react to the wholesale slaughter of the script she'd been labouring over during the eight years they'd been together. But knowing that didn't make it any less true.

It *was* George, in fact, who had brought them together, a story that Deacon had heard her tell a half-dozen times and that he'd told once himself in a slightly redacted version, owing to her parents being present, during the toast he'd made at their wedding. That George had been dead for almost two years when they'd met made their union seem all the more miraculous, something that Dylan had only been more than happy to exploit to his own advantage. While his sister and her new husband were sharing their first dance as a married couple, he'd sought out Deacon, who was doing his best imitation of the potted eucalyptus tree beside the chair in which he'd secreted himself, in the far back corner of the Rosedale Country Club's dining room.

"That George sure is a marvel, ain't he?" Dylan had said, drawing up his own chair and slumping down in it beside Deacon. "I wonder what he's going to cook up next."

He'd patted Deacon's leg. Recalling that, Deacon felt the same twitch jerking at his arm and the same sudden desire to flee as he had then.

In the driver's seat, Crystal was busy with her wireless headset, as she had been ever since she'd ordered Deacon to "go on, read." Whoever was on the other end of the line was doing most of the talking and seemed to have had a stabilizing effect on Crystal's mood. Her tone still bore traces of acrimony but it was leavened by the stifled laughter released in sporadic outbursts to punctuate her mostly one- and two-word replies. "Fuck me" and "Fucking dimshit!" were most common among these — minute exclamations of disdain at what the other person was saying. The longest — "You got to be fucking kidding me. He really said that?" — was followed by a short pause and chuckling-snort at something the other said.

"Well, he is an actor, after all. What do you expect?"

Another pause.

"No, no. I say keep it in. He's the one who'll come across looking like an idiot. It'll serve him right, that fucking dimshit. And who knows, maybe there'll even be a scandal."

It didn't take Deacon long to surmise that she and whoever was on the other end of the line — her assistant, Janine, most likely — must have been reviewing the commentary tracks for the upcoming DVD release of *Beast Planet*. It was the third film in her and her husband's *Beast* franchise and the first in which she'd been given a full writing credit. She'd earned the producer credit on all three, and the "Screen Story By" on the original and its sequel. On *Beasts*, the latter, she'd shared the credit alongside none other than Deacon himself.

No one had been more surprised than Deacon when he'd attended *Beasts'* opening gala at the Toronto International Film Festival — the first horror movie to ever be given that honour — and saw his name up there on the screen. Crystal had kept it a closely guarded secret so that, he later mused, she could revel in the look on his face when it appeared.

"How do you feel about wearing that tux now?" she'd then whispered in his ear, a flagrant knock at how virulently he'd protested when she'd shown up in a limousine at the house some four hours previous with the offending outfit protected in a garment bag.

Tugging at his collar, he'd answered, "I don't know, it still seems pretty tight to me."

She chastised him with a light backhanded slap to his arm, smiling in a most beguiling manner, like maybe she knew something else that Deacon didn't.

And maybe she did.

Beasts had gone on to gross over $250 million worldwide, five times what the original had. The credit earned Deacon enough to pay off the *Chronicle*'s debts, invest a sizeable down payment on the house on Baker Street, which Grover had previously bought from the Clearys after George's death, and also to put a fair chunk in trust for Tawyne.

Not a bad return on an offhand comment he'd made to Crystal after watching the cast-and-crew screening of the original *Beast* at the Kingsway repertory theatre on Toronto's Bloor Street. The moment the screen had faded to black he'd slipped out, unnoticed, on the pretence of grabbing a smoke, though really that was just an excuse so he could delay that inevitably awkward moment when Crystal turned to him from the next seat and asked, "So what'd you think?"

He'd been trying, unsuccessfully, to formulate a response to that for much of the show's ninety minutes and hadn't been able to muster anything beyond a rather limp "It was good. I- I liked it." A blatant lie: the film, in his mind, was a decidedly lame composite of a dozen far better films, self-conscious almost to the point of parody, amateurish even in its depiction of a group of castaways stranded on a deserted island who, one by one, are picked off by the titular Beast. His disdain, he'd later concede, might have been spurred by the fact that it was mainly shot on the ubiquitous iPhones carried by each of the castaways and on the GoPros worn by two surfer dudes, the action augmented in the film's latter half by a fleet of drones and a network of surveillance cameras revealed to be hidden about the island. This placed the film squarely in the found-footage genre — in Deacon's opinion a played-out breed of film that generally only served to give him a splitting headache centred somewhere in and around his optic nerves.

And his eyes were throbbing plenty as he stepped out onto the sidewalk and lit a smoke. He'd only managed two puffs when he heard the theatre's door slamming open. He was leaning against the brick partition that separated the theatre from the dry cleaner's beside it and was well out of sight as Crystal strode onto the sidewalk. From the way she scanned down the street to where his Cherokee was parked, it was clear she'd expected it to be long gone. As she turned around, the consternation tightening her features gave way to a smile of the mildly irritated variety.

"I thought you'd taken off," she said, snatching his cigarette and taking a long and lusty drag, giving no sign she was planning on giving it back.

"Just grabbing a smoke," Deacon said.

He was already sticking another in his mouth as she took a second puff off hers and then flicked the cigarette on a wide arc into the street — a momentary reprieve, for he knew that awkward moment was quickly drawing nigh.

And Crystal didn't disappoint.

"So?" she asked, turning back to him. "What did you think?"

Back then he was still wearing George's old green corduroy jacket but it was on its last legs. The collar was frayed and darkened by sweat. Two of its four buttons were missing and one of its pockets shredded by wear so that anything he put in it had a habit of working its way deep into the jacket's lining. Probing into the hole after his lighter, his fingers had brushed against what could only have been a roach. Lighting the fresh cigarette and then sparking the roach off its cherry mercifully gave him an extra few moments to come up with something — anything — positive to say.

"I like the ending," he said after exhaling a lungful of stale skunk.

That much was at least partway true.

Beast's big reveal had been that the whole thing was merely an entertainment for a bunch of rich people who'd been watching the fate of the castaways in a theatre at the heart of a complex hidden within the island's dormant volcano. The lone survivor, a pretty, young medical student short on tuition, had been in on it and when she'd come into the complex's courtyard to collect her reward, the spectators had gathered around her, clapping and hollering, "Bravo! Bravo!" But really what they should have been shouting was, "Encore!" because that's exactly what they'd been given after the Host had handed the med student an envelope with a jovial, "I hope you don't mind cash."

"Cash is good," she'd replied, reaching out for it, only to have the Host seemingly reconsider.

"I'll need your pendant first."

It was hanging around her neck on a chain — a small gold rendering of a savage- and mythical-looking creature. Evidently it was what had kept her safe and though the viewer had yet to get a clear shot of the titular Beast, the glowing red eyes above its snarling maw made it readily apparent that the charm was a miniature version of the same. After she'd handed over the pendant, the Host gave her the envelope but when she opened it, she found that it was stuffed full of blank pieces of paper cut to bill-size.

"What the fuck?" Her indignation quickly turned to horror as one by one the assembled spectators pulled out their own pendants, concealed until then under their shirts or blouses or deep within the cleavage of low-cut evening dresses.

"Now wait just a minute . . ."

A plea that fell on deaf ears and eager eyes as a half-dozen drones swooped down from the shadowed ceiling, their cameras trained to a one on the med student, who backed away as a hidden door in the courtyard slid open. Red eyes appeared from within its dark chasm, first a pair and then another and another after that. The scene then shifted to a wall of monitors in the Games Master's lair. Onscreen, the med student was being ripped apart by three of the genetically engineered beasts from six different angles.

When she'd been suitably reduced to a bloody mangle, the Host's voice announced, "Dinner will be served in the dining room in fifteen minutes, if anyone wants to freshen up." A moment later, the screens all went black. But just for a second. The screens clicked back on as the guests entered their rooms, the men loosening their ties and pouring themselves drinks, and the women removing high heels to soothe aching feet, a young couple toppling feverishly onto their bed, tearing at each other's clothes, ripping them off and growling in merry re-enactment of the scene they'd just witnessed. The camera then panned past an older man saying to his wife, "That was the best one so far. It'll be hard to top that." It settled on a screen in the bottom-most left, in front of which the Games Master could be seen from the back, sitting on what could only be described as a throne. Beyond him, the bank of monitors was clearly visible as the older man's wife remarked, "I'm sure he'll come up with something spectacular. He always does," the implication being that he already had and the spectators were going to be in for quite a surprise themselves.

And maybe that's indeed how *Beasts* would have played out had Crystal not then remarked, "That was my idea. The very last shot from behind the Games Master, I mean."

"Sets it up nicely for a sequel, I suppose."

"That's the point. Of course, a sequel will depend on how well this one does."

Beast would go on to gross a shade over fifty million, a pretty good return for an independent film made for under ten, but Deacon didn't know that yet. Neither was he was aware that he was about to make himself a quick three hundred thousand dollars and change.

"You know what'd be funny," he said rather offhandedly.

"What's that?" she asked.

Deacon shaking his head. "No, it's stupid."

"What?"

"Um —"

"What?!"

Bolstered by her delicate plead and the weed smoke and further by the certainty that it'd be a miracle if *Beast* even made it to theatres, much less produced a progeny, he ventured, "It'd be funny, you know, if in the sequel you got together a bunch of famous Canadians and, I don't know, made 'em out to be the world's best hunters or soldiers or something. Bring *them* to the island."

In later years he'd often muse upon where he'd got the idea without coming to any definite conclusions except that when Crystal had first told him she was producing a film, what had most excited her about it was, "And it's going to be one hundred percent Canadian! Actors, crew, locations, everything!"

"I thought you said it was set on a tropical island," Deacon had countered. "Last I recall, there aren't too many tropical islands in Canada."

"Ward's father owns an island off Turks and Caicos," she replied rather smugly, "so I guess you aren't so smart as you think after all."

That conversation must have been nibbling at his subconscious and maybe at Crystal's too, for her brow had suddenly furrowed, deep in thought.

"Jim Carrey could be the Games Master," Deacon offered, since the latter's face had never been revealed and Jim Carrey was about the most famous Canadian he could think of.

She shot him a smirk like it was the dumbest idea she'd ever heard.

"No," she said with the finality of a done deal. "Bruce Greenwood should play the Games Master."

"Who's that?" Deacon asked.

"You've never heard of Bruce Greenwood?"

"I'd tell you if I had."

"But I bet you've seen him in a dozen films. *The Sweet Hereafter?* *Meek's Cutoff?* 'Hell is full of bears!'" The last line was delivered in a deep and guttural snarl. And when that only produced another blank stare: "He even played Captain Pike in J.J. Abrams's reboot of *Star Trek.*"

Deacon had only a vague memory of that, not enough to place a face to a name.

"How about Jim Carrey plays some deranged Rambo type then," he countered, for it all of a sudden seemed to make a whole lot of sense to him. "And Keanu Reeves could play his arch-nemesis —"

"A mercenary," Crystal interrupted, "who's been tracking him ever since he killed his brother or son. Maybe his entire family."

"Hell, why not." Then after a puff on his smoke: "What about that stoner guy. Uh . . ."

"Seth Rogen? Yeah, yeah. He's a little fat to be a stone-cold killer. Maybe he could be the Games Master's half-baked son who's lured everyone to the island."

"Yeah, Rogen's good — funny as hell — but I was thinking . . . Chong. Tommy Chong."

"Is he even still alive?"

"If he is, he could be like, I don't know, the survivor of a past game, living in a cave."

Crystal was shaking her head. "I see Callum Keith Rennie in *that* role."

Deacon had never heard of him either.

"And what about Rachel McAdams," Crystal barged on, "the camera just loves her. And Elliot Page. He'd be great as a tough-as-nails investigative journalist, I always thought so. And the Two Ryans and Taylor Kitsch and Graham Greene. And Drake and

Biebs. Wouldn't you love to see *him* ripped to shreds? And, of course, Shatner would just have to have a cameo."

From her malevolent grin and the sheen to her eyes, Deacon began to suspect that her enthusiasm was chemically enhanced. Nonetheless, it was proving to be contagious. He was halfway to the point of believing such a thing was possible when his burgeoning good mood was itself suddenly ripped to shreds by Dylan's voice, raised in exuberant declaration from the theatre door.

"So that's where you two have been hiding!"

Seeing Dylan's shit-eating grin all over again as the snow plough ahead of them slowed to a near crawl, knowing Dylan would have been wearing a facsimile of the same expression as he wrote the text. Hell, he was probably still wearing it now, transmitting it across time and space, searching out Deacon like he was a satellite designed to receive an endless barrage of his ill intentions. How else to explain how practically every train of thought Deacon had had over the past decade ended in the calamitous wreckage of Dylan's leering smile?

"I'll see you tomorrow," Crystal was saying into her headset. "Two? You can't make it by noon? . . . I know it's New Year's . . . Okay, okay. See you at two. Bye."

The snowplough had lifted its blade and was doing a U-turn, sweeping in a wide circle around a bulge in this, what appeared to be the end of the road. It shuddered to a halt facing back the way they'd come and a snowmobile pulled alongside. The skidoo was black and its rider dressed all in black too, from his snow boots to his shiny black helmet. The snowplough's driver eased himself out of the cab with the stiff gait of man who'd spent the better part of his days behind the wheel, the flap of belly skin that oozed out from beneath a tattered T-shirt telling Deacon he'd spent most of his nights drinking beer in front of the TV.

The skidooer had fished a manila envelope from inside his snowsuit and was handing it to the driver, Deacon only then realizing that it wasn't a coincidence they'd been following the snowplough after all, that he must have been hired to make sure Crystal arrived safe and sound. Thinking, *Boy, it sure does pay to be rich*, he watched the driver scurrying back towards the warmth of his truck without feeling the need to count his score.

Crystal was by then turning into an even narrower lane cut between two snowbanks just short of ten feet high. Beyond, a freshly ploughed driveway dipped into a valley winding on a circuitous and seemingly arbitrary route amongst snow-laden conifers towering on all sides out of the rippling ocean of white. Exhaling a deep sigh of relief, her hand once again sought out her belly and while she was looking at Deacon when she spoke next, it seemed her assurance was meant solely for the benefit of the baby inside.

"We made it!"

3

"**Y**ou've got to be shitting me!"

Crystal was shaking her head and clenching the wheel hard enough to make Deacon think she was imagining wrapping her hands around her husband's neck.

The Land Rover had just crested the valley's far slope. Below them the driveway straightened as it slanted downwards, bottoming out onto a span of immaculately snow-blown cobblestones about half the size of your average football field. The trees between them and it were all of the deciduous variety — mostly maples, with a few elms and oaks filling out the spaces in between. Their leaf-free branches were unencumbered by snow except for a light frosting so even though they numbered as many as the conifers they did little to obscure the sweeping breadth of the Swanson family's so-called cottage.

In the novel *A Precious Few*, the reader had first glimpsed the same structure through the eyes of Tom Willis, a science fiction writer of ill repute who also just happened to be the father of two of its owner's grandchildren.

> *It looked to Tom as the plane pitched steeply, descending towards the lake at the base of the ridge upon which the building was perched, more like an airport terminal than his idea of a cottage. It was easily two hundred feet in length and each of its two storeys was comprised entirely of tinted picture windows, twelve or fifteen feet high and framed by grey concrete. The foundation was made of the same grey concrete, as was the rooftop patio. Half of the latter was engulfed by a swimming pool ringed with a rainbow's worth of Muskoka chairs. A set of steel steps on its far side switchbacked twenty feet upwards onto another slab of grey concrete that might have been mistaken for a high-dive platform if it wasn't for the helicopter stationed on the pad there. It was sleek and jet-black except for the Parsons' ancestral coat of arms decaled in gold leaf on its tail.*
>
> *His youngest son had seen it too.*
>
> *He'd pressed his nose up against the window's glass and there was a scowl souring his lips in stark contrast to how excited he'd been when his mother had informed him they were heading up to the cottage in her beaver float plane.*
>
> *Hey, why didn't we get to come in a helicopter!*

It was a sentiment sharply in tune with Deacon's, spying the similarly adorned helicopter just setting down on the landing pad above the pool.

In Crystal's words, her husband's New Year's party was supposed to have been a modest affair confined to a few close friends and business associates. But from Deacon's vantage it was eminently clear that there was nothing in the leastways modest about it. The rooftop patio was lit up like a mall at Christmas and further ringed with heat lamps, the throngs of revellers in between these seething with the frenetic activity of an anthill set on fire. Above them, the helicopter's doors were swinging open, unleashing a foursome of ski-jacket-clad twenty-somethings carrying snowboards and ducking low, the two women amongst them pulling hoods over their heads to protect their hair from the ravages of the swirling blades. A man wearing a black parka was motioning the quartet towards the stairs with the neon-orange baton he held in one hand. The moment they'd reached the top rung, he waved the baton over his head, a signal the pilot took to mean it was okay for him to take off. He did and before he was clear of the platform another helicopter was already swooping towards the landing pad.

"I'm going to strangle him," Crystal fumed, pulling to a stop at the foot of five granite slabs fashioned into stairs leading up to the so-called cottage's front door.

Cue the propulsive bass-heavy bleat of trip-hop, for that's exactly what Deacon heard when she threw her door open, easing herself out of the driver's seat, gripping one hand beneath her pregnancy bump as if the baby inside was somehow in danger of tumbling out.

"Where is he?!"

Crystal was shouting above the din and striding past the skidoo driver from before, who had somehow beaten them there and was just dismounting his machine. He was still wearing his helmet and Deacon couldn't see his lips move nor could he hear a response, if there was any. Either way, Crystal didn't seem to care. She bounded up the stairs with an alacrity belying her condition and by the time she'd reached the top step the door in front of her was opening of its own accord. From within blared a staccato *bwawmp bwawmp bwawmp* that did sound a little like a siren if it had been submerged in water. It was soon accented by the playful dance of funk guitar riffing in challenge to the rooftop patio's frenetic techno beat.

The skidoo driver had since removed his helmet and was talking into a wireless headset. Deacon couldn't hear what he was saying above the music but it wasn't much of a leap to imagine it was "The eagle has landed," or some other loosely coded message informing his boss that his wife had arrived. The driver was big, six-foot-five, as white as any man Deacon had ever known and sporting a military-style crew cut with a nettle of thorny-looking tattoos swarming up his neck, almost to his chin. It was those that told Deacon this was the same man who'd been driving the limousine the night Crystal had picked him up for the gala screening of *Beasts*. His first thought upon seeing his ink back then was that it been chosen expressly to mirror his disposition, for when he'd caught Deacon staring, he'd responded with such a look of disdain that it had Deacon wincing same as if he'd just been pricked.

"I see you've got a new driver," Deacon had commented once they were underway, an involuntary spasm that had more to do with how uncomfortable he'd felt wearing a tux and sharing the back of a stretch limo with Crystal's parents.

"His name's Wyatt," Crystal had answered, assuming a suddenly serious tone that seemed entirely out of whack when discussing a new hire. "He was Dylan's lieutenant in Afghanistan."

"You don't say."

"He was the one who pulled him out of the LAV after they hit that IED. You know, when he got his scar. Giving him a job seemed the least we could do, since he was the one who saved my brother's life and all."

Recognizing him as such had Deacon now prickling all over again and he hurried up the stairs after Crystal, suddenly quite eager to join the party after all.

4

The front door opened into a room that, unencumbered by walls, took up the entire main floor.

A flotilla of bubbles cascaded in waves amongst streamers of smoke tinted blue by the miasma of strobing lights, lending Deacon the impression that he'd entered a giant aquarium. To his right, a sunken pit some fifty feet square was crowded with another throng of partygoers too numerous to count, their forms reduced to silhouettes bobbing ecstatically to the *bwawmp bwawmp bwawmp* within the murky effluence, driven into an ever-increasing frenzy by a DJ wearing a deep-sea diver's helmet on an elevated platform.

A legion of statuesque servers wearing dresses cut from a thousand mirrored shards, their skin dazzled with glitter, swarmed amongst the revellers, hefting trays laden with sushi and dim sum. One descended into the pit, where she offered her treats to those lounging on the ring of couches surrounding the swirling mass of ravers; another circled past a crowd of a dozen or so, all with drinks in their hands, gathered around a pool table in the middle of the room, on her way towards an elevator's stainless-steel facade in the far left corner; a third snaked through the automatic sliding doors some thirty paces in a straight line from where Deacon stood, trying to absorb it all in a dozen parcelled glances.

The last of these located Crystal.

She was halfway up the stairs ascending towards the second floor on the other side of the pit. The entire north-facing wall was comprised of hand-hewn logs that, if George's description of the same in *A Precious Few* could be trusted, were remnants from the original one-room cabin that had once resided here. The stairs were made from a stealthy projection of similar beams emerging from the wall on an upward trajectory with neither any means of support between nor a balustrade. At their foot, a man in a black suit, verging on seven feet tall, stood with his arms crossed and his eyes blanked by dark sunglasses. Even the most cursory glance at him gave Deacon every indication that he'd be on his own, at least until Crystal came back down.

He was already feeling a little dizzy from the room's smoky heat and the unrelenting throb of the music and his gums were aching for want of a cigarette. That last problem was at least one he could solve. Fixing his eyes on the sliding doors, he set off across the room.

He was dressed in his usual snow-blowing outfit — George's old pair of insulated rubber boots, two sizes too big, and a pair of George's even older work pants, worn through at the knees and exposing the long johns Deacon had bought in a pack of three on sale at Walmart five or six years ago. His jacket was a plain blue winter parka he'd picked up at the Salvation Army Thrift Store on the main street in town and which had borne a crude square of stitch marks — lime-green — on its right sleeve ever since he'd caught it on a sharp corner of the metal utility shelves in the garage one time when he was fetching the blower. Weaving amongst young men and woman wearing, he'd have guessed, outfits that cost as much as he'd spent on food in any calendar year, he'd never felt more out of place and was only spared any further indignity in his meek shamble because he appeared to have turned invisible.

Finally, the pane of glass was sliding open in front of him and he was stepping onto the back deck. He was greeted with a welcome whoosh of cold air and he welcomed it back by lighting the cigarette already in his mouth. The deck was of the cedar variety and ran the entire length of the "cottage." Any hope that it'd provide a refuge where he could bide his time in blissful solitude while he waited for Crystal to seek him out was quickly dispelled, for the party was in full swing there too, and also as far as the eye could see.

The deck's steps led down into what could only be described as a raucous winter wonderland for the idle rich. A pathway made out of ice led away from the bottom step, splitting about twenty paces hence, one branch leading to a full-sized hockey rink bordered by snow banks and populated by four shifts' worth of players so serious in their intent that it seemed a playoff spot must have been on the line. The other branch trailed off into the lightly forested grounds, the skaters there gliding mostly in pairs with the awkward grace of lovers on a first date, stolen kisses and frivolous laughs captured within the orange glow of the electrified torches strung from the trees. On the left sat a structure resembling the helicopter pad but made of latticed wood. From this there descended a snow-covered ramp and a succession of snowboarders whipping into view, releasing primal shouts or catcalls as they hurtled down the path dipping along the edge of the ridge, sloping steeply towards the frozen lake below.

For the less energetic there were snowmobiles — he could spot the lights of several zipping through the woods. Two free machines were stationed off to the right side of the deck's stairs and Deacon was thinking maybe he'd like to take a ride on one of those, if only because the roar of its engine would blot out the propulsive throb of music from the rooftop patio. But he'd forgotten his gloves in the Land Rover and the chill air was already nipping at his bare hands. He was trying to think his way around that when he caught a whiff of skunk.

It was coming from under the awning that cordoned off half of the deck on its right-hand side. Heating lamps were strung from its rafters, below which a half-dozen tables were filled to capacity by those taking breaks from their winter frolic. On the table closest to him was an eight-tentacled hookah and for every person taking a puff there was another waiting behind to take his or her place. Deacon had begun to shuffle towards it, thinking it wouldn't do him any harm to at least join one of the lines, but was halted by someone tugging at his jacket's sleeve.

He turned around, hoping to see Crystal. Instead, he was confronted by what appeared to be a thirteen-year-old girl peering up at him. She had straight black hair down to her waist and pale skin with an asymmetrical spattering of freckles, like finely ground pepper, on either cheek. She was wearing a loosely hung pink one-piece sleeveless jumper unbuttoned halfway to her navel, with nothing underneath. If her intent had been to show off her budding pubescence she'd achieved that in spades and even the sparest of downward glances had Deacon feeling like a dirty old man. His gaze jumped upwards with such dire alarm that it seemed his eyes were about to lunge out of his sockets and make a run for it.

"You don't remember me," the girl said and that was enough to make him cast her another quick glance centred, for propriety's sake, on the middle of her forehead.

She'd since produced a tube approximating a cigarillo, though the green tufts he saw fraying its butt-end as she stuck it in her mouth told him it wasn't likely filled with tobacco. The shock of seeing such a young girl dressed like that was nothing compared to seeing her lighting a giant blunt with the casual air of a chronic and he inched away from her, feeling a sudden guilt by association just standing there.

"It's Grace," the girl said with her first exhale.

And then he did remember her.

Eight years ago, at Crystal's wedding, he'd been hiding out from Dylan at the dessert table when a girl he'd have guessed was eleven or twelve approached him.

"I'm Grace," she'd said with the formal countenance of a tween about to ask a man almost three times her age for a dance. "Ward's sister."

"Deacon," he'd replied brusquely, reaching for his third Nanaimo bar. "Crystal's, uh, uncle."

"Crystal told me you needed someone to dance with."

"She did, did she?"

"She said you wouldn't want to."

"She's sure right about that."

"She also told me not to take no for an answer."

Grabbing at his hand, she gave him a tug towards the dance floor.

"No, really —" Deacon protested.

But really, she wasn't taking no for an answer and his resistance only served to firm her grip on his hand, surprisingly strong for a girl her size.

Carried along by her eager insistence, he'd let himself be dragged onto the dance floor, his appearance there earning a warm smile from Crystal, dancing with her father to a rather laconic swing rendition of "Heart-Shaped Box." Grace took the lead, guiding him in a simple three-step, and Deacon doing his best not to trample on her toes.

"Actually, I'm only Ward's half-sister," she said after a few awkward seconds.

"You don't say," he muttered, trying to sound interested.

"We have the same fathers. Father, I mean, since he's the only one."

"I see." Then, after another three-step, Deacon asked, "Is he around here somewhere?"

"Who?"

"Your dad. I saw him at the church but —"

"Oh, he doesn't do parties," Grace interrupted.

"Too bad. I was kind of hoping to meet him."

"Why?"

"Uh —"

"Because he's the richest person in the country?"

"No," he answered, which was at least partway the truth.

Why he wanted to meet Michael Swanson mostly had to do with what Crystal had said after the first time she and Ward recounted to him how they'd come to meet.

"That's quite a coincidence," Deacon had commented when they were through, for it certainly was that.

Crystal had smirked as if it wasn't a coincidence at all but divine providence. "But did you know Howard Parsons was based on Ward's grandfather?" she'd then asked. "How's that for a . . ." making air quotes with upraised fingers on either side of her head ". . . 'coincidence'?"

Howard Parsons was the elderly patriarch of the richest family in the country in *A Precious Few* and the revelation that his character was inspired by the father of the actual richest man in the country did come as a shock to Deacon. He hadn't quite recovered from it before Crystal was speaking again.

"Turns out Grams was his second wife's cousin. They'd grown up together in some religious commune back in the forties."

That too had come as a surprise, since Deacon knew absolutely nothing about her grandmother Adele's life before she'd become a Cleary by marrying George.

"It was more like a cult," Ward had piped in.

"They were crazy, anyhow. You should have heard the stories Grams told. She and Howard's second wife —"

"Virginia."

"— escaped when they were teenagers. Just after she'd married Howard Swanson, she invited Grams and Gramps to visit their cottage and that was what inspired him to write *A Precious Few*."

Ward's father, Michael Swanson, was Howard's son from his first marriage and so Deacon had plenty of other reasons why he'd want to meet him. He hadn't figured a way to verbalize any of that so instead he said, "I own a newspaper. He owns a newspaper. Figured we could exchange a few tricks of the trade."

That Michael Swanson's paper was just one facet of the largest media conglomerate in the country and Deacon's a small-town weekly didn't exactly have him exuding confidence and Grace took eager advantage of that.

"You're lying," she snapped back with such vehemence that it made him wonder if maybe he was. "If he wasn't the richest person in the country, nobody would *ever* want to meet him. He's actually really very boring otherwise."

Shortly after Crystal and Ward had told him what they'd come to call "Our Origin Story," Deacon had googled "The Richest Man in Canada" to get a little supplementary background on Ward's father. He hadn't learned much except that Michael Swanson was a highly secretive man. That had made him seem pretty damned interesting in Deacon's mind but then, of course, his own daughter would probably know better.

"My mom used to say being in a room with him was like watching milk curdle," Grace insisted. "I'm much more interesting than he is."

"I don't doubt it," Deacon said, and he didn't.

"But do you know why?"

"Why?"

"Because I have a secret."

"And what's that?"

"Wouldn't you like to know?" she asked, flashing him a coquettish smile that no eleven- or twelve-year-old girl had any right laying on a man almost three times her age.

It was only a few minutes later that Crystal had filled him in on Grace's secret, which apparently wasn't much of a closely guarded one after all.

"Can you believe she's nineteen!" she'd enthused with genuine wonder after she'd tracked him to the open bar. Seeing Deacon's stunned expression of disbelief, she'd then explained, "Something about a recessive gene. Her condition is actually kind of tragic. She's not expected to live much beyond thirty. Poor little thing."

That had been eight years ago and while Grace looked like she hadn't aged more than a few months, a quick calculation told Deacon that she must be twenty-seven now.

"I thought you were only his half-sister," he said, to temper the unease he felt looking at someone as young as she appeared to be who was smoking a giant blunt and would also probably be dead within three years.

It earned him a gracious smile.

"So you do remember me."

"Hard to forget someone like you."

"I'll take that as a compliment."

She nudged his hand with the back of hers and gave him another one of those coquettish smiles that had him feeling like a dirty old man all over again. His expression must have betrayed his unease, for in the next moment she was offering up the joint daintily between her thumb and forefinger.

"You look like you could use a puff," she said and Deacon didn't need to be asked twice.

"Don't mind if I do."

I t couldn't have been more than ten minutes later that he was standing in what could have passed for the presidential suite at any number of five-star hotels, with no clear memory of how he'd got there. He was naked save for a pair of boxer briefs and staring into what appeared to be a funhouse mirror from the way the reflection staring back at him was melting into a gelatinous blob.

His skin was losing all cohesion and oozing down his chest and his hands were grappling after it, in a vain effort to keep himself from turning into a puddle on the floor. But it was like trying to get a grip on greased lard, from the way he was sweating so. His hair was soaked through too, and suddenly felt as heavy as chain-link. The heft of it was tearing at its roots and dragging his head towards the floor. He clutched two handfuls' worth, holding them above his head and the weight of that driving him to his knees.

He heard someone screaming, "What the hell was in that joint!?"

It must have been himself.

"Here," a voice was then calling out to him as from across a great divide, could have a been a desert or an ocean, might as well have been from the damn moon, "drink this."

Turning and startled by the proximity of a glass a few inches from his face. It was filled with something. Something clear.

Sloshing. He couldn't quite place it. His eyes were roving over the surface of the glass, twisted into the shape of a funnel cloud. Drips were trickling in spirals along its ridges and he was mesmerized by the way they circled the glass like marbles on a rollercoaster's track, so unlike how a drip was supposed to behave.

The glass was pressing to his lips and the cold and wet — he still couldn't remember the word — was splashing into his mouth, his lips and tongue lapping after it, slurping it back, the cold and wet feeling like an ice cube — was that what it was called? — rammed down his throat, choking him.

He came up for air, gasping and spewing . . .

Water!

He must have spoken it aloud, for the voice was answering, "You'll get more in a second. First take this. It'll even you out."

A spot of something blue materialized before his eyes. A finger was pushing it into his mouth and he was helpless but to let it. Then the cup was pressing up against his lips again, parcelling the water in staggered sips. He drained the glass and was chasing after its last few drops with a desperately lunging tongue as it moved away. All the while he was still clutching two handfuls of his hair, holding them above his head, he could no longer remember why. He was trying to ease his grip but it seemed that his hands had become as stuck fast as with Krazy Glue, and then Grace was speaking again.

"Crockett or Tubbs?" she asked.

She was standing in front of a walk-in closet and holding up two suits. One was white linen and overlaid with a splash of pink — a shirt of some sort — and the other a deep, glossy purple with a white collared shirt accented by a pink tie.

"Crockett, I think," she said, Deacon trying to figure out how she could remain so calm and more so what the hell she was talking about. Crockett? It was a name, he was certain about that but not what it could mean, bandying it about his mind, trying to make sense of it with a delirious urgency like it was a key that might unlock the secret of the very universe.

It would come to him hours-that-felt-days later, when it seemed like nothing could have been so unimportant as a reference to some cheesy cop show that was off the air before he was even born.

He was lying in bed in a room coloured all in pink — pink walls, pink ceiling, pink canopy, pink sheets. The latter were soaking wet and growing cold beneath him. He was no longer even wearing a pair of boxers to ward off the chill and he was gazing, stupefied, down at his limp and glistening manhood, wet even more so than the sheets.

He had a vague memory of dancing, for how long he couldn't say. The windows' drapes brokered no light so it couldn't have been all night, though from the way his body ached he felt like he might as well have been dancing for going on a week. One song bleeding into the next, thrashing about first on the rooftop patio and then the first floor's pit, carried along like a stick of driftwood battered about a stormy sea, flouncing along like it would have meant the end of the world if he'd dared try to free himself from the gyrating throng.

That's how it had felt dancing with Grace and it was also how they'd fucked, longer maybe even than they'd danced. Rain had never fucked him like that, nor Laney, the woman he'd dated after her, and definitely not Rebecca, his latest fling, whom he'd only seen naked once, though they'd lain together a dozen times. With any of them he'd certainly never laid in bed afterwards feeling both of his nipples on fire and one crusted with blood, his head still throbbing to the reverberation of trip-hop and a taste in his mouth like a fish washed up on the beach, parched and shrivelled in the summer heat.

He could hear the shower's trickling spray from the bathroom and he was telling himself that he ought to get up, get dressed and get the hell out of there before Grace came back — for no particular reason except he was certain her reappearance would spell his no-uncertain doom.

But he barely had the strength to blink, much less go through all that.

He could hear a droning buzz from somewhere. It sounded almost like a fly caught behind a screen, but it couldn't have been. There were no screens on the windows and it took another buzz for him to realize it was coming from his phone, set to vibrate. It was sitting on the nightstand beside the bed, not more than four feet from his head, just out of his reach.

It buzzed a third time and lay quiet. The shower had gone off in the interval and after a moment Grace came striding out of the bathroom, towelling her hair. Otherwise she was stark naked and as she executed a full turn — scanning about the room, looking for something — she'd never looked more like a thirteen-year-old girl than she did right then.

There was a voice screaming in his head, *What the fuck have you done?!*, and then Grace was talking to him.

"I heard a buzzing noise," she said, like nothing could have been more natural. "Did you hear a buzzing noise?"

Doing another full turn, her glance fell on the nightstand as if by chance, though there was something in her look of smug satisfaction that made it seem like more than mere providence.

"Do you know you have thirty-eight unanswered messages?" she asked after she'd picked up the phone.

Deacon grunted something not even halfway resembling an answer and she thumbed the screen.

"The last one's from someone named Dylan?"

That was enough to get his full attention, but couldn't elicit any degree of coherence when he tried, unsuccessfully, to speak again.

"—ey Deke," Dylan was then saying through the cell phone's speaker. "Crystal ran into some trouble at that party last night, you know the one I'm talking about. She's up at the hospital in North Bay. I'm going to be here all night. If you're heading this way I sure could use a coffee."

The familiarity of that drove Deacon bolt upright, for it was almost exactly the same thing Dylan said in the message he'd left for him after Ronald Crane had been found burnt to death in his van. He stared at the phone held out in Grace's hand, his mind flashing back to ten years ago, when Rain had done the same.

Then Dylan was speaking again, his voice quieter, almost a whisper.

"She's lost the baby," he said and then paused again just long enough for Grace to gasp, "Oh my god. That's horrible!"

The timing suggested to Deacon that her reaction had been scripted but when he looked to Grace her face was blanched with genuine horror so maybe he was wrong.

"If you ask me," Dylan continued on cue, "it weren't no accident. Looks like —"

He cut himself off with an urgency that suggested there was someone shouting at him as there had been before, though there was no indication of that at all. Deacon now waiting out the moment of dead air, knowing full well what he'd say next, and that hardly diminishing its menace.

"Oh shit," Dylan finally said, "I've got to go. See you when I do."

JODY

H e was late getting home.

The town plough had been by since he'd left and the entrance to his driveway was barricaded with a wall of snow. In the cascade from his headlights he could see the gouge in the ten-foot snowbank on its far side where the driver had used his blade to topple it backwards, filling the driveway with glacial chunks four feet high and almost twice as deep. It was, Jody was sure, Byron Chance who'd done this and it was no mystery to him why he'd been doing it all winter long. Byron's dad had been a constable with the Ontario Provincial Police, which is how Byron found out Jody's dad had been arrested for hitting a cop when they were in grade seven. Byron had made some dumb-fuck comment — Jody could no longer remember what — so Jody had punched him in the face, making him cry in front of the whole class. He'd been suspended for two weeks because of it and that should have been the end of the matter.

Yet here Byron was, almost ten years later, filling his driveway with snow every time he left the property, as if he was hell-bent on proving beyond a shadow of a doubt that he was still the same breed of asshole he'd been back in school.

Through the speakers, Tom Araya was screaming about tearing someone's fucking eyes out and ripping their fucking flesh off and Jody shouted along, his and the singer's combined fury rising to a crescendo as he flicked the switch beneath the dash to lower the blade hitched to the front of his Toyota Tacoma. Gunning the engine, he spun the wheel, angling the truck into the driveway. The blade struck the ground an inch or two before the embankment and the pick-up bucked in protest as it slammed into the icy wall.

Downshifting, he growled, "Motherfucker!" along with the song and floored the gas.

The tires spun for a revolution or two, then caught and the truck even straightened out a little as it punched its way, fish-tailing, through. He'd have to come back out and clear the rest away later but he was too tired now to do anything but flick the switch again and ease off the throttle as the blade ascended. He let the truck coast to its parking space in front of the garage and sat there a moment, waiting for Slayer's caustic drone to wear itself out before switching off the ignition.

It had been the third major blizzard since the one they'd called the Storm of the Century and here it was only the middle of February. For the past eight weeks he'd been working twelve- and fourteen-hour days, seven days a week, ploughing driveways and blowing paths to front doors, shovelling off roofs and decks, mostly for an elderly clientele who could no longer do it themselves. Not that he had any right to complain — he'd already made more in two months than he had all of last year — and if it came down to it, his wife, Tina, had no right to complain either.

With all the extra work, he'd had to add a second coffee can to the one already full of twenty-dollar bills in the kitchen cupboard he'd labelled *OUR NEW HOUSE* with a permanent marker.

Still, he knew she would. Especially since it was clear from her Sunfire in the driveway that the town plough had been by before she'd been able to get off to town, as she usually did on Saturdays, to do a little shopping and to let their eighteen-month-old son, Clyde, play for a couple of hours at the Early Years program in the basement of the United church. The car was coated with a light dusting from the remnants of the storm, which had tapered to a few errant snowflakes while he'd cleaned it off before leaving that morning just after five.

And here it was going on eight in the evening.

The temperature hadn't risen above minus fifteen all day and when Jody snatched his phone from its holder on the dash, the weather app showing on his lock screen told him it was back to the minus thirty-two it had been when he'd left. Still he didn't bother zipping his snowsuit, though he was only wearing a T-shirt underneath. He also didn't bother with his gloves, tucking them under his arm as he lit a cigarette, all the while telling himself he really ought to put the blower strapped in the truck's bed back in the garage, or at least throw a tarp over it, in case it snowed again.

It wasn't supposed to but then they'd been wrong about that before.

Hell, as far as Jody could tell, these days they were wrong about the weather more often than they were right.

Really, except for the blower, it didn't matter to him much either way. His internal clock would have him up at four regard-less of whether he'd have to leave by five, which he always did when it had snowed, to make sure he'd be able to get through all the driveways he'd been paid a premium for, on the promise they'd be done by eight. If it hadn't snowed he'd leave at seven, spend most of his day behind the blower or up on one of a dozen or so roofs around town, manning a shovel and a scoop.

Tomorrow was a Sunday and that shouldn't have made a difference either, though he knew it would to Tina. How many times had she barked, "But it's Sunday! Would it kill you to stay and have breakfast with us once in a while? It's not like I'm asking you to come to church or anything."

He'd come around the back of the truck, the cold reducing the drags off the cigarette to quick nips that scalded his throat. The curtain in the window looking out from the trailer's kitchen was open and he could see Tina's face framed in its yellow glow. He couldn't tell of her expression but he knew what it'd be — a look of tremulous concern, like it was some stranger pulling into the driveway in the middle of the night, and her all alone with an eighteen-month-old and a dog that would just as soon lick you to death as bite, the closest neighbour a half-klick away on either side.

It was all for show, he knew, since it would have been impossible to mistake the battered Toyota Tacoma equipped with a snowplough and four overhead lights for any but the one he'd been driving since he'd moved in with Tina five years ago, inheriting it from her father, who'd been driving the same vehicle since Tina was ten. As usual, she waited until she was sure he'd seen her before letting the curtain drop and Jody took one last quick pull off the cigarette before pitching it into the dark.

He knew exactly what she'd say the moment he opened the door, and also that her voice would be curdled with a healthy dose of snark.

"You said you'd be home by six," she'd scowl, "seven at the latest."

It was already putting him on the defensive, which likely wasn't going to improve Tina's mood. He took a deep breath, trying to settle himself as he stepped up onto the porch. It wasn't much of one as porches go, just a hastily contrived frame that he'd built from the dozen two-by-fours Tina's father had stored in the rafters of the garage that they'd inherited along with the truck, the plough and ten acres, most of which was scrub brush or swamp. Over the frame he'd tacked a double layer of clear plastic from a three-quarter roll he'd scavenged from the reuse shed at the Maynard Falls landfill site. It didn't do much against the cold but it did, in the least, keep the wind at bay when they were having a smoke or a puff. The screen door he'd bought for twenty bucks at the Habitat for Humanity store in Tildon. His hand was already going numb from the cold but it was still warm enough that when he reached for the door's latch the skin on his fingers stuck to the metal as fast as Velcro. He popped it open and tore loose his grip and was reaching for the knob on the inside door when he remembered, *The block heater! You forgot to plug in the fucking block heater.*

Cursing, "Goddammit," he spun around and tromped back towards the garage.

A half-moon was creeping out from behind a wisp of cloud just above the treeline and casting a pale glow over the four-foot droop of snow sagging from the garage's roof. He'd have to get to that soon or the garage would end up no better than the house that had once sat where the trailer did now, though it was fire that had done the house in. Maybe he would stick around in the morning after all. He could shovel the garage's roof and the trailer's too. And the truck was overdue for an oil change and so was the snowblower, he might as well do them both. He could even make his mom's blueberry rollover pancakes, which Tina refused to make herself though the recipe was stuck to the fridge and it was Clyde's favourite breakfast.

Thin strands of shadow from the poplars lining the far side of the dirt road telescoped over the blunter shadows from the chunks the town plough had left in the driveway.

Hell, Jody thought as he rounded the truck, *if you stick around long enough maybe Byron'll make another pass.*

Revelling in the thought as he reached for the extension cord hanging on a hook beside the garage's door.

You could go after that asshole, run him right off the road. An unlikely proposition at best, since the town ploughs had a couple of tons, at least, on his and would probably be carrying a load of sand to boot. Still, that didn't keep him from follow-ing the thought to its logical conclusion — dragging that son of a bitch from his truck, beating him to death with the claw-end of a hammer, pissing on his remains and then leaving those for the ki-yotes.

He'd plugged in the cord and was walking back towards the house.

It'd bloody well serve that motherfucker right!

"Did I miss Clyde?" he asked, though he knew she'd have put Clyde down an hour ago.

He was kicking his boots off by the door and, with friendly, eager eyes, imploring Tina, clipping her nails on the couch, but she refused to even glance his way. Scout, her German shepherd cross, nuzzled her snout into his groin, sniffing, as she always did when he stepped through the door. The one time he'd told her to bugger off, Tina had countered, "She's just keeping you honest," and that was the last time he'd said anything about that.

Nudging the dog away, he scanned towards the couch.

Tina was wearing the grey flannel reindeer jammy-pants he'd bought her for Christmas "from Clyde" and the Ramones T-shirt he'd given her "from Scout." She must have just showered for her hair was wet, its thin drape of sandy-blonde brushed back over her forehead, the skin there dotted with a mottle of red bumps, same as she'd had since she'd turned thirteen and had never managed to shed. The wireless Beats he'd given her "from Jody" were strung around her neck and so she'd have heard him just fine, though she was doing her best to pretend otherwise.

Setting aside her clippers, she lit a cigarette and made a conscious effort to blow the first exhale in a dismissive billow in his general direction.

Ever since Clyde had been born they'd agreed they wouldn't smoke in the trailer, the only exception being after they'd fucked and only then through the screen on the window behind their bed. She must have been sore mad at him to be smoking so brazenly in the living room and he found his own irritation creeping through the feint of his good humour.

"You said you would be home by six," she said, taking another drag. "Seven at the latest."

He resisted the urge to bark, "Have you looked the fuck outside lately!" and instead walked to the fridge. Grabbing himself a bottle of Carling, he popped the cap and drained half of the beer before speaking.

"You wouldn't believe what's going on out there," he said trying to keep his tone on an even keel. "People are such fucking idiots. I saw not one but two cars go into the ditch, and that was just on my way home."

That much was true anyway but only seemed to add fodder to her ire.

"And it never occurred to you to call a tow truck?"

He drained the rest of the bottle in four gulps before answering.

"Hell, every tow truck between here and Orillia is busy up on the 11. It's a fifty-car pileup, they're saying, and getting bigger by the minute." A feeble attempt at levity that fell on deaf ears and he added, "It's been on the radio all afternoon."

She must have heard something about that, for her eyes scrunched. When they'd relaxed, she took only one more drag off her smoke before dropping it in the can of raspberry cooler on the coffee table and that gave Jody every reason to keep on talking.

"I pulled the first car out myself," he said stepping out of his snowsuit, "but the other, he must have been going one-twenty when he went off the road. It was buried up to its roof. It's going to take a crane to get it out. Shoot, it took me damn near fifteen minutes before I could even get his door open."

"I suppose you think that makes you some kind of hero?"

She was halfway smiling when she said it and he knew that even if she really had been sore at him, her mood was on a definite upswing.

"Could be," he answered, hanging the snowsuit on the rack beside the door and turning on the space heater beside that so the suit would be dry come morning. "Too bad it pays more to play the fool these days than the hero."

It was a line his father had picked up somewhere. He'd used it as an excuse to get out of doing anyone a good turn and Jody had taken to using it to justify quite the opposite.

"I guess then next time I'm going to have to find me a fool," Tina countered with a pointed smirk.

He was walking towards her. He must have been itching at the fresh tattoo on his chest, for she was snatching up one of the pillows from the couch and heaving it his way, scolding, "Quit scratching."

The pillow hit him in the belly and he used it as an excuse to veer towards the couch, setting the pillow against one of the futon's wooden arms and bending down to give her a quick peck on the forehead.

He'd barely mustered a congenial "Yes ma'am" before she was pushing at his chest with both hands. She was five-foot-four

50

and barely weighed a hundred pounds to his six-foot-three and 205, most of that hard-earned muscle. He'd have to be a lot more tired than he was for her to hold him back and he pressed forward that last inch, licking her forehead instead of kissing it.

"God, you stink," she chided, wiping the lick off with the palm of her hand.

"I thought you liked my stink."

"Yeah, when you were, like, fifteen."

"Well, I still like your stink plenty fine."

He pushed in for another lick and this time she planted her palm over his mouth, pushing back again.

"Shower," she said. "Now!"

He was already veering towards the bathroom.

"Don't forget to put the cream on the new tat," she called after him. "It itches because you never put the cream on it."

"Roger that."

"And make it quick." Her voice then taking on a playfully ominous tone. "I still got plans for you tonight."

A fter he'd showered and towelled himself off, he took the antiseptic gel from his shelf beside the sink and squeezed a daub into his palm, smearing that over Tina's latest creation, inked on his right breast.

It was a reproduction of the first picture taken of Tina and him with their newborn son, the same one he'd been using as the wallpaper on his phone ever since Clyde was all of two minutes old. Jody had just cut the umbilical cord with the pair of stainless-steel surgical scissors the eldest of the three midwives in attendance had handed him and he was feeling a little woozy from his part in the birth and more so from staying up all night. Most of that he'd spent keeping out of the midwives' way as they'd prepared Tina to give birth, something she'd steadfastly refused to do in a hospital, choosing instead to give birth at home on the same bed, point of fact, on which Clyde had been conceived. Previous to cutting the cord, Jody's only job had been to prime her with a steady supply of raspberry leaf tea — brewed from the reserves she'd harvested that spring and had kept in an oversized Ziploc bag in their freezer — and to keep his phone handy in case something went wrong.

That *had* given him some cause for concern.

It would have taken an ambulance the long side of thirty minutes to get out there, meaning it'd be at least an hour before she'd get to the hospital. But in the end the birth had gone off without a hitch and after he'd cut the cord the youngest of the midwives had asked him if he wanted her to take a picture of the three of them together.

What struck him most about the photo she'd taken was just how different he and Tina appeared. She was red-faced and sweat-soaked and yet beaming with a youthful vitality at stark odds with someone who'd just endured nine hours of hard labour, and himself, hollow-eyed with nary a trace of a smile, looking like he was having his mug shot taken after an all-night bender had landed him in the drunk tank. When she'd first shown him the sketch she'd made of it — delicately rendered as she always did in pencil on onion paper before she started a new tattoo — he'd asked her to cut him out of it. She'd refused, same as she always did on the rare occasion he'd balked at her latest creation, as if she had more of a claim to his body than he did.

And he'd never balked more than he had that first time, five years ago.

He was seventeen and Tina two years younger. She'd just moved into the house he'd lived in with his mother at the end of Talon Lake Road, a half-kilometre from the house Tina herself had been born in and which would burn down not a year later. A week before Tina had come to live with him and his mother, Jody's father, Lenny, had been sentenced to twelve years under a new law which compelled prosecutors to impose a manslaughter charge on anyone found to have sold a narcotic that resulted in its user's death. A police investigation had tied twenty-five overdoses over the course of a week to the same batch of fentanyl they'd found in Lenny's trunk during what the paper called a "routine traffic stop," though Jody had good reason to suspect there was nothing routine about it at all.

Four of those overdoses had resulted in deaths. While that hardly seemed a reason to celebrate, his mother had treated the verdict like it was Christmas, Thanksgiving and Easter all rolled into one.

By then, Tina was already spending more consecutive nights at his house than his father ever had. Over the next five years she'd cover his back with sixteen discrete tattoos, all of them together doing a fair job of recounting the story of Jody and Tina's relationship thus far. So it made sense that the first tattoo, inked at the nape of his neck, would also depict the first clear memory he had of meeting her.

It had happened one morning on the school bus, when he was in grade seven and she in grade five. His stop was either the first or the last, depending on whether it was the morning or the afternoon, and hers the one immediately before or after. Since he was the first to get on in the morning, he always got his choice of seats. He'd have preferred to sit right in the back but those seats were reserved for the high schoolers so instead he always chose the seat right behind the driver, biding his time on the forty-five-minute ride staring out the window and wishing he was anywhere but there.

On that particular morning, he hadn't slept a wink the night before and had other reasons besides to be filled with inconsolable dread at the thought of wasting yet another goddamned day at school. He was sitting in the seat with his backpack beside him to deter anyone else from sitting there — though nobody ever did — and he'd abandoned his usual habit of staring out the window for slumping in his seat with his arms crossed to hide the maxi-pad his mother had Scotch-taped over the gash on his right hand since they'd been out of Band-Aids.

It had taken every ounce of his will to keep himself from cursing "Motherfuckers!" under his breath, which he'd been doing at regular intervals all night as he lay awake in bed, unable to sleep for the memory of what he'd just done. It was also what he'd screamed when he punched the tiles surrounding the tub while he was in the shower an hour ago, startling himself by how easily one of them had shattered and more so by how its broken shards had sliced a ragged crescent over three of his knuckles.

"We have to get you to the hospital!" his mother had screamed, panic-struck, when she'd opened the bathroom door to see what was taking him so long and found him wrapping his hand with toilet paper, though no amount of that could stem the flow that had turned the tub and the sink and the floor into a virtual slaughterhouse.

He could smell the stink of skunk on her breath and knew she'd already had a couple of dabs of the weed oil she called "shatter."

"You're high," he'd countered. "I ain't going to the hospital with you when you're stoned."

She'd reacted like she'd been slapped and for a moment he regretted what he'd said. Truth was, she functioned far better stoned than she ever did straight. Not wanting to let her drive him to the hospital had almost nothing to do with her current state of mind and everything to do with his.

"Looks like you punched something you shouldn't have," the doctor might say, examining his hand. "Do you want to tell me what you punched?"

Under his scrutinizing glare, Jody'd be helpless but to answer, "The wall in the shower. I punched my hand right through it."

"And why would you do something like that?"

"I guess it was because I was angry."

"Angry? And what could have made you angry enough to punch a hole right through the wall in your shower?"

"I- I —" he'd stutter, trying not to cry as the memory of what he'd done the previous night came hurtling back to him. "I —"

Then maybe he would start crying and he'd be helpless but to be carried along by the flood of tears, what had happened to him spilling out of his mouth and the doctor, and his mother, growing more alarmed with every passing word. By the time he'd have reached the end, he'd be blubbering like some little baby who'd lost his rattle and the doctor might ask: "Do you remember the police officer's name?"

Jody shaking his head and the doctor excusing himself, no doubt to call the police station to confirm what he'd just heard.

No, there was no fucking way he was going to the hospital.

His mother seemed to get that and had bandaged him up the best she could. And here he was, then, sitting on the bus and doing his best to hide the fact that she'd used Scotch tape and a maxi-pad. They'd evidently reached the school. The kids were all filing off, getting in a last few shoves and jibes before the bell,

Jody waiting until they'd streamed past, trying to summon the will to join them. Taking a deep breath and turning to the aisle, seeing that little girl from down the road standing there.

"You look like you could use a rainbow," she said in a delicately preening voice that immediately raised his hackles.

She was holding up a piece of paper on which there was indeed the drawing of a rainbow and he had the sudden urge to grab at it, tear it to shreds, if only to wipe the stupid grin off that little girl's face. And maybe he would have too, except the picture had been drawn on the see-through onion paper they sometimes used in art class. The sunlight was shining through it and also through the arching lines of colour filled in with some sort of translucent gel so that it looked almost like stained glass. His hand twitched with the memory of slicing his knuckles open on the broken tile and he'd felt the shock of pain all over again and that had stayed his venom.

Muttering a rather feeble "Thanks," he'd reached out and taken the picture.

So it wasn't really much of a surprise that the first time she'd asked him if she could ink something on his back, she'd answered his "That depends on what" by pointing to the same picture of the rainbow that he'd taped to his window five years previous as a constant reminder of what happened when he let his anger get away from him.

"No fucking way!" he'd spat back at her. "Everyone'll think I'm a fucking faggot!"

"Nobody will think you're gay."

He'd gritted his teeth and shaken his head and she'd set her hand on his arm.

"And even if they do, you'll get to kick their ass. It's a win-win, if you ask me."

He'd seen a strange sort of logic in that and after a fair bit of hemming and hawing he'd grudgingly consented. It had taken her two hours using her father's old needle gun to ink the rainbow onto the back of his neck, high enough that his uneven crop of shoulder-length hair concealed it anyway. It was a few moments after she'd finished that they'd fucked for the first time, and that *had* come as a big surprise, since she was still three months shy of her sixteenth birthday, the date she'd set to lose her virginity so that, in her words, "I'd be legal."

E ven thinking about that first time was still enough to set his groin a-tingle, and as he smeared the antiseptic gel over the picture of his new family, his groin was tingling plenty. The shower, and more so the beer, had renewed his energy and he teased himself with the thought of how in a few short moments he'd be burying his face in Tina's sex, feeling her thighs tightening around his head, parting her lips with his tongue, tasting of her salty-sweetness . . .

He was already rising to the occasion.

He dispensed with the modesty of a towel since he planned to be under the covers in two seconds flat. As he turned into the hallway, his pace was verging on a run, hurrying him past Clyde's closed door. It was of the accordion variety and made of thin vinyl. It didn't do much to block out the sound from the living room and as a buffer Tina always played a recording of waves crashing gently onto a beach in an endless loop whenever she put the boy down.

Music, he thought, hearing it now. *You forgot the music.*

He looped back around, trying to recall where he might have put his phone and knowing it was probably still in his snowsuit.

And so it was. It buzzed when he clicked it on and there was an orange banner over the family photo reading, *You have messages.* Ignoring that, he clicked on the musical note as he headed back for the bedroom, thumbing down his fifty-odd playlists, waiting for one to catch his fancy.

He was waffling between "Alison Hell" and "Stoned Again" when his phone buzzed again. A message was scrolling across the top of the screen. *He's out!* it read and that stopped him in his tracks. He'd come to Clyde's bedroom door. He knew the "He" could only have been his father and thinking of him, the waves all of a sudden didn't seem so gentle anymore. Amplified in his suddenly pounding head, they seemed fierce and wild, about to wash him under, and then the phone was buzzing again.

He's out!!

He pressed the home button and then the message icon. It had a red *2* already on it and by the time he'd confirmed it was from his mother — though he needn't have — a fourth message then a fifth and a sixth were already coming through.

He's out!!!

He's out!!!!

He's fucking out!!!!!

She was liable to keep it up all night, adding one exclamation after another, as she'd always done when Jody was growing up and didn't reply right away. He keyed, *I'm on my way,* even as Tina's voice assailed him with an irritated whisper-shout through the open door at the end of the hall.

"Jody!" she said. "Are you coming or not?"

He forced his legs forward, no longer in much of a rush to get to the end of the hall and having no idea what he'd say to Tina when he got there.

The phone buzzed again with the message: *Hurry!* That only served to further slacken his pace but it did give him an idea.

Planting the phone against his ear, he took a deep breath before pushing the door open.

"Really, Mom," he half-whispered into the mic to keep his voice from waking the baby, "it's not a good time. I —"

Shaking his head as if she was being unreasonable and looking pleadingly to Tina. She was sitting on top of the covers wearing only the T-shirt and rolling a joint in her lap, making a tray of the lid from the antique tea tin in which they kept their stash.

"But —" Jody said in feigned answer to whatever demand his mother was supposed to be imposing on him.

"Tell her we're fucking!" Tina shouted with no consideration for Clyde at all, and Jody turned his back on her, nodding and saying, "Okay, okay."

He pretend-clicked *End Call* and turned back to Tina with grave reluctance. She was already lighting the joint they were meant to smoke together and Jody was searching about for an excuse to explain why he'd be running off to his mom that wouldn't include mention of his father getting out of jail, since Tina knew all too well what plans Jody had laid for when he did.

"If it's not one damn thing it's another," he finally said, assuming an air of frustration that wasn't entirely put on. "Her car's stuck."

"Well, you can unstuck it in the morning."

"She tried to run the ridge the plough left in her driveway. It's half on the road. If the plough comes by again and doesn't see it . . ."

He was already at his dresser, opening his socks-and-underwear drawer, and cast her a quick glance. There was nothing about her expression — lips pursed, eyes like laser beams — that suggested she believed the lie, and why would she? She'd have known he'd have circled past his mom's place before coming home, for that very reason.

"Well, let her dig herself out then," she said.

"You know she can't, not with her hand," he answered. Carpal tunnel syndrome and early-onset osteoarthritis had conspired to render his mom's right hand about as useful as a lobster's claw, a fact Tina knew as well as he did.

Slipping on a pair of boxers and grabbing a pair of socks, he offered, "I'll be back in fifteen."

But Tina plainly didn't believe that either.

"Boy," she snarked, "I've sure heard *that* before."

F ive minutes later, he was pulling into his mom's driveway and parking behind her Outback.

He'd brushed it off just that morning after he'd ploughed her driveway, his second of the day after his own. Its windows were covered with a plate of frost, both inside and out, the same as they'd been for the past week, which meant she hadn't been out of the house for at least as long.

The porch light was on and when he came around the car he found his mother sitting on the front steps. She was wearing a one-piece grey flannel nightgown and a pair of slippers and nothing else. Her head was craned forward and her hair — a messy tangle of grey-streaked auburn curls — concealed her face. The crunch of his boots on the hard-packed snow didn't raise so much as a twitch from her and as he approached it was beginning to seem to Jody like she'd frozen solid.

"Mom?" he said and finally she looked up.

Her curls fell away and in the stark light from the bare bulb overhead it looked like her face had been run through a meat grinder. Her nose was squashed and oozed bloody mucus and her lips were mashed and the skin on her cheeks pummelled into hamburger. Her right eye was swollen shut and her left pooled with blood and the gash on her one cheek was deep enough to see bone. Her bare arms were criss-crossed with slash marks and on the whole she looked like she'd been thrown through a plate glass window and had landed in a threshing machine, which maybe wasn't too far from the truth, Jody knowing his father as he did.

"Jesus Christ, Mom!" he gasped, rushing towards her.

"Jody?" she asked, as if she couldn't see it was her son bending down to her.

At his touch, her body convulsed in an icy shiver and he wrapped one arm around her waist while cinching the other under her legs.

"We got to get you inside."

When he picked her up, she groaned, wincing in pain.

"Goddamn, that son of a bitch!" Jody cursed, popping open the screen door latch with a free finger.

The smell of cat piss and shit assaulted him in the mud room as it always did and he hurried forward. The door to the house was open and the window in its top half was shattered, leaving shards of glass like crooked teeth along its frame. One of her cats — she'd "saved" eight at last count — meowed and brushed against his leg, almost tripping him as he carried his mom into the living room.

She'd never been one to keep a clean house but what confronted him there was beyond all reckoning. It didn't look so much like the work of a man as some crazed bull moose on a drunken rampage. There wasn't an inch left untouched by its violence — lamps smashed and the coffee table in splinters, the TV screen a spider's web of cracks splayed around an impact point, shelves toppled, spilling books and scattering her collection of miniature ceramic cats over the bare hardwood floor among four of her real cats, all of them mangled and bloody. In the middle of the room, Whiskers, her prized angora, lay with its head crushed in a sticky pool bearing the imprint of the boot heel that had done it — an exclamation point maybe to his father's rage.

Cold blew in crisp gusts through the room's two windows, the one in the front a picture and the one on the side wall a small two-pane, the both smashed. A baseball bat — the one his father had bought Jody for his eighth birthday and which had likely done most of the damage — was imbedded in the drywall over the couch, the cushions of which were festooned with broken glass too. Setting his mother down on her feet and holding her around the waist, he pulled off the comforter folded over it, shaking the shards from it and easing her down onto the couch, tucking the blanket over her to ward against the chill.

"We need to get you to the hospital," he said.

She shook her head. "No!" The look of fright in her eyes brokered no argument and he knew exactly why.

The day after her ex-husband was convicted of manslaughter for selling that deadly batch of fentanyl, two of his friends had showed up at her house. One had held her down while the other broke her arm over a stick of firewood because they thought she'd been the one who'd turned him in. With two priors, a conviction for an assault like this would get Lenny life. If Jody took her to the hospital in her current state there'd be questions, and even in the asking she'd be as good as dead.

But from the look of her it seemed unlikely she'd survive the night anyway without immediate medical attention. Weighing that against the alternative, he took out his phone. He only managed to dial 9-1- before she lashed out, grabbing him by the hand, clenching tight.

"It won't matter what they do to you if you're already dead," he said shrugging her off.

"It'll be okay," she pleaded. "I called Julie."

Julie was a co-worker from when his mother had worked as a personal support worker for the Red Cross. But unless she'd taken some surgical training in the meantime, it didn't seem to Jody that Julie would be able to do much for his mother.

"She'll fix me up," she was saying and that got her coughing, Jody helpless to do anything but watch his mother as the fit consumed her.

Bloody strains of spittle spewed over her lips and speckled her nightdress as the cat from before — a tabby — wrapped his tail around Jody's leg. He got then a sudden image in his mind of Whiskers doing the same to Lenny, his father raising his foot, stomping its head to mush. Suspecting then that it wasn't an exclamation point at the end of his father's rampage but rather marked its beginning.

Seeing his mother — already bruised but not yet quite so bloody — flailing madly at Lenny, all reason lost to the sight of her precious Whiskers being crushed to death before her very eyes. Probably she'd had the bat in her hand. She'd stored it behind the couch for years so that it'd always be in easy reach when she was watching television, because, she'd said, "You just never know."

Jody knowing now the real reason she'd put it there — because she did know — and that it hadn't done her a damn bit of good, and neither had he. Now here she was likely coughing herself to death and there was nothing he could do about that either except reach over her and grab the bat — his bat — from the wall, clenching it tight, wishing for nothing more than to see the familiar image of his father sauntering out of the kitchen popping open a beer, about the only thing he ever did when he was home besides eat, shit and sleep.

His mother's coughing had eased and she was talking again.

"He was looking for something," she croaked through phlegm, and that got Jody's attention.

"Looking for what?" Jody asked, though he had a pretty good idea.

"He didn't say. Only that he'd buried it out behind the garage. Do you know anything about that?"

Jody did but shook his head nonetheless.

"When he couldn't find it . . . That's why he got so mad. Before, he only . . ."

The "only" hanging there between them, for it was hardly an "only" at all. The rage surging again, for what his father had done and the worst of it because of him.

"Did you tell him where I was?" he asked, and she shook her head.

"I told him you'd lit off for Fort Mac over a year ago."

Lights flashed over the room, someone pulling into the driveway. Jody's hand tightened again on the bat as he prowled to the front window, looking out.

"It's a blue SUV," he said.

"That'll be Julie."

His mom was trying to stand, as if she was planning on meeting Julie at the door. But she didn't have the strength and slumped back down. Another of her cats — a marmalade — was nuzzling at her arm and that's how Jody left her, turning towards the door and seeing through its broken window Julie's short and squat figure bundled into an ankle-length green parka and bustling up the driveway.

"What are you going to do?" his mother asked after him and he turned back, fixing her with a hard stare so there'd be no doubt about it.

"You know what I'm going to do."

Her one good eye was alight with something he'd never seen in her before — joyful malice or a freakish sort of glee. A smile then, or at least what her ravaged lips could muster. Between those lips, an open space where her two top front teeth had once been and that leaving no doubt in Jody's mind that there was no turning back now.

Charging through the mud room and kicking open the screen door hard enough that Julie, almost at the stairs, let out a startled gasp. Storming past her, trying to think of where he might find Lenny and pretty sure he knew the answer to that.

Hearing then the buzz of his phone.

It was still in his hand and when he looked down he saw Tina's name.

I'm starting without you, the text read. *You better get here before I finish.*

Turning it off and tucking it into his pocket as he came to his truck, reaching into his pocket for his keys.

He was going to catch serious hell when he got back home.

5

"I guess maybe George was wrong after all!"

They'd been standing on the bridge for five minutes
before either of them had spoken. It was Grover who'd finally
broken the silence, shouting over the thunderous roar of the
falls raging beneath them. The daytime high had been pushing fifteen degrees since the last week of February. With the
record-breaking snowfall over the winter, the river was already
threatening to engulf the bridge leading into the downtown,
and here it was only the third week of March with the thaw not
even halfway over yet.

Fifteen minutes ago, Loretta had popped her head into
Deacon's office, telling him that Grover wanted to go and check
on the river's progress and asking him to go along to make sure,
in her words, "he doesn't fall in." Deacon had grabbed George's
old green rain poncho off the hook behind his door and a fringe
of tiny icicles now clung to the rim of its hood. Before answering
Grover, he swiped at them with his hand.

"How's that?" Deacon shouted back, though he'd been thinking pretty much the same thing himself.

The curls of Grover's snow-white beard were glaciated with clumps of ice from the spray churned up by the madly roiling water, which had already crystallized the bridge's braces with a layer some four inches thick. They were glimmering now in the morning sun and making Grover squint, reducing his eyes to but two more wrinkles among a multitude, yet it was hard not to detect within their fold a familiar sparkle.

"He always said it would be by fire next time," he answered. Tossing then a quick glance up at the sky, whether at God or George Deacon couldn't say, and turning back to Deacon. "That sure isn't how it's looking from here."

"You can say that again."

The river was already almost two metres above its normal level for this time of year. The homes on River Road, just across the train tracks from downtown, had borne the brunt of the flooding thus far. A legion of volunteers had been filling sandbags for the past week to help save the six houses there as well as the River Road Apartments, a four-storey brick building advertised as "assisted living" and filled mainly with retirees. In yesterday's paper Deacon had run a two-page photo spread of the relief effort to go along with the front-page story under a headline of *Hundreds Rally to Save Seniors*. Even then he'd known their efforts, though valiant, were likely in vain, or so said Frank Darling, head of the town's Flood Management Team. The TFMT had been formed after the flood in 2019, which had resulted in the declaration of a state of emergency in Tildon and damages later assessed in the tens of millions. Back then the mayor had declared it a "One Hundred Year Flood," and yet here it was only six years later.

This year's thaw, in Frank's words — strictly off the record — was shaping up to make that one look like no more than a busted water main compared to what was coming, placing most of the blame on the record snowfall combined with a forecast of heavy showers expected by the weekend. In anticipation of those, the mayor had pre-emptively declared another state of emergency. He'd put in a request for help to the army, only to be informed that they already had their hands full in the nation's capital, where the Ottawa River was threatening the evacuation of several suburbs.

Tildon's residents would be on their own and if Frank Darling's predictions held true, it'd be a miracle if half the town hadn't been washed into Lake Mesaquakee come Monday.

"It's lucky I'm building a boat," Grover said, as if he'd been reading Deacon's mind.

"You're building a boat?" It was the first time Deacon had heard tell of it. "Since when?"

"Oh, ever since George appeared to me in a dream. He says to me" — assuming then the zealous bluster of an old drunk — "'The end of all flesh has come before me; for the earth is filled with violence through them; and, behold, I will destroy them with the earth.'"

"That sure sounds like George all right," Deacon said, for it did.

It had been a terrible blow to both Deacon and Grover when George had died ten years ago. For his part Grover had been doing his utmost to keep the *Chronicle*'s former owner's memory alive, taking every opportunity he could to channel George's indomitable spirit with such keenly rendered impersonations that it really did seem at times like George was speaking through him. And never more so than when Grover was quoting Genesis 6:13, for George had often done the same after one too many ryes and had also referenced it no less than five times in his fictions, being as it was the message his villainous Sons of Adam used as their calling card after going on one of their murderous rampages.

"Seemed like a pretty clear sign to me," Grover continued, nudging Deacon in the ribs with his elbow as if he hadn't already figured out it was all in jest. "Started building it the next morning. Three hundred cubits long, fifty cubits wide and thirty high. Already got the two cats and the two dogs. I'm expecting the rest of the animals along any day now."

A *ba-weep* sounded from down Ecclestone Drive and drew Deacon's attention to the ambulance accelerating past a pulled-over minivan on the slope leading towards the bridge. It was only a quick glance upwards to the Meadows' familiar house perched at the edge of the cliff. There was a figure standing on its widow's watch that couldn't have been anyone but Rain. She appeared to be looking through a pair of binoculars and the sudden shiver Deacon felt like ice running down his spine gave him every indication that she was looking down at him.

It had been five years now since he'd caught more than a fleeting glimpse of her. To stifle the memory of the last time they'd spoken he turned back to Grover.

"You be sure to save me a seat," he said as the ambulance sped past.

"Will do," Grover said with a wink. "As long as you don't mind shovelling shit."

The breast pocket of Deacon's jacket gave out a vibrating buzz. He reached under his poncho for the phone, expecting it to be Rain. He wasn't much relieved when he saw it was Rebecca, whom he'd never really thought of as his girlfriend, though she — and half the damned town, it seemed — apparently did. She'd texted him a dozen times since New Year's, mostly in her official capacity as a dispatcher for the Tildon Police Service but twice to ask him over for dinner. He'd declined both times, unwilling to face her after what had happened with Grace on New Year's Eve, even if that seemed like a poor excuse to keep dodging her.

The text read: *Suspicious Death. Algonquin Rd & Highland*

The intersection, he guessed, was probably where the ambulance had been headed. He punched in a quick *Thanks!*, hoping that would be the end of it, and waited a moment for her to text back. When she didn't, he pocketed the phone. Grover had gone back to staring down at the falls, lost in the rapture of its tumult. Deacon touched him on the arm to get his attention.

"Duty calls," he said and Grover turned to him, swiping his hand over his face, wiping away the ice lodged in his eyebrows and lashes.

"I'm about done playing popsicle anyway!"

They were approaching the four-way stop between the bridge and downtown before Grover spoke again. He'd taken Deacon's arm in his so as to bolster himself against a fall on the sidewalk-encrusting ice that no amount of the beet-based solution the town had spread in record amounts seemed able to disperse.

"I read that piece Tawyne wrote in yesterday's paper," Grover said, clenching Deacon's arm a little tighter as they manoeuvred through a stream of yellow-stained slush.

Here it comes, Deacon thought, meaning the real reason Grover had paid him a visit.

Grover's lips were pursed and his eyes scrunched and Deacon knew he was gearing up for a good old-fashioned tongue-lashing.

"I suppose that was your idea," he scowled, to start things off.

It was.

Deacon had been walking to work when he'd been alerted to an unfolding drama by a distant wail of sirens accompanying a few screams and a conglomeration of bystanders who'd gathered in the parking lot of the 7-Eleven on Main Street. The only person he recognized among them was the town's oldest veteran, Arne Milner, who always wore his dress uniform and whom Deacon interviewed every year for the paper's Remembrance Day edition. When he asked Arne what had happened, the old man answered, "Some kid walking around with an axe, is what I heard."

He'd later find out that the kid was a fourteen-year-old named Kylie Farmer. Apparently, he'd chosen to celebrate the first day of March break by taking his father's splitting axe for a walk down Main, using it to take whacks at anyone who'd dared cross his path. He'd injured three pedestrians — the worst with a gash in his arm that required sixteen stitches — before four officers in tactical gear tackled the boy in front of the Norwood movie theatre.

The photo accompanying the article had been taken by Deacon himself a few minutes after he'd asked Arne where the kid was now. Arne had pointed him in the direction of downtown and Deacon had arrived at the Norwood in time to snap a few shots of the handcuffed teenager being forced into the back of a police cruiser by two of the tactical officers. He was interrupted in this by a third officer walking towards him, also dressed in tactical gear, so Deacon didn't recognize him right away. But there was no mistaking his voice when he cried out, "It's just like in Chapter 10, eh, Deke?"

It was Dylan, and he was carrying the Farmer kid's axe. Blood had stained the blade red and spattered the handle and Deacon had felt plenty menaced by the way Dylan was spinning it in a deftly lackadaisical twirl, the blade blurring into a fair approximation of an airplane's propeller, zeroing in on him. That had been enough to send Deacon scurrying away, ducking down Mary Street and taking the stairs to the parking lot behind the old feed store, cutting back up onto Main by way of the alley between the old townhall building that housed the clock tower and the Royal Bank.

When he'd finally reached the *Chronicle*, he'd found Tawyne behind the front counter, helping himself to the tray of donuts Cheryl had bought from the Tim Hortons on her way to work. During the three years Tawyne had been living in the apartment above the paper, he'd grown to a lanky six-foot-one and, if his aunt Jean could be trusted, was the spitting image of his father when he was that age, though René himself had never managed more than five foot ten. Tawyne had shown a natural aversion to cutting his hair and tended to use it as a screen between him and the outside world, letting it hang loose over his face — a strange affectation, for otherwise he was about as chipper a seventeen-year-old as Deacon had ever met.

He'd greeted Deacon with his standard "Hey, Chief," which he'd been calling him ever since Cheryl had made a stink about her husband addressing him that way. Cheryl had let it slide, perhaps figuring even if they didn't share exactly the same cultural heritage — his father being Iroquois and Deacon's mother Chippewa — their skin at least shared a similar enough pigmentation.

"Someone took the last maple cream," Tawyne said with a mischievous smirk as he took a bite out of what was plainly a maple cream, Deacon's avowed favourite. Then, lowering his voice to a conspiratorial whisper, "I think it was Gabe."

But Deacon had more important matters on his mind than donuts.

"Didn't you hear the sirens?"

"Yeah," Tawyne answered, "I was wondering what was going on."

"Then I guess it's lucky it's your job to find out!" Deacon snapped, hurrying down the hall leading to his office.

Until then Tawyne had only covered the high school beat, science fairs and basketball games, that sort of thing. He'd proven a certain proclivity and in the name of professional development Deacon had been looking to assign him something a little meatier. A teenage boy walking down Main Street taking swipes at passersby with a splitting axe was certainly that and it further spoke to Deacon of the article he himself had written about those two pit bulls which had attacked a three-year-old boy while he was playing in his sandbox — the first real news story George had assigned to him, almost twenty years ago now.

Relating such to Grover might have provided suitable context as to why it was that he'd given the story to Tawyne. But he also knew that it'd have mattered less than a grain of sand against the coming deluge when measured against Grover's opinion on the matter, for they'd had this argument a dozen times before.

"I'd never have printed an article like that," Grover was saying. "And neither would've George."

"I guess it's just a sign of the times," Deacon answered, playing his part. "It's a different world than it was in your day."

"Different world my ass," Grover growled. "What you young 'uns can't seem to grasp is that in a town like Tildon, bad news always gets around well enough on its own. It's our responsibility to spread the good news. You got to pound it into them! Otherwise people might just as well read the damn *Sun*."

"You'll have to take that up with Gabe," Deacon countered, feeling quite justified since it had been Gabe, in fact, who'd changed the paper's masthead from Grover's "How About Some Good News for a Change?" to the somewhat punchier "Our Town. Our Stories."

But that just got him a dismissive wave and Deacon was thinking *Robbie Smart* an even second before Grover spat out, "Just look at Robbie Smart!"

One fall morning in 1988, Robbie Smart, a grade eleven student, had shown up at school with a sawed-off baseball bat. He'd beaten two other students and the vice principal half to death with it and the way Grover went on about it you'd have thought that his greatest accomplishment as a journalist was keeping that out of the paper.

"He's married now, you know," Grover continued. "Has two kids. He's the best damn stucco man in Mesaquakee, last I heard. What use would it have been dragging the worst day of his life through the damn paper? I'll tell you —"

But Deacon had just spotted a familiar blue Toyota Highlander Hybrid pulling into a parking spot in front of the *Chronicle*.

"Oh look," he said, happy for the last-minute reprieve, "there's Loretta now!"

6

Tawyne must have still been in bed when Deacon knocked at his apartment a few minutes later.

It took three knocks before he opened the door and when he finally did he was wearing nothing but a pair of grey boxer shorts and wincing as if the encroaching daylight caused him no inconsiderable amount of pain.

Deacon heard a soft click from somewhere within — the bathroom door closing, likely — and from the way Tawyne refused to open the door more than a crack, all indications led Deacon to suspect he wasn't alone.

That thought gave him every reason to pause. After then-Sergeant Marchand had shot Tawyne's father dead, Deacon had assumed a mentorship role for the boy and over the past decade he'd done his best not to treat Tawyne like the son he'd never had, though he often thought of him that way. Whenever he felt Tawyne needed a push in one direction or another, he'd gener-ally deferred any and all of those responsibilities to the boy's aunt

Jean, or just let it be, trusting Tawyne to work it out for himself. But one of the conditions Jean had made before she let Tawyne move to town was that he wasn't to have any overnight visitors. Though she hadn't exactly said as much, Deacon was certain she was worried he'd fall into the same trap as his father, who, in her opinion, had started down his particular slippery slope after spending one too many nights in the company of "That Fields Girl."

If there was one lesson Deacon had learned over the past three years, it was the value of maintaining plausible deniability. Fronting his best good morning smile, he ignored what was plainly the pop of a shower coming on in favour of a congenial "You feel like taking a drive this morning?"

Tawyne opened his mouth, no doubt to conjure some excuse, and Deacon beat him to the punch.

"If you've got something better to do . . ."

"No, it's not that —" Casting an ill-disguised glance back into the room. "Can you give me a couple of minutes?"

Deacon was just finishing a cigarette, leaning against his Jeep in the parking space beneath the building's back staircase, when Tawyne finally appeared on the platform above. He was wearing a light black hoodie and jeans, the same as he'd been wearing all winter regardless of how low the mercury dipped. He paused a moment to look over the rail, maybe hoping Deacon had already left without him.

"You're not going to lock up?" Deacon asked when the teenager had descended in a stomping clomp to the midway point.

Tawyne paused mid-step and turned as if he meant to go back, and then turned around again.

"I already did," he said, plainly a lie.

Walking his cigarette butt to the coffee can he'd put by the *Chronicle*'s back door to serve as an ashtray, Deacon was thinking, *Maybe it's time you see about getting him another set of keys.*

But that was a conversation for another day.

Tawyne was circling the Jeep in his gangly slump towards the passenger side door and Deacon intercepted him.

"You know how to get to Algonquin Road?" he asked, holding out his key chain.

That earned him a smile.

After he'd got his first royalty check for *Beasts*, the one concession Deacon had made to his vanity was to trade in his old Jeep for a maroon 2019 Grand Cherokee. He'd thus far been successful in thwarting Tawyne's every attempt to get behind its wheel but thinking of Tawyne sneaking someone into his room last night had him swelling with a sense of paternal pride, however misplaced, and he felt like honouring the occasion.

"That's down Highland, ain't it?" Tawyne asked, snatching up the keys.

"I guess there's only one way to find out."

Highland Road cut off the 118 on the far side of the highway from the Rainbow Ridge Retirement Villa and bisected the Highland Golf & Country Club, ascending on an uphill climb between its ninth and tenth fairways. Just past the clubhouse the road switched from asphalt to gravel. The winter and the ensuing thaw had reduced its dirt to a rippling expanse of icy ruts that seemed ever in danger of shaking the Jeep apart.

"Take it easy, now," Deacon told Tawyne, though the speedometer was already dipping towards thirty.

"If I go any slower," Tawyne shot back with a scowl, "we might as well just get out and walk."

Still he eased off the gas a touch and as the Jeep bounced past the fenced-in rolling hills on either side that would shortly become cow pastures, Deacon could feel that familiar dread churning in his stomach, thinking Dylan, no doubt, was waiting for him at the end of the road.

"It's just like in Chapter 10, eh Deke?"

Those were the very last words Dylan had spoken to him and it wasn't much of a mystery as to what he'd meant. Every year on the anniversary of George's death Deacon had found an envelope marked *FOR DEACON* in his mailbox, each of which contained the next chapter in George's last book, *No Quarter*. With the two Dylan had left him on George's desk ten years ago, he now had twelve. While he'd brooded in his office after sending Tawyne off to cover the Kylie Farmer story, Deacon had wanted nothing more than to get his ass back home so he could reread the whole lot of them all over again. But the tremble to his hands and the erratic thumping in his chest already had him feeling like a marionette with Dylan's hand on the strings. And Dylan, he was sure, would have liked nothing better than to see him scurry back to the old brick barn behind the house on Baker Street that he'd refashioned into a bunkie, to pore over the manuscript for the hundredth time, looking for clues as to what might happen next.

Not that it was likely Dylan had anything to do with a four-teen-year-old boy going whack-happy with an axe on the main street of town. But then that was kind of the point of Chapter 10, which had started with reports of a fifteen-year-old boy hacking up his stepfather with a machete before heading out the front door, taking a swipe at anyone who had the misfortune of cross-ing his path as he made his way towards his ex-girlfriend's house where, he'd tweeted, he'd meant to exact his revenge for all the times she'd fucked around on him.

Aside from the prologue of George's novel, the chapters alter-nated between the perspective of the boy, Del, who had witnessed the murder of the man in the minivan in Chapter 1, and Mason

Lowry, introduced in the second chapter as the man taking Rain from behind on her living room couch. Deacon would shortly learn that he was a retired small-town police chief who would be hired by the father of the real estate developer who'd been found burnt up in the van to make a few discreet inquiries into the murder of his son.

Over the following ten chapters, there'd be five increasingly savage, and apparently random, murders perpetrated against Mesaquakee's wealthy tourist population. The RCMP were investigating and while the official consensus was that the same individual or individuals responsible for murdering the real estate developer were also responsible for these other killings, Mason had begun to suspect that something more dire was afoot. The teenager hacking up his father had brought these suspicions to a head. Chapter 10 had ended with a conversation between Lowry and James Latham, Lowry's predecessor, an eighty-three-year-old former police chief who'd returned to his family's farm after retiring from the Tildon Police Service some two decades previous.

> If you ask me, the old man said, spitting the half-chewed plug of tobacco into his front yard, it all started going to hell when the school board outlawed the strap.
>
> Mason had heard him say the same thing a dozen times and hadn't yet made up his mind on the matter, though he had his doubts by then that any sort of violence could accomplish anything but begetting more of the same.
>
> If parents won't discipline their kids, Latham continued, then the schools have got to step up. And if they don't, you know who's going to pay the

price. You and me and every other damn person out there still fool enough to put on a badge and a uniform.

He was veering off topic; trying to get him back on track, Lowry rephrased the question.

So you think it's possible I'm looking for multiple perps here?

You're asking the wrong man about that. I'm just an old farmer. But I will say this, the world's become a pressure cooker and we all seem hellbent on turning up the —

Here he cut himself off, having just spied his Irish setter gulping down the plug he'd spit into the yard a few seconds ago, and was lunging out of his chair.

Get away from there! he yelled as he snatched up his cane, hurtling down the stairs. Goddammit, Red, spit it out! You're going to make yourself sick. Spit it out!

The dog was scurrying out of his reach. He was barking and pouncing at the ground as if nothing could have pleased him more than his master swinging after him with a stick and as Lowry watched the old man pursue the dog in looping swirls around the yard, he turned the old man's last words over in his mind.

A pressure cooker, he thought. He's sure right about that.

And with five increasingly savage, and apparently random, murders in as many months — and seemingly no end to them in sight — it was looking ever more likely that it was getting ready to explode.

When Deacon had first read that, he'd been immediately reminded of something he himself had written some years earlier. "Mayor Threatens to Cancel Summer Amid Covid Concerns" the headline had read on the front page the week before the May Two-Four weekend was to have signalled the start of the 2020 tourist season. In the accompanying article he'd quoted Barry Wylde, Tildon's mayor, as saying, "If cancelling summer is what it takes to halt the spread of Covid-19 from the cities in the south to Mesaquakee, then that's what I'm going to do!" which seemed like a dodgy piece of logic, given that summer was going to happen regardless of what he, or any pandemic, had to say about it.

Grover had dismissed it as mere electioneering but Deacon couldn't so easily disregard the underlying sentiment. It spoke well, he thought, to the escalating friction between Tildon's "year-round" and its "seasonal" residents, the former worried that a rapid influx of tourists would inundate Mesaquakee with new cases of the virus and the latter countering that they paid their fair share of property taxes and had the right to come up to their cottages any time they damn well felt like it.

In the end though, the increased tension seemed to have turned inward. While the Tildon Police Service reported a sharp spike in domestic disturbance calls over the previous spring, there weren't any overtly suspicious deaths during the crisis, nor since, and certainly none that could be deemed "savage."

Of course, in *No Quarter* the murder of the real estate developer had gone unsolved, meaning the killer was still at large and thus, or so George would have the reader believe, provided the perfect screen for any number of copycat killers who had a grudge against someone in Mesaquakee's cottage community. In real life, the only suspect in the Wane family murders — Tawyne's father, René Descartes — had been shot by then-Sergeant Marchand.

Deacon had spent a lot of time thinking on that, wondering if maybe Marchand had inadvertently foiled Dylan's plans or whether maybe Dylan had simply used the Wanes as a dry run, the murder of Crystal's unborn child giving Deacon every reason to suspect that Dylan's cryptic warning of "we ain't hardly yet just begun" meant the worst was still to come.

Recovering from the miscarriage, Crystal had spent a couple of weeks in February at her parents' place, not more than a five-minute drive from Deacon's house on Baker, and Deacon had dropped by three times, intending to share with her his fears regarding Dylan's warning. On his first two visits her mother had told him she was sleeping and wouldn't even let him in the front door. His third had found her awake and when he'd knocked on her bedroom door she'd answered with a highly agitated "What?"

He'd poked his head in and found her sitting on her bed with her laptop propped against her knees, apparently working on a script.

"It's just me," he'd said and she gave him a cursory glance punctuated with a token smile.

"Sorry, Deacon," she'd replied, "but I'm kind of on a roll here. Can you come back in a few hours?"

"Will do," he'd answered and while he'd meant it, he never had come back, telling himself it was best just to let her recover before burdening her with any more grief.

It was the same excuse he'd used to conceal from Tawyne the circumstances surrounding his father's untimely demise and here he was on his way to another suspicious death with the real killer likely waiting for him at the scene.

It was a thought amplified and also rent in two by Tawyne yelling:

"Jesus Christ!"

His hands were clenched white-knuckle on the wheel and his foot sprung from the gas as the orange blur from a pick-up truck sped past in the left-hand lane, clocking close to a hundred kilometres an hour. Its back end was shuddering against the bumps with the frenzy of water on a hot plate and as it swerved back into their lane its rear tires were kicking up a storm, pelting the windshield with sand and slush and reducing their visibility to just this side of nil. A sharp *tack!* sounded against the spatter — a pebble striking the glass. From its impact point in the middle of the windshield radiated a sudden splay of cracks tapering to points as fine as gossamer and those growing longer with every bump and bounce.

"Son of a bitch!" Tawyne was cursing as he activated the wipers and Deacon was thinking much the same as twin jets washed over the mucky effluence, bringing the road back into view.

The truck was speeding away and Tawyne pressed his foot down on the gas as if he meant to pursue, coming back to his senses only after the truck had disappeared over a hump in the road. Easing off the throttle, he looked to Deacon with a truly mystified gape, asking then as if he hadn't himself been sitting right there:

"Did you see what that asshole just did to your windshield?"

7

"**D**o you want me to pull over, so you can say something?"

They'd just turned onto Algonquin and found the orange pick-up pulled to the side of the road a hundred or so metres away. Its body was raised an extra foot off the ground by its oversized tires, and its monster-truck-like appearance was further complemented by two chrome exhaust pipes, like horns, extending over its cab.

Hard not to notice something like that driving around town.

Deacon had seen it a few times before and knew well of the two decals stuck on its rear window. The one on the right had a buxom woman with tires for feet, bent over with her rear end raised in the air beside the caption *My Other Ride Has Tits*. The one on the left was a somewhat anomalous Confederate flag. Anything he might say to a driver who'd have the latter emblazoned on his truck seemed too much like giving him an excuse and Deacon shook his head.

"Keep driving," he said.

"But —"

"Insurance will cover it."

"You're still going to be out the deductible."

"It's okay."

"You really ought to say something."

Tawyne had slowed the Jeep to a virtual crawl as they passed the truck. The driver was sitting behind the wheel. With his elevation all Deacon could make out of him was the toothy crocodile's grin tattooed on his arm and the cigarette wedged between two of his fingers. A ways down the road, another man stood at the top of what Deacon knew to be a long, curving downward slope. He couldn't have been taller than five-six and was dressed in a black leather jacket and black jeans and holding what appeared to be a telescope to his one eye.

As they approached, he lowered it with a sudden jerk, as if they'd caught him doing something he shouldn't have, and Deacon saw it wasn't a telescope but the sight from a rifle. He also saw that the man had a horn like a ram's tattooed on either side of his neck, which immediately made sense to Deacon, since his face bore an uncommon similarity to that of a billy goat. As the man walked back towards the orange pick-up, Deacon stared straight ahead, trying to avoid any and all eye contact, while Tawyne did quite the opposite, staring at the man brazenly through the passenger window as they passed him by.

"God," he said as the Jeep dipped down the hill, "they sure breed rednecks ugly around here."

The gully was surrounded on either side by a regiment of Jack pines, planted in evenly spaced rows, and at the bottom of the slope the road swung a hard left to follow along the valley floor. A tow truck was pulling a vintage grey sedan — a Buick Regal, Deacon would have guessed — from the ditch on the far side of the curve. A cop car was parked diagonally across both lanes there and an officer wearing a neon safety vest was standing in front of that. He had his back to them as Tawyne eased the Jeep down the well-sanded slope but the officer looked enough like Dylan that Deacon didn't feel inclined to get a closer look.

"Here's fine," Deacon said when they'd come to within fifty yards of the cruiser and Tawyne jammed on the brakes hard, just to be funny.

"Right here?" he asked with a playful smirk.

Deacon disregarded that by popping open his door and stepping out, easing it shut softly behind him so as not to attract any undue notice. Tawyne wasn't so inclined towards stealth and slammed the door hard enough to get the officer's attention. When he shot a vaguely irritated glance backwards, Deacon saw it was Officer Rhimes and not Dylan at all.

"Don't forget the camera," Deacon called over the hood and Tawyne opened the back door to retrieve it. When he had, he started off towards the scene and then stopped.

"You're not coming?" he asked backwards and Deacon shook his head.

"I'd just get in your way."

Tawyne nodded like he understood exactly what Deacon meant and set off on a jogging walk. Deacon scanned past him, searching amongst the four police officers and two paramedics crowding around the sedan as the tow truck's winch lowered its front end to the road. Dylan wasn't among them but he did see the familiar bob of Officer Myers's auburn ponytail.

It had been three years since Elaine "Laney" Myers had ghosted Deacon and yet every time he'd come across her in the interval she'd greeted him with a disembodied gape — meant, he supposed, to be a reflection of his own expression on the night they'd parted ways. Recollections of that gave him reason enough to maintain his distance. Lighting a cigarette, he stepped to the front of the Jeep and leaned against its bumper, watching Tawyne snap a few pictures of the sedan from several different angles.

He'd smoked his cigarette to the butt and was lighting another when Marchand appeared from behind the treeline masking a curve in the road, walking straight towards Tawyne. He said something to him. It must have been along the lines of "Your boss around somewhere?" because Tawyne responded by pointing directly at Deacon.

If Tawyne held a grudge against Marchand for his father's death, he'd never said as much, though it was hard not to intuit a resonant glower in the way he stared after him as Marchand made his way towards the roadblock. And while Marchand was smiling on the outside as he approached Officer Rhimes, Deacon knew that he was probably feeling quite the opposite on the in.

The discovery that René hadn't been carrying a rifle but a fishing rod he'd meant to give his son on his birthday had come as a terrible blow to Marchand. After the police board had cleared him of the killing, he'd taken a few months off and during that time Dylan must have told him another René had met a similar fate in one of George's books. The night before he was scheduled to return to duty he'd shown up at Baker Street with a six-pack of Keith's tall cans and a well-worn copy of George's eleventh book, *The Unnamed*, though he'd be well into his fourth of the former before he finally got around to referring to the latter.

"Can I ask you something?" he'd asked after taking a healthy swig from the can.

"What's that?" Deacon had asked.

"I —" Pausing and shaking his head as if he couldn't quite verbalize what was bothering him. Looking up at Deacon then with nervous eyes, more akin to an awkward teenage girl asking the captain of the football team to the prom than a police sergeant in his late fifties who suspected the local reporter was holding out on him. "I mean . . . You've read it, right?"

He glanced down at *The Unnamed* so there'd be no mistaking what he'd meant.

"Sure," Deacon answered, "a half-dozen times."

Marchand nodded like that was exactly the answer he was looking for.

"You ever talk to George about it?"

"On occasion."

"You ever ask him about . . . René? I mean the character in the book. How he came to, you know, call him that?"

Deacon had, in fact, asked George about that on multiple occasions, since it had always seemed damned strange to Deacon how a character George had created would seemingly spring to life right off the page so many years later. The only answer he'd ever got was a wry smile and a variation of, "Yeah, that's a helluva thing. Kind of makes me think I might have been onto something all along."

Deacon told Marchand the same and when that did little to satisfy him, he added, "Probably it was just a coincidence."

He gave Marchand a quick summary of how George had come to write the book and added, by way of a conclusion, "Guy's last name was Descartes and so it wasn't really much of a stretch to think that someone in his family would eventually end up calling their son René."

That didn't seem to satisfy Marchand much either but for whatever reason he wasn't inclined to press the point. He sat for another moment, thumbing at the pages and looking at the ground, before speaking again.

"Do you think —" he started then stopped and the grave deliberation with which he next spoke gave Deacon every indication that this was what had been on his mind all along. "Do you think René — The real René, I mean. Do you think he might have been innocent too?"

There was despair in his eyes and Deacon would have liked nothing more than to tell him that he was wrong, that René had brutally murdered the Wane family and that Marchand shouldn't have felt any worse about shooting him than he would've a rabid dog. But Deacon had also gleaned something else in his eyes. It might have been a genuine longing for the truth, though it could have just as easily been a desperate plea for Deacon to tell such an exacting lie that it would erase all doubt.

Deacon hadn't had the will to muster such a deception and so instead he said, "It always struck me that way."

Marchand's expression had hardened and he'd nodded and swallowed like he had cement in his throat before pushing himself to his feet and stumbling off towards the driveway without bothering even to say goodbye. And that was the last either of them had ever spoken about that.

In the intervening years, Marchand had made a careful point to always come over and say hello whenever their paths crossed, where before he'd never paid Deacon more than a passing glance. After Tawyne had been accepted into the Accelerator Program at Tildon High, and for convenience's sake had moved into the apartment above the *Chronicle*, Marchand always gave Deacon a crisp fifty on Tawyne's birthday and a hundred-dollar bill at Christmas "to buy him something nice." It had also become his habit to start or end their conversations asking after the boy, token gestures which in the grand scheme of things didn't amount to much but had come to mean a great deal to Deacon.

At the roadblock, Officer Rhimes was saying something that Deacon couldn't hear and Marchand answered him with a jovial smile, calling back, "And I thought I was stiff when I got up in the morning!" Officer Rhimes laughed and Deacon took the exchange to mean that the *Suspicious Death* must have still been in the car, frozen solid.

Marchand picked up his pace as he walked past the cruiser and force of habit had Deacon reaching into his pocket for a stick of the gum he used to hide the smell of weed on his breath even though he hadn't yet had his first toke of the day.

"I see you've finally put the lad to work," Marchand offered by way of a greeting.

"Well, you know what they say," Deacon answered. "Idle hands do the devil's work."

"You're sure right about that."

It was a phrase Mason Lowry had himself used twice by Chapter II and it lent weight to Deacon's increasing suspicion that Aubrey Marchand had been George's inspiration for the retired police chief, whom he'd described in *No Quarter* as perambulating about town on his nightly jaunts with the proudly obstinate gait of an old-time Wild West sheriff who'd gone to seed after too many fallow years chained behind a desk.

George would later add to that:

> He'd let his already formidable moustache grow long enough that he wouldn't have had much trouble tying it into a bow beneath his chin and whenever he was mulling something over he tugged at one of its ends, as if he was trying to spring loose a trapdoor in his mind that'd send the solution to whatever was beguiling him tumbling out through his lips.

Chief Marchand's moustache was certainly getting there and he took a moment to give it a tug before speaking again.

"I see you got my message," he said. The look of confusion on Deacon's face must have been plain to see, for he then added, "I damn near had to make it an order before Becca would send it. You two on the outs or something?"

All Deacon could manage in answer was a facsimile of the expression Laney had been feeding him these past three years. He'd always been careful to keep his relationships with both Laney and Rebecca private, worried more for their sake than his that if someone found out they were his "undisclosed source" within the Tildon Police Service it'd mean their jobs. Evidently, Rebecca hadn't been quite so discreet. To keep from thinking about what else she might have said about him around the station he stuck the piece of gum in his mouth and gave it a few good chews, trying to think of how he might respond.

"That's news to me," he finally offered, and then couldn't help himself but add: "Why? Did she say something?"

"Not to me. But I did hear your name come up when she was talking to Laney the other day. Seemed pretty pissed. Something about a . . . pot roast?"

That too was news to Deacon and he took Marchand's wry smile as being as good an excuse as any to steer the conversation towards business.

"Your message," he said between chews, "mentioned something about a suspicious death?"

"You could say that," Marchand said, casting a quick glance back at the scene.

The four officers were affixing a tarp over the sedan's roof and window, using bungee cords to secure it to the car's frame. The body must have been frozen fast to the seat, and they were prepping it for a drive to the station, probably to thaw it out in their service garage. Beyond, the trench the car had left dipped through the snowbank and down into the ravine. It followed a

91

straight line with the road and looked to Deacon like someone, driving too fast, had simply failed to make the corner.

He said as much to Marchand.

"And that's what we thought at first too," he answered, reaching into his jacket's inside pocket and pulling out a smallish clear-plastic evidence bag. "Then we found this tacked to the steering wheel."

He passed it over. It contained a piece of yellow paper, about the size of your standard stick-it note. On it was clearly hand-printed in black ink:

> *Dear camerado! I confess I have urged you onward with*
> *me, and still urge you, without the least idea of what is*
> *our destination,*
> > *Or whether we shall be victorious, or utterly quell'd*
> > *and defeated.*

How long Deacon had been staring at it he couldn't say and maybe he'd be staring at it still if Marchand had not then said, "It's something George wrote, isn't it?"

Deacon shook his head.

"No, it was, uh . . . Walt Whitman."

"But I thought —" Marchand started and Deacon cut him off.

"George quoted it in one of his books."

Point of fact, he'd used it as the epigraph in *The Road Ahead*, a book he'd dedicated "to David," David being his publisher's first name. George had often said, "I reckon he was the only person in the country who had the gumption to publish my fictions," and while he'd always only expressed the utmost respect for David, George had told Deacon he'd meant the Whitman quote, and more so the book itself, as a bit of lark.

The Road Ahead was the seventh novel he'd written and the sixth novel published by Shade Tree Press, the only exception being *My Brother's Keeper*, which he'd self-published for purely personal reasons. None of his books had sold even half of their English-language run and while the three translated into German had sold a few thousand copies each, George had begun to suspect that maybe his publisher was losing patience with him, sales-wise. It hadn't helped matters that his previous fiction had taken his propensity for violence and sexual deviance to hitherto unexplored depths of depravity. There wasn't a single reviewer in the entire country — nor librarian, aside from Loretta — who'd been willing to give it even an inch of space, whether in a column or a catalogue. It had sold a meagre one hundred and fifty copies, a resounding failure even by George's standards, and it was perhaps with this in mind that his publisher had sent him a handwritten note at the bottom of his so-called royalty statement.

The note had simply asked, *Do you want to give me some idea as to where the hell you're going with this?* George, or so he'd said, had taped it to the hood of his Remington Rand typewriter while he wrote *The Road Ahead*, his answer to that.

Knowing the book as Deacon did, he could well understand why Dylan would have chosen to leave its epigraph at the scene of a crime. He, himself, had been circling around it for years and had finally conceded that if there was a key to unlocking the mystery of what game Dylan was playing at, it wasn't likely he'd find a better candidate than *The Road Ahead*. But any discussion of that could only serve to make him sound like some sort of raving lunatic — he didn't have to look further than his last conversation with Rain to be reminded of that.

Trying to think of what he might say now, his thoughts wandered back to the text Dylan had sent him on New Year's Eve. It seemed as good a place to start as any and he asked Marchand, "You have any idea of how long it's been buried in the snow?"

"The car?" Marchand asked him back, though Deacon thought the inference was clear. "It couldn't have been more than a month, since its driver was in jail until then."

That placed it in mid-February, which didn't tell Deacon much but did, in the very least, provide him with another question.

"You have a name?" he asked.

Marchand tugged on his moustache and for a moment Deacon thought he wouldn't answer, next-of-kin needing to be notified and all. But after two tugs he said, "Leonard Stokes. That name mean anything to you?"

"Rings a bell," Deacon answered, though he couldn't quite place it.

"He was the one who sold that bad batch of fentanyl killed those people a few years back."

Deacon remembered the case well. Dylan had been the arresting officer, having pulled over Leonard Stokes for driving without a left taillight. Stokes had just smoked a joint in his car and that gave Officer Cleary sufficient cause to search the vehicle. In the trunk he'd found two thousand pills and ten thousand in cash. When tested, the former were found to be from the same batch of fentanyl as the ones that had already killed four people, the youngest victim only fifteen.

It was seeming less and less likely now that Dylan had been conducting a "routine traffic stop," as Deacon had reported in the article he'd written on the trial, and there was little doubt in his mind that the late Leonard Stokes was somehow wrapped up in whatever scheme Dylan was hatching next. A name and a tenuous connection wasn't much to go on — certainly not enough to make a convincing case to Marchand, anyway — but the memory of the trial did in the very least provide him with another question.

"Didn't the judge give Stokes twelve years?" he asked, the verdict having been handed down a meagre five years earlier.

"You'd have to take that up with the parole board."

The grate in his tone suggested what he thought about the board but the timing did give Deacon a new direction.

"You say he was released in the middle of February?" he asked.

"Roundabouts. Why? That mean something to you?"

"No. I mean — The snowbanks would have been ten feet high in the middle of February."

"I've been thinking the same thing."

"He'd have needed a nudge to get him that far off the road."

"Hell, he would have needed a damn sight more'n a nudge."

Trying to wind his thoughts around that and then taking a stab, however unlikely, at bringing Dylan into, at least, the periphery of the conversation, Deacon asked, "Who called it in?"

"A couple of skidooers. Saw something poking through the snow. Turned out to be the antenna. They'd half-dug the car out before they saw the body."

A dead end so he asked another obvious question.

"You know where he was staying? Leonard, I mean."

"He used to live over on Talon Lake Road. His ex-wife still lives there, far as I know. I'll be heading over there shortly."

"Talon Lake Road, you say?" Deacon asked, mulling over that.

"That mean something to you?"

It did.

Five years previously a husband and wife had burnt up in a house fire on Talon Lake Road. The victims' bodies were found in their basement, surrounded by what was left of their couch. The fire inspector's report indicated that the blaze that had consumed them and reduced their house to a charred foundation had likely been the result of one of them falling asleep watching TV with a lit cigarette still in his or her hand. A dozen-odd liquor bottles had been discovered amongst the wreckage so it wasn't much of a mystery as to why neither had woken up and likely

Deacon wouldn't have had cause to remember it at all had it not been for the text he'd received ten seconds before the first siren had alerted him to the tragedy.

You better get out to Talon Lake Road, Unknown Caller had written. *Another world's about to end in fire.*

If the dead couple had any connection to Dylan, Deacon had never found it, and since an "anonymous" tip alone wasn't much to go on, he answered now, "It's probably nothing."

Marchand opened his mouth to maybe press the point but was interrupted by the roar of an engine. The tow truck was muscling up the slope with the tarped-over sedan and the two men paused to watch it pass. Tawyne was trailing after it, taking his time to get back to the Jeep, and once the truck had passed, Marchand gave him a quick glance. He couldn't help but have noticed that it caused a certain hesitation in Tawyne's stride and that, apparently, was reason enough for Marchand to be on his way.

"I'm going to need that back," Marchand said, holding out his hand.

It took Deacon a moment to realize he was asking for the evidence bag. He passed it over and Marchand gave the quote another look, perhaps seeking further inspiration and apparently finding a little.

"You know," he said, "I asked George one time if he made any money writing books. You know what he told me?"

"What's that?" Deacon answered, though he had a pretty good idea of what George would have said.

"He said he couldn't even get his family to read his books, much less the general public. Seemed to rankle him some. But on the upside, it sure does narrow down our list of possible suspects."

To practically one, Deacon was thinking, though he held his tongue, not ready to play that card yet.

Marchand was already heading down the slope and he turned back.

"Oh, and that reminds me," he said. "You haven't seen Dylan around lately, have you?"

"Dylan? No. Why?"

"Last anyone heard he was on his way back to the station last Monday with that Farmer kid's splitting axe. He was supposed to enter it into evidence."

"He never showed up?" It was hard for Deacon to conceal the trace of panic in his voice.

"And nobody's heard from him since," Marchand said.

He'd gone back to tugging at his moustache and Deacon offered: "You check his house?"

"I swung by yesterday. There was a moving truck in his driveway."

"That's strange."

"I thought so too."

"Was it moving stuff in or out?"

"In. Turns out he sold the place two months ago. Didn't tell anyone either."

"Hmm."

"Hmm is right."

Marchand's eyes had narrowed in their scrutiny, which planted the thought in Deacon's head that maybe Marchand had already devised his own list of one and everything he'd said up until then was just pretence.

"You'll keep me posted," Marchand was then saying.

"Sorry?"

"If you can think of anyone who might have written this."

He held up the evidence bag as if there might still have been any doubt as to what he'd meant.

"You'll be the first to know," Deacon assured him and Marchand flashed him his congenial smile, though that hardly diminished the pointed glare in his eyes.

Turning down the slope, Marchand let gravity pull him past Tawyne, the boy turning after him, maybe to get in one last glower. Habit had Deacon circling the Jeep towards the driver-side door. It was only after he'd slipped inside and was reaching for his keys that he remembered Tawyne was driving.

Looking then through the windshield, tracing over the cracks radiating outwards from where the pebble had struck, quartering its glass, and thinking of the road ahead, not meaning George's book but Highland, rutted with ice and thawing mud.

It'd be a miracle if they made it back home before the whole damned thing came crashing down.

CRYSTAL

S he'd been back in her old bedroom at her parents' house for over a week.

Two hours ago, Ward had slipped from between the covers at seven, trying his best to be quiet, but had awoken her nonetheless. He'd left his skiing outfit neatly folded on the dresser the night before and had stolen out the door with it tucked under his arm, as silent as a practised thief. After that she'd heard the toilet flush and the muffled voice of her mother greeting Ward in the hall and then all was quiet. She'd shortly fallen into a restless sleep, awoken every half-hour or so by a cramp in her abdomen and then just after nine by a sharp pain, like a needle being thrust into her stomach.

Gasping awake and clutching at her belly, the pain folding time, as it had so often over the past three weeks, catapulting her back to New Year's morning. Then a searing agony like a hot poker rammed into her stomach had her clutching at her bump, its flesh as taut as a drum and yet alive, tiny hands and feet battering at her insides, the pain unimaginable like it wasn't a child in there but a porcupine trying to claw its way out.

Clamping her teeth now, refusing to cry out, to alert her mother, the thought of her racing into the room — panic-stricken and out of breath, clutching feebly in her cancer-ridden stupor at the door frame for support, barely able to stand — almost worse than the pain. Holding her breath, she waited for the cramp to subside long enough for her to chance another breath. Her fingers were kneading at her belly, its flesh as soft and warm as bread dough, and its deflated sag speaking to Crystal even more so than the pain of what she had lost, or rather what had been taken from her.

"It's goddamned murder!"

What she'd screamed at Ward shortly after she'd awoken in the ICU at the North Bay Regional Health Centre. He was sitting beside her on the bed, with her hand in his, as he had for three days, ever since the "extraction" that had saved her life but not their baby's.

"There must be another explanation — I mean —"

Shaking his head, wrangling his thoughts around how his wife had come to have a near-lethal dose of the abortion drug misoprostol in her blood. Failing in that, he passed a skittish sideways glance at Crystal, which seemed to suggest he hadn't ruled her out as a prime suspect in their child's death. Crystal, after all, had expressed plenty of misgivings about having a baby and with the way she'd been acting these past few months . . .

Ward was then biting his bottom lip and shaking his head again, as if he couldn't bear to even entertain such a thought.

"I was poisoned," Crystal had stated bluntly, trying to put the matter to rest once and for all. "Someone must have switched out my vitamins, which means Baby Rose was murdered and you're just going to sit there —"

A stabbing pain then, almost as bad as the one that had awoken her just past midnight on New Year's morning. Clutching at Ward's hand hard enough to leave three fingernail gouges on the back of it, Ward crying out, "Nurse! Help! Someone! Nurse!"

They hadn't spoken of it since and Crystal again shrank from the memory, rolling over and reaching towards the nightstand, feeling for the two Percocets Ward had left for her. She plucked up one then the other, dry-swallowing both and then lying back down, closing her eyes and breathing shallow breaths against a lesser cramp like an aftershock.

Tears squeezed from her eyes, rolling down her cheeks. She wiped at them with the palms of her hands, anything to keep them from searching her belly again. Breathing in shallow gasps until she could feel the Percs weaving their spell, not so much taking the pain away from her as taking her away from it. Drifting her off not towards sleep but into an ever-receding wakefulness, her eyes open and her world blissfully reduced to four sepia-toned walls devoid of anything except a few thumbtack holes and an empty corkboard, a wisp of a spider's web in one corner — a veritable tomb compared to what it had looked like just four months ago.

Up until then, it had remained the same as it had on the morning she'd left for the University of Toronto, a virtual museum of the tastes and preferences of a small-town girl with big-city dreams. After the dinner at which she and Ward had told her parents that they were pregnant, she'd come up to the room, just to take a look. Standing at the door, she'd been overwhelmed with an undeniable urge to box up all of her posters, her books, the corkboard of photographs and inspirational messages, her record collection and assorted knick-knacks and stuffed animals, to preserve them for a day when together she and her daughter could sift through it all with the wonder of archaeologists unearthing artifacts from a lost civilization, what they might have called "the

Nesting Instinct" in any number of the pregnancy books gifted to her by well-meaning friends and which had been gathering into a tottering stack, mostly unread, on her nightstand.

But lying back in her old bed, doped out on Percocet, it had begun to seem to her that stripping the room bare had simply been the first stirrings of a madness that, three months later, would hurtle her on some lunatic drive into the northern wilds, firm in the belief that her husband was sabotaging her efforts to realize their dream of bringing *A Precious Few* to life on the big screen.

Poor Ward, she thought, thinking about what she'd said to him on New Year's Eve and feeling only shame in that.

Without him . . .

An errant thought that sometimes sprung upon her unawares, most often when she wasn't thinking about him at all and which she'd cut off not because she hated to think of where *she* might have ended up if it wasn't for *him* but because it seemed so disingenuous, like she was an awkward ninth-grader daydreaming in class about some boy who'd smiled at her when they'd passed in the hall. And if there was one thing she knew for certain, it was that *she* had made *him* as much as *he* had made *her*, that itself feeling disingenuous, this setting one against the other, the language of *him* and *her* itself unequal to the task of trying to untangle the feelings she had about *them* or *they* and *we* or *us*. The exercise would quickly degenerate into the equivalent of a semantic Sudoku, *I* seeming to capture the spirit of what they had better than any but that not making sense either since *I* was a singular. There wasn't supposed to be room for two in there and really she knew two could never become one. But between them, and of this she was certain, there was a space where in any true marriage two not only could become one but must.

How had Howard Parsons put it in *A Precious Few*?

Love, he was certain, was an accumulation of things;
kisses and secrets and time and patience. And love grows
or wanes, it never remains still. Silent at times, but
never still. Like faith, it is a longing with a foreseeable
outcome. Companionship, a purpose. And nothing more?
No, it's arbitrary — the ultimate coincidence. A looking
at something and then the sudden awareness that some-
one else is looking at the same thing right alongside you.
As when you stand in a room with mirrors on opposite
walls and try to see beyond your own reflection but your
head gets in the way. Two people standing side by side
likewise can't see beyond their heads but between them
there is a space which does see and that space is love.

The fact that Howard Parsons was a degenerate old man
lusting after his teenage granddaughter hardly diminished the
impression the passage had made on Crystal the first time she'd
read it. For what were the circumstances surrounding how she
and Ward had met if not the Ultimate Coincidence?

They had told what they'd come to call *"Our* Origin Story"
together so many times that it seemed like even thinking about it
alone was just short of a betrayal. But lying stoned in her old bed
with her thoughts swirling like a dervish around how she'd acted
on New Year's Eve, it had begun to seem that her momentary
bout of insanity had nothing to do with being pregnant at all
and everything to do with her losing faith in *their* story. So here
she was poring over it once more, like some old priest suffering
a crisis of faith who'd returned to the place of his own personal
Road to Damascus, seeking to rekindle it once again.

She'd been twenty-five and had just completed her MBA at
the U of T. She'd had plenty of ideas as to what she might do next
but no firm plans beyond the promise she'd made to herself that

she'd never go back to living in Tildon. For the past two years she'd supplemented her meagre teaching assistant's income by working as a concessions manager at the Cineplex in the Yonge Eglinton Centre of midtown Toronto and in the three months after she'd got her degree her life had fallen into a predictable pattern: counting candy and cash from six until eleven, five or six days a week, and then changing out of her office greys and into something bright and skimpy, hitting a dance club or an all-night rave with the delirious abandon of a recent grad who had the luxury of sleeping all day long if she so desired.

Most often she did this in the company of Kendra Tinsdale, one of the theatre's floor managers. Kendra had been three years into an accounting degree when she decided to take a year off, in her words, "to, you know, live a little." She was a somewhat mousy woman at work who turned into a veritable hellcat with a few drinks or a couple of pills in her. She was also from a small town — Lindsay — and that had lent them a natural affinity, though where Crystal had spent most of her off hours studying, Kendra had spent her time honing an almost preternatural ability to what she called "suss out a good time."

Often their nights started at the Purple Onion, a skeezy little bar on the outskirts of the city's entertainment district. The Onion's walls were adorned with a motley collection of neon-embossed black-and-white photographs depicting various aspects of Las Vegas nightlife circa 1971. Between those, the perennially low lighting and the art deco proclivities of whoever had designed the furniture, The Onion always struck Crystal as exactly the kind of place any number of down-on-their-luck gamblers might search out to drown a losing streak in cheap tequila. It was, however, an altogether unlikely place for two young women such as they were to embark on their nightly frolics, made only slightly less unremarkable by the "arrangement" Kendra had with the bartender, Randy.

Whenever they'd come in, he'd nod to her and a short while later she'd follow him into the storeroom, returning to the table after their quickie with a half-dozen free shots to wash down whatever else he'd given her, usually a couple of mollies or Percs, a couple of lines of blow, once two tabs of acid.

So it had been a great disappointment when they'd shown up one Thursday night to discover that Randy had, in the new bartender's words, "moved on."

In its redacted family-friendly version, Crystal would leave out the matter of Randy altogether, saying only that they'd stopped by the Purple Onion on that particular night because she had to "take a seriously wicked piss." That much at least was true and when she and Ward had told the story to her parents, even her rather mild use of the vernacular had been enough to make her mother scold, "Oh, Crystal, don't be so crass!" Her mother might have thus appreciated that the sign on the door to the woman's bathroom at the Purple Onion read *The Powder Room*, a detail that Crystal neglected to mention, saying only that when she returned after "powdering her nose," she found the new bartender pouring them two shots of tequila.

"From the gentlemen in the back," he said by way of explanation, motioning to a table on the far side of the lounge.

In the family-friendly version, Ward was one of the two young men sitting there, the only other two people in the bar at all. But the truth was, the two young men were actually Ward's roommates and she wouldn't meet her future husband until the next morning. One was Black and the other white and both were dressed in what could only have been called casual beach wear — garish Hawaiian shirts and the Black guy with a straw fedora, the white one sporting a translucent red visor that gave Crystal the impression he was aspiring towards a career in gonzo journalism. But they were both plenty cute and from the way they were ogling the two young women at the bar they certainly seemed eager for some company.

Kendra was playing it cool, not looking their way until after she and Crystal downed their shots and then only to hold up two fingers, indicating another round. The one in the fedora nodded to the bartender and when he approached them Kendra declined a second shot for swiping the bottle, adding a well-choreographed wobble — for dramatic effect — to her step as she carried it on a circuitous path among the empty tables on her way towards theirs in the back.

The next half-hour proceeded with the terminal velocity of a slow-rolling tsunami. At one point the guy in the fedora, Brad, who would later serve as the DP on all three movies in the *Beast* franchise, mentioned that both he and Garland — a wannabe screenwriter who'd end up running the service department at his father's Mazda dealership in Brampton — were film students at York University. Kendra had answered that by pouring them all another drink on her way to saying, "That's funny, because we're both actresses."

"I guess this must be fate then," Garland said and they'd raised a toast to that.

At this point in the telling, if they were among friends, Crystal would say, "And then Brad said what were the magic words for me in those days." If Brad was in fact present, as he often was, he'd lean towards Crystal as he had then and in a conspiratorial whisper he'd say, "I've got some coke back at my place."

Ward, who had been silent until then since he wouldn't appear in the story for another twelve hours, would scrunch his face and shake his head. Aside from smoking a little pot and doing mushrooms — twice — he'd never developed a taste for substances of the mind-altering variety. And while he never held judgment over anyone who did, still he'd say, "Boy, I tell you, if I knew then what I know now . . ."

Crystal would gently chastise him with a backhanded slap on his arm before returning her attention to her audience. "He's such a prude," she'd say and then, feigning befuddlement, she'd ask, "Now where was I?"

Really this was just another pretext to include Ward and he'd play his assigned role by answering, "I believe you were just about to let Brad fuck you up the ass."

To that she'd chastise him again: "No silly, it was Garland who fucked me up the ass. Brad came all over my tits."

"Sorry, my mistake." Then, propping his index finger under his right cheekbone, he'd settle his chin on his knuckles, assuming the guise of a seasoned therapist listening attentively to his most degenerate patient. "By all means, continue."

The truth was that she had no coherent memory of what followed, only that she'd awoken in a strange bed with a dull throb in her posterior that did suggest someone had indeed fucked her in the ass. Someone had also come on her tits and, evidently, in her hair too. She was feeling sticky and weak and slightly nauseous but really no more so than on any other morning she'd awoken hungover in a stranger's bed. Whoever's room this was, he'd at least left the drapes shut so she was spared the scalding light of day, the traces of which were straining at the edges, their exuberant bright telling her it must have been approaching noon. A few minutes later, when she finally summoned the energy to sit up, she discovered that whoever's room it was had left her a glass of water and two Tylenol extra-strengths. After she'd washed the latter down with the former, she found he'd also taken the time to write her a note.

Had class, it read. *There's coffee in the kitchen. Lock up when you leave. Brad.*

She'd shortly discover that the room was on the second floor of a three-storey brick Tudor on a double-wide lot in the upscale Beaches district of Toronto. It was the same house, in fact, that she'd been living in ever since and in later years she'd always answer admiring comments about what she'd done with the place with a rather caustic "You should have seen it the first time *I* did."

"Bad?" the other person would infer.

"Three university students — males — had been living in it for four years. And nary a broom to be found. Bad? It was a fucking disaster!"

What she'd really wanted to do more than anything was to take a hot shower. But the tub in the bathroom down the hall was being used as a de facto laundry hamper, which didn't seem to have stopped someone from puking in it several times in the meanwhile. After relieving herself in a toilet that very likely hadn't seen more than a quick wipe since the turn of the millennium, she cleaned herself at the sink the best she could. She checked behind every one of the hallway's other four unexplored doors for Kendra and finding no sign of her, she'd followed a narrow set of stairs down into the kitchen.

The sink and the surrounding countertops were ensconced with plates of congealed food and the garbage can beside the fridge was overflowing with takeout containers, the occupants' obvious solution to the lack of any clean dishes remaining in the cupboards. There was a pervasive odour as if a bottle of bleach had been poured over three-day-old roadkill and the lurch she felt in her stomach upon smelling that was giving her every reason to find the quickest way out. But she'd forgotten her purse upstairs — she was hoping it was upstairs, anyway — and then there was the matter of the drunken pact she'd once made with Kendra. During one of their nightly debauches, they'd promised each other they'd "leave no woman behind," the unspoken inference being that such applied equally to the morning after. But she was feeling light-headed and weak-kneed, and mounting a full search of the premises without at least the bracing influence of a hot cup of coffee seemed like a fool's errand at best.

Without the benefit of any dish detergent — the dispenser by the sink was empty — she rinsed out a coffee mug and poured herself a cup. There was a two-litre carton of milk in the fridge and it seemed a miracle that when she gave it a whiff it smelled at least halfway fresh. The same couldn't be said for the sugar bowl on the table. The sides of it were imbedded with yellow crustules as hard as cement and she was glancing about for something to chip away at that when her eyes passed over the book sitting in front of the table's only chair. It was face down so she couldn't see its title but the picture of the author on the back struck her as vaguely recognizable. It only took her a second to realize why: it was none other than her grandfather, George.

His eyes were wide in static surprise as if whoever had taken the photo had snuck up behind him. It had been exactly how her grandfather had looked at her the time she'd snuck into the old barn he used as his den. She was with Corey Vance, the son of a local physician who fancied himself a writer and who'd goaded her into letting him take a peek at where a "real" author worked. They'd ended up fucking on the floor behind the desk and she was just standing back up, unravelling the underwear that had become bunched around her knees, when she caught sight of her grandfather gaping back at her from the door. His frozen shock quickly gave way to panicked befuddlement. He'd glanced away, mumbling something about looking for a book. His eyes were casting about the stacks piled around the shelves and his hand grabbing at the closest one within reach, muttering more to himself than her, "Here it is," before making a quick escape.

III

Seeing her grandfather now peering at her with the same startled mortification as he had then, it seemed — it did — like he was somehow admonishing her from beyond the grave. It had an immediately disorienting effect and to hide from his castigating gaze, she'd flipped the book over. It was only then that she saw that the book in question was *A Precious Few*.

Below the title, the cover read, *A Novel*, and beneath that, *George Cleary*. Otherwise, its cover was a photograph of a towering pine tree perched at the edge of a granite cliff overlooking a wilderness expanse that stretched all the way to a distant horizon. The sky there was simmering with the reddish hues of dusk, the sky above fading towards a star-fraught dark and the forest below speckled in equal measure by what appeared to be fireflies, though she'd later learn they were actually torches.

The picture didn't mean much to her at the time — regardless of the assurances she'd made to Deacon some years previous, she'd never yet read any of her grandfather's fictions — but there was something else about the book that did make quite an impression. Dozens, or perhaps hundreds, of multicoloured stick-its protruded from its pages and when, out of idle curiosity, she'd opened the book at random to see to what they might portend, she'd found the page, and every subsequent page thereafter, embossed with a delicate, almost girlish, litany of handwritten notes. The margins were full of them, and huge swaths of the text were underlined and some highlighted and further emphasized by an accumulation of *s and *!*s, the latter most often in batches of twos and threes.

In her weakened state — flipping through page after page of the same — her vision began to blur and her head to spin. She'd eased herself into the chair and closed her eyes, holding them shut and waiting for the world to stop reeling, when she heard a gentle click from behind — the front door opening. It had a similar effect on her as had seeing her grandfather staring up at her from the back cover and she hastily flipped the book back over as the tromp of footsteps grew louder. They were definitely heading her way. Trying to muster a casual air that seemed well beyond the current state of her hangover, she took a sip from her cup.

"Ah, coffee," Ward would chime in at this point in the telling, for that is exactly what he said when, finally, he'd made this, his first appearance in the story. A brief moment later he would add, "Perfect."

It was while he was pouring himself a cup, seemingly oblivious to the woman sitting at the table, that Crystal got her first glimpse of her future husband. He was wearing blue athletic shorts, a trifle too short for her taste, and a plain blue T-shirt stained with sweat, both of which hung loose over his lank — almost to the point of being skeletal — legs, arms and chest. She'd shortly discover that he was twenty-four — a mere one year younger than herself — but right then he looked no older than nineteen. There was a plaintive awkwardness about the way he cast her a nervous glance on his way to the fridge, as if he was scared half to death at the prospect of finding, sitting in his kitchen, the much older woman he'd heard fucking both his roommates last night.

He'd just taken his first sip of coffee before he spoke again.

"Oh," he said, "let me get that out of your way."

In his haste, he set his cup a little too hard down on the counter and the liquid lapped over its rim and onto his hand. Wincing against its heat and licking at the splash, he snatched up *A Precious Few*. He was careful to avoid any and all eye contact as he cradled it to his chest. Under Crystal's stalwart gaze, he seemed to have forgotten all about his coffee and was looking ever so much like he was about to flee. His eyes were straining towards the living room, though that seemed to offer little hope of escape either.

"Um," he said, looking back in Crystal's general direction but still avoiding her eyes, "I don't suppose you know who that is passed out on the couch?"

Crystal craned her head back far enough that she could see down the hall and into the living room. A lone foot drooped over the couch's arm and she didn't have to look further than its silver anklet to know whose it was.

"That'd be Kendra," she said. "I was just looking for her."

She companioned this with a rather goofy thumbs up and that made Ward cringe even as his eyes sought out the back stairway — his quickest means of escape. Everything about him seemed to suggest he was on the verge of making a run for it and in the telling Crystal would say the same, adding to that: "And maybe he would have too and Our Story wouldn't have been much of one at all had I not then said, 'And who might you be?'"

"Oh, um, I'm um, uh —" Ward would stammer in perfect mimicry of his reaction then, as he held out a nervously proffered hand.

"I'm Ward."

It was only when she took his hand in hers that he finally did meet her eyes, if only ever so briefly, so that Crystal could see that they were the most piercing shade of steel-grey she'd ever seen. There was something else about them not quite so tangible — a mischievous, almost malevolent, glint that told her at once she'd been wrong about him being nervous around women, that his awkwardness was all part of some act he'd contrived for moments just like this, all the better to catch his quarry unawares. And in that moment it struck Crystal that his eyes looked just like a wolf's eyes sizing up its prey.

When she related this, there wasn't a friend who hadn't nodded in mutual understanding, for there was not one among them who hadn't had a similar experience the first time they'd met Ward. By virtue of their friendship, each in their own way had risen to the challenge inherent in his gaze, though none among them had risen quite so high as she, holding fast when he'd tried to withdraw his hand, challenging *him* to look at *her* again so he could see the glint in her own eyes, bolder still.

"I'm Crystal," she said. ". . . Cleary."

All these years later, thinking about it still gave her the chills. Lying in bed, revelling in the moment and feeling the hairs hackling at the back of her neck, she heard the door click and then saw it open a crack. Ward's face appeared in the gap a moment later, his eyes prying, cautious, as if he'd expected to find her asleep and didn't want to disturb her.

"Oh," he said opening the door wider and taking a tenuous first step into the room, "you're awake."

"I just woke up now," she lied, fake-wiping sleep from her eyes and yawning to complete the illusion.

"Can I get you anything?"

She shook her head and yawned again, this time for real, for she really was quite tired.

Taking another step into the room, he closed the door behind him. As he walked towards the bed, she couldn't help but notice that he glanced ever so casually at the laptop sitting on the dresser in the exact same spot he'd put it six days previous, setting his script of *A Precious Few* and the annotated novel of the same name on top. While he'd never spoken a word about why he might have done so, there they were nevertheless.

To stop herself from thinking about that, she asked, "How was your ski?"

"It was good." Bending over then and kissing her on the forehead. "Real good."

Crystal nodded and smiled, trying to think of something else to say. But she'd never been one for chit-chat and besides there was something else she'd been wanting to talk about, though she'd yet to formulate exactly how she might broach the issue.

"Listen," she said, which seemed as good a place to begin as any, "I've been thinking . . . Maybe it's about time for you to . . . leave."

Ward opened his mouth to protest, as he had every time she'd even suggested that maybe his energies could be better spent than hovering perpetually by her side.

"It's not you," she cut him off, "it's Mom. The longer you stay, the longer she'll expect me to stay" — lowering her voice then — "and I really just want to get the fuck back home."

And while that was plainly another lie, he nodded, seeing the apparent logic in what she'd said even as the scrunch to his eyes told her he was wavering still.

"And you've been putting off that meeting with HBO for two weeks now," she added trying to seal the deal.

She and Ward had recently sold HBO on a limited-run miniseries that, in his pitch, Ward had called "a *Great Gatsby* for our generation," but there'd been a few niggling points in the contract that still needed to be hashed out in person down in L.A.

"You should be there for that," he protested.

"It's more your thing than mine," she countered, which was true. "And besides, a couple of days in the sun would do you a world of good."

"And if it takes longer than a couple of days?"

"Then I'll get to join you. It's a win-win."

He scrunched his eyes again but she knew she had him.

"Now go on, git," she prodded, "before I change my mind."

That was enough to get him on his feet. He took a reluctant step towards the door and his glance again sought out the laptop on the dresser. He paused in his deliberation long enough that Crystal knew it spoke to him of something he'd also wanted to say but hadn't managed to figure out how to without it coming across as pushy — or, worse, insensitive.

He took another step, more resolute, and she knew it would have to be up to her.

"Would you mind bringing me my laptop before you go?" she asked. "I thought I might get a little writing done today."

When he glanced back at her, the surprise in his eyes harkened back to all those years ago when she'd first told him her name.

"What?" she asked, meeting his gaze with the same pointed stare she'd given him back then. "You didn't think I was just going to lie around in bed while you're off playing Mister Big Shot down in La La Land?"

So here's Crystal now, an hour later, the laptop propped open on her legs, staring at a blank screen.

The tyranny of the words as of yet unwritten, is what she'd once heard her grandfather call it whenever he'd faced a blank page. It was a tyranny made doubly so because lying in another bed on New Year's Eve, her quarrel with Ward behind her and Ward behind her as well, spooning against her back and his one hand cupped lovingly beneath her — *their* — pregnancy bump, the whole movie had seemed so clear in her mind that it might as well have been projected onto a screen wrapped around the inside of her skull.

She'd goaded herself to get up and write it down but she'd left her notepad in the Rover and besides she was perfectly happy spooning with Ward and too tired anyway to even open her eyes.

If it's worth remembering, she'd assured herself as she passed into sleep, *then you'll remember it in the morning.*

But that had been three weeks ago and in the meantime she'd been too doped up or in too much pain to give it more than a passing thought. Now, staring at the blank screen, she found she'd lost its thread entirely.

When she'd asked for the laptop, Ward had also brought her the script and his annotated copy of *A Precious Few*. She picked up the latter and flipped idly through its pages, seeking inspiration, knowing already that looking for any there was all but a lost cause.

What was it that Ward had said while he'd made them a conciliatory pot of tea shortly after she'd confronted him on New Year's Eve?

"You've been going about it the wrong way. Forget about the book. It's not your grandfather's story anymore. It has to be about you. Make it your own story."

And while it seemed paradoxical, his advice had her reaching for the script — *his* script. Flipping through the pages, she first sought out the once-reviled page 60.

In her grandfather's *A Precious Few*, the Parsons family — fleeing an unspecified and possibly civilization-ending catastrophe — had sought sanctuary in their isolated wilderness retreat only to find themselves at the mercy of a biker-gang-cum-doomsday-cult bent on burning the world back to Eden. He'd described the so-called Sons of Adam as having *shaven heads and faces painted as white as bone, their mouths tattooed with the imprint of skeletal grins so that they more resembled ghouls than men and their flesh impaled with the rib bones of their victims pierced like armour through the ashen plate of their skin.*

Suitably menacing for sure but not enough, apparently, for Ward. In his adaptation he'd pilfered a half-century's worth of horror icons to serve as his villains — a lazy bit of writing, in

Crystal's mind, justified solely on the basis of the caption that was to appear at the beginning of the film. *Halloween, Next Year*, it read, the inference being that the bad guys were really just regular folk all costumed up for the holiday.

It was indeed a plot point revealed on page 60, when Michael Myers, Freddy Krueger and Jason Voorhees showed up at the isolated cabin to which a group of twenty-something dot-com millionaires had fled in the opening scene after seeing, through the window of the private jet returning them from a drug-fuelled weekend in Whistler, Toronto consumed by a mushroom cloud.

To quote from the offending passage:

EXT. ROOFTOP PATIO NIGHT

They all gaze terror-struck at the sight
of the three horror icons standing
in the lightly wooded glade beneath
them, their ghastly masks rendered
in the flickering orange of the torch
each holds in his hand. Polly clutches
at Brad's arm, cringing, and Brad
shrugs her off, raising the rifle to his
shoulder, taking a bead on Voorhees.

His finger is itching on the trigger
when another torch alights from behind
Jason, illuminating Pinhead's pale and
prickly face. It's shortly followed
by another and another and another
until the whole forest has become one
seething mass of ghastly visages and
flickering flames surging forward with

the sudden frenzy of a colony of ants
doused with gasoline and set on fire.

Bang!

The shot hits Voorhees in the chest but
slows his progress about as much as if
it had struck his fictional counterpart.

He must be wearing a bulletproof vest!

THROUGH THE RIFLE'S SIGHT:

The crosshairs target the hockey mask,
dead centre, but before he can fire

ROOFTOP PATIO:

Polly is grabbing at his arm, pulling
him away from the rail.

                    POLLY
          Goddamn it, run!

It continued along in this vein for the next twenty pages and the
first time she'd read it, that's as far as she'd got before throwing it at
the wall in abject fury. She was sitting on her bed in her old room,
just as she was now, having blocked off the week after Christmas
to spend with her mother. Her mom's cancer had returned but this
time she'd rejected any and all suggestions of another round of
chemo, even if refusing treatment meant she wouldn't likely live
long enough to see the birth of her first grandchild.

It was a stressful time, to say the least, one exacerbated by the argument she'd had with Ward on the tarmac at the Mesaquakee airport. Their helicopter had dropped her off on the way to ferrying Ward to his family's "cottage" three hundred kilometres north, where, he'd said, he was going to rough out a first draft of what he'd taken to calling his "*Gatsby* reboot."

After kissing her goodbye, he'd said, "Try to get a little writing done if you can. It will make you feel better."

Though his tone was conciliatory, it had immediately struck her as deeply insensitive and she'd spat back at him, "Feel better? 'Feeling better' is the last thing on my mind right now. I mean, you know she's dying, right?"

He was clearly surprised by the venom in her tone. His expression had sagged into a disembodied gape and his inability to answer only further incensed her.

"You know what," she fumed, turning and storming towards the airport's lone terminal, "go fuck yourself!"

Through the terminal's window both of her parents were waving ecstatically and the sight of her emaciated mother clutching her father's arm for support only served to make her angrier still.

Ward had texted her a few dozen times in the meanwhile but she'd ignored every one of those. Then, six days later, on New Year's Eve, he'd couriered her his version of the script. By page 80 she was too angry to do anything except hurl it across the room. A few hours later she'd hurl it into his face as well.

"What the fuck is this!" she'd scream as Ward's hand shot up to deflect the screenplay-cum-projectile.

He was standing in the cottage's elevator at the time. Its door had opened as she stormed down the second-floor hallway towards the same, knowing exactly where Ward was likely to be: in the Cold War–era fallout shelter his grandfather had blasted into the granite beneath the Swanson family's summer retreat and which Ward had since made into his own little warren. The only way to get there was by means of the elevator and the only way to get its control panel to even acknowledge the existence of the bunker was by means of a DNA scanner, coded to allow access solely to blood members of the Swanson family. The thought that he was hiding out down there and that once again she was at his mercy didn't do much to improve her mood, and neither did the ironic smile with which he greeted her outburst.

He was wearing the pink linen suit Robert Redford had worn during his turn as Jay Gatsby and that Ward had bought at auction as a birthday present for himself last year, though it fit his wiry frame about as well as a potato sack would a beanpole. He'd doffed the jacket, probably for that very reason, and was wearing the vest loose and his shirtsleeves rolled up to the elbows so that when the script hit his forearm one of its brass fasteners scratched a wide arc over his skin. It was already beading blood by the time Crystal reached the end of the hall. Ward's expression was distinctly wounded and when he looked up at her his eyes didn't so much resemble a wolf's as a puppy dog's whose master had just swatted him with a rolled-up newspaper for shitting on the floor.

That he'd feign such obliviousness in the face of her bile was giving her every reason to slap the stupid right out of him.

"Do you think that's fucking funny?" she'd spat instead.

"N-no," he stuttered. "I mean, yes. I mean — Kind of. I thought —"

"You thought what?"

"I thought — I mean, I thought you'd understand."

"Understand what? You butchered it."

"Butchered it? What? I —"

"If you don't want to make the movie, you could have just fucking said so. You didn't have to go through this . . . charade!"

"Not make the movie? Charade? I —"

Shaking his head and giving her a sideways glance, something seemed to dawn on him.

"You didn't make it to the end, did you?" he finally asked.

"The end? Are you fucking kidding me? You're lucky I made it past page 60."

He was already bending down and grabbing the script from the floor. Flipping through its pages until he'd come to its last four or five pages he held the script out to her, ordering in no uncertain terms, "Read!"

It was a tone he'd rarely, if ever, taken with her and it planted enough of a seed of doubt that she scanned down the page before her.

INT. NUCLEAR FALLOUT SHELTER NIGHT

Polly lunges through the gap created by the opening door, which she can now see is fashioned out of eighteen inches of steel like one guarding a bank vault. The shelter beyond is concealed in shadow and as the door comes to a rest against the wall with a muffled thud she pauses in the square of light cast from the corridor she's just come through, seemingly unwilling to venture into the darkness.

She hears the rapid pound of footsteps coming down the stairs on the far side

of the hall and her hands grapple
feverishly with the door, trying to
force it shut but it's locked in place.

Her breath is as ragged as her torn and
bloodstained dress as she hammers at
the door to no avail.

                    POLLY
        Close, goddamn you!

The square of light all of a sudden
vanishes and she turns back to the now
darkened corridor. From its far end
sparks the glint from four fingers worth
of knives scraping off the cement wall,
moving towards her with increasing
rapidity.

It's Freddy!

Here Crystal paused long enough to scoff, to which Ward
responded, "Just keep going. You'll understand, I promise."
Reading again:

Snatching her phone from her pocket
Polly hits the torch symbol and scans
its light over the shelter's wall,
searching for something, anything,
that'll close the door.

A large red button!

She pounds against it. An orange
light flares overhead, flashing, and an
alarm bleats in warning as the door
finally begins moving, closing with an
interminable leisure at drastic odds
with the four-fingered sparks now racing
towards her.

Polly leans her weight against the
door's steel veneer, pushing hard, and
that doing nothing to accelerate its
pace. Freddy's burnt face appears in the
narrowing gap and then just as quickly
disappears as the door clanks shut.

                    POLLY
            (with both middle fingers
             upraised)
          Fuck you, Freddy!

The alarm quiets and the light stops
flashing. A distant whirring then
sounds. A generator starting. A moment
later fluorescents flare overhead and
Polly turns, getting her first glimpse
of the shelter.

The rows of fluorescent lights in its
ceiling pop on one after the other,
cascading into the concrete-lined
bunker fifty feet wide and of seemingly
infinite depth, spreading their glow

into its nether regions over banks of
shelves ten feet high and packed with a
Walmart's worth of goods and supplies.

Polly walks forward as if it's all thin
ice ahead, her horror slowly turning
to wonder as she comes to grasp the
enormity of the structure.

The quiet is then suddenly rent by a
familiar voice.

> BRAD
> (whimpering)
> No. Please. Please. No!

It's coming from the six-by-twelve-foot-
long screen affixed to the left-side
wall in place of a window and draws her
into the shelter's makeshift living
room, fashioned out of two couches and a
couple of easy chairs. As she approaches
the screen we see that the screen is
divided into four quadrants, each wired
into one of the cottage's exterior
surveillance cameras pointing north,
south, east and west.

In the top leftmost, Brad can be seen
on his knees in the driveway. His shirt
is bathed in blood and his guts are

spilling out through a gash in his
stomach and onto the cobbled stones.

Pausing again briefly here, intuiting that it wasn't a coincidence that Ward had named Polly's boyfriend Brad. While he'd never once expressed any hostility over her dalliance with his best friend, she saw now that it must have rankled him at least a little. She couldn't think of what to make of that and so quickly returned to the page.

Jason Voorhees is standing behind him,
holding his head up by the hair so
that Brad is looking directly into the
camera — at Polly — as Jason slashes
downwards, severing his head with one
blow of the machete.

As Brad's body slumps onto the ground,
Jason strides forward, holding his
head up and advancing toward the camera
until Brad's ghastly visage fills the
quadrant.

Shaking her head in terror and
disbelief, Polly backs away from the
scene, bringing the other quadrants
into view. All of them are now filled
with a half-century's worth of monsters
and cinematic psycho-killers glaring
at the camera and stamping their feet
in unison, creating a thunderous din

filling the shelter, and Polly, with the
menace of their solidarity.

It's their world now!

Bumping up against a desk on the far
wall, Polly crumples to the ground,
pressing her eyes shut and screaming
against the vociferous pounding.

                    POLLY
          No! No. It can't end like
          this. Please, God, no!

As the pounding increases in volume and
tenor, a sharp *clack* pierces its chorus
and the camera sweeps upwards, revealing
an old typewriter sitting on the desk
behind her. It's an ancient Remington
Rand inserted with a blank piece of
paper, in the middle of which resides
the letter *T*. Another clack and an *H*
appears and then an *E* and after that a
space and then another *E* and an *N* and
a *D* and finally a *?* as if there was still
some doubt in the unseen author's mind
as to whether this really was the way
things should pan out.

Six years ago, while Ward was editing *Beast*, Crystal had
sequestered herself in her grandfather's old barn, telling Deacon
she wanted to use George's Remington Rand to mount her first

attempt at adapting *A Precious Few* so, she said, she could "steal a little of its magic." She'd hammered through a draft in nine short days and never before, or since, had she felt so alive, seeing, or rather feeling, a whole world springing to life, right off the page. She'd barely been able to contain her excitement when she'd related the experience to Ward and in the sharing she'd never seen him become so excited about anything either.

"I know, I know," he'd enthused. "There's nothing quite like it, is there?"

"Hell, it's better even than fucking," she'd gushed, whereupon a shade of that wolfish glint had come back into Ward's eyes.

"Well, I guess we're just going to have to see about that."

It seemed hardly a coincidence, thus, that her grandfather's typewriter would make a sudden, if somewhat anomalous, appearance in his script. All at once, it was painfully clear to her that Ward had been using that to send her a message. She saw now she'd misinterpreted it completely and that thought was enough to have her on the verge of tears.

There was still one page left and to forestall that inevitable moment when she looked up at Ward, she flipped to it.

In Memory of George Cleary
Who Brought Us Together

And there it was again, the memory of how they'd met, pushing away all traces of her venom and bile. On its heels another image arose just as clear: Ward bent feverishly over his laptop, hammering out the script when really he should have been working on his own. Whereas before she'd cursed him for the hackneyed job he'd made of it, full of flagrant errors in both grammar and continuity, she now saw that what he'd done was not an act of malice but one of love.

And then she was crying in great braying sobs, not thinking of *them*, nor the script at all, but of her mother, who wouldn't likely live to see the birth of her first grandchild, and no one to blame for that but Crystal herself. Ward was wrapping his arms around her, holding her tight, waiting for her to cry herself out.

Only when she had did he speak to her again.

"Come on downstairs," he said kissing her on the side of her neck, "I'll make us a pot of tea."

Lying in one of the bunker's five bedrooms, two hours later, with Ward spooning her so lovingly from behind and what he'd said about making it *her* story so fresh in her mind, she'd thought over her life these past six years, how far she'd come since hammering out that first draft of the script. Remembering then something else her grandfather had once remarked: "The first draft is always shit. Hell, even Hemingway said that."

She saw clearly now that she'd never really got beyond a first draft and also that the exhilaration she'd felt writing it had been like a Chinese finger trap — the more she tinkered with it, the more ensnared she'd become. While the multiple perspectives and rather meandering structure of her grandfather's novel had worked well enough on the page, the same would have meant a slow death on the screen. But convinced, above all, that she had to honour the source material, the endless bickering among the Parsons clan had steered the first two acts of her script into melodrama, and the ill-explained arrival of The Sons of Adam in the third act had further reduced that — there was no denying it now — to nothing more, and maybe something a whole lot less, than a cheap slasher film.

Trying to think her way out of that and recalling a piece of dialogue from Ward's script.

```
             WILT
You worry too much, Doug. If
this was a movie, wouldn't
it be more an apocalyptic
thriller than a horror?


             POLLY
Why couldn't it be a
miraculous tale of survival?


             WILT
That's the spirit!
```

Seeing then that the real problem with her screenplay was that she hadn't taken the time to decide exactly what kind of movie she was writing in the first place.

Thinking back to how she'd felt the first time she'd read the book, the answer to that popped into her head seemingly of its own accord.

It's a horror movie, silly.

Certain that Ward had planted that exchange in his script for that very reason, she'd pored over what he'd written in minute detail, seeking further clues as to how she might proceed. As the producer on the *Beast* trilogy she'd engaged in a similar practice, breaking the script into easily quantifiable compartments in advance of devising a budget, and fell quite naturally into that process again. Her first consideration was always actors and she sorted through his characters, coming up with her dream cast, envisioning them as they would appear and setting them down, as by the hand of God, into a variety of locations, shuffling them within individual scenes and creating conflicts amongst them, following those towards their inevitable conclusions.

If there was anything Ward excelled at, it was structure. He preferred five acts rather than three, as a talisman against the dreaded second-act doldrums. She saw then that he'd given her that as well, the climax of each progressive act escalating the conflict beyond the last and leading to a reversal of some sort, alternating between the negative and the positive and ending with a combination of the two — Polly's survival matched against her virtual entombment and the ensuing chaos of the world outside.

It was their world now!

Another signpost along the way, trying to get her to think of what that might entail.

Recalling another morsel, how Polly hosted a popular entertainment blog called *Polly's World* — a subplot which had led nowhere but that she now saw maybe held the key to the whole damn thing. From her habit of signing "air quotes" around words with two fingers on each hand to express irony and how she twisted her fingers around a strand of her curly red hair when she was nervous to her propensity for using the pejorative "dimshit" and her favourite turn of phrase — "And how's that working out for you?" — it was clear that Ward had based Polly on her. Where before it had seemed he was poking fun, she saw now that he was trying to get her to see it was *her* story all along.

So he'd given her the framework and most of the pieces, not the least of which was the hero. Really, all that was left for her to come up with now was . . . a villain.

The obvious villain of her grandfather's book was Howard Parsons. After hiring a group of mercenaries to free his granddaughter from The Sons of Adam, he'd brought Cassandra to his isolated retreat both for safekeeping and to provide her with the treatment needed to counter the brainwashing she'd incurred at the hands of the cult. There he allowed himself, quite willingly, to be seduced by the teenager and the book's central conflict revolved around him keeping that a secret from his family after the civilization-ending catastrophe had sent his five children, their eight kids, and all three of his ex-wives fleeing to his door, seeking refuge. The book had ended with him leaving the surviving members of his family to die at the hands of The Sons of Adam. He'd spared only Cassandra, with whom he'd fled into the fallout shelter beneath the cottage. There, he would shortly discover that this had been her plan all along, since only Howard knew the combination to the bunker's vault, and during her "captivity" she'd promised to deliver that to The Sons of Adam.

In the book George had portrayed Cassandra as more of a victim but a fresh start required a fresh villain and there was no denying that she lent herself easily to that role.

And who do I see playing her? she mused, trying to think of the perfect someone-someone to fit that role.

But it wasn't an actress's face that sprung to mind.

Grace! she thought, a sudden inspiration spawned from the last time she'd seen her.

It was three hours previous, just after Crystal had stormed through the cottage's front door, incensed by how it had opened ahead of her because it meant that Ward was down in the bunker, watching her on closed-circuit TV. Further enraged by all the clamour and the smoke, and pushing her way through the legions of thin young-and-lovelies — both hands guarding her belly against an errant elbow or a drunken swoon — and seeing Grace appear as if out of thin air amongst the throng.

She was standing ten feet ahead, wearing that ridiculous pink jumper, playing a twelve-year-old girl as she often did to catch people unawares, though there was nothing tween about the way she was looking right then. She was standing with her arms rigid at her sides, her fingers fanned and her eyes enflamed, glaring at her with an expression of such seething rage that it called to Crystal's mind Carrie White after they'd dumped that bucket of pig's blood over her. Such hate that it had stopped Crystal mid-stride, long enough for one of the servers to pass. A sudden bright reflecting off the fragmented mirrors on the server's dress had momentarily blinded her. She'd glanced away for no longer than a second but when she'd looked back Grace was gone.

And it was that memory which came back to her full bore, lying in her old bed some three weeks later, recalling then how she'd muttered, "Fucking freak!" on her way up the cottage's stairs, cursing more herself than Grace for how she'd let the other rattle her so.

Seeing then, as if by divine intervention, Grace running through the woods, dodging trees, frantic in her flight, maybe an opening scene for the film.

But what was she fleeing?

Answering herself:

Her grandfather, Howard Parsons, of course.

Stymied then by all the baggage that would entail, trying to think her way around it.

Maybe she isn't his granddaughter. Maybe she's just some kid from a nearby town. Maybe he kidnapped her, could have been years ago. And now she's escaped. Or maybe he's let her escape because he likes hunting her. Maybe she's running through the woods and SNAP! she's caught in a rope snare.

Seeing her jerked off her feet and that seeming all too familiar.

But, no, that's how No One Lives *starts*, she reminded herself, it being one of her favourite horror flicks.

Hearing then the distant bark of dogs from a neighbour's yard and recalling how Howard Parsons had been an avid hunter who kept a brood of hounds for that very purpose.

So Grace is running through the woods and she hears dogs barking behind her. Cut to a brood of hounds pulling at their leashes held by Howard Parsons. Except he wouldn't go after her himself. He'd send someone else. His kennel master then. His rifle is slung over his shoulder and there is a walkie-talkie clipped to his collar. The dogs have come to a muddy hollow and are sniffing at a flurry of footprints in the muck.

A burst of static through the walkie-talkie and then: Do you see her?

The kennel master answering, She's close. Don't you worry, sir, we'll find her.

The dogs are already off again, the kennel master hurrying to keep up, except now we're watching from behind the cover of trees.

Someone else is watching him!

Feeling then a trace of the familiar exhilaration that had so consumed her before and looking down at her blank screen, her hands finding the keyboard as if by their own volition and typing this:

EXT. WOODS AFTERNOON

And that was all it took to catapult her fingers into a mad flurry, hammering at the keys, trying to keep up with the flood of words tumbling into her mind as *her* vision took hold.

Nothing could stop her now.

8

"**D**o you want to grab a bite?"

Deacon was angling the Jeep into the alleyway behind the shops on Main when he spoke, the first time either of them had said anything on the drive back from Algonquin Road. Tawyne had been texting the whole time. Deacon figured it was probably with whoever had spent the night at his apartment. He'd been stealing quick glances at him, trying to catch a hint of a name on the screen but Tawyne was covering the phone behind his hand, apparently wise to his game. As he turned into the alley, the clock on the dash read 11:53 so it seemed an easy way to break the silence.

"Thanks," Tawyne said, pocketing the phone altogether, "but I've got some homework I need to catch up on."

Deacon dropped him off without bothering to pull into the parking space behind the *Chronicle* but lingered a moment on the pretence of texting Gabe. *Heading home for lunch*, he typed, then added, *Anything I need to know?* to give himself a few extra seconds before pressing send.

Almost immediately Gabe texted back, *We're all good here.*

Tawyne had since reached the top of the stairs and was biding his time kicking the slush off his shoes on the door's frame while chancing furtive glances at Deacon over his shoulder, maybe worried that whoever was inside had locked it after all and he'd have to knock. It was exactly what Deacon was hoping for so he could catch a glimpse, and Tawyne was obviously wise to that game too. He cast a last glance Deacon's way. Deacon offered him a sprightly wave before shifting into drive, letting gravity draw the Jeep down the alley without help from the gas pedal and assuring himself, *When he wants you to know who it is, he'll tell you.*

Just past the clock tower in the middle of downtown, he swung a right at the lights, turning onto Entrance Drive and then a left onto the next street. The sign at the corner called it Hiram, the street which would lead him to Baker, but most people still referred to the stretch between there and Anne Street as The Albion Expressway, though the hotel/bar/strip club it had been named after had been torn down some twenty years ago.

Plans for a new hotel to replace it had been approved by town council eighteen months previous but all those had amounted to thus far was a movie-screen-sized billboard in the vacant lot advertising *The Weekender, Coming Soon.* Beneath that was an artist's rendering of a rather quaint, almost anachronistic, four-storey brick building across from a futuristic-looking train disembarking a flood of passengers, the idea being that the Weekender's proximity to the train station on the other side of Hiram made it an ideal destination for city-dwellers living south of Toronto who are eager to make a quick getaway to cottage country without the trouble of having to fight through traffic on the 401, a highway which routinely topped the list of the busiest in North America.

A thoroughly modern idea, for sure, but the idyllic future depicted there stood in sharp contrast to the equally compelling scene playing out on the far side of the tracks. The flooding had turned River Road into an extension of its namesake and to keep the water from engulfing Entrance Drive too, the town had barricaded it on this end with four overlapping cement slabs of the kind used to block off lanes during highway construction. These were further bolstered with sandbags and between those and the four-foot-high, five-foot-deep wall of sandbags mustered along the sidewalk to protect the houses and the River Road Apartments, it was looking like the beleaguered residents were getting ready for an enemy attack as much as a deluge.

George, he was sure, would have had plenty to say regarding the disparity between the future-oh-so-bright depicted on the billboard and the increasingly dire one prognosticated by the meteorologist from Environment Canada, the latter cast in vivid and immediate detail by the dirty froth of water splashing in near-tidal surges against the wall of sandbags. This enduring conflict — between the world as it really was and how we merely imagined, or wished, it to be — was a central motif in his fictions, and never more so than in *The Road Ahead*. And regardless of what he'd texted Gabe, it was thoughts of that book which had sent Deacon scurrying for home.

Tawyne's steadying influence had kept him from slipping into the mania that often accompanied his ruminations over what endgame Dylan might be working towards. Alone in the vehicle, with only a few short blocks between him and yet another afternoon spent poring over George's fictions trying to knit together the futures depicted there with the ever-present seemingly exploding in his face whichever way he turned, he could feel the familiar mania begin to take hold though, truth be told, it felt more like the comforting embrace of an old friend rather than the stultifying neurosis that Rain had persistently claimed it was.

With *The Road Ahead*'s epigraph so fresh in his mind, he started there. It was actually only the last three lines of the Whitman poem whence it originated. Later in the book George would include the poem in its entirety, having his lead character, Cotton Bland, recite it over and over instead of counting sheep to combat yet another sleepless night wrestling with a past overwhelmed by omissions and regrets. At the height of his "investigation" Deacon had handwritten the poem over two index cards he'd then tacked to the wall in the barn's loft along with all the other "clues" he'd thus far divined. For some months afterwards, reciting it had served as a kind of reset button to help him clear his mind.

"As I lay with my head in your lap camerado," he started, the rest spilling forth from his lips with the mumbling whisper of a mantra, or perhaps a prayer.

> *The confession I made I resume, what I said to you and*
> *the open air, I resume,*
> *I know I am restless and make others so,*
> *I know my words are weapons full of danger, full*
> *of death,*
> *For I confront peace, security, and all the settled*
> *laws, to unsettle them,*
> *I am more resolute because all have denied me than I*
> *could ever have been had all accepted me,*
> *I heed not and have never heeded either experience,*
> *cautions, majorities, nor ridicule,*
> *And the threat of what is call'd hell is little or nothing*
> *to me,*
> *And the lure of what is call'd heaven is little or noth-*
> *ing to me,*
> *Dear camerado! I confess I have urged you onward*
> *with me, and still urge you, without the least idea of*
> *what is our destination,*

Or whether we shall be victorious, or utterly quell'd
and defeated.

Over the ensuing years the epigraph had come to reside in
Deacon's mind as a declaration of George's resolve and it was
hard not to intuit that Cotton Bland was but a surrogate for
George himself. It was a notion lent further weight in that Cotton
was described as *an obscure writer of even obscurer fictions . . . a hulk-*
ing shambles of a man whose shock of coal-black hair was so unused
to a comb that it would have taken a pair of scissors to tame its wild.

Following the breakdown of his marriage, Cotton had
retreated to the isolated cabin his grandfather had built on the
shores of a small northern lake, when he himself was but a young
man. Cotton hadn't written a word since the death of his eight-
year-old son, Adam, and his plan was to finish the book he'd been
writing before joining the boy in The Great Beyond by means
of the hunting rifle he'd brought with him, the same gun with
which Adam had accidentally shot himself after Cotton had left
it loaded in his den. The novel, also called *The Road Ahead*, was
to be the simple story of a family — a father, mother and son —
who were holed up in an isolated cabin following an unnamed
cataclysm, probably a nuclear war, since it was written in the late
1970s. Cotton had since reimagined it as both an apology to his
wife and a suicide note. After reading what he'd already written,
and finding it lacking, he used it to kindle a fire in the cabin's
woodstove then set to rewriting it from scratch on his Remington
Rand typewriter.

As the novel within a novel begins, the family is travelling
north in a Beaver float plane, the only allusion to the disaster that
has prompted their flight being the dark spectre of a cloud bank
that has pursued them on their journey north and seemed ever
on the verge of engulfing them.

No sooner had he written those words when he was harkened from the page by an ominous darkening of the light streaming through the window beside his desk. When he looked outside the sky was indeed a billowing mass of utter dark. He discounted it as mere coincidence, given that the region was prone to such storms at that time of year. He returned to his typewriter and had just written how the plane is struck by a bolt of lightning of unnatural predation when lo and behold, he himself heard the distant whine of an engine followed immediately by a bright flash.

Hurrying out onto his front stoop, he saw an aircraft trailing a fume of smoke and fighting to regain its altitude then, failing that, swooping down onto the lake at a drastic angle, its wing dipping into the water and its fuselage pinwheeling end over end in a violent palsy.

Rescuing its occupants, by means of his grandfather's old rowboat, Cotton discovers that they are indeed a father, mother and son, though they aren't exactly the ones he'd described in his novel. They are a family of Cree, for one, and they aren't fleeing to a cabin but returning home to their reserve. The boy, Nikosis, has suffered a broken ankle in the crash and after they patch him up as best they can, the father, Nohtawiy, sets off to walk the fifty or so miles to the reserve to get help.

He'd only been gone for a few short hours when the wind rose into a furious gale. Shortly, hailstones the size of softballs assaulted the roof with such virulence that it felt like the cabin might come apart at any moment and when they chanced a look out the window, the lake below seemed to have become a seething cauldron. The boy was naturally worried for his father's safety but Cotton, sitting at his desk, assured him that he'd make out just fine. When the boy asked him how he knew, the writer replied, Because I will make it so.

He began to type:

As quick as it began the storm relented and a column of light extended through the clouds, shining on the cabin as if God himself had seen fit to ordain these beleaguered refugees with proof of His mercy.

Such is exactly what came to pass. Cotton takes no more than a breath to revel in his handiwork before setting himself to the task of seeing Nikosis's father safely back to the reserve and *while, in the past, writing had most often felt to Cotton like he was trying to force a sliver out of his thumb with a ball peen hammer, when he sat back down at the typewriter the words began to appear on the page before him with the delirious ease of water flowing through his fingers.*

Every night, by the light of the cabin's lone lantern, Cotton reads Nikosis and his mother, Nikowiy, what he has written and *such a deft proclivity he has with words that the story seemed to spring to life in the flicker of shadows cast upon the wall with the lucidity of a film projected upon a screen though, as this story was about his father, no movie had ever enraptured Nikosis so.*

Everywhere his father goes he finds fires ravaging the landscape. At first, Nohtawiy believes them to be the result of the same lightning storm that downed his plane but after he chances upon a cherry tree festooned with the heads of a dozen men he begins to fear there is something more diabolical afoot. With mounting dread at what he might discover next, he continues on his way. Finally he reaches the town not ten kilometres from his reserve to find it burnt to the ground. His alarm is tempered when he runs into his older brother, Nistis, who has come to investigate the fire. But any hope of a joyful reunion is quashed by the sight of dozens of headless bodies littering the streets. Fearing their reserve will shortly suffer the same fate, they set off to find the people who committed such an atrocity and the smell of cooking meat leads them to an encampment not more than an hour's walk from their reserve. From the vantage of a grove of cedars on its outskirts, they observe:

> Torches were spaced at intervals around the perimeter of the clearing and there was a firepit at its centre, over which roasted a hog on a spit. In the flickering light they could divine a dozen men, all near giants with skin as pale as ash, and naked save for hide-sewn loincloths. Their ears were punctured with the bite of a half-dozen teeth and their chests adorned with what appeared to be sharpened rib bones, perhaps those of their victims. They wore shaved heads with their bald pates dipped in red so that it looked like their skin had been sheared off with their hair and their faces were tattooed with a skeletal imprint so that they more resembled ghouls than men. All were using stones to whet the blades on weapons of a medieval design — axes and machetes and barbed shafts of steel.
>
> This is greatly troubling, Nohtawiy whispered to his brother.
>
> Yes, Nistis whispered back.
>
> But what troubles me more is that you are smiling. How can you take pleasure in such fearsome creatures?

Brother, it is not in their countenance that I
derive pleasure, it is solely in their armaments.

You derive pleasure in weapons of such a crude
and cruel design?!

Yes brother, he whispered, clapping his brother
on the back and offering him a most malevolent
grin, but only because, unlike the last time foreign
invaders sought our annihilation, we are now the
ones who possess the guns.

So it will come to pass that the men and a good number of
the women from the reserve exact a rare victory over The Sons
of Adam, who Nohtawiy comes to call Echoes, for, or so he said,
they are but yet another reverberation in the endless symphony
of destruction the white devil has been orchestrating for time
immemorial. As Cotton reads what he has written that night,
Nikowiy grows increasingly dismayed that he could imagine her
people capable of such acts of wanton brutality as depicted in the
book's climax but she can't help but take a certain satisfaction in
the Echoes' resounding defeat, as does the boy. Such is his delight
in the carnage that he spends the next morning re-enacting it
after his mother leaves him sitting on the porch while she fishes
for their lunch down at the dock.

All the while the boy was using his walking stick to
shoot at imaginary Echoes appearing from behind the
trunks of trees, the clackety-clack of Cotton's typewriter
had been hammering through the door at his back with
such a thunder that it seemed it might, at any moment,
bring the whole cabin crashing down. The clamour then
stuttered to a sudden quiet that gave no indication that
Cotton had just written this line:

> And so, at long last, the two brothers paddled the
> canoe out from behind the peninsula secreting
> this cove from the rest of the lake and finally came
> into sight of the cabin perched at the edge of the
> ridge on its far side.

Cotton watches the tearful reunion through the cabin's window and, having demonstrated his power to conjure this family into being and then towards safety, it only makes sense that his thoughts would then turn towards his own. He wants for nothing more than to bring Adam back to life but, unable to conceive of a plausible means to achieve this, he settles for having his wife arrive at the cabin.

> The door bursts open as if by a sudden gust of
> wind and there she is. Her swollen belly bears the
> promise of a new son to replace the old and her
> journey north is catalogued in the tattered fray of
> her dress, the dirt mired upon her cheeks and the
> wantonness turning her eyes into hollowed-out
> mirrors in which Cotton can't help but see a dim
> reflection of his own sins.

His ex-wife June appears just as written but to Cotton's alarm she is not alone, she is accompanied by a man named Jordan Clay, with whom Cotton has long suspected his wife has been having an affair. Jordan also happens to be a writer, one who is vastly more successful than Cotton and who, in one reviewer's words, "may be the first truly great novelist this country has ever produced," a claim substantiated by the sales figures for his wildly popular trilogy — *The Tides of History* — which, in another reviewer's words, "uses the backdrop of World War I to free The Canadian Experience from its colonial tether and in so doing elevates us all.'"

It's an insult further compounded by his own inability to write a bestseller and his conviction that Jordan was a hack, a mere propagandist, and Cotton's first impulse is to shoot the man where he stands. He goes so far as to reach for his rifle but Jordan is spared from this fate when Cotton's wife suddenly goes into labour.

Nikowiy takes charge of the birth, leading June to the bed and telling her son to run down to the lake and fetch some water. It's then that Cotton conceives of a plan to win his wife back. He confides to Jordan that whatever is written on his typewriter will come to pass and challenges him to a contest to see which writer truly has the power to shift the tides of history. Naturally, Jordan is skeptical but Cotton reminds him that there's a gun pointed at his head so, really, he doesn't have much of a choice. Certain, in his vanity, that it's his prowess as a writer that has placed such divine influence in his hands, he allows Jordan to go first.

Sitting at the typewriter Jordan stares at the blank page, his hands suspended above the typewriter's keys as if waiting on inspiration.

What's the matter? Cotton asks him rather smugly when it looks like he'll never begin. You already hit a wall?

It's just that I'm not used to writing with a gun pointed at my head, Jordan answers.

Well, I'd say that's as good a place to start as any.

Jordan nods, takes a deep breath and then begins to type.

Bestselling author Jordan Clay is sitting at a typewriter with a gun pointed at his head. He starts to type and he's only midway through the second line when he hears a strangled gasp. He glances up and that miserable old sod Cotton Bland is clutching his chest, his eyes rolling back into their sockets, his body stiff and teetering backwards on its heels. Foam drips from his mouth like from a rabid dog as he keels over. He is dead before he even hits the floor.

To his amazement, Jordan does indeed hear a dull thud followed by the clatter of the rifle knocking against wood and when he looks up from the page, Cotton is lying on the floor, white foam oozing from his mouth, bubbling over his lips with his dying breath. Just then, the door slams open and the boy runs in carrying a bucket of water. He barely makes it past the threshold before he begins to fade. The bucket, deprived of its holder, pitches to the ground, its contents lapping up against the bearskin rug beside the bed where just seconds before his mother had stood lighting a kerosene lamp to chase away the encroaching dark. The lamp, also thus deprived of its holder, has smashed to the floor, releasing a sudden gust of flame which quickly engulfs the bed upon which June is gasping against her birthing pains.

Jordan! she cries out but Jordan has already turned back to the typewriter.

It's okay honey, he assures her, everything's going to be just fine.

And with that he begins hammering away at the keys, secure in the knowledge that, unlike that grim son of a bitch Bland, his books always have a happy ending.

9

Deacon was sitting in George's reading chair, staring down at the last line, could have been for a few minutes, could have been for an hour or more.

He was thinking the same thing he'd thought every one of the four times he'd read it over the past ten years: that if Dylan's plan, half-baked as it may have been, really was to bring George's final book to life, then he was well on his way. Thinking back then to the night he'd first read *No Quarter*'s opening chapters, knowing even then that it'd end with a world on fire in some fashion or another and then events progressing towards a real-life climax! worse than any he could have possibly imagined.

A sudden and resounding *Knock! Knock! Knock!* startled him from his musings and also lent them added weight, recalling how he'd been similarly startled by Dylan knocking at his door ten years ago, after he'd left him that first couple of chapters. Then Dylan had poked his head into the barn, wearing his shit-eating grin like he couldn't have been happier with the way things were working out. The door's knob was rattling now and thoughts of Dylan shortly doing the same again were giving Deacon every reason to crawl into a dark hole, maybe never to come out.

Then, after a moment, a woman's voice was shouting, "I know you're in there, Deacon!"

With its tenor of escalating virulence it couldn't have been anyone but Rain.

He had about as much desire to see her as he did Dylan and he sat there holding his breath, wishing her away, knowing that'd be about as fruitful as wishing away the sun in the noonday sky. His fears manifested a moment later at the sound of a key being inserted in the door's lock. Probably she'd got it from under the rock, where he'd left it in memory of George. Nothing he could do about that now and he leapt out of his chair, making for the stairs. He was halfway up when she came bursting in and he turned around, fronting his best casual air.

He opened his mouth, to say not even he knew what — probably something about being in the bathroom when he heard someone at the door — but she beat him to the punch.

"Cut the bullshit, Deacon," she said. "We need to talk."

She'd grown her hair out since the last time he'd seen her and let her natural grey wash away the blond. It was hanging in a billowing drape over the chaotic explosion of pastel colours that made up her handsewn dress and was halfway concealing her face, the cheeks of which he could see were undercut with the sag of deep wrinkles radiating from her mouth like cracks in old cement.

"Talk?" Deacon countered. "I thought you were done talking."

That stopped her short and she took a moment to brush the hair out of her face with a flip of her hand, like she was shooing away a particularly troublesome fly.

"Why do you always have to be such an asshole?" she asked.

"I'm not the one who just broke into someone else's house."

"I wouldn't have had to break in if you'd answered your damn door."

"A door, I might add, that was locked."

It was the kind of back and forth that might go on for hours if they'd let it. Rain at least had the good sense to nip her end in the bud, though she was hardly admitting defeat. Her eyes were scanning about the room, taking it all in. Since she'd last been there, Deacon had cleared away the stacks of books, keeping only the ones he might conceivably read and otherwise could find room for on the shelves. The rest he'd shipped off to the Sally Ann and their departure had freed up enough space for him to create a modest living room in the alcove opposite the door consisting of a couch, a coffee table and a thirty-two-inch television. He hadn't the will to get rid of George's desk and had left it and the Remington Rand where they'd always been, along with George's reading chair, his lamp and his end table.

It was on the latter that Rain's wandering eyes finally settled.

"A-ha!" she said, striding towards it, Deacon trailing after her, pleading, "A-ha! what?"

Her one hand was already reaching into her bag and pulling out something with the deft theatrics of a practised magician.

"This," she said, slamming a book down on the table with Deacon leaning forward so he could see it was her copy of *The Road Ahead*.

There was a time when such a thing would have made him gasp "How in the hell —", but those days were long past. Knowing her like he did, he immediately surmised that someone had told her about the note tacked to the steering wheel in Leonard Stokes's car.

She'd have known as soon as she heard that you'd gone scurrying home, just like every other time Dylan had you dancing to his puppet-master routine. She'd of course have brought along her own copy of The Road Ahead, no doubt to use as a prop in whatever lunatic story she was planning to unload on you now.

He was bristling all over with thoughts of what that might entail. Trying to regain a measure of control, for dignity's sake, he reached past her, snatching up his copy of the book and walking it to the shelf behind the desk.

"I don't know what you're talking about," he said, sliding it into the gap between The Sons of Adam and Into the After and hoping against hope that that would put an end to the matter.

It didn't.

"Eleanor Wilson," Rain stated flatly. "Does that name mean anything to you?"

"No," Deacon said, relieved to be able to answer with the truth. "As a matter of fact, it doesn't."

"What about Stokes then? That's her married name."

And though Deacon didn't say a word, his expression must have betrayed him, for Rain was pointing an accusatory finger at his chest and exclaiming, "I knew it!"

Deacon shaking his head, knowing this was just the opening salvo of yet another petty skirmish in the endless war she was waging against all reason. Mounting his own offensive had never served him well in the past and instead he chose a tactical retreat.

"You going to tell me what this is about or not?" he asked with an air of tired resignation that wasn't altogether put on.

That earned him a pointed glare.

"You first."

There was no way around her needling gaze. He knew she'd stand there all night if that's what it took to get him to speak.

Best just to get it over with, he thought, searching backwards in time, thinking about where he might begin.

Dylan's text might have seemed like the obvious choice but that led into the quagmire that was Grace Swanson and he couldn't fathom how he might try to account for what had happened with her.

"Stokes, you say?" he said after a moment.

"I did."

She sure wasn't itching to make this easy.

"I don't suppose you know the name of Eleanor's husband?"

Rain clamped her lips shut and Deacon gritted his teeth. It was a stand-off of sorts. If this was a movie, it would most definitely be of the Mexican variety. The only way out of that would have been for someone to start shooting, a notion that had Deacon thinking about the revolver Rain had given him ten years ago, telling him George had told her he might need it before this was over. It seemed a little early to be reaching for that, though, and Deacon settled instead for picking up his cigarette case from the table. He fished out a smoke and was just searching about his pockets for a light when a flame flickered at the end of the cigarette in his mouth — Rain lighting his and then lighting the one that had appeared in her mouth as well.

He took a drag and tried to reason how Rain might have come to know Eleanor Stokes who — there was no use denying it now — couldn't have been anyone other than Leonard Stokes's ex-wife. That Leonard's body was even then thawing out in the service garage up at the police station suggested that Rain also had a contact within Tildon's Police Service. Hell, it could have even been Marchand himself. After all, he — not George, as Deacon had originally thought — had been the one fucking Rain in *No Quarter*, though Deacon was pretty sure she and George had also exchanged their fair share of intimacies. It was a slippery slope thinking that Rain might have been making a little money on the side servicing Tildon's aging male population in such a fashion and he sidestepped that in favour of thinking of how she serviced her female clientele instead.

Mostly they were elderly themselves, widows pining after their dearly departed, and Rain offering them her assurances that they were waiting with open arms on the other side. No doubt Rain would eventually get around to intimating that this was how she'd met Eleanor Stokes (née Wilson) and so it seemed as good a place to begin as any.

"I suppose you're going to tell me that Eleanor came to see you," he said with the bluster of a general ordering his troops into battle.

That caught Rain a little off guard and she hid her obvious chagrin by tapping her cigarette in the ashtray.

"Well, maybe she did."

Deacon thought it was doubtful at best, and that she was simply using what Marchand had likely told her to insinuate herself back into the story. Why she'd want to do such a thing wasn't clear but it did give him a line on how he might proceed.

"And when was that?" he asked.

"This morning."

"What time?"

"I was just sitting down to my coffee when she knocked at the door. It must have been around eight."

Which made perfect sense to Deacon, since the body hadn't been found until nine.

"Let me guess," Deacon asked with a healthy dose of sarcasm, "she was looking for her husband? Wanted to find out if he was dead?"

"She already knew her husband was dead. Said she'd known that for over a month."

"Did she say how she knew?"

"Woman's intuition."

"Woman's intuition?"

"That's what she said."

"But you didn't believe her."

"Of course I believed her. That's what she was paying for, somebody to believe her when no one else would." Tapping her cigarette again and then: "I take it you knew him."

"Her ex?"

She shot him a look of exasperation, as if she was wasting her valuable time.

"All I know is that his name was Leonard and he spent the last month sitting in his car, parked under five feet of snow. They dug him out this morning."

Rain was nodding, like it meant something. Whatever it was, she didn't seem inclined to let him in on it and instead said, "They found something with him, didn't they?"

Deacon was certain she knew very well what they'd found and yet here she was trying to pretend she'd heard about it from one of her spirit guides, or whatever she called them. It was enough to make him want to run screaming for the hills.

"What'd they find, Deacon?" She was nudging his arm with a knuckle and showed no sign she was planning to stop.

"They found a note," he said.

"What kind of note?"

Biting his lip, refusing to speak.

"What did the note say, Deacon?"

"You know what it said."

"How would I know what it said?" Nudge, nudge. "Well, are you going to tell me or not?"

"If I had the choice —"

"It was something George wrote, wasn't it?"

"As matter of fact it wasn't. It was Walt Whitman who wrote it."

154

"Oh," Rain said, in mild disappointment. Her eyes then drifted down to the book on the table as if it had somehow misled her and then Deacon's meaning did begin to dawn.

"Oh!" she said. Then: "How's that go again?"

"You know damned well how it goes."

"But not nearly as well as you do. You still reciting it instead of counting sheep?"

"At least I don't go around talking to ghosts."

Rain shook her head ruefully, eyes narrowed, looking like she was about to smack him upside the head.

"I never talked to a ghost in my life," she said through pursed lips.

"That's right. I forgot. You only get 'more-like-impressions.'"

That earned him a smirk.

"So what did your 'more-like-impressions' tell you when you spoke with Eleanor?"

"If you're just going to make fun of me —"

She was turning for the door and everything in Deacon told him he should let her leave. Still, he said, "No, I'm interested. Really. What did your impressions tell you?"

"It wasn't so much an impression as —"

"As what?"

"It was . . . George."

"You talked to George."

It came out sounding like an accusation regarding the current state of her mental health and he'd meant it to.

"I told you, that's not how it works," she said through gritted teeth. "But he was there. I felt him. He was there as sure as I'm standing here in front of you."

"So George was just standing there."

"At first."

"Then what happened?"

"It got real cold, freezing cold. So cold we could see our breath."

"You and Eleanor?"

"Yes, me and Eleanor."

"And that was all."

"Then we heard a thud."

"A thud?"

"From upstairs."

"Naturally you investigated."

"If you mean, did I go upstairs . . ."

"And when you did?"

"I found . . ."

Looking then down at the book.

"It had fallen right off the shelf in my bedroom."

"You mean to suggest George knocked it off."

"If you don't believe me, you can ask Eleanor. She was standing right there behind me."

"And what did she have to say about that?"

"Nothing. I mean, what could she say? We went back downstairs and finished our session."

"Did she get what she came for?"

"Yes. I mean — Actually, she seemed a trifle disappointed."

"Imagine that."

"With the cold, I mean. She was kind of hoping to find out her ex was burning in hell."

"That's what she said?"

"It's why she'd come to me in the first place. One of her friends is a regular and —"

"And why would she want her ex to burn in hell?"

"For what he did to her."

"And what was that?"

"You'd have to ask her that yourself."

"But I'm asking you."

"And I'm telling you, you're going to have to ask her yourself. It's what George wants."

"George wants me to talk to Eleanor Stokes?"

She opened her mouth to reply but was interrupted by a tinkling like wind chimes sounding from her bag. Reaching into it, she retrieved her cell phone. She gave it a quick glance and then dropped it back in.

"I've got to go," she said, turning for the door. "Talk to her. I mean it, Deacon. She lives on Talon Lake Road. The last house at the end, that's what she told me. Go and see her. Today!"

"And you expect me to do that alone?"

"She can't know I was talking to you. It'd mean my business if word got around I was blabbing about my clients all over town." Her cell phone chimed again and this time she disregarded it in favour of casting Deacon a most impetuous smile. "And besides, I'm late for a date."

"A date?"

"Yes, a date. And if you looked any more surprised, I might be inclined to take offence."

She was staring at him with an expression he'd only caught fleeting glimpses of before, usually out of the corner of his eye when she thought he was looking elsewhere. A deep sort of longing that had always made him wonder if maybe they could have had a real life together after all, a stark contrast to how she'd usually made him feel — like she wished he'd find someone his own age so the both of them could finally get on with their lives.

It had a softening effect on his mood and he even felt the first stirrings of the affection that had kept them together for so long.

He opened his mouth, about to say, "There's nothing about you that could surprise me anymore," but she was already heading for the door.

Deacon watched her leave, feeling the same sinking sensation he'd felt when she'd stormed out on him five years ago and finding only a dim sort of comfort from that by telling himself, *It's probably best if you keep that thought to yourself anyway.*

10

Any of the residual goodwill he'd felt towards Rain was long gone by the time he was driving north out of town on Highway 4. He was back to feeling like a marionette and with Rain's hands on the strings it felt like maybe she was intent on using them to strangle him.

George wants me to talk to Eleanor Stokes, he fumed. *What kind of an idiot does she take me for? Why can't she just tell me the goddamned truth for once? She's always got to cloak everything in smoke and mirrors. Well, I say fuck her. I'm done playing her games!*

He was already reaching for the signal light, ready to turn into the next road, get his ass back to town, if only to spite her.

Just ahead, on the right, he could see a familiar red brick building, its windows, as ever, covered with sheets of plywood — one of the many "settlers' churches" scattered about Mesaquakee that had been left to fall into ruin. It was directly across from Falconbridge Road and for most of his childhood had stood as his own personal way marker, telling him he was almost home.

Lest his thoughts be cast back to the day his father had swerved to miss a moose and hit a tree instead, he'd done his best to avoid Highway 4 altogether, taking the 11 to Highway 142 just south of Huntsville and cutting back if a story for the paper required him to drive out that way or he was going to see Laney, who lived in Utterson. But he'd forgotten where Talon Lake Road was, and the Jeep's GPS had guided him to Highway 4. So here he was with his left blinker flashing and him about as inclined to turn onto Falconbridge as to turn right, drive the Jeep up the church's stairs and go crashing through its front door.

But keeping his eyes pinned to the road ahead didn't do anything to prevent him from hearing a voice — his own — rising inside his head.

Maybe it wouldn't be such a bad thing if Abel drowned himself in the creek after all.

A tremor coursing through his body at the memory of the swarm of hornets funnelling up from their nest in the ground not two seconds after he'd thought that, seeing the insects attacking him and his brother Abel as they fled, Abel then convulsing in the throes of anaphylactic shock, his face a scourge of fiery red bumps, peering up at Deacon with crazed fear in his eyes, the two memories intimately linked in Deacon's mind as if it was his cursing his little brother that had brought forth the plague of hornets. Hearing himself screaming, "Ma! Pa!" and then there he was wedged on the floor in the back of the Jeep, bouncing around like a Mexican jumping bean, listening rapt with dread to the spiralling confusion in his father's voice — "It doesn't make any goddamned sense" — and hearing his mother screaming, "Watch out!" A noise then like a train wreck and the weight of the world pressing down on him, turning his world black. But only for a split second. Hearing a sudden tearing noise like an elastic band snapping, jarring him awake, seeing his father's body catapulted halfway through the windshield, a coyote as big as a wolf standing over him on the hood, chewing on his face.

Then, he'd slammed his eyes shut and thrown himself backwards in the space between the seats. He must have passed out because the next thing he remembered was a hand tugging at his broken arm, the pain so fierce he was hurtled into wakefulness, screaming. Opening his eyes and seeing a vaguely familiar face — one of the men his father sold cordwood to. Tears were streaming down the man's face but when he spoke it was with an exclamation of joy not sorrow.

"Deacon!" he gasped. "Thank god. You're alive!"

Deacon had clutched at him same as if he'd been drowning, braying great heaving sobs such that it felt like his ribs were about to shatter.

Thinking now, *The bravest soul George had ever met. What a load of horsesh—*

A horn was blaring in frantic alarm and that snapped Deacon back.

The Jeep had drifted into the oncoming lane and a white cube van was swerving onto the shoulder to avoid a head-on collision. Deacon jerked the wheel right, overcompensating and finding his own shoulder, the Jeep shimmying against the loose gravel and Deacon certain that he was about to get sucked into the ditch, any hope of a soft landing there lost in the face of a protrusion of granite as big as a Mack truck. He jerked the wheel left and came back onto the road, fishtailing. He brought it back under control, gasping for breath and feeling a trickle of sweat rolling down his temple, his chest heaving as the vehicle straightened out.

Shouting, "Fucking Rain!" and tyrannized again by the thought of her barging into his house, spewing some cockamamie line of bullshit. It reminding him enough of the good times they'd had together to send him off on some wild goose chase, or worse, and her begging off because she had a "date."

I'll bet, he thought. *More like a client. How many old geezers do you think she's fucked? Half the town probably. That fucking whore!*

His stomach clenched as the shame of even thinking such a thing wound itself into a knot. Taking a deep breath, trying to calm himself down, looking through the cracked windshield.

A small green sign in the shape of an arrow was just passing by. *Talon Lake Road,* it read, and that had him cursing all over again.

11

Talon Lake Road was in worse shape even than Highland.

Its ruts were accompanied by a patchwork of potholes deep and wide enough to breed frogs and he eased his way through these, in no real hurry to get to the last house at its end. The creaking of cracked windshield glass rubbing against itself provided a perfect accompaniment to his mood, as did the seams creeping noticeably outwards before his eyes.

His GPS told him that Talon Lake Road was less than two kilometres long and a chapter in *They Came Here to Be Free*, Grover's history of black settlements in the area, had informed him that it had originally been built by a group of emancipated slaves to service the lumber mill they'd built on the eastern shore of its namesake. The mill had survived only a few years before it and the houses in the settlement that had sprung up around it burnt up under what Grover had called *suspicious circumstances*. Most of the residents had migrated back to Toronto and, in Grover's words, *all that remained of this once thriving community* was a few old foundations, none of which were any more remarkable than the piles of mossed-over rocks tumbled into what had once been their dwellings' root cellars.

The houses etched into the surrounding scrub brush and swampland over the past century hadn't fared much better. They were all ramshackle bungalows with sun-curled shingles, sided with weathered vinyl or painted press-wood, one with only Typar, its flaps sprung loose from their staples, revealing tattered strips of tarpaper beneath. Rusted-out cars and trucks littered front lawns, emerging from beneath the melting snow alongside disused play structures for children and dilapidated doghouses and bags of garbage that must have been tossed out front doors mid-winter and had since provided easy forage for all manner of woodland creatures.

It was the second-to-last house before the road's end that had burnt down in 2020. As Deacon approached it he slowed the vehicle to a crawl, scanning down the driveway, searching out anything that might have been left of the house and finding a large trailer-home in its stead. It was mostly concealed behind a mound of ploughed snow almost ten feet tall and there was a child, couldn't have been much older than one, playing in the driveway leading up to a porch built out of what looked like scrap lumber and wrapped with clear plastic. The boy was wearing a snowsuit and rubber boots and carrying a stick almost as tall as him as he waded through a puddle as big as a small pond under the watchful gaze of a German shepherd.

When the dog caught sight of Deacon's Jeep, she let out a bark and charged down the driveway, looking for all intents and purposes like she was getting ready to attack, the boy frozen in mid-stride, staring after her with a static amaze that wouldn't have been out of place had he just seen a UFO flying past.

The dog reached the edge of the driveway, holding up there

and barking in clamorous reproach as a man strode out from behind the pick-up truck parked in front of the garage to the left of the driveway. He was tall — six-foot-two at least — and wearing a pair of grease-stained coveralls unzipped to the navel, his bare chest exposed within. He was holding a wrench about the size of a moose's femur and was clenching it more like a bludgeon than a tool as he peered after Deacon with a similar intensity as his son, though it wasn't so much in amaze as in bitter recrimination.

That was enough for Deacon to turn back to the road and apply a little gas. The way the man had been looking at him had him checking his rear-view mirror every few seconds and sure enough, he'd just come into view of the black-and-yellow checkered sign marking the end of the road a half-kilometre hence when he saw the pick-up truck pulling out of the driveway, heading after him.

The last house was only a few metres from where the road expanded into a circular bulge large enough to allow a school bus, or a snowplough, to turn around. Deacon used it to loop back the way he'd come and pulled to a stop on his side of the house's driveway, watching the pick-up truck barreling towards him. He saw now that it had a snowplough hitched to its front and it was moving at such a clip that it seemed to Deacon its driver was intent on ramming him. But at the last moment, the truck swerved into the driveway. It had barely shuddered to a stop behind a white Outback when the man surged out of its driver's front door.

He was still carrying the oversized wrench and, as he charged towards the road with it clenched firmly at his side, the sight once again called to Deacon's mind a moose, though it wasn't the tool but the look in the man's eye — like a bull on the rut — that inspired him thus. As a reporter in a small town such as Tildon, where a long, cold winter such as they'd had could unhinge even the best of men, his pursuit of a story had often brought him face to face with similarly irascible characters. He'd found that a welcoming smile as he greeted them with his credentials had served him well in the past and, as he opened the door, he slipped one of his cards from the holder he'd Velcroed to the dash.

"Good afternoon," he said, approaching the man, though it was closer to evening by then. "Deacon Riis. I'm with the *Chronicle*."

He held out the card in his hand and the man reacted as if he'd been offered a fresh turd. The rabid glare in his eyes made Deacon think he was just looking for an excuse and, trying to avoid giving him just that, Deacon looked away. His gaze passed in a downward sweep over the man's chest, catching a glimpse of the joyfully beaming face of a young woman tattooed over his bare breast, before Deacon sought out the clapboard bungalow nestled beyond a thin row of poplar trees. The drapes in its front window were parted and framed within the opening's glow he could just make out a woman's face. Whether it was just the glare or not, there seemed to be something off about it. It was bent all out of proportion and bore a crude patchwork of stitches so that it didn't look like a face at all but a mask, like the one that hillbilly freak in *The Texas Chainsaw Massacre* had worn over his own hideous visage.

What was it Rain had said about Eleanor's ex?

"She was hoping he was burning in hell. For what he'd done to her."

There was no mistaking then who the woman in the window was but still he turned back to the man and asked, "Can you tell me if Eleanor Wilson lives here?"

He snuck a quick peek back to see if the name indeed meant something to the man. It must have, because he was gritting his teeth. It looked to Deacon like he could play the strong, silent type all day and so he was surprised when the man actually did speak.

"What's it to you?" he asked.

"As I say, I'm a reporter with the *Chronicle*. I just wanted to ask her a few questions."

"Questions about what?"

"Leonard Stokes."

The man's eyes narrowed at the mention of the name, seething with undisguised hate, and yet he said, "Never heard of him. And neither has she."

"But —"

It was all Deacon could get out before the man was taking a step forward, his hand twitching on the wrench.

"I said she's never heard of him."

"Fair enough," Deacon said and turned back for the Jeep, offering a backwards wave of his hand. "You have a good afternoon, now."

Sitting back into the driver's seat, he took a moment to thread the business card back into the holder before keying the ignition and looking up through the cracked windshield. The man was still standing where he was before, but it wasn't towards him that Deacon's gaze wandered as he started the vehicle and shifted into gear, it was towards the truck.

"He'd have needed a nudge to get him that far off the road."

What he'd said to Marchand just that morning.

Marchand had answered, "Hell, he would have needed a damn sight more than a nudge."

But what whoever had buried Leonard and his car in the ravine on Algonquin Road really would have needed was a snowplough, a snowplough exactly like the one hitched to the front of the young man's pick-up.

Shifting into gear, Deacon turned the wheel a hard left, giving the man as wide a berth as possible on his way past, all the while thinking, *Maybe Rain was right and George was trying to tell you something after all.*

JODY

"Looks like he's headin' for your ma's."

Jody was strapping Clyde into the car seat in the Sunfire and when he looked up at the road he saw a black Chevrolet Tahoe with *Tildon Police* decaled over its doors driving past. Tina was standing behind him, carrying an armload of reusable shopping bags, and the both of them stood stock-still, watching the vehicle until it disappeared behind the grove of cedars on the far side of the garage.

"You think it's about your dad?"

"Could be," Jody answered, casting her a sideways glance, trying to get a sense of what she might have thought about that.

He'd been gone the better part of thirty-six hours after he'd seen what Lenny had done to his mother. He'd halfway expected Tina to have changed the locks by the time he got home but when he finally did return, two mornings later, the door was open. He'd found her at the stove, dishing a ham and cheese omelette from a frying pan and as he took off his coat, she'd set the plate on the table in front of his chair, though clearly the breakfast had been meant for her. She sat across from him, breastfeeding Clyde while he ate, and didn't say a word until he was wiping the grease from his plate with a crust of toast.

"So," she said, "I dropped by your *mom's* yesterday . . ."

Her tone was all casual, like she was just making conversation, Jody knowing full well that his mother's face would have been all it took for Tina to know why he'd up and disappeared, for he'd often told her what he'd do to Lenny if ever again he laid a hand on his mother.

They hadn't spoken of it since but from the way she'd been biting the corner of her lip as the Tahoe drove past he knew she'd been brooding over it, waiting for the day when it would come back to haunt them.

"What are you going to do?" she asked.

"I guess I better go and see what he wants."

"So we're not going shopping?" The uplift to her voice at the end vented her irritation as if groceries were their biggest concern right then.

"I won't be more'n a couple of ticks," he answered but she mustn't have believed him. He'd barely turned out of the driveway when he saw a streak of red in his rear-view mirror — her Sunfire speeding away in the opposite direction.

When he got to his mom's, the Tahoe was parked on the road. The cop was already inside and to occupy himself while he waited for him to come back out, Jody fetched his toolbox from the passenger seat. Two days ago his mother's Outback had refused to start and he'd tracked the problem to the alternator. He'd put in an order for a new one at True North Auto Parts in town and at eight o'clock that morning had got the call it had arrived. Tina said she'd go in with him since she had some shopping to do and now that was just one more damn thing he was going to catch hell for.

Ten minutes later he was craned under the Outback's hood, using a propane torch to loosen one of the alternator's corroded bolts. He heard the front door open and a husky voice saying, "If you can think of anything else, you have my card." The door clicked shut and then all that stood between him and the cop was the heavy clomp of boots coming down the stairs. The passage of time had dulled the urgency that had driven him there and he was kind of hoping the cop would just walk on past. But sure enough he stopped a few feet behind him, showing no signs he was going to leave until Jody at least turned his way.

Jody obliged, giving him a dismissive backwards glance.

The cop was in his late fifties or maybe early sixties. He was wearing what appeared to be his dress uniform and from the way its buttons were on the verge of popping against the pressure from his bulging gut, it seemed to Jody that he mustn't have worn it very often. He had a curiously overgrown moustache of the handlebar variety and, the uniform notwithstanding, it lent him the appearance of an aging Texas lawman from some old western. While he stood there staring back at Jody he tugged twice on one end of its drape and that seemed to activate a lever connected to his mouth.

"You Jody Stokes?" he asked.

In his dealings with cops, playing local-yokel had always served him well in the past and so, fronting his best squirrel-eyed grin, he replied with a question of his own: "What can I do ya fer?"

"Aubrey Marchand," the man said. "I'm chief of the Tildon Police. I'm afraid I have some bad news for you."

When Jody didn't respond, he forged ahead, telling Jody what he already suspected: "Your father was found dead this morning."

Trying to keep his voice on an even keel, Jody answered, "You don't say?"

"You don't sound overly surprised about it."

"I guess it's because I knew him."

"How's that?"

"Lenny never did know when to keep his mouth shut and from what I've heard of the joint, I'd've expected him to have got shanked years ago."

"And what do you know about 'the joint'?"

"Only what I seen on TV and in movies."

"So not much."

"Enough to know I'd rather be about anywhere else."

"That why you never visited your father in prison."

He wasn't sure if it was meant as a question or a statement of fact and to play it safe he answered, "It was one of the reasons."

"I take it then, you two weren't . . . close."

As close as the back of his hand, Jody was thinking as he answered, "He weren't exactly the kin'a dad who'd take me to little league games, if that's what you mean."

"When was the last time you saw him?"

"Before he went away."

"And you haven't had any contact with him since."

"You jus' told me I ain't never visited him."

"I did. But then that doesn't account for the fact he was released from the Central North Correctional Centre almost a month ago."

"First I'm hearing about it."

"So you haven't had any contact with him since he got out?"

"Nope."

He hadn't looked back at the cop since the first time, worried that he'd have guilty written all over his face. When the cop hadn't said anything for a couple of breaths, he snuck another backwards glance. The cop was staring right at him, squint-eyed and resolute, like he really was an old-time Texas lawman and Jody was the leader of a band of outlaws he was squaring off against on the main street of some one-horse town. It was clear from the look that the cop hadn't believed a word he'd said. But if he did have any proof that he was at fault for what had happened to his father Jody figured he'd already be in handcuffs and he went back to massaging the bolt with the flame, trying to wrangle his thoughts around why the chief of police would be so interested in a piece of shit like Leonard Stokes.

But then maybe, he thought, *the chief always took it upon himself to be the one who delivered the bad news to families who'd lost a loved one, which might explain the dress uniform.*

A mild bit of reassurance shattered to bits by the way the cop's eyes squinted narrower still when he asked, "I don't suppose you can think of anyone who might have a reason to want him dead?"

It struck Jody when he said it that maybe, seeing his mother's face, the chief had put two and two together. The scars had never quite healed and the one on her forehead had made her come to resemble a mental patient after undergoing a frontal lobotomy, which is how she'd been acting more or less ever since. It wouldn't have taken more than a quick call to the hospital to know that her friend Julie had called an ambulance to his mom's address on February 16th, presumably the same day Leonard Stokes had been released from prison. Probably the cop had already done that and was keeping Jody talking in the hope of catching him in a lie. Best thing to do right now would be to shut his mouth, at least until he spoke with his mom, find out what she told him, but that didn't account for the matter of the cop's question hanging in the air between them.

"You're saying someone killed him?" Jody finally asked.

"Could be."

"You don't know?"

"All we know for certain is that he was found in his car this morning. Frozen solid."

"Frozen, you say?"

"Solid."

"He go off the road drunk or sumpin?" It came out before he realized it was about the absolute stupidest thing he could possibly have said.

"Why would you say that?" the cop asked.

"It wouldn't've been the first time," he answered, covering.

In fact, it would have been the second that Jody knew of. The first, he'd been eleven and was sitting in the passenger seat when Lenny had tried to take that corner on Algonquin going ninety. They'd plowed through the snow bank and ended up at the bottom of the ravine, which is what had given Jody the idea of dumping him and his car down there in the first place.

"And when was the first time?"

"Hell if I know. Probably the same day he got his licence. He never did have any sense when he got behind the wheel. Especially when he'd been drinking."

"So you're saying it was an accident."

"How would I know?"

The cop seemed to be mulling that over and it was a moment before he spoke again.

"Well, the funny thing is," he offered, "it did look just like he'd gone off the road, like you said. Could have been he bumped his head, knocked himself out. Froze to death before he woke up. And that's probably how the official record would have read if we hadn't found this tacked to the steering wheel."

Jody chanced another look behind. The cop was holding up a clear plastic baggy with a slip of yellow paper inside and that did come as a big surprise since it sure as hell wasn't there when he'd left Lenny, doped unconscious but still very much alive, in the driver's seat of his car before burying it under five feet of snow.

Written on the paper in black ink he could clearly read:

> *Dear camerado! I confess I have urged you onward with me, and still urge you, without the least idea of what is our destination,*
> > *Or whether we shall be victorious, or utterly quell'd and defeated.*

It struck him as oddly familiar, though he couldn't quite place it.

"It's part of a poem," the cop said, filling him in, "by a fellow named Walt Whitman. You ever heard of him?"

"Can't say as I have," he answered, which was the truth.

"What about George Cleary?"

Jody opened his mouth to reply but hearing that particular name had sucked the breath right out him. The cop was talking again and it took a moment before Jody realized he'd said, "That bolt's getting a trifle hot there, wouldn't you say?"

Jody looked and sure enough the bolt's head was glowing red. He jerked his hand back same as if he'd been burnt and then the cop was asking him another question.

"So," he was saying, "have you heard of him or not?"

"Heard of who?"

His throat had become a desert and the words came out parched, which certainly didn't much help his cause either.

"George Cleary."

Jody paused a moment like he was thinking hard on it before he lied, "Nope. Don't ring a bell."

"You sure?"

"Like I said, it don't ring a bell."

The cop was back to playing sheriff again, squint-eyed and surly. His one hand was tugging at his moustache and his other rigid by his side as if to get ready for a quick draw, though he wasn't wearing a piece as far as Jody could tell. The whole routine was giving Jody the jitters and to cover he turned off the torch and reached for the socket wrench he'd propped on the engine block.

"This particular poem here was from one of his books."

"Whose books?" Jody asked, playing dumb again.

"George Cleary's."

His voice carried more than a hint of accusation, like he knew exactly what game Jody was playing at and would have liked nothing more than to slap him into handcuffs right then and there.

"He some kind of a writer or something?" Jody asked before he could stop himself.

"One of a kind, some might say."

"Well, I guess then that's why I never heard of him. I ain't never been one much fer readin'."

That much was also true, the only exception being George Cleary himself. If it had been up to Jody, he'd have as soon read any of his books as pull out his fingernails with a pair of needle-nose pliers but then Dylan hadn't given him much of a choice. George Cleary, he knew, was Dylan's grandfather, which suggested that Dylan had found a way to mix himself up in Lenny's death. Why he'd do that wasn't immediately clear to Jody and the cop didn't give him more than a couple of ticks to ponder on that.

"You never answered my question," he said.

Jody's silence prompted him to repeat it.

"Do you know of anyone who might have a reason to want your father dead?"

"I can think of one or two," Jody answered.

"And who's that?"

"The parents of that kid who overdosed, I guess they'd be at the top of the list. The father, I recall, made some threats during the trial."

"And that's all?"

"Off the top of my head."

Jody had affixed the ratchet's bit to the bolt. He was applying a little pressure, just enough to see if it might spring loose, and even that little bit was enough to snap the bolt's head clean off.

Muttering "Son of a bitch!" under his breath, he stared in rueful contemplation at what was left of the bolt. Its stem was rusted almost to its core, meaning he'd have to drill it out, and he'd probably have to do the same with the other three bolts as well.

The cop seemed to have got a sense of that too.

"Looks like you got your work cut out for you there," he said. He was craning forward, looking past Jody in the general direction of the alternator. "Well, I'll leave you to it, then."

The crunch of his boots on the driveway's snow-encrusted gravel told Jody he was walking away. The bolt's head had become lodged in the socket wrench's bit and he bided his time tapping it against the battery, hoping to knock it loose and thinking about Dylan, trying to figure out what game he might be playing at.

He'd seen him a few dozen times over the past five years. Mostly it was when he was shovelling snow or mowing lawns at a house in town and he'd look up and see the ghost cruiser Dylan always drove passing by. Dylan had never offered him so much as a smile or a nod to say that he'd seen him too, but it had happened frequently enough that Jody had long begun to suspect it hadn't been a coincidence, that he was trying to tell him something, if only that he was keeping tabs on him.

It didn't seem much of a coincidence either that a quote from one of Dylan's grandfather's books suddenly turned up alongside Lenny's body. He was still trying to think of what message he might be sending him now when he heard the front door of his mother's house banging open.

When Jody glanced over at it, his mom was standing on the top step, watching the Tahoe driving away. He was thinking he ought to ask her what she told the cop but he was afraid of what she might say and went back to banging the socket wrench against the battery, knowing already he'd need a screwdriver if he had any hope of popping the bolt's head out.

"Is it fixed?"

His mom was hobbling down the steps, taking one at a time and holding fast to the rail to guard against a fall as she had ever since Lenny had beat her near to death that one last time. All it took was one look at the strained expression on her face to know that she didn't much want to talk about what the cop had said either, and Jody was thankful for that.

"No, it ain't fixed," he replied. "I toldya, I'm waiting on a new alternator."

"And when do you expect that?"

"It came in this morning."

"Is that what you're doing now? Putting it in?"

"I ain't picked it up yet."

She'd made it to the bottom of the stairs and stared at him with her mental-patient gape, like she had no idea what the hell he might have been talking about.

"I was planning on going to pick it up now," he offered and that snapped her back to it.

"You're going to town?" she asked.

"Well, it sure as hell ain't gonna come to me."

"Do you mind if I go with you? I've got some shopping to do."

"The more the merrier, I always say."

Her eyes brightened and her face relaxed. For a fleeting moment she looked almost like his old mother again as she said,

"Just let me fetch my purse," before wheeling around and clutching at the rail, dragging herself upwards and lurching back into the house.

She'd done a couple or three dabs of shatter while she was inside. Happily buzzed, she spent the twenty-five-minute ride into town staring listlessly out the passenger window and that gave Jody plenty of time to reflect on what Dylan might have been trying to tell him.

He'd been keeping tabs on him these past five years, there was no doubt about that. Maybe he'd even been following him the night he buried Lenny alive. Or maybe he'd been keeping tabs on Lenny too.

He must have known Lenny'd been released from prison, he deduced. Maybe he'd been following him, hoping he'd slip up and he'd be able to put him away again. That's how he'd come to see what you'd done. But why then the note? It didn't make any goddamned sense. Unless . . . Unless he figured you'd be the prime suspect and was simply trying to muddy the waters, deflect the blame. But hadn't the cop himself said they'd have treated it like an accident if it hadn't been for the note?

No, it didn't make any goddamned sense at all.

The only thing he could be certain of was that whatever Dylan was playing at must have had something to do with his grandfather. Why else would he leave a quote from one of his books at the scene of the crime?

George Cleary, he thought.

The name had rattled him plenty when the cop had said it and there was absolutely no mystery as to why that might have been. Thinking then back to the first time he'd heard the name, or rather read it off the cover of one of his books.

It had also been the first time he'd stayed overnight at Nickel Down, what Dylan called that old nuclear fallout shelter on two-hundred-plus acres just north of Algonquin Park that his grandfather had left him in his will. They'd already been there the previous four or five Saturdays, heading off at four a.m. so they could get in a couple or three hours of dirt-biking in the morning. Dylan would always bring lunch — sandwiches and bags of chips, mostly — and in the afternoon, they'd go hunting or fishing, cooking whatever they'd caught or killed in the evening, eating that and then heading for home as soon as the sun had dropped below the treeline. It had become Jody's job to start a fire in the ring of cinder blocks in the clearing behind the bunker, over which they'd roast or fry their bounty, and on that particular evening he was feeling more than a little apprehensive as he stacked the kindling around several crumpled-up wads of newspaper.

Dylan had told his mother some cock-and-bull story about how they'd be camping with a bunch of other cops and kids from "the program." That had been enough to ease her concerns about letting her son stay out overnight, but hardly Jody's. It was just the two of them, as always, and while he'd initially been excited about the chance of getting in an extra day of dirt-biking, his niggling doubts over spending the night with a man who was practically a stranger, and a cop at that, had resurfaced, escalating at even pace with the setting sun. As he put match to paper, he kept them at bay, assuring himself that if Dylan had been planning to perv out on him, he'd have done it by now, where so far he'd treated Jody like he was his long-lost brother and was eager to make up for the time they'd spent apart.

Still, with what he owed Dylan it was a pretty good bet he'd someday come to collect and so why not tonight?

With that *still* . . . hovering about his thoughts, he stood up from lighting the fire only to have Dylan slap a book against his chest.

"What's this?" Jody had asked, though it was plain for all to see.

"What does it look like?"

"A book."

"There's no fooling you."

"What am I supposed to do with it?"

"A book's for reading, son. Ain't they taught you that in school?"

Dylan was grinning at him with obvious condescension and that gave Jody reason enough to look away, his gaze immediately settling on the book in his hand.

It was called *A Bad Man's Son*. The name *George Cleary* was written below the title and below that was a charcoal drawing of a cowboy with his hat pulled down over his eyes, sitting against the trunk of a spindly old tree. A noose was draped from its lone branch as if the man was just sitting there waiting for the hangman to arrive. The picture spoke to Jody plenty, conjuring into his mind the all-consuming dread he'd felt every single night over the past few months as he lay in bed, feeling like there was a noose hanging over his own head. And when he took another glance at the title it spoke to him even more so, being as he was *his* father's son.

"Go on, then," Dylan prompted after Jody had been staring at it for a few too many breaths. "It ain't going to read itself."

"Do I really have to?" Jody asked, unable to keep the whine from creeping into his tone.

"No," Dylan had answered before quickly adding, "that is, if you don't mind walking home."

It would be a two-kilometre hike along an overgrown wagon trail from the bunker to the wrought iron gate guarding its entrance and then twenty kilometres along a dirt road back to the highway. There wasn't a single house on the whole stretch, meaning it'd be a five-hour walk before he'd have any hope of thumbing a ride. Most of the surrounding area was muskeg so he'd be battling mosquitoes and black and deer flies the whole way. And then there was the matter of hitchhiking. He had his own reasons for never wanting to do that again and while he thought it unlikely Dylan really would have made good on his threat, even the suggestion gave him enough of an incentive to sit down in one of the two lawn chairs at the firepit and at least make a go of it.

The book wasn't very long — a hundred and fifty or so pages — and that gave him some consolation as he flipped forward to Chapter 1.

Halfway down the page, it read: *He was a long way from home.*

Given that he was a fair way from home himself, reading that had a strangely disorienting effect on him. For a moment he couldn't shake the feeling that somehow the book was going to be all about him and that Dylan had chosen it for that exact reason. Knowing what Dylan knew about him, the dread he'd been feeling turned the pit in his stomach into a bottomless chasm, thinking about having to face that all over again. It was threatening to swallow him whole when he felt Dylan's hand on his shoulder.

"It'll get easier as you go," he said.

The reassurance in his voice — like he knew exactly why Jody was having a hard time getting past the first line and also that he wouldn't have given it to him unless he knew he could handle it — gave him the necessary nerve to read on.

> *They were huddled behind the counter of the bank in a town called Merryweather, as dumb a name for a town as Clyde had ever heard. There wasn't much to it except a hotel, a livery stable, a sundry store, the bank, and a church, the side yard of which was occupied by a dozen or so wooden crosses. When they'd rode into town, there was a woman dressed in black standing in solemn*

mourning over one of the graves. It was that woman Clyde was thinking of now, wondering if it was her son who'd died and would his own ma come to visit him when he was buried there too.

But more'n likely, he told himself, they'd just bury an outlaw like him in a common pit alongside his pa and his pa's gang, all the latter of whom were lying dead on the other side of the counter.

His pa hadn't fared much better.

He'd been gut-shot by one of the tellers. As he loaded his last two bullets, one into each of his twin Colt .45s, his hands were shaking as with the palsy and it pained the boy, seeing such a strong man as his pa had proven himself to be enfeebled so.

It had only been two months since Tyrone Yates had shown up at his younger brother's farm, where Clyde and his mom had been living ever since his uncle, Cyril, had taken pity on her when Clyde had been nothing more than a bump in her belly. They'd rode out together not twenty minutes later, Tyrone on his Appaloosa and Clyde on the pinto his father had brought for him and which he'd said was called Misty. As they'd headed south through the pasture, they'd passed the elm tree where their animals sought refuge from the noonday heat and Clyde had looked back, hoping to catch a glimpse of his ma one last time. But his pa had reached over, pushing at his chin with the barrel of his gun, forcing him to look ahead.

Never look back, son, he'd said. Looking back'll kill an outlaw quicker than any Tin Star.

It had made sense to him at the time, with his own future so perfectly rendered in the plume of steam rising

*from his pony's mouth in the chill morning air. It spoke
to him of the adventure awaiting him maybe just over
the next rise, as did how the stranger who'd only just
introduced himself as his pa yelled, Hyah!, slapping his
horse's rear-end with his reins, commanding it forward
at a hard gallop, Clyde doing the same, chasing after his
pa and never feeling freer than he did right then.*

*Huddled now behind the counter of a bank in some
podunk town surrounded by the posse that had been
dogging them ever since they'd shot that preacher, his
wife and their boy — younger even than Clyde — and
thinking about those crosses, hoping against hope that
they would make one for him so his ma'd have a place
to come and visit, it was hard not to look back, if'n only
so the last thing he'd see before he met his fate was that
tender look in his ma's eyes whenever she smiled at him.*

It had taken Jody almost five minutes to get that far and he
could already feel a pressure building in his frontal lobe, same as
always happened whenever he had to read something in school.
When he looked up from the page, Dylan was walking back from
the well with a fire-charred pot of water he'd hand-pumped. He'd
use the water, once it had boiled, to blanch the two grouse they'd
shot that afternoon in advance of plucking them.

"How you making out?" Dylan asked.

"Barely made it halfway through page 2," he answered.

"Better than plucking grouse, though, I bet."

He'd set the pot on the iron grate suspended over one half of
the pit's cinderblock ring and was reaching for a log from the pile
beside to add to the fire.

"Ah hell, anything's better'n plucking grouse."

"You don't have to tell me."

Bolstered by Dylan's wry grin, Jody looked back down at the page.

Pass me that looking glass of yours, his pa said, chambering the last round, and Clyde fetched the retractable telescope from his coat's breast pocket, where he'd kept it ever since Tyrone had gifted it to him two minutes after they'd met.

Extending it, his father pressed its thick end through a shotgun hole in the counter's wall, placing his eye against the sight and swivelling it right to left. Finally, he found what he was looking for and bade his son to take a peep.

Through the glass, Clyde found a man dressed all in black — black duster, black chaps, black boots, black hat — and if it wasn't for the tin star pinned to his lapel he would've hardly looked like a lawman at all. He was surrounded by five deputies on the street in front of the bank's bullet-pocked front door and was lighting a cigar and puffing hard on that.

You see that man? his pa asked.

I see 'im.

He's the one goin' kill yer pa.

Then he's goin' t'ave to kill us both!

And while Tyrone Yates had never felt more pride in his son, or any man, than he did right then, he delivered a sharp slap to the back of the boy's head.

You listen up and you listen good. Ain' but two reasons we Yates have been put on this'n here earth: fightin' and fuckin'. And you ain' done near 'nough of neither to make it worth the trip.

But pa —

That earned him another smack.

Time'll come when you'll understand why I done what I'm about to do. But fer now you just take a good look at that man. Remember his face. Can ya do that fer me?

I will. I swear it!

Through the looking glass the man in black was lighting the fuse on a stick of dynamite with his cigar and shouting out, Yates, you got to the count of three before we'll be picking bits a you outta the rafters!

Pa, he's got a — ! the boy exclaimed only to be cut off by his father swinging downwards with the butt-end of one of his pistols. It caught the boy in the back of his head and knocked him sprawling onto the floor, out cold.

Safe travels, son, his father said, running the back of his knuckles over the boy's cheek, the first time he'd ever shown him any kind of affection at all.

One! the man in black was calling from the street and the urgency carried in his voice was enough to get Yates on his feet.

Two!

Taking a single breath, Tyrone yelled out, I'ma comin' for ya, Tin Star! and with that he charged out from behind the counter, his arms snapping to as if they were spring-loaded and both hands coming up guns a-blazin'.

He read on for an hour or so, pausing only when Dylan set a plate in Jody's lap loaded with one of the roasted grouse, a cob of buttered corn and a mound of store-bought potato salad.

"I told you it'd get easier," Dylan said and when that barely got him a passing glance he asked, "What part are you at now?"

"The part where he kills them two whores," Jody answered, his eyes never wavering from the page.

"That's a good'un," Dylan said. "Though you might not want to mention it to your mom. She's liable to have a fit, she finds out I let you read something like that."

And it was true. If his mom found out that Officer Cleary, as she always called him, had not only allowed but forced him to read something as vile as what was happening on the page now, it'd be the last time she'd let him anywhere near Dylan.

To quote:

> The red-haired whore was staring at him with a look of startled confusion, as if he'd just run a feather over her skin and not a straight razor. Her neck then lolled backwards as if on a hinge and the gash in her throat opened up so wide it looked for a moment that her head might come toppling off. Blood erupted in a geyser, spraying over Clyde sitting up on the bed as naked as the day he'd sprung from his mother's womb. And in that moment it did feel like he'd been reborn, covered with another woman's effluence and hearing a piercing wail, louder even than a birthing pain.
>
> It was the blonde-haired whore who was screaming. She was still sitting in the chair at the foot of the bed, her hips spread straddle-legged and the fingers of her one hand buried in her sex, the ones on the other clamped over a nipple, as he'd commanded her to so he'd have something to look at while he was having at her friend. The horror of seeing the other's throat cut had frozen her body as stiff as a corpse, leaving only

her mouth alive enough to vent her terror. It formed as
perfect a circle as any bullseye and Clyde was thinking
just that as he fetched his piece from the mattress beside
him, levelling the barrel at its gaping hole, thumbing the
cock back and the click stilling the woman's voice same
as if he'd pulled the trigger.

Now that yer done hollerin', he said, why'n't you
put yer mouth to the use God intended. And ah hell,
if'n you manage to wring a few more drops outta old
Johnson here, I might even let you live.

But it wasn't so much the violence and the increasingly deviant acts that accompanied it that kept Jody reading, it was the recurring feeling that the book was speaking directly to him. But where before the same thought had filled him with dread, as he read on it began to offer a strange sort of comfort. It was as if in Clyde Yates's mad quest to become the man hard enough to avenge his father's death he saw his own possible future spreading out ahead of him, for how many times had he himself imagined becoming the same if only so he might have the guts to kill Lenny?

He saw now that such was a fool's game, that he'd stand to lose a whole lot more than he could ever hope to gain. Clyde's hatred towards a world that had killed his pa and treated him — a halfbreed — like a pariah had turned toxic, destroying everything he touched, so that when finally he'd tracked and killed every man in the posse, saving the Tin Star in black for last, he was a burnt-out husk of a man, feared by all and loved by none. In the last chapter, he'd fallen asleep in the saddle and his horse, *on orders from God or the devil no mere mortal could have divined*, had carried him back to the farm he'd left so many years before.

He was jolted awake as the nag came to a nickering halt.

The gathering dark had reduced the landscape to mere shadows but there was no mistaking the familiar outline of a house and a barn. There were two figures — a tall one and a short — traversing the distance between. The taller was carrying a lantern in an upraised hand and though Clyde couldn't make out a face, the man's lopsided gait told him it was none other than his uncle, Cyril. The smaller one was carrying what looked to be a milk bucket and that couldn't have been anyone but his half-brother, Joseph.

Scanning away from them, Clyde sought out the pasture's elm tree, hoping to maybe see his ma, for she and him had often sat on its lowest branch as dusk approached so they could, in her words, glory in the Lord's mercy for seeing them through yet another day.

The tree was cast against a diffusion of reds and oranges painting the horizon with a cavalcade of such colour that, in that moment, it spoke to him, if not of the Lord's mercy, then in the very least to the splendour of the world the Lord had created. As his eyes adjusted to its radiance, he was able then to divine something else that spoke to his mother's God — a lone cross erected beneath the tree's billow — and there wasn't anything even the slightest bit merciful about that.

A short while later he was staring down at the "Beloved Wife & Mother" etched over the grave marker's crossbeam and *even that wasn't enough to stir a trace of feeling in his long-dead heart. He tried to conjure an image of her tender-hearted smile, hoping to feel something, anything, but found he could no longer even remember what it looked like.*

Then there was a voice calling out his name.

Clyde! it shouted and he spun around, his hand instinctively feeling for his sidearm.

Out of the gloom, Cyril Yates was limping towards him and the barrel of the shotgun in his hands was levelled at Clyde's chest.

You got a lot of nerve coming back here, his uncle said and quicker'n a rattlesnake's bite Clyde drew his gun, shooting the man square between the eyes.

Joseph was standing a ways off, holding up the lantern and frozen as still as a statue. Coming abreast of the boy, Clyde snatched up the lantern, coaxing his horse then in the direction of the house. He stopped in front of its porch, tossing the lantern through its front window and waiting until the flames had taken hold before wheeling his horse back towards Joseph.

You comin' or not? he said as he passed him by and the boy didn't have to be asked twice.

The book ended with the two of them riding out side by side along the same path that had taken Clyde away from the farm so long ago.

As they crested the pasture's rise, beyond which the world was engulfed in an almost preternatural dark, Joseph looked back to catch one last glimpse of his mother's grave, and his brother reached over, pushing his chin forward with the barrel of his Colt .45.

Never look back, son, he said. Looking back'll kill an outlaw quicker than any Tin Star.

And with that he yelled, Hyah!, slapping the reins over the horse's rear end and galloping off. Joseph spurred his horse too and as he chased after his half-brother he was already hatching a plan as to how he might go about avenging his own father's death.

Jody had read the last few chapters by the light of the fire, the orange glow from the flames dancing in ribbons over the words and their flicker, as much as what was written, bringing it to life right off the page.

When he'd reached *The End*, he looked up, seeking the fire's comforting embrace. Instead he found Dylan's eyes, narrowed and black, staring at him with ill-concealed amuse. It was hard not to see in them a reflection of the book, for he could well imagine the two half-brothers camping out for the night and Clyde gazing over their own fire at Joseph just like that, goading him towards a ruin as dire as his own, that thought enough to dig a well — deep and dark — into Jody's gut.

Recalling the *Beloved Wife & Mother* etched over the grave marker's crossbeams and how when *that wasn't enough to stir a trace of feeling in his long-dead heart, Clyde had tried to conjure an image of her tender-hearted smile, hoping to feel something, anything, but found he could no longer even remember what it looked like.* Thinking then of his own mother's face, how she'd smile at him sometimes when she thought he wasn't looking and how good that made him feel, because he knew she was thinking, *At least I got him.* He'd be thinking right back at her, *At least we got each other*, and maybe that wasn't much but at least it was something.

Firming the memory of her face in his own mind, telling himself he'd never get so bad as to forget it, and that thought letting him breathe easy, maybe for the first time since the night he'd killed the man he'd later find out was named Ronald Crane.

Over the next six months' worth of Saturday evenings, he read the rest of what Dylan called his grandfather's "fictions."

While most of them were as chock full of sex and violence as *A Bad Man's Son*, none made quite the impression as had that first. Still, he read every one that Dylan gave him, figuring it was a small price to pay for getting to go dirt-biking on Sundays too and then, after the first snow, having an extra day behind the wheel of one of Dylan's snowmobiles. There was even one fiction, he'd learn, called *Nickel Down*. Dylan introduced it as "the true story of how the bunker came to get its name," which seemed kind of strange to Jody, since *Nickel Down*, the book, took place in a dark and distant future, described on the back cover as *a burnt-out district of mythic savagery over which the course of empire runs in reverse.*

The fallout shelter itself was described as *being the mere skeleton of a much grander building. The only sign that its hollowed-out frame of eighteen-inch-thick poured concrete had ever been adorned by anything other than creep-vines and moss was a single unhewn cedar log running its length, which must have, in some distant past, supported a roof long since crumbled into dust.*

That was exactly how it looked on every day he'd spent there and the idea that it might still look the same in a few hundred years added to the ever-deepening impression he felt when he was at Nickel Down that it existed as a world apart, outside of the very bounds of time and space. It was a feeling he'd come to relish as much as the cup of hot chocolate Dylan always gave him while he read by the fire. The feeling of unease that Dylan was somehow using their world apart to goad him towards ruin had never fully departed him, but over the months it was chipped away by the growing assurance that Dylan's grandfather seemed to have quite the opposite intention in mind for the reader while he was writing his fictions.

There was rarely a book that passed in which he didn't have one character or another say a variation of *the road to hell is paved with good intentions*. It was one of his mother's favourite sayings as well and the more he read on the more he began to suspect that it offered him a clue, though a vague one, in trying to understand what George Cleary was up to beyond a mere cataloguing of the horrors that men do. His English teacher might have called it a "theme," but it seemed to Jody more like that thread George had mentioned in *The Pines* which some Greek princess — Ariadne, he'd called her — had given to her boyfriend — Theseus — so he might find his way out of a labyrinth. Where that thread was leading *him* Jody couldn't exactly say but it must have had something to do with "Indians," since every book had at least one or two in it and most a whole lot more than that.

His teachers always called *them* Indigenous or by the name of their Nation, trying to be respectful, though his father, on the rare occasion he had anything to say about *them* at all, rarely was. But his teachers, no less than his father, always made *them* seem like they were some sort of entirely different species, as different from him as a bear was from a moose. But as he read on, he began to see that the "Indians" in George's books weren't all that different from him and in a lot of ways he had more in common with *them* than he did with most of the other kids in his class, a no-uncertain truth added weight when he recalled that Clyde and Joseph Yates's mother was a full-blooded Plains Cree.

And never did he feel more like an "Indian" than when he read the last fiction George wrote before he died. It was called *No Quarter* and unlike the others it wasn't really a book at all, it was simply a stack of photocopied pages held together by three brass fasteners.

"I got a real treat for you tonight," Dylan had said by way of an introduction as he held it out to him. Adding then: "Mind you don't get it too dirty, now."

The spring had come early that year and though it was only the first week of March there weren't but a few patches of snow left clinging to the shade. Dylan had brought hotdogs for lunch and canned chili and nacho chips for dinner and they'd celebrated the warm weather by dirt-biking all day. Both Jody and Dylan were coated from head to foot in muck and the selfie Dylan had snapped of them afterwards spoke to Jody well of the kinship he'd come to feel with Dylan. He was still feeling that abiding sense of fraternity when he'd opened up the stack of photocopies to the first page. There was a quote there and he skipped past that without giving it more than a glance, turning to the next page and reading the opening line:

How long it had been following her she couldn't say.

He'd become a pretty fast reader since he'd had to slave over *A Bad Man's Son* so it was only a few sparse minutes later that he'd reached page 4 and come upon this paragraph:

As another vehicle approached from the opposite direction, two glints of light shone back at her. They couldn't have been anything but eyes . . .

Thinking of how he'd seen the same two glints staring back at him from the ditch one night when he was ten and was dragging their garbage can to the road, of how panicked he'd felt seeing them staring back at him under a sky so black it looked to have been painted on. For a moment it had seemed that there was nothing left of the world but him and those two yellow glints. After a breathless moment the coyote had simply slunk away but never had Jody felt so afraid, peering into the dark, terrified that the coyote was still out there just waiting for him to turn around so it could pounce.

Reading on and shortly coming to this:

> She heard the rat-a-tat-tat of the stones pelting the
> ground and even before they'd settled she was back-
> ing away, reaching for the knife in the back pocket of
> her jeans. It had been her brother's, what he called
> a butterfly knife. She'd been carrying it ever since
> she was nine and her neighbour, a man she'd known
> as Uncle Pete her whole life, had followed her one
> morning when she'd gone down to the river to pick
> fiddleheads for her mother. He'd said he'd snap her
> neck if she ever told anyone what he'd done to her,
> wrapping his hands around her throat and squeez-
> ing just a little so she'd know how easy it'd be.

Here he then slammed the book shut and gritted his teeth, his
rage rearing with the force of a tidal wave, threatening to wash
over him, trying not to think about how one of Lenny's friends —
he never knew exactly which — had crawled into his tent that one
time his dad had taken him hunting. He'd been startled awake
by a hand clenched around his neck. He could smell the stink of
whisky and weed on the man's breath as a voice warned in a dry
rasp, "I could snap your neck as easy as a chicken's. You think
about that if'n you get the urge to scream."

The man had then reached one hand into Jody's boxer briefs
and the other into his own pants and all the while he'd jerked
them both off he'd been cooing, "Easy there, son. It'll all be over
soon. You just take it easy there. Easy. Easy. Easy!"

Jody had had a few wet dreams by then and he'd been overcome by the same shame he always felt whenever he'd woken
up to a moist patch in his briefs, as he did when he came a few
seconds later, the man grunting almost at the same time so Jody

knew he'd come too. The man was then wiping his hand on his shirt even as his other hand latched tight around Jody's throat.

"A fuckin' chicken!" he'd rasped as a final warning before slipping back out of the tent.

Jody's shame had quickly turned to anger. He'd hung the hunting knife his father had given him on one of the tent's clips in easy reach and, as he stared up at it, he'd cursed himself for not grabbing the knife, sticking it in that motherfucker's throat. Taking it down and easing it from the sheath, staring at the blade in the moonglow that brightened his tent almost as much as in the day, and promising himself that he'd kill any man who ever laid a hand on him again.

"You okay there, Jody?"

It was Dylan who'd spoken and Jody flashed his eyes towards him. There must have been something in those eyes that startled the cop, because he immediately shied away from their menace. There was a look on his face that Jody had never seen before, a wavering uncertainty as if, seeing the rage turning Jody's eyes to pinpricks of hate, he'd suddenly wished he'd never given him *that* book after all. Jody was of the same mind and he was even then raising it in his hand, about to throw it in Dylan's face, or better yet into the fire, when there flared in his mind again an image of those two yellow glints of light — the coyote's eyes peering back at the girl stranded on that dark and lonely stretch of road, same as they'd once stared back at him.

You can't just leave her there!

His own voice, screaming in his head, and its fury brokering no argument. Lowering his trembling hand and peering down with mortal dread at the mud-splattered sheaf of papers now in his lap, seeing again the girl facing off against that coyote same as he once had and hoping against hope as he opened the book again that everything would turn out okay for the both of them.

"I don't know who you think is gonna eat all this food."

Jody was manoeuvring one of the two shopping carts his mother had filled with almost four hundred dollars' worth of groceries through the parking lot's maze of ice and slush.

"Milt and Alice and Raymond are coming home on Friday," his mother answered, following after him with the other cart. "I told you that. And Milt's three boys alone could eat through all of this in less than a day."

Milt and Alice and Raymond were Jody's older brothers and sister. As far as he knew none of them had spoken to their mother in years so his tone took on a skeptical note when he asked, "They said they were coming home? I mean, you talked to them?"

"Well, no. I didn't talk to them. But it's my birthday on Saturday and they always come home for my birthday."

That was a blatant lie and one that didn't seem likely of being disproved this year either. Milt was in Calgary and Raymond in Edmonton and Jody had no idea where Alice was. Prison or dead, for all he knew. None of them would be coming home for their mother's birthday and that sobering reality had him projecting ahead to what he could expect come Saturday. If it was anything like her last birthday it'd be just Jody and Tina and Clyde and Julie, who'd only stopped by for a moment between house calls as a PSW for the Red Cross. His mother had made enough food for a football team and most of that was still sitting on the counter two days later when Jody had stopped by again. The "party" had ended with her locking herself in her room and Jody eating three pieces of the pineapple upside-down cake she'd made, since Tina hated pineapple and it seemed a shame to let the whole thing go to waste.

At least Clyde's old enough to have a piece this year, he thought as he steered the cart along a river of slush, *and he likes pineapple just fine.*

A whistle of such piercing intent sounded then that he was powerless but to jerk his head on a quick lateral, knowing right off that the whistle was meant for him, since it was how Dylan often whistled whenever he wanted to get his attention up at Nickel Down. He tracked the sound to the other side of the cart corral and saw, sure enough, that's who it was. Dylan was wearing a full-body camo suit decorated with swirls like falling leaves and a matching cap with earflaps, the fur lining of which blended perfectly with the shag of his beard, bushy and full except for a bald patch on his left cheek revealing a checkerboard of seared flesh.

Dylan had seen him looking and was oscillating his outstretched index finger back and forth in front of his nose like a horizontal piston, pointing towards the row of cars on Jody's left. Jody followed the finger to a customized orange pick-up truck parked directly across from the corral. He didn't need more than a cursory look through its windshield to see it was two of his father's buddies inside. The driver he knew only as Gator, a nickname he'd earned because he'd grown up in Florida and had even spent time wrestling his namesake for tourists when he was a teenager. The man in the passenger seat was named Roger, although Jody had rarely heard him called anything but Ram on account, he'd surmised, of the horns he'd had tattooed in spiralling loops on either side of his neck and because he was about as ugly, and ornery, as a billy goat.

What the hell are they doing here? Jody thought, though both were staring right at him so the answer was all too clear.

They were waiting for him, there was no doubt of that, and he also had a pretty good idea as to why they'd be doing so. Seeking out Dylan again, he glanced back at the cart corral but Dylan had since vanished. A crashing noise erupted from behind and he spun around to find his mother's cart had toppled over. It must have run aground on an icy shoal and got away from her.

She was standing over it, looking down in moribund despair at the groceries spilling out of the bags and into the slushy muck as if it was a tragedy beyond all reckoning.

A roar then from Jody's left — Gator starting the pick-up. He was revving the engine and black smoke was pouring out of the truck's dual exhaust. Ram had since cranked his window down and was wearing the lecherous grin of someone who positively revelled in calamity.

"Hey, Jode," he called out, "ain't you goin' to help yer ma?"

The orange pick-up truck followed his Tacoma out of the parking lot.

Jody was sure it would turn left at the light, same as him, but instead it peeled off right with such a screeching roar that it had his mother clutching at her chest in startled fright and hollering after it, "Give an old lady a heart attack, why don't you!"

There was a green light at the intersection of Highway 118 and Wellington, a block away, but the hand signal was flashing. He pressed his foot down hard on the gas and the Tacoma was surging towards eighty as it raced under the now red light. As he eased off the gas, Jody checked his rear-view mirror for any sign of a cop and sure enough there was one turning left on the advance green, following after him. He wasn't overly concerned, though, since the cop was Dylan and the fact that he was driving a green Forester and wearing camo gear instead of a uniform surely meant he was off duty.

Just past the lights, Jody swung left onto Wellington Street North. The salt-encrusted asphalt sloped on a steep rise, leading upwards onto what his mom called Snob Hill. This was mostly due to the house at its summit. It had been built in the 1970s by

Franz Mueller, the late patriarch of the so-called Mesaquakee Kennedys, who'd obviously derived his inspiration from the Southern plantations, though the house was smaller, by a half, than any of the ones Jody had seen in movies. Between its four columns and gabled roof, its circular driveway and meticulously manicured yard, it had once been the town's most coveted property, though with the proliferation of so many McMansions in the town's subdivisions, it'd be lucky to make even the top twenty now.

Its current owner, a retired electrician named Phillip Grant, was one of Jody's clients. He paid him a premium to have his driveway ploughed by eight a.m. and a lesser fee to shovel off his roof and also to clean out his eavestroughs in the fall. He'd given Jody a hundred-dollar bonus at Christmas and otherwise had never been anything but friendly to him. Hardly a snob, but whenever they were taking the shortcut to Highway 4 by means of Wellington Street North, the Mueller Mansion never ceased to give his mother cause to shake her head and sneer in bitter reproach, mostly because it was Franz's son, Russ, who owned the car dealership where, in her words, she'd been swindled into buying that piece-of-shit Outback.

And no doubt she'd have been doing the same as the house approached when, no sooner than they'd crested the hill, the green Forester suddenly swerved into the left-hand lane. It sped past them at, best guess, sixty klicks over the posted speed of 40 kph and then blew through the three-way stop a few hundred metres hence, going faster still.

That gave his mother plenty of reason to forget, for once, about the no-end-to-grief she suffered on account of her car but still gave her plenty of reason to shake her head and scoff, "He's going to kill someone driving like that! We should call the cops. Did you get his number?"

Jody ignored her, watching the Forester disappear around the bend leading to the stop sign at Highway 4. As he applied the brakes at the three-way, he waited for its flash of green to reappear so he'd know it was heading towards Talon Lake Road too, but it never did, meaning it was heading back towards town.

"I swear to god," his mother was saying in the seat beside him as she lit a cigarette with no thoughts whatsoever of rolling down the window to vent the smoke, "the drivers in this town have all gone crazy!"

Hard to argue with that, though, truth be told, Dylan had never been what Jody would have called anything even resembling sane when he got behind the wheel. But where Lenny's brand of reckless abandon always had Jody clutching at the vehicle's armrest, terrified for his life, there was something about the casual grace with which Dylan handled the steering wheel that always set him at ease. The twenty-odd kilometres between the highway and Nickel Down's wrought iron gate was a stretch of potholed gravel leading them on a rollercoaster ride vacillating between lowland swamps and granite bluffs but no matter how fast Dylan drove, Jody never felt so much as a twinge of fear. He even took to enjoying how his stomach seemed to jump into his mouth whenever the truck took a sudden drop as it plummeted down one of the steeper grades.

Probably that had to do as much with where they were going as with how they'd got there, for the times they'd spent together at Nickel Down were the happiest of his childhood, really the only happy memories he had at all before he started going out with Tina. That his very worst childhood memory had brought him and Dylan together had only served to validate his mother's oft-repeated assurance that even the darkest cloud can sometimes have a silver lining. It was something she said, more to herself than to Jody, whenever Lenny had, in her words, "let his hand slip again," though the state she was often in afterwards suggested he'd let both fists, his steel-toed work boots and a stick of firewood slip, too. While the way she looked at Jody whenever she said it told him that the silver lining she was talking about was none other than himself, the only silver lining he could ever divine was that the worse a beating his dad gave his mom, the longer Lenny tended to stay away afterwards.

If they were lucky, he'd be gone for a couple of weeks, or maybe a month, and every night he was gone Jody would lie in bed wishing that he'd never come back at all, knowing that was a fool's game — he didn't have to look any further than one of his father's favourite sayings to know that.

"A wish in one hand and shit in the other," he'd answer pretty near every time Jody asked him for something, "put them together and what do you got?" He'd be holding each hand out when he said the first part and, when he came to the second, he'd clap his hands together and Jody could practically see the shit fly.

No, either way you sliced it, any wish he could have made wouldn't have amounted to anything but two handfuls of splattered excrement and maybe he'd still be thinking that if it hadn't been for Officer Cleary.

After Dylan had dropped Jody off at his house on the night he'd killed Ronald Crane, Jody hadn't seen him for almost three months. Then, one afternoon as his bus was pulling up to his house, he'd spotted a cop cruiser parked beside his mom's car. He'd waited at the end of his driveway until the bus had turned around and was heading back towards the highway, and then he'd waited a few moments more.

If the cop car was there because of what he'd done to that fat fucking perv . . .

With every passing heartbeat spent staring at the cop car, he was thinking more and more that his only hope of not going to jail was making a run for it. In the second week of September there'd be plenty of empty cottages within an hour's walk through the bush. While the owners often paid millions for their summer homes, they mostly spent only a few weeks there, if that. Such had always seemed like a waste to Jody but it did mean that anyone looking for a place to hide out didn't have to look far.

The best way would be to follow that old deer trail from the end of the road. It'd take you to the back side of Talon Lake and, if none of its cottages were empty, it was only a short hike over to Lake Joseph.

He was turning that way, about to set off in a hard sprint. And maybe he would have, too, had his mother not then hollered at him from the top step leading into the mudroom:

"What the hell are you doing out there? Get on in here!"

She was wearing a pair of jeans and her favourite cardigan sweater — pink — which she must have put on for their visitor, since usually when Jody got home she was only wearing a bathrobe and a T-shirt. He was thinking even then that it'd take her at least two or three minutes to put on her shoes, what with her lobster-claw hand, and that would have given him plenty enough of a head start. He'd then caught a hint of movement off to her right and tracked it to the front window. Even with the glare in the glass it was hard to mistake the man peering out for anybody but *that* cop from *that* night, since the one side of his face looked like something out of a horror movie.

Jody had trudged up the driveway, his footfalls growing heavier with every step. By the time he'd come to the house's stairs, the cop was standing behind his mother in the mudroom, grinning over the top of her head like he was the devil himself and that didn't do much to elevate Jody's mood.

"Don't look so glum," his mother enthused, as cheerful as he'd ever seen her. "I've just heard some good news, for a change."

The good news, she'd tell him once he'd got inside, was that his father was in jail.

"For how long?" Jody asked, looking at his mother, though it was the cop who answered.

"He struck an officer of the law," he said, "so I'd say he's going to be away for a good while yet."

While he spoke, he craned his head ever so slightly to one side, all the better for Jody to see the swollen bruise puffing out the skin over his right eye. He added to that a discreet wink so Jody knew that it hadn't been a coincidence that it was him his father had struck. Perhaps he should have been thinking, *so maybe silver linings do exist after all,* but his belly had started to squirm like there was a den of snakes living in there as he thought of how they'd met, knowing all along that he'd have to pay a price for the cop letting him off the way he had and certain that this was the day when his debt had come due.

He'd taken an inadvertent step backwards and felt his mother's hand on his shoulder, lending him a measure of resolve.

"Officer Cleary has something he wants to ask you," she said and he turned back to the cop.

He spoke at some length, though Jody didn't catch much of what he said. Something about a new program kind of like Big Brothers that paired police officers with children who had one or both parents in jail, so as they wouldn't grow up hating lawmen. Jody was having a hard time following what Officer Cleary was saying because every time he looked up at the cop and saw the scar on his cheek, he'd got a sudden flash in his mind of the first time he'd seen it.

He'd been sitting in the passenger seat of that fat fucking perv's minivan. He was holding the hunting knife his father had given to him for his tenth birthday clenched in his hand, its hilt resting on his leg and its blade upright. Blood was draining over its tang and dribbling down his fingers and he could feel a trickle from the arterial spray that had spurted out of the man's neck dripping off his cheek in perfect synchronicity with the *ding ding ding* sounding from the open driver's side door. A voice from the radio was crooning about hearing something through the grapevine. It was a song he knew well since his mother often listened to the oldies station, and he was singing along in a tenuous croak as if, as long as he kept singing, he wouldn't have to think about the man he'd just stabbed in the neck and who was now lying on the ground, maybe dead, outside the open driver's side door.

A gentle rap at the passenger window had startled him and when he jerked towards it there was that face staring back at him. The checkerboard of seared flesh engulfing its left cheek immediately called to mind Freddy Krueger and wasn't he a child-killer before his neighbours burnt him alive? Could have been he was a friend of the man he'd just stabbed. Maybe he'd been waiting in the shadows to get his turn with their latest victim and seeing his friend murdered he was about to exact his revenge. Such anyway were the thoughts cascading through Jody's mind, sending him reeling into the driver's seat and scurrying out the open door.

Instead of the ground his feet found one of the dead man's legs and his foot slipped off it like he was stepping onto a floating log. He went down hard and landed soft, sprawling over the man's prodigious belly, his flailing hands slapping at the perv's face, sticky with blood and feeling like wet bread dough lathered with melted butter, his fingers grappling at it trying to find something solid to latch onto. But it was like he was caught in quicksand and it was sucking him under, into the man's very chest. In a sheer panic by then, thrashing about and feeling the prickle of raspberry brambles lashing at his face as he finally managed to scramble off. Looking up and finding the other man standing a few feet away. He was framed in the moonglow as if by an otherworldly light and Jody could see from the man's uniform he was a cop, which didn't exactly set his mind at ease. His one hand was resting on the butt of the gun in his holster but his other hand was reaching out, beseeching Jody towards calm, as was his voice when finally he spoke.

"It's okay," he said. "You're safe now. Everything's going to be okay."

Dredged then from the memory by his mother's hand prodding at his shoulder.

"Well, aren't you going to say something, honey?" she asked and Jody glanced upwards at the cop, trying to recall what he'd been talking about and having absolutely no idea.

The cop seemed to get that and offered in a conciliatory tone, "If you don't like dirt-biking, we can always figure something else out."

That got Jody's attention. He'd been after his mom to buy him a dirt bike for years but she'd always vetoed the idea because, in her words, she'd have to use two hands to count all the people she knew who've been crippled or killed riding a motorcycle.

"Dirt-biking?" he asked and the gleam in his eyes must have betrayed his interest for the cop then answered:

"Like I said, we just got two in at the station, one just about your size too. Proceeds of crime, you know. They's just sitting there . . ."

Letting the sentence trail off into Jody's imagination as the boy looked to his mom. She was smiling in her fragile way, suggesting that even if she was not necessarily enthused, she was at least open to the idea, and that was as good as consent for the cop.

"Now that that's settled," Dylan said, clapping Jody on the shoulder and a gleam coming into his eyes as he smiled down at him, "when do you want to start?"

A tenuous beginning for sure but one that had led to five years' worth of weekends dirt-biking and hunting up at Nickel Down, cooking what they killed over an open fire, and Dylan teaching him how to fight after the mandatory one-hour minimum of reading in the evening. Later, they'd also spent a fair share of weekdays together there too, chainsawing the property's hardwoods and chopping them into cords, which Dylan would then sell by the trailer-load, mostly to his neighbours or his fellow cops. In the meantime, Jody had grown big and strong and tough. Because they split the profits fifty-fifty, he always had a little money in his pocket, enough to buy his own dirt bike anyway, and later, after he'd got his licence, a used Ford F-150. Driving the truck back from school one afternoon, he'd picked up Tina hitchhiking. Though she'd always say their relationship began the day she'd given him that rainbow, in Jody's mind it didn't really begin until he'd offered her a ride which is why he'd insisted the black pick-up truck be the second tattoo she'd inked on his back.

It got so that he was driving her to and from school every day and then spending most of his free time with her as well. The only time they were ever really apart after that was when he went up to Nickel Down with Dylan. She was never shy about telling him how she thought "it was weird" that he was spending so much time up in the woods with an older man, practically a stranger and a cop to boot. Probably she was just jealous since she was also always badgering him to ask Dylan if maybe she could come along with them too. Jody didn't really want her to intrude on his and Dylan's world apart but, during what she'd come to call "Covid Summer," she'd taken to harassing him non-stop, arguing that it wasn't right that he'd get to go off every weekend while she was mostly stuck at home, and finally he'd relented.

When he asked Dylan, the very next Saturday, he could tell from the way Dylan paused before answering that he wasn't overly keen on the idea either. Still he'd said, "Ah hell, why not? The more the merrier, I always say."

Tina had been hiding around the corner of the house and when she'd heard that she'd come bounding out, skipping towards Dylan's Bronco, her face aglow just like when she'd first spotted the picture of her rainbow in Jody's bedroom window.

After she'd planted herself in the Bronco's front seat with her knapsack, Dylan had turned to Jody, smiling his wry grin and giving him a wink on his way to whispering, "She sure is an eager little beaver, ain't she?"

Her eagerness lasted about two minutes after they'd arrived at Nickel Down, deflated almost at once by the relentless assault of a million or so mosquitoes and black and deer flies.

"Once we get on the dirt bike," Jody had assured her, "you'll forget all about them."

They'd set off along the trail with her clutching him tight from behind but before they'd even made the first bend, she'd scalded her leg on the cycle's exhaust and that put a quick end to the ride. She'd spent the rest of the day in the tent, hiding from the bugs and tending to her bites and her burn. It was only with dusk fast approaching that Jody had been able to entice her back out.

"Come on," he'd said, "I want to show you something."

"What?"

"It's a surprise."

"What kind of surprise?"

"You'll see when we get there. Come on, now, we're losing the light."

What he'd wanted to show her was that old apple tree perched at the top of the granite ridge that split the property almost in half, about the biggest apple tree he'd ever seen. One of the bike paths led them straight there and after the fifteen-minute hike Tina's face had taken to looking like she had the pox, she was so bitten up by bugs.

"This is what you dragged me out here for?" she'd fumed, swatting at the horde that had gathered into a furious assault around them. "A fucking apple tree!"

"Just wait until you see the view from up top," Jody assured her. "It ain't like nothing else in the whole wide world. Come on, now, I'll give you a boost."

He cupped his hands for her to step into and she'd snarled at him, "I don't need no damn boost to climb a fucking apple tree."

She motioned for him to get out of the way. After Jody had taken a couple of steps back, she'd run at the tree, scampering up its trunk with the ease of a squirrel and then standing on its lowest branch, sneering down at him and sticking out her tongue. The lowest branch was some seven feet off the ground, within easy reach of Jody's six-foot-two. He pulled himself up and climbed past Tina, and then kept climbing until he'd reached what Dylan called the sitting branch. It was less than twenty feet above the ridge's summit but the way it jutted out over the cliff meant it was a good fifty feet to the dense canopy of treetops below, and maybe another forty below that to the forest floor.

Jody had been plenty scared the first time Dylan had coaxed him out onto the sitting branch and it had taken him two years before he'd summoned the nerve to tightrope-walk to the middle of it, where Dylan preferred to sit. Tina had followed him up but the expression on her face told him it was unlikely she'd follow him out there and he forsook the thrill of that for sitting down a few meagre feet along the branch from where she was clinging desperately to the trunk.

"Come on," he'd said, "sit beside me."

He was holding out his one hand and she was looking at it like it was a rattlesnake coiled and ready to strike.

"Come on, now," he said, "I won't let you fall. Whatsa matter, don't you trust me?"

She'd answered with a frown but had taken his hand, holding fast to the trunk until she was sitting down and then wrapping both hands around his arm, too terrified to look down. Until then, the sun had been hiding behind a furrow of bluish-grey clouds splayed over the horizon. It was only a few seconds later that it reappeared, radiating out from within the thin screen as it passed behind the ridge on the far side of the valley and infusing the sky with such a splendour of reds and oranges that the sight of its majesty stilled them both.

Tina had wrapped one arm around his waist and leaned her head on his shoulder and they sat there in quiet awe until the last traces of light were leaking out of the sky. Jody honoured that by bending down and kissing her on the top of the head, nestling his nose into her hair and inhaling deeply the scent of strawberries from her shampoo. That roused her enough that she looked up at him and never before or since had he seen such a look of tranquil serenity in her eyes. She'd then gone back to leaning her head on his shoulder and looking back towards the horizon. There was a sudden flourish of light rimming the clouds with a golden hue, like the sun was giving them a final wave goodbye before relinquishing its dominion to the emerging stars and the sliver of a crescent moon.

A cool evening breeze had chased away the bugs and there was not a single sound except for the gentle rustle of the apple tree's leaves as the colour drained from the clouds and the dark crept deeper into their furrows, Jody and Tina watching in muted reverence, as if they were witnessing not just one sunset but the end of all sunsets, and after this only the night.

A perfect little moment, for sure.

Thinking that, a sudden and involuntary shudder rippled

through Jody such that it caused Tina to startle and clutch at him with a fevered hand as if she'd been shocked awake from a falling dream just before she'd hit the ground.

"Hey, I was thinking," Jody said after she'd relaxed again, "you ought to tattoo this on my back."

"What?" she asked, a little drowsy. "The sunset?"

"No. I mean — Yeah. The sunset and this tree and us sitting in it."

"A perfect little moment," Tina said as if she'd been reading his mind.

"You think you could do that?"

"I'd like to see you try and stop me," she'd said, looking up at him with an oddly misplaced, though by now familiar, sheen of defiance adding a twinkle to her eyes.

She'd begun work on it the very next day.

It would be Dylan who'd make the connection between the tree she would ink onto the small of his back and George Cleary.

They'd been chopping up a yellow birch into cordwood. Jody was manning the chainsaw and Dylan the axe and Jody had just stopped for a moment to gas up. It was hot that day and he'd taken off his shirt, the first time he'd done so since Tina had finished her latest creation.

"I didn't know you'd joined The Sons," Dylan said, using that as an excuse to take a break of his own.

"What?" Jody asked, for he had no clue as to what Dylan was talking about.

"I figured you must have, since only The Sons are allowed to wear their banner, it'd mean the rope for anyone else who did."

"What the hell are you talking about?" He still had no clue.

"Your new tattoo. An apple tree cast against a setting sun? It's The Sons of Adam's banner, ain't it?"

"No," Jody protested, "it's —"

Cutting himself off because he'd suddenly realized, aside from the silhouettes of him and Tina sitting on a high branch, it was actually a pretty fair approximation. It had come as a bit of a shock, since that had hardly been his intention. His befuddlement must have been written on his face, because Dylan was then slapping him jovially on the back and saying, "It's okay. I never did take you much for the hero-type anyway."

It was a line from one of George's books, Jody couldn't remember which, and while the wry grin teasing at the corners of Dylan's lips suggested he couldn't have been happier at the thought, Jody wasn't able to dismiss the sentiment so lightly.

As far as he knew, The Sons of Adam were just a bunch of fictional characters. Dylan treating them like they were real recalled to him the night he'd finished reading *A Bad Man's Son* and Dylan had been gazing at him across the fire as if positively revelling in thoughts of his imminent ruin. And there could be nothing in George's world more ruinous than joining The Sons. They were about the most evil sons of bitches Jody had ever heard about. With the current pandemic hinting that the apocalyptic world in which they so thrived wasn't maybe too far removed from our own, the idea that Dylan would so delight in counting him amongst their creed enflamed his niggling doubts over why Dylan had spared him as he had. It became like they were hot embers burrowing into his hair, burning at the back of his head, and as he finished cutting up the tree into eighteen-inch lengths, he bided his time trying to remember what he could of the book George had named after his murderous band of outlaw-bikers-cum-doomsday-cultists.

In *The Sons of Adam*, Nickel Down was where the titular motorcycle club had built themselves a new Eden and they'd taken the apple tree perched at the edge of the cliff as their emblem, setting it *against a diffusion of reds and oranges as might* colour a sky approaching dusk to symbolize how the sun itself seemed about to set on a world gone mad, maybe never to rise again.

It was an obvious reference to the threat of nuclear winter, given that the book had been written in the 1970s. They'd taken the threat of the impending disaster *hanging like a noose over the entire planet* as an excuse to proclaim themselves God's Chosen Few, *charged with a sacred mission to burn the world back to Eden, what He himself had ordained by means of the rainbow that had appeared after the flood.*

Such an orgy of violence and despair they left in their wake that it had given Jody nightmares for weeks on end. All of it was witnessed through the eyes of the local coroner, Hubert Cairn, who'd started off documenting their rampage only to be captured by The Sons on the final page of the next-to-last chapter. They'd let him live *for reasons only God or perhaps the devil could surmise* and had brought him back to Nickel Down, where he'd been shocked to learn that the men he'd begun to think of *as demons cast upon this earth to show humankind, and himself too, the errors of our ways* were also devoted fathers and husbands, *as likely to lavish their children and wives with hugs and kisses as they were to rend their fellow men limb from limb.*

In the final chapter, a series of bright flashes appeared on the horizon, *chasing away the encroaching dusk as surely as the dawn did the night.* The end of the world had apparently come. The Sons and their families treated that as a cause for celebration and the coroner, disturbed by their *callous ebullience*, fled from the compound, following a path, *made by deer or man he couldn't say,* to a high ridge *upon the crest of which resided an apple tree whose size and the lushness of its fruit made it seem almost divine in origin.*

Cairn immediately recognized the tree from the banner The Sons affixed to their bikes and tattooed on their chests and backs. It was cast against a similar diffusion of red and oranges, *its lustre emboldened by particles cast into the air from the disaster he was certain had consumed the cities to the south in a whelm of fire.*

> *So this is where it all must have begun, he thought, staring up at the tree. Hard to believe such evil could come from something so beautiful but then maybe that's the very nature of evil itself — it could spring forth from anything.*
>
> *Far from a reassuring notion, though thinking it immediately set his mind at ease. For if evil could come out of anything, he thought, then maybe that meant good could as well.*
>
> *And it was with this in mind that he turned back towards The Sons' compound, thinking of all the smiling, happy faces that were no doubt waiting to greet him, perhaps the only smiling, happy faces left anywhere in the entire world.*

Dylan kept his copies of George's fictions in an army footlocker in the bunker's basement and Jody took *The Sons of Adam* into his tent with him that night. After he'd finished it, he lay down musing upon what he'd just read and telling himself, *Maybe Cairn was right and good could come out of anything, same as evil.* It struck him as somewhat overly optimistic but did plant within his addled mind a small seed of hope, for if good could really come out of anything, then maybe that meant it could even come out of someone like him.

Thinking then back over all the time they'd spent at Nickel Down, it seemed that maybe that was the lesson Dylan had been trying to teach him all along. Later, when he thought about the five years they'd spent together, it would come to make sense that that night was also the last night they'd spend together, though in the weeks immediately following it, Dylan shunning him had come as a terrible blow.

For the next few weekends afterwards, Dylan had simply begged off, citing work, and then Tina's house had burnt down with her parents passed out in the basement. He and Tina had been at his mom's house and had been alerted, just before four o'clock in the morning, to the fire by the wail of sirens screaming down Talon Lake Road. By the time they'd got there all that was left of the house was smouldering wreckage and Jody had spent the next three hours sitting with Tina behind the garage in the car seat her father had ripped out of his old Buick Cutlass Cruiser station wagon because, or so he'd said, "It was more comfortable than any couch he'd ever owned." Tina's head was propped on his shoulder and Jody's arm was draped over hers. She'd just cried herself back to sleep a few moments before Dylan poked his head around the side of the building.

"There you are," he'd said with his characteristic jocularity. "I was just looking for you."

Jody hadn't much to say to that and Dylan seemed to understand, for he'd then turned to the house where a fireman was using a hose to soak the last of its remnants lest a hidden ember might cause it to flare up again.

"It's a helluva thing," Dylan had then said, shaking his head. "But at least they won't be accusing you of corruptin' their daughter no more."

While it was true that neither Tina's mother nor father had taken much of a shine to Jody, and had even threatened to call the cops on him on account she wasn't legal when she'd moved into his room, it seemed to Jody like a painfully callous thing for Dylan to say.

The wry grin curdling Dylan's face didn't do much to ease Jody's discomfort, nor did the way he was staring with such earnest approbation, as if he was seeking confirmation that things had indeed worked out for the best. Since Jody didn't know what to say to that, he'd kept his tongue and it was only a few moments later that Dylan had said, "Well, I guess I best get back to it. See you when I do."

They were the last words he'd spoken to Jody and they'd long since come to reside in his mind as a bookend, demarcating the end of their time together. He now saw that maybe he'd been overly optimistic about that too. Why else would Dylan have insinuated himself into his father's death and then shown up in the parking lot of the grocery store to warn him that he was being tailed by two of Lenny's friends?

He was still pondering on that some hours later as he heaved a stack of four ancient wicker lawn chairs into the back of the Tacoma. He was cleaning out the garage, the one task he'd set for himself on this, his first proper day off in almost two weeks, and something Tina had been after him to do for years. Her mother, Marnie, had once dreamed of opening an "antique" store in town but her years of going to yard sales and auctions, or just picking up other people's junk from the side of the road, had amounted to nothing more than a garage packed to the rafters with mouldy old furniture, boxes of knick-knacks and other assorted detritus.

He'd meant to get to it just after lunch and here it was after dinner and he still hadn't managed to fill his truck with but a half a load, even that seeming like a waste of time since the town dump had closed at six, a half-hour past.

When he turned back to the garage, he saw Tina had climbed up onto a grey metal desk piled with boxes and was trying to untangle the cord from a standing lamp that had become wrapped around a pair of wooden cross-country skis.

"You be careful up there," he cautioned, "that pile comes down it'll bury us both."

She mustn't have thought that deserved an answer and Jody watched her yanking at the skis. They wouldn't budge and she paused a moment, breathing hard and wiping the spiderwebs off her face with a frenzied sweep of her hand.

"You want me to give it a go?" he asked and she threw him a dismissive scowl to show him what she thought of that.

"You just keep your eyes on Clyde," she said.

It had been maybe thirty seconds since he'd last looked at the boy. He'd been trying to climb what was left of the snow-mound at the end of the driveway then but when Jody glanced back at it now, Clyde was nowhere to be seen. Stepping out the door, he tracked him to the middle of the puddle turning their drive-way into a lake. He was carrying a stick almost as tall as himself, whacking it at the water and shouting "Ha!" every time he made a splash. His snowsuit was soaked to the chin and Jody cursed himself, since the last thing Tina had told him before climbing onto the desk was "Don't let Clyde out of your sight and what-ever you do make sure he stays away from that damn puddle, he's liable to drown himself."

Didn't seem much chance of that but still Jody knew he'd catch hell for letting him get sopping wet and he had a sudden vision of the future, Tina carrying Clyde kicking and screaming into the house; just one more reason, among the multitude he'd already given her that day, for her to be pissed off at him.

The boy seemed to be having the time of his life, though, and to forestall the inevitable, if only for a few moments, Jody turned back to Tina. She'd apparently given up any hope of untangling the skis and was instead passing him down a rusted old wrench, about as big as one of his arms. He was sizing it up, trying to think of whether he might have a use for it, when he heard Scout give out a growl. The dog followed that up with a caterwauling of barks as she tore off down the driveway and Jody stepped out from behind the truck, seeing the source of her ire was a maroon Grand Cherokee driving slowly past on the road. The driver had caught sight of her too and was already picking up speed as Jody rounded the front of the pick-up. Unless the driver was lost, he knew, there was only one place he could have been going.

"Jesus Christ!"

This from Tina striding out of the garage.

"I told you to keep him out of that fucking puddle!" she was yelling and Jody, as a buffer against having to face the now very real future he'd imagined only moments ago, turned back to the Jeep hurtling down the road.

"You finish loading the truck?"

Tina was sitting on the couch with Clyde in her lap, his favourite pop-up book spread over the boy's legs. She'd let Jody get his boots off before she'd asked the question, the answer to which she'd have already known, since Jody'd heard Scout barking ever since he'd pulled into the driveway not thirty seconds ago.

"You mind if I take a squirt first," he answered, a little more gruffly than he'd intended.

He was walking past, heading for the bathroom, though he didn't really have to go. He was feeling a little jittery after scaring off that reporter and what he really wanted was a toke and a beer, to calm his nerves. He saw now the latter would have to wait and the toke would have to be from his pipe, though he preferred the elevated high he'd have got from smoking a joint. But that'd take time, even if it was only a minute or two. Best to get back outside as quick as he could, finish loading up the truck before Clyde went to bed, so he could kiss him goodnight, which only gave him fifteen minutes or so.

When he came back out of the bedroom, secreting the pipe in his pants pocket, she was still reading to Clyde. She ignored him completely as he walked past, detouring towards the kitchen and thinking, *Maybe I'll have that beer after all.* He retrieved a bottle of Carling from the fridge and was just popping its cap when Scout let out a low growl. Lights flashed through the window — someone turning into the driveway — and the dog bounded off the floor, barking up a storm as she stalked towards the door.

God, Jody thought taking a sip from the bottle, *what now?*

It didn't take more than a quick peep through the kitchen's window to find out.

He'd halfway expected it to be the chief of police coming back to arrest him and wasn't much relieved when he saw it was Gator's pick-up truck. It had come to a stop ten feet from the porch, its headlights glaring directly at the kitchen window, its engine gunning. Black smoke poured out of its twin exhausts, billowing in a noxious cloud against the stars winking from above the treeline, tarnishing their bright.

"Who is it?" Tina asked, standing from the couch. She was clasping Clyde to her chest and the boy was shouting "Bah!" in protest, wriggling in her grip and straining his hands for the book she'd set on the coffee table.

"It's a couple of Lenny's friends," Jody answered.

"Well, what do they want?"

"How the hell should I know?" he spat back, though he had a pretty good idea. "Maybe they've come to pay their respects."

It didn't seem likely. If they'd wanted to pay their respects, they could have done so in the parking lot at the grocery store. No, they were here for something else and he was betting it was what he'd found in that duffel bag he'd seen Lenny burying behind his mom's garage five years previous, on what would prove to be the hottest night of Covid Summer. It had been too stifling to sleep in the house so Jody had set up the tent in the backyard, lining it with cushions from both the living room's and the rec room's couches for comfort's sake. They'd smoked a joint and that had knocked Tina out but Jody hadn't been so lucky.

Or maybe he had been lucky. He'd certainly thought so a few weeks after Dylan had pulled Lenny over and found all that fentanyl in his trunk. With his dad out of the picture, for a few years at least, curiosity had gotten the better of him. He'd dug up the duffel bag on a day Tina had gone into town with his mom and discovered it was stuffed with just short of two hundred and fifty thousand dollars, a Ziploc freezer bag full of pills and a gun that looked to him just like the Scorpion machine pistol he'd often used while playing *Call of Duty*. The money and the drugs weren't much of a surprise to him — the newspaper article he'd read about his dad's arrest had said fentanyl dealers in Northern Ontario could make upwards of twenty thousand dollars a week — but the SMG sure was. The question of why his father would own such an exotic, and lethal, firearm was shortly eclipsed by thoughts of what he might have been planning to do with it.

Whatever it was, he told himself, *it's best you forget you ever saw it*.

He'd reburied the bag, being careful to spread a few layers of leaves over the ground as his father had. And maybe he would have forgotten all about it, or would have at least left well enough alone, had Tina's parents not been burnt up in that fire a few weeks later. They hadn't left any insurance, only debts, and to consolidate those they'd recently refinanced the house to within a few thousand dollars of what it was worth. Either someone would have to start paying the mortgage for them or the bank would seize the property. After what Tina had lost already, losing the house seemed like adding salt to an open wound and so Jody had dug up the bag again. He'd paid the bank five grand, enough for six months' worth of payments, telling Tina that the loan officer he spoke with gave him a two-month extension to make good.

The last four months of school the previous spring had been cancelled due to the pandemic. Even if they were planning to resume again in the fall, it didn't seem to Jody it'd be much use him going back and he'd gone through the address book Tina's father had kept in the Tacoma's glovebox, calling every one of his clients and offering to carry on with whatever landscaping and snow removal services he'd provided.

He'd promised himself he'd replace every last dollar he'd taken before Lenny got out but then Tina had spotted an ad for a mobile home for sale on the community notice board when they were shopping at the FreshCo in Huntsville.

Pointing it out to him, she'd said, "That's what we need. We could live in it until we get together the money to build a new house."

It was really only a piece of wishful thinking on her part, as the price tag was twenty-five thousand dollars, way out of their reach. But at the sight of the picture on the ad, a look had come into her eyes — maybe it was hope. Jody hadn't seen anything but grief in those eyes since her parents had died and while Tina was fetching a cart, he'd called the number. He arranged to view the trailer after dropping Tina off at school the next day and an hour later he'd handed the owner twenty grand in cash, which strictly speaking wasn't legal but the owner'd seemed more than happy to turn a blind eye. It cost another three grand to have it moved and hooked up to water, power and septic but it was well worth it, if only because he'd never seen Tina so elated as she was when she'd spotted it sitting at the end of her driveway.

They'd moved in the very same day.

He hadn't taken a single withdrawal from the bag since. If he hadn't exactly forgotten about it, he'd at least pushed it far enough into the back of his mind that he didn't much think about it again until he was driving away from his mom's on the night Lenny had beat her near to death after being released from prison.

He figured it a good bet Lenny'd be staying at Gator's place, a clapboard bungalow on one of the side roads just this side of Maynard Falls. He'd staked the place out and was rewarded for his vigilance when his father appeared a few hours later, grabbing an armload of firewood from the stack under the carport. After finding the duffel, Jody had devised what he thought was a fool-proof plan on how to deal with Lenny, but it wasn't for another twenty-four hours that he'd get a chance to put it into motion.

Just after ten the following night, Lenny had come out of the house again, this time slipping into the Buick Regal parked in the driveway next to Gator's truck. Jody followed him down the road, driving up right behind and then signalling him by flashing the Tacoma's high beams. That had got Lenny to stop. When he'd got out of the car to see who it was, he'd been quite plainly tucking something into the back of his pants. Jody guessed it was a gun and lest he give Lenny any reason to use it, he stepped out of the truck keeping his hands raised and palms out in front of him.

"Well, don't that beat all," his father had said when he'd seen who it was, "I was just coming to look for you."

The way his hand was inching towards the back of his pants got Jody to thinking his dad would just as soon shoot him dead as give him a hug.

"I got something of yours," Jody said.

"I was hoping you might. Well go on then, son, you best be fetchin' it."

"I don't have it on me."

"So where is it?"

"Not far. If you'll follow me, I'll take you right to it."

Now, thinking back to that day, Jody realized that as Lenny followed him out to that ravine on Algonquin Road, he must have called Gator and told him what was what. When Lenny never showed up after that, Gator might have figured Lenny had just taken off with his stash and not thought much of it until Lenny turned up frozen solid in his car. That might have got Gator and Ram to thinking about the two hundred and fifty grand, and the pills worth almost as much, except Jody had dumped the pills down the toilet before he'd stashed the duffel under their trailer. He'd saved only five, which he'd dissolved in saline, using that to fill a syringe, telling himself that if Lenny ever touched his mother again maybe the cops'd figure it was poetic justice that a piece-of-shit dealer like him would go off the road doped up on his own supply and leave it at that.

But of course, Gator didn't know Jody had dumped the pills and it wasn't much of a leap to suppose what a couple of guys like Gator and Ram would be willing to do to get their hands on almost a half-million dollars. Whatever that was, it didn't seem they were going to be overly subtle about it.

Scout was battering her paws against the door's window, barking and snarling, and all that racket was making it hard for Jody to think his way around how he might go about stopping them.

"Shut that goddamned dog up!" he shouted, turning back to Tina.

The alarm in his tone registered in her face, blanching it white. Setting Clyde down, she hurried to the door, grabbing the dog by her collar and dragging her back into the living room. Clyde had since retrieved his book. He was holding it out and shouting "Bah!" at his mother. Tina was kneeling beside him, stroking the dog's fur, hackled in furrows over the back of her neck.

"You know what we're here for, Jody!" Ram was yelling from outside. "Be a good lad now, and don't make us go through your wife and kid to get it!"

Through the kitchen window Jody saw Ram turning towards Gator, who was stepping out from behind the truck's rear, carrying a sawed-off shotgun. Ram said something to Gator that Jody couldn't hear and Gator responded by cocking the weapon and shouting, "He ain't coming out?! Well, I guess we'll have to see what Terror has to say about that."

Ram reacted by walking towards the back of the truck. He boosted himself up on its rear tire, reaching inside the truck's bed for something, Jody couldn't see what. A second later he saw it was a chain and also that the chain was attached to a dog. It leapt over the side of the truck, landing with the grace of a cougar and looking about as fierce. It was big and black and its size and the shape of its head told Jody it must have had some mastiff in it.

"You want to tell me what the hell's going on?" Tina asked as Jody stood staring out the window, tilting the bottle of beer to his lips, draining it in four gulps and that lending him a small measure of courage.

"Hey, Jode," Ram was calling out. "I don't think you've met my dog, Terror. But boy, is he sure eager to meet you."

Terror was aptly demonstrating his eagerness, pulling at its lead and snarling, Ram all the while acting like he could barely restrain the dog.

That finally got Jody moving.

"Take Clyde into our room!" he ordered, marching into the living room.

When that only got him a vacant stare, he set the beer bottle on the coffee table and grabbed Tina by the arm.

"Goddammit, do what I tell you!"

Scout seemed to take offence at his tone and the way he'd jerked her master roughly to her feet. She lunged, nipping, at Jody's arm. Her teeth gnashed at his skin hard enough to draw blood. Jody was just raising his hand to smack back but Tina got to the dog first, dragging her away, and Jody stepping around the both of them, snatching Clyde up off the floor and hurrying down the hall.

Behind him, Tina was saying, "Mommy's room. Go to mommy's room!" and the dog bounded after Jody, bristling past and almost tripping him up. Spinning back to Tina, Jody handed her Clyde. The boy was still holding the book and slapped Tina across the head with it, shouting "Bah!" again. Tina took the blow as if it was her duty as a mother to accept such abuse. Such tolerance hardly extended to her husband, though.

"Are you going to tell me what the fuck's going on?"

There was enough venom in her tone to have paralyzed a dozen men and on any other night Jody would have withered under its vitriol. But right then the most important thing was to make sure she and Clyde were safe, and also away from any windows lest either of them were to see what he was about to do. He'd have to deal with the consequences of his actions later.

"Get in the closet," he ordered, "and don't come out until I say!"

"But —" she started, only to be cut off by Jody slamming the door in her face.

He was already turning towards the hall, hurrying back into the living room.

The rumble of the truck's engine had since quieted but he could still see the bright of its lights in the fringe around the kitchen window's drapes.

"I'm giving you to the count of ten to get your ass out here!" Ram was calling out and that was fine by Jody.

Ten seconds was all that he'd need.

Shoving aside the coffee table, he pulled up the rug, tossing it onto the couch and bending over the trap door the previous owner, he'd never said why, had cut into the floor. Finding that door had given him the idea of hiding the duffel down there, figuring it was best to have it close at hand. Pulling at the trap door's ring, he pried it loose, shuttling it aside and lowering himself into the breach.

"Ten . . ."

Shafts of light from the truck in the driveway shone through the lattice skirting the trailer's base, glimmering off the cobwebs, remaking the three-foot crawlspace into one vast spider kingdom of crystalline threads. The dank air carried the heady odour of wet dirt and mould, infected with the sting of fibreglass from the pink insulation lining the underside of the floor. It prickled at his throat as he probed with flattened hands over the frozen earth, searching out the piece of plywood that marked his cache. A sudden flickering of shadows passed through the light: Ram and his dog converging on the porch.

". . . nine . . ."

Jody's hands had found the board but when he tried to lift it off, the dirt he used as a cover was as hard as ice and it wouldn't budge.

". . . eight . . ."

Reaching for the knife on his belt, he slipped it from its sheath and used it to chip away at the frozen mud.

". . . seven . . ."

He could hear the scuff of nails on the porch and jammed the blade into the gap he'd made, pulling hard on the hilt and prying the board up. It made a sound like nails popping as it tore free from the ice but it was too late to worry about that right now.

"...six..."

Tossing the plywood aside, Jody reached into the two-foot hole, grabbing at one of the duffel's straps and yanking at it and it holding fast. The bag must have frozen to the ground too and he plunged his hands back into the hole, feeling for the zipper.

"...five..."

He found it and flung it open, reaching into the bag and feeling past the wads of money and finally latching onto the machine gun. Grabbing it and ducking backwards a step, he came out of the trap door, the weapon gripped at his chest, its muzzle angled at the front door, and his finger feeling for the trigger.

"...four!" Ram yelled and then there was a vociferous crashing, Ram smashing the trailer's door open with a sledgehammer, three and a half seconds early.

But it was he who'd get the bigger surprise.

From the startled alarm on his face as he sighted what was plainly a nasty little piece of hardware pointed directly at him, it was clear that Lenny had never mentioned the Scorpion. Ram took a step back, trying to drag the dog with him, but it wouldn't budge. It was so big it took up half the doorway and the rabid menace of its slobbering maw had Jody squeezing at the trigger without a second thought. But he might as well have been pressing the trigger on a squirt gun for all the good it did him. Must have been the safety was on or he hadn't cocked it or maybe it was jammed. Either way, the trigger didn't even give so much as a hair.

Seeing Jody's folly, Ram was grinning like the fool he most surely was. Terror was grinning too and Ram was opening his mouth, no doubt to offer some parting witticism, but he never got the chance. His body stiffened all of a sudden and he lurched forward, his free hand clutching at his chest, grasping at something protruding from his jacket. It looked like an arrow.

No time to think of where that might have come from. The moment Ram had lurched forward, Terror had sprung from his grasp and was already bearing down on Jody, stuck as fast to the hole as if in cement and precious little between him and a rack of teeth meant for crushing bone. He flung the Scorpion tomahawk-like, sending it pinwheeling towards the dog and hitting it in the shoulder but hardly slowing its rampage.

Ram was screaming, "Goddammit, I've been shot!" and then the dog was upon Jody, going straight for his throat when really it should have been going for his arm. His right hand had lashed out and had grabbed the upturned rug and was flinging it downwards over the dog, not six inches before it would have tasted blood. Jody heaved himself over it, smothering the dog under the carpet and bringing the knife in his left hand down in a vicious stab, thrusting it into what must have been the dog's neck and back once, twice, thrice, knowing already the dog was dead but giving it an extra stab, then two, just to be sure.

As he clambered out of the hole, he could hear Ram screaming, "Where the fuck is he? Goddammit, where the fuck is he?!" and as he bent to pick up the machine pistol from the floor, he could hear Tina screaming too.

"Jody, don't!"

She was standing at the open bedroom door with a look of such utter despair warping her face that it wouldn't likely have been much different if she'd been standing there watching him being ripped apart by Terror.

"Close the goddamned door!" Jody yelled back at her but Scout was already hurtling through that, Tina calling after him,

"Scout! Goddammit Scout, get back here!" and her voice having about as much effect on the dog as it did on Jody.

He'd just flipped a switch on the gun's breech that he hoped was the safety and was jerking at what he knew was its cock when Scout brushed past him. She careened onto the porch, her nails raking against the unpainted plywood floor and her tail end fishtailing in a mad frenzy as she swerved towards the driveway, Jody following her, his finger teasing on the trigger. It seemed to give a little now but that didn't offer him much comfort as he approached the door.

Ram had since gone quiet and the only noise now was Scout barking and growling. There was a small hole in the plastic covering the porch's frame at about chest level. Must have been from the arrow and there was now little doubt in Jody's mind who'd shot that. Dylan had always hunted with a bow to, in his words, "honour the animals with at least a sporting chance," though it seemed a fool's game to Jody that he'd have offered Ram or Gator the same. But then a gunshot might have alerted the neighbours, a thought that rendered the machine pistol in Jody's hands about as useful as a stick of wood as he craned his head out the front door.

A quick peek revealed Ram crumpled to his knees on the ground in front of the pick-up. The stark glow of its headlights blurred his form, turning it hazy but not so much that Jody couldn't see he'd been shot two more times in the meanwhile. There was also now an arrowhead protruding through the thigh of his right leg and another through his left arm just above the elbow. There was a spatter of blood on his cheek and more draining into a pool on the ground but Ram seemed to have forgotten about his injuries, his eyes trained as they were in dire pursuit of Scout, prowling back and forth in front of him, barking and snarling, looking like she was about to chomp.

Jody heard a whistle then and that diverted the dog's attention. She bolted right and out of frame and Jody took a first, cautious step onto the porch. That led to another and another still, the latter bringing him to the top of the porch steps and affording him a full panorama of the scene that had already played out in his driveway.

Dylan was kneeling on the ground at the side of the truck, feeding Scout what looked to be a piece of the jerky he always kept in his glove compartment and scratching the dog behind the ears, cooing, "Hey there pup, ain't *you* a friendly one."

Scout responded by licking his face and Jody turned his gaze towards Gator. He was pinned against his truck by two arrows stuck through each of his arms and another in his gut. His eyes were straining toward the shotgun discarded at his feet, as if it still offered him some hope of getting out of this night alive.

"There you are," Dylan was saying to Jody as he came to the bottom of the stairs. "I was wondering when you'd show up."

It was the same thing he'd said after the first time they'd gone dirt-biking together. Dylan had raced off ahead and Jody had followed his tracks for two hours before they'd circled him back to the bunker. Then, Jody had been too enthralled with the ride to answer and finally Dylan had prompted, "So was that fun or what?"

Dylan was beaming at him the same way he had then and so it wasn't much of a surprise when he added, "What do you say? You up for a little more fun?"

Standing then and drawing his hunting knife from the sheath on his belt so that there wouldn't be any confusion as to what he meant.

"I'll even let you have first pick."

Scout had padded over to Jody and was nuzzling at his hand, Jody ignoring her as he scanned from Gator to Ram. Gator was glaring at him with hate in his eyes, daring him, it seemed, to do his worst, but when his glance touched upon the other, Ram lowered his gaze. There was shame in the way he was watching Jody out of the corner of his eyes, as if he was all too aware that he'd brought his impending demise down upon himself. Jody had always suspected it was Ram who'd crawled into the tent that night he was camping with Lenny. He was certain now it was and his gathering rage found its full expression in how his hand was tightening on the hilt of his knife.

Ram seemed to have accepted his fate and was now looking up at Jody with *the resigned recalcitrance of a sinner on his way to the confession box*. That was how George Cleary had described the Tin Star who'd killed Tyrone Yates in *A Bad Man's Son* after he'd awoken with the barrel of a Colt .45 pressed up against his forehead, the moment before Clyde shot him between the eyes.

That had been the final coffin-nail sealing Clyde into an emotionless void. But Jody's reminding himself of that, and of how he'd sworn he'd never let that happen to him, barely put a hitch into his step as he faced the man who was on his knees in front of him now. The rage he'd felt after Ram had jerked them both off was coming back into him full bore. He thought then of all he stood to lose — of Tina and what they'd been through together, and of Clyde, whose name he'd chosen to prove to himself that something good really could come out of anything. Yet that only firmed his conviction, knowing as he did right then — beyond even a sliver of a doubt — that no matter what he did, he'd love them both until the day he died.

His hand seemed to know that too, for it was already drawing his knife, eager, from its sheath.

"If it's all the same to you," he said, "I'll take this one right here."

12

It started to rain just after seven on Friday night.

Deacon was sitting on his couch, rolling a joint, when he heard the first patter of drops — a premonitory burst sounding more like hail than rain on the roof's sheet metal. It was followed by a torrential gust of wind he could feel in the way the bunkie seemed to shudder. Branches from the maples crowding the building on the ravine side raked against the corrugated steel above, and the weather vane he'd installed on a whim squeaked into life, Deacon sitting there listening to its wobbling whirr and this shortly overcome by a sudden deluge pounding at the barn with the force of a hurricane.

It was only a couple of seconds later that his phone started to buzz, which it had been doing at steady intervals for the past couple of hours, mostly on account of the Mesaquakee Emergency Alert System. MEAS, as Frank Darling commonly referred to it, had been implemented several years ago to warn residents of potential threats — forest fires and floods, tornadoes and toxic spills, missing children and seniors. Its previous four texts had all warned, *Flood Watch! Record Rainfall Expected Over The Next 24 Hours. Residents Advised To Stay Away From All Active Rivers In The Mesaquakee Watershed*, and after he'd finished rolling the joint and checked the latest, it was a mild variation of the same.

Setting aside his phone, he sparked the joint, thinking maybe he'd watch a bit of the news. But the remote was sitting on the desk he used for a TV stand and by the third puff the weed had sapped him of the will to get up and fetch it. So instead he sat listening to the storm's fury, trying to summon the energy to go upstairs, take a shower, do the dishes, watch a little porn, jerk off, anything to keep his eyes from wandering to the picture tucked into the middle frame of the triptych of photos on the mantel over his TV.

It was of Crystal's first ultrasound and had come in a greeting card announcing, *It's a Girl!* — how she'd informed him she was pregnant. On the inside of the card she'd written, *Hey Unc, Meet Rose Lily Swanson-Cleary*, and seeing that Crystal planned on honouring his mother by using her name for her daughter's had almost reduced him to tears.

The photo behind it was the sepia-toned eight-by-ten George had once taken of the Riises and which he'd later given to Deacon's parents as a Christmas present. The whole family was gathered on the front porch and if you didn't know any better, you'd have thought it was a family of homesteaders from some bygone era, which had been George's stated intent. Deacon was four at the time and was standing in front of Bergin, his pa's hands resting on his shoulders and the both of them staring straight at the camera, dour-faced and resolute as George had instructed, for authenticity's sake. Rose was always shy about having her picture taken and in most of the photos Bergin had snapped of his wife, she'd turned away at the last moment or was hiding behind an outstretched hand. And maybe she would have been doing that in this one too, except she was cradling baby Abel at her breast. The moment before George snapped the shot, Abel had snatched a loose strand of her hair and jerked down on it. Rose had just reached over and was grasping his hand, to keep him from pulling any harder, and if there was one expression that sprung most often to mind when thinking of his ma, it was the one she was wearing on her face right then. A kind of blossoming joy as if she really was a flower and looking into her newborn son's gleaming eyes and hearing his giggle was to her as if the sun had just come out, opening her petals and revealing the true beauty that lay buried beneath all those scars.

When Deacon was six she'd started the first of the three photo albums she'd use to document the life of her family and she'd taken the framed photograph down from its place of honour on their mantel to use for its front page. Bergin had protested, saying it wasn't right to be hiding it away like that.

"I'm not hiding it," she'd answered. "I'm preserving it, is all."

It hadn't made a lick of sense to Deacon at the time. A photo hardly needed to be preserved like the stewed vegetables from her garden she sealed in mason jars for the winter and even if it did, you could do so in a frame as well as in an album. But over the years he'd begun to glean a definite sort of logic to what his mother had done. Seeing the photo every day on the mantel had reduced it to just another thing, no different really than their bookshelf or that old bearskin rug. Putting it in the album made it special since Rose usually only brought those out on birthdays, when she'd sit on the couch with Abel on one side and Deacon on the other. Bergin would be leaning over her shoulder so he could see too and as soon as she opened to the first page he'd always say the exact same thing.

"I don't know what it is you got against having your picture taken. You're a right beauty, you ask me."

The proof of that was right there in her lap. Still, she'd always dismiss what he said with a backwards wave but would sit staring at the picture a moment longer as if she herself couldn't believe it really was her until Abel or Deacon — though usually it was Abel — would urge her impatiently, "Come on ma, what are you waitin' for? Turn the page already!"

Some months after he'd come to live with the Clearys, George had left the three albums sitting on his dresser and Deacon had recoiled in horror coming upon them. He wasn't yet ready to face all those pictures of his family, nor the funny little comments his mother had written in captions beneath each. He'd put them on the top shelf in his bedroom closet, hiding them underneath two hand-me-down wool sweaters that Adele had given him and he knew he'd never wear. He wouldn't think of them again until he was moving into the apartment over the *Chronicle* and then only for long enough to transfer them to a box with a few other childhood relics.

The box would remain sequestered in another closet for the next five years and he wouldn't open it again until after he'd finished renovating the barn into a bunkie. The first time he did, he found the album sitting on top and when he opened it, the sight of his family had hit him like a sledgehammer to the gut. Looking at his mother cradling Abel and remembering how she'd clutched him just like that after he'd been stung by those hornets, hearing then her next-to-last words echoing in his head: "He's not breathing!"

He'd clamped the book shut but that hadn't done a damned thing to stop the tears from rolling down his cheeks and time had seemed to fold around him, taking him right back to the last time he'd cried. He'd been chasing after that parrot and Adele had found him in the backyard, sobbing, his whole body shaking like he couldn't contain all that grief. Holding him tight, she'd stroked the back of his head and cooed, "There, there. It's all right. Get it out. It's okay."

Such a deep longing he'd felt then for her comforting embrace. But, of course, she was dead and all that he had left of her was a few pictures he'd scavenged from the pile Louise had arranged on their dining room table after George's funeral so whoever wanted any could take what they liked. Louise had also given each member of the immediate family a copy of the framed triptych of photos she'd displayed at George's funeral. It had come as a shock at the time that she'd given one to him as well, since she'd never treated him much like family, immediate or otherwise. The photos had ended up in another box and, wiping the tears from his cheeks, he'd sought them out from the stack piled in his living room. Finding them and seeing Adele's warm shining bright smiling back at him he'd felt her working a little of her old magic. To preserve that he'd put the photos on the mantel over the TV, though he knew exactly what George would have had to say about that.

Thereafter, whenever he looked at them, he thought of the photo George had taken of his family, how it too had started out framed and on a mantel, and how seeing it every day had made it into just another thing. With that in mind, he'd taken out the middle picture of George and Adele from the triptych and put in that one in its stead. For almost ten years, he'd preserved both of his families together in this way and so when Crystal had sent him the card with the ultrasound of her daughter, he'd tucked the picture in the bottom corner of the frame just below her namesake, hoping maybe that a little bit of *his* Rose would rub off on *hers*.

On the day he'd returned home after Crystal had lost the baby, he'd felt like crying all over again, seeing the ultrasound tucked into the corner of a frame that had practically become a graveyard. His sorrow had quickly turned to rage thinking of what Dylan had done.

That fucking monster!

But blaming Dylan for killing Baby Rose felt like blaming the sun for rising. If he was looking for a place to plant the real blame, he didn't have to look much further than the face staring back at him in reflection from within the picture frame's glass.

What was it that Rain had said on their last, fateful evening together?

"I'll tellya one thing, brooding endlessly over it sure as hell ain't done you any favours!"

They were lying in his bed, arguing, as they often did, about his lack of progress on the book she'd proposed he write. It had all seemed so vivid to him the morning after George's funeral when *He heard the first siren just after midnight* had taken him right back to the beginning, thinking through everything that had happened, and that leading him right back to where he'd started, so that he'd got it in mind that maybe his opening line could also be used as the book's last. But regardless of what George, or even Rain, had said, knowing where it began, and also where it ended, wasn't enough to get him past those first eight words. For five years they were as far as he'd got and Rain's constant needling had been the thin end of the wedge that would eventually drive them apart.

"You ought to just sit down and write it," she'd chided yet again on what would be their last evening together. "At least it would be something. Better than doing nothing, that's for damned sure."

"I've tried," Deacon protested rather feebly. "You know I have."

"Oh, horseshit. Walking around half the day mumbling one line over and over and over to yourself ain't trying, it's more like giving up one word at a time."

"But —"

But she'd already heard too many excuses over the years.

"Write it or don't write it, I don't care," she'd spat at him, storming out. "Either way, get on with your damn life and if you can't do that, you can bloody well do it alone!"

While he might have been able to raise sufficient protest regarding her syntax, there was no contesting the veracity of what she'd said. He'd embraced indecision as if that was an end in itself and where had that got him? Discarding maybe his only real chance for any kind of a life outside of chasing a ghost into the deep and dark and that amounting to nothing more tangible than a foreboding sense of doom. It's what had driven Laney away and kept him at a careful remove from Rebecca, and had his gaze ever circling back to the ultrasound of Crystal's dead baby like a moth drawn towards a flame, helpless to do anything about that either.

You ought to just walk up to him and shoot him in the face, that's what you ought to do!

A reoccurring thought that had hounded him during many of the sleepless wrestles he'd endured since New Year's Day. He'd gone so far as to retrieve George's old seven-shooter from where he'd secreted it under the towels in the bathroom closet, stashing it in the Jeep's glove box. But the only time he'd seen Dylan since was after Kylie Farmer had gone on a rampage with his father's splitting axe. Deacon had been walking to work at the time and hadn't even thought about the gun until a few hours later, when it had only served to further underscore his impotence.

Dylan's disappearance had rendered the gun nothing more than a useless hunk of metal but still, after coming home from the *Chronicle* that evening, he'd brought it in with him from the Jeep. He picked it up from the coffee table now, feeling its heft lighten as he took it by the grip and laid his finger on the trigger, thinking about how, if George was telling the truth in *My Brother's Keeper*, it had already killed six men, the last of whom was the last man in the posse of four who had come after William for shooting the man who'd killed his brother.

Blood was frothing at his lips, George had written, and he was gasping what would amount to his dying breath, though he hadn't quite given up the ghost yet. His hand was reaching with a palsied jitter into his parka's fur, could have been for a gun, and William kicked at his arm, knocking it away and pinning it to the ground under the heel of his boot.

Please, the man begged, beseeching him with desperate eyes. Pleeeasssse . . .

The last word trailed out of his mouth along with a final staggered wheeze and William bent to him, reaching under the man's coat. It wasn't a gun, though, he'd been reaching for but a small wooden box. It was in his breast pocket and was about the size of a deck of cards. It had a bronze latch on one side and when William flipped it up and opened the lid he found that the only things inside were a lock of hair and a photograph of a young woman, must have been the dead man's wife or sweetheart.

She was smiling but it was a strained smile and it immediately recalled to William his own mother, who was smiling the exact same way the last time he'd seen her. He'd been eight and she'd been laid out in a pine box and when he'd looked down at her it seemed she'd been smiling just for him, telling him it was all going to be okay, the same way she'd often smile when she'd crawled into his bed after her old man, his father, had once again laid the beats into her.

I'm going to kill that son of a bitch, he'd told her one of those times and she'd grasped his hand and dug her nails harshly into his palm, so he'd have the memory of pain to remind him of what she'd had to say.

It'll mean the hell-fire for you, if you do. You got to learn to turn the other cheek, like I done, for we the meek shall inherit the earth, the good Lord promised us at least that.

She'd inherited the earth turning the other cheek, all right — a six-foot plot to call her own — and he'd always thought her a fool because of it. But looking at the picture of the man's wife or sweetheart — a man she'd never see again and all because of him — he finally saw the truth in her words. Violence had only begotten more violence and it had damned him in life as surely as it would in whatever he might find in the great beyond.

William's first impulse had been to throw the gun away but in the end he'd kept it to serve as a constant reminder of the terrible price — his brother's death — he'd paid for shooting his father and made a solemn vow with himself that he would safeguard it against ever harming another living soul.

But if George had really meant what he'd written, Deacon now asked himself, *why then did he pass it on to you through Rain, telling her you might need it before this was over?*

It didn't make sense, unless . . .

Unless George feared you'd someday face a night just like this, when it seemed that your only hope of salvation might come through the barrel of a gun.

His finger was fretting restlessly with its trigger and as he stared unbidden at Crystal's ultrasound — his anger rising at an even pitch with the rain and gale-force winds battering the barn — the thought provided him with a small reprieve from the shame he'd felt. And even the smallest reprieve from that seemed to him the most precious kind of mercy, especially on a night like this one was shaping up to be.

13

I t was still raining the next morning when he awoke stiff-backed and cramped-necked from sleeping upright on the couch.

The wind had died down but Deacon could barely see out the windows, such was the veil of water streaming off the barn's roof. That wasn't giving him much of a reason to get up, though the pressure in his bladder would soon make that an imperative. The gun was still sitting in his lap and he set that on the coffee table as he reached for his pack of smokes. His phone buzzed while he was lighting the cigarette — the first time it had since just before ten the previous night — and it buzzed again while he was butting the stub in the ashtray.

Both, he'd learn moments later, started off with the now-familiar heading *Flood Watch!* but were really more in the way of a courtesy than a warning good and proper. The first advised residents that *Entrance Drive Is Closed Between Front And Main Streets Due To Elevated Water Levels* and the second to warn that Santa's Village Road was flooded between Brobst and Golden

Beach. Each ended with instructions to *Please Follow Detour Signs*. Satisfied that, despite Frank Darling's dire prognostications, Tildon wasn't likely to be washed into Mesaquakee Lake, he took his time in the shower and then made himself his standard breakfast: a banana-blueberry-yogurt shake and a travel mug of coffee, both of which he drank at intervals while smoking two more cigarettes.

He spent the rest of the morning and a fair share of the afternoon driving around, documenting the flood waters' progress. The barriers along River Road had succumbed that morning which, as MEAS indicated, had resulted in the water washing up over Entrance Drive, closing the bridge leading into downtown and also engulfing a section of the railway tracks. Trains were supposed to have been rerouted but when, in the early afternoon, Deacon parked at the barriers erected at the top of the hill on Charles Street and walked to the railway crossing halfway down the slope, he found a CN engineer standing there under an umbrella with his train parked fifty metres down the tracks. The man's name was Martin Crosby and Deacon learned from him that he was pulling freight from Calgary — mostly petroleum, crude oil and natural gas. He'd been stopped there for eight hours already and the only order he'd received so far was to wait by his train for further instructions.

Marty, as he liked to be called, was easy to talk to, and Deacon spent a few minutes jawing with him, asking him about where he was from — Capreol — and how long he'd been with CN — eighteen years — and enough other questions to pass for a journalist of the investigative variety while the two of them watched, with no more than idle curiosity, the water lapping in swirls of frothy brown at the foot of the embankment. That gave it a good ten feet before it reached the train, meaning something truly dire would have had to happen before it did.

The four houses on the lower section of Charles Street hadn't been so lucky.

The two on either side of the street at the base of the hill were engulfed by four feet of water and the two below them, six or seven. A beaver-felled tree had lodged itself in the picture glass window on the one closest to the river. Water was spewing in makeshift falls out and around this, having gained entrance no doubt through a back window.

Charles Street dead-ended at a three-way stop, where it intersected with River Road. Turning left would bring you onto the two kilometres' worth of gravel snaking along the river on its way to Wilsons Falls and turning right would take you back to town. It was towards the latter his gaze had drifted. From where he stood, he could see the backside of the River Road Apartments. They were flooded to the balconies on their second floor and Deacon scanned the balconies above, halfway expecting some crotchety old holdout who'd evaded the evacuation team to be standing on one of these, thumbing his nose at Mother Nature's rampage. A photo of that would have made a helluva front page for the *Chronicle*'s next edition. But the balconies were unmanned and the apartments all dark and, saying his goodbyes to Marty, he tromped back up the hill towards his Jeep.

George's rain poncho hadn't done much beyond delay the inevitable. He was thoroughly soaked and shivering and that gave him reason enough to call it a day. Two minutes later he was turning onto Baker Street. There was a purple Mercedes parked in his spot in the driveway, which he knew belonged to Louise Brennan, née Cleary.

Louise was about the last person he'd have wanted to see right then, or ever. She'd never really got over George leaving him the *Chronicle*. Every time he'd seen her since, she'd been scowling at him like he'd robbed her children of their birthright, though

Gabe, her eldest son, seemed more than happy — even relieved — to be its managing editor rather than the person responsible for keeping a small-town newspaper afloat in such perilous times as these were for print journalism.

Pulling past the driveway, he parked in front of the black-and-yellow checkerboard sign warning of the street's terminus. Drips leaking through the crack in the windshield splattered on the dash in parcelled intervals and he sat there watching them for a moment with static futility. The splay of lines radiating out from where the pebble had hit the glass had once struck him as an all-too-obvious metaphor for how the world seemed on the verge of crashing down around him. But it didn't appear to him like that now, it just looked like a cracked windshield — one more hassle in a day already filled to its brim.

He'd have to make an appointment to get it fixed.

First thing Monday, he told himself, *I'll call . . . what in the hell is the name of that place? The autobody shop where you got the rocker panels fixed on the old Jeep that one time?*

He couldn't remember but it'd be in the phone book, or just as likely he'd have taken one of their cards. It'd be in the bureau's drawer he reserved for odds and ends, which had filled up with so much junk he'd barely been able to close it the last time he'd put something in there. Maybe he ought to sort through it and while he was at it, he might as well sweep the kitchen floor and give the bathroom a good wipe. Hell, maybe he'd have a puff and clean the whole damned bunkie. He could even open the windows and let in some fresh air, it had been years since he'd done that.

It wouldn't be much but at least it would be something. Better than doing nothing anyway.

That thought, at last, was enough to get his hand reaching for the door.

As he skirted through the cover of the pine trees barricading the yard from the road, he could hear the rush of water from the ravine below, the stream that wound through it engorged with the runoff and turned into a gnashing tumult of rapids such that it shook the smaller trees engulfed within its plunder. Walking towards the barn, he kept to the shadows lest Gabe spotted him through a window and felt inclined to invite him in for dessert, as was his habit whenever his parents visited. As he approached the barn's door though, the motion-activated halogen he'd installed above it flared to life, freezing him like he was an escaped convict trapped in a searchlight, waiting for a shout, or a shot, from the guard's tower.

And sure enough, he was just reaching for his keys when he heard Gabe calling to him from the house.

"Hey, Deacon, hold up!"

Gabe was hurrying towards him under shelter of a large umbrella with *The Highland Golf & Country Club* printed over its canopy. He was dressed in a grey sport jacket and tie, dressier than anything he ever wore to work. His already ruddy cheeks were flushed red, which always happened when he'd been drinking.

In his free hand he was carrying a large manila envelope.

"You got a (*hic*) delivery," he said, holding the envelope out and swallowing against the hiccup, his lips pursing as if he'd had to swallow a little bile along with it.

"Thanks," Deacon said, accepting the package.

In bold black marker on the front it read, *FOR DEACON*, and that was enough to make his heart skip a beat. Every one of the ten chapters Dylan had sent him so far had been delivered in the exact same fashion, except this package's heft told him there were two, maybe three hundred pages in the envelope — way too many for it to be a single chapter. His eyes must have been widening with the realization of what that might have meant, for Gabe was then asking, "Is something wrong?"

Deacon had no idea how to answer that, and instead deflected the question by asking one of his own.

"When did it get here?"

"Two, maybe three minutes ago."

That would have meant he was sitting in the Jeep when it had arrived. A discomforting thought he evaded by asking, "Did you see who delivered it?"

Gabe shook his head.

"The doorbell rang and when Cheryl answered, it was sitting on the welcome mat. You sure nothing's wrong? You look a little pale."

"No. It's — It's just been a long day, is all." Then looking up, trying to front a smile. "Thanks."

He was already turning towards the barn.

"There's still some leftovers from lunch," Gabe offered. "It's baked ham, scalloped potatoes and corn on the cob, Mom's apple crumble for dessert. We might even be able to spare a scoop of ice cream. If you want to drop by, I know Louise would just *love* to see ya."

But his rather feeble attempt at levity wasn't able to penetrate the anxious fury with which Deacon was fumbling his key into the lock.

"Sure, fine, sounds good," he offered back, though he'd barely heard a word Gabe had said.

By then the door was swinging open in front of him and he was stepping into the dark and closing it behind, leaning against its window glass, clutching the envelope to his breast, knowing that Dylan sending it to him now must mean something — an escalation, no doubt — and barely able to breathe for fear of what that might be.

14

He'd set the envelope on the table in front of George's green leather chair some twenty minutes earlier but had yet to open it.

In the meantime, he'd made himself a fresh pot of coffee and indulged in a long, hot shower to ease the chill that had penetrated, it seemed, to his very marrow. He thought about rolling himself a joint but told himself it'd be best to keep his head clear. Having a few nips, he'd found, served that well enough. Retrieving from the cupboard over the stove the bottle of Canadian Club Special Reserve that Gabe had bought him last Christmas, he poured a good three fingers of it into his travel mug then filled the rest with coffee, a dash of cream and two spoonfuls of sugar.

Presently, he was settling down in the reading chair. He took a healthy sip from the mug to steel his resolve and then there was nothing to do but slip the sheaf of paper from the envelope. When Dylan had left him those first two chapters — the same night he'd killed the Wane family and burnt their summer residence to the ground — he'd alerted him to the impending climax! by typing that into the photocopied manuscript. Maybe he'd done something similar with this one. With thoughts of finding a possible shortcut to Dylan's endgame, he flipped the stack of papers over, setting it face down on the table. He ran his flattened hand over that, trying to detect any indents made by a typewriter's keys. Finding none, he did the same with the next page and the next and the next. By the time he'd done this with fifty or so pages, he'd given up any hope that Dylan might have been inclined to make it easier for him and flipped what was left back over.

There was nothing to do now but just get to it. Taking another gulp of the spiked coffee, he set the stack in his lap and began to read.

The first chapter — 13 — was one of Del's, which made sense since the last had been Mason Lowry's. After the boy had witnessed Emma killing the man in the van — whom George had named Reinhold Kranich — he'd reported what he'd seen to Emma's big brother, William Dupuis (aka Big Willy). Ever since, so as to maintain around-the-clock surveillance on his sister, Big Willy had stationed a man in the old fort he'd built when he was a kid in the woods behind his parents' house. As the chapter began, Del, newly initiated into his gang, was himself taking a turn on watch.

> For the past four hours he hadn't seen anything except a couple of squirrels and a chipmunk. It was just after four o'clock in the afternoon and the only thing he'd had to occupy his time thus far was swatting at the mosquitoes swarming in droves around his head and feeding at the back of his neck. The fort had become as hot as a sweat lodge. He was feeling drowsy and to keep himself

awake until his relief arrived at six he churned over in his mind something William had said two days earlier while he and the rest of his gang were cutting up a moose in his kitchen.

He'd been going on about what he called "So-Called Truth & Recycled Shit," as he often did whenever he had a captive audience, saying it was just one more way the white devil was trying to pull the wool over our eyes, like we's too drunk or stoned or just too plain stupid to know any better.

But, he'd conceded, there was one line in that whitewash of a report they'd written that did have at least a smudge of truth about it. I quote, he'd then said, taking on the weaselly nasal drawl of some petty bureaucrat: "It would not be inconceivable that the unrest we see today among young Aboriginal people could grow to become a challenge to the country's own sense of well-being and its very security." That's a fancy way of saying they's worried we Indians are gonna declare open revolt against them's that's oppressed us, and by them's I mean every goddamned white motherfucker in this whole shithole excuse for a country.

But what that report didn't have the guts to say, he continued, was how they owe us five hundred years of back dues, and I ain't talkin' about money here neither, I'm talking about pain, I'm talking about deprivation, I'm talking about fucking sacrifice. And it don't matter how many reports they write, when it comes time to collect on that debt, them white devils — you'll see — won't even spend the measure of a single goddamned penny!

He'd been using a cleaver to hack one of the moose's back legs from its haunches and punctuated his final pronouncement with one last vicious slash that cut through the remaining cartilage and imbedded the blade into the countertop. Yanking it out provided a small break in his rant, long enough for Del to ask a question that had been percolating in his mind.

But, I mean — he said, his voice wavering and then faltering altogether under William's tyrannical gaze.

What's on your mind, son? William had then offered, running a scaling knife under the hide on the moose's shank, peeling back the skin.

Um.

Go on, we's all brothers here, don't be shy.

Taking a deep breath and summoning his resolve.

Not all white people are bad, are they? he asked. I mean, we can't — We can't hate 'em all, can we?

The hell we can't, and what's more we must. If we don't we'll lose any real hope of making things right.

Hate's our only way of making things right?

Hate's just a means, the only one of any real value they've left us. Single-mindedness, that's our real weapon, and that's where they've been beating us all the way back to day one. And who's had to pay the price for their single-minded greed? Our sisters and our mothers and our grandmothers and our aunts and our uncles, our brothers, our fathers and our grandfathers — every one of us who's gone missing or was outright murdered these past few hundred years while they all turned a blind eye.

And then when the slaughter became impossible to ignore, what was their response? A chorus of voices ringing out in disbelief across the land: "I- I- I had no idea what was going on!" Like they were living in a whole 'nother country or something. Well, I call bullshit on that and if I had my way, son, I'd turn myself into one giant flame and burn this country into fucking ash! If you ask me, it don't even have a right to exist at all.

Here Deacon paused a moment to ruminate on what he'd read. It was that last line that had made him stop, for he'd heard George read something similar to him once before.

He was fifteen, or maybe sixteen, and had gone out to the barn to call George in for dinner. He'd found him reading in the very chair in which Deacon himself now sat.

"Sup's on," Deacon had said, popping his head in through the door.

When George had looked up from his book, his eyes were bedazzled with wonder and awe, as they so often were when he'd just read something too precious not to share.

"Listen to this," he'd said without so much as a hello. Flipping back a few pages, he'd found the passage he was looking for and read it with his characteristic zeal: "Wouldn't you hate all white people if they kept you in prison here? Kept you here, and stunted you and starved you and made you watch your mother and father and sister and lover and brother and son and daughter go mad or go under, before your very eyes? And not in a hurry, like from one day to the next, but, every day, every day, for years, for generations? Shit. They keep you here because you're Black . . . while they go around jerking themselves off with all that jazz about the land of the free and the home of the brave. And they want you to jerk yourself off with that same music, too, only keep your distance. Some days, honey, I wish I could turn myself into one big fist and grind this miserable country to powder. Some days, I don't believe it has a right to exist."

Then looking up at Deacon again with that sprightly bedazzle: "And that was a Black man — a gay — writing back in the sixties. Talk about some balls on him!" Shaking his head as if he couldn't believe such a thing was even possible and then a sudden dour turn coming over his face, transforming his brow into a restless sea of quivering wrinkles. "Can't imagine what it'd take for a *Canadian* to muster the guts to write with such unabashed vitriol, even now."

Could have been that was the moment that he *had* imagined it, for his gaze had then taken on a contemplative air as he scratched at his beard and here now it was staring up at Deacon right there on the page. All it had taken, apparently, was an old white man grown too tired of waiting, and sufficient bile to see it through.

Thinking then of what George had said next.

"Not that it'd matter anyway since, even if they did, there isn't a publisher in this country who'd have the guts to see it into print."

Deacon ruminated a few more moments on that and then turned back to the manuscript in his lap, eager to find out what George might have written next.

15

He came to Chapter 24 — the third from last — with the clock just striking five.

The sun was still an hour from going down but from the dull pallor of the light penetrating the rain- and dirt-spackled windows, it might as well have set ages ago. Deacon hadn't yet turned on the reading lamp but he did so before draining the last of the spiked coffee in his mug and turning back to the thinned-out sheaf of twenty or so pages, all that remained of the book in his lap.

The epidemic of increasingly savage, and apparently random murders had since swollen to twelve, most of them committed against Mesaquakee's cottagers and four of them of the mass variety in which entire families were butchered. The RCMP were still adamant that a single person was responsible for all of them, and their only real suspect so far was William Dupuis. Mason Lowry, however, was more than ever convinced that he'd had nothing to do with any of them. Previously, he'd hypothesized that the lion's share of murders were perpetrated by disgruntled former

employees of the victims who were using the spectre of a psycho-
pathic killer at large as a smokescreen to wage their own personal
vendettas against these privileged few who had so wronged them.

He'd said as much in Chapter 24, when he was delivering his
final report to the elder Kranich.

> It's just like my daddy always used to say, Mason
> concluded, when you treat a man like dirt long
> enough, sooner or later it'll be mud in your eye.
>
> If the old man heard him, he made no sign and
> continued staring out the window, gazing at the
> last traces of light leaking between the trees on the
> southern shore of Lake Mesaquakee. The hiss of gas
> from his oxygen tank and the staggered wheeze of
> his laboured breaths was all there was left to fill
> the space between them and in that moment they
> spoke volumes to Mason as to the true nature of
> the particular breed of man standing before him. It
> seemed like the setting sun and the elder Kranich
> were one and the same and that neither would be
> wholly satisfied unless the passing of their light
> meant the passing of all light unto a darkness so
> complete it'd swallow the earth in its gloom, and all
> of humankind along with it.

Mason had meant his concluding statement to be provoca-
tive, a barb at the elder Mr. Kranich who, he'd begun to suspect,
had himself been using the murders as his own personal smokescreen — a means of eliminating a business rival who also owned
a summer residence on Lake Mesaquakee. Seeking confirmation,
before he was escorted out of the den by the elder Kranich's
head of security, Mason planted a bug on the underside of the

old man's desk. By means of this he later discovered not only that his suspicions were correct but also that the chief of security had been conducting his own investigation into Reinhold Kranich's murder.

All evidence, he reported, indicated it had been committed by a young girl from the reserve, name of Emma Dupuis.

Whatever Kranich intended to do about that he never explicitly said, though the final exchange between him and his chief of security informed Mason it was going to happen that very night.

> Do you think that's wise, us going in tonight?
> What with the RCMP raiding her brother's house
> at the same time?
>
> The note of uncertainty in the security chief's
> voice was met with a gruff rebuff from his boss.
>
> You're being paid too much to be getting cold
> feet now! he growled back. You'll go in by boat, like
> we discussed.

Chapter 25 found Del back in the fort, watching over Emma. She'd retired that night into the tent in her backyard, Del supposed, seeking relief from the swelter that had rendered his own house about as habitable as a sweat lodge built over a volcano.

The swelter in the fort wasn't much better and he was on the point of passing out from the heat himself but was spared from this by a sharp *rat-a-tat-tat*.

> At first it sounded to him like someone was setting
> off a string of firecrackers but it was shortly
> accompanied by a resounding blast that couldn't
> have originated from anything other than a shot-
> gun. It was coming from the woods to the north

and the only house that was down there, he knew, was the one owned by William Dupuis.

The police! Del thought. They must be raiding Big Willy's!

William had often said what he'd do to any cop fool enough to trespass on his property and the ensuing barrage of weapon fire told Del that he and his gang were making good on that promise.

You ought to be there, Del told himself, cursing his bad luck for being stuck out here when he should have been fighting, and maybe dying, right alongside of them.

Fuck it, he said, reaching for his bow and that seeming no more than a child's toy when measured against the relentless barrage. That thought gave him reason enough to pause — for no longer than a breath — and it was just as he was exhaling that he heard Emma's voice calling out from her backyard.

Grams! she was yelling, then, Gramps!

When Del looked through one of the knotholes in the fort's wall, he saw her hurrying towards her back door when, suddenly, she stopped. Her hand went to the back of her neck like she'd been stung and then just as suddenly she dropped like a marionette whose strings had been cut, Del watching in mounting confusion as she crumpled to the ground and seeing two black figures — no more than shadows — emerging from the forest dark on the far side of her tent.

One was hunkered low, skulking at a fast clip towards where Emma lay, but it was the other that Del had become fixated on. He was clearly holding a gun of the submachine variety and peering with a widening scan through what Del could only assume were night-vision goggles as his partner scooped Emma up, tossing her roughly over his shoulder like she didn't mean more to him than a sack of rotten potatoes.

Chapter 26 began with Mason Lowry sitting in his old aluminum fishing boat hidden beneath the cover provided by the many-tentacled screen of a weeping willow growing along the shore on the eastern edge of the Kranich's property, watching a speedboat coasting into their boathouse with the ominous glide of a hawk or an eagle returning to its roost, clutching its prey.

And there was no doubt in his mind what that prey was: it couldn't have been anyone but Emma Dupuis.

So she was his endgame all along, he thought. He wasn't seeking justice as he'd said, he only wanted revenge. Or maybe . . . Maybe that's not all he'd wanted from the girl either.

Recalling then the first time he'd met the elder Kranich, during his first month with the Tildon Police Service. A girl, no older than Emma, had gone missing and when her mother and aunt came into the station to file a report they'd said she'd recently been hired as a babysitter by the Kranich family. The last time anyone had seen her was the previous morning, when she'd left for work on her bicycle. The case was assigned to Officer Darby, the twenty-year veteran who Mason was shadowing, and together they'd driven up to the Kraniches' summer residence on Brackenridge Road to have a few words with her employer.

Someone must have told them they were coming, because it was Mr. Kranich himself who'd met them in the driveway. When asked about the girl, he'd replied that she'd only been working for them for a couple weeks, taking care of his four-year-old son, Reinhold.

Two days ago she'd simply stopped showing up, he'd said and then quickly added: That's the problem with hiring Indians, they either show up for work drunk or they don't show up at all.

Shoot, you don't have to tell me, Darby had answered, immediately following this with: Sorry for bothering you, sir. You have a nice day now.

During the forty years Mason was on the force, more than a dozen other girls, and as many boys, had gone missing from the reserve. The investigations, when there even were any, always reached the same conclusion: the girls, or boys, had either run away or had met an unfortunate end at the hands of their father, or maybe an uncle, who'd no doubt hit them a little too hard one night when he was drinking and then buried the evidence somewhere deep in the bush.

Once in a while, if the family made too much of a stink about it, they'd question a suspect, usually whatever "Indian" they had in their holding cell at the time. Mason had participated in a few of these "interviews" himself and knew they generally ended with the bruised and bloodied "suspect" being dumped on some deserted road to serve as a warning to his fellow "Indians" about what happened when they made a big stink about something or, rather, anything.

One "interview" in particular had stuck in his mind all these years. It was in the late seventies, he couldn't remember the exact date, and the "suspect" was a brash young man who'd been picked up the night before for smoking a joint outside the Albion. He'd "resisted" arrest and by the time Mason had come to speak with him, his face looked like it had been used as a battering ram to open his cell door. He was missing his front teeth and his nose was broken and he was having trouble breathing, likely the result of a broken rib, or two.

Still, Mason had gone through the motions of asking him if he knew anything about a fifteen-year-old girl from the reserve who'd last been seen hitchhiking back from the Maynard Falls General Store.

You should ask yer buddy about that, the young man had replied, with a defiant air belied by his condition.

My buddy?

Him that was just in here . . . beatin' on me. Last anyone ever saw of her, she was gettin' into the back-a his cruiser.

Mason had heard plenty of such "unfounded" accusations before and knew better than to include it in his report. And neither did he include it in the report he'd filed a few days later when the same man turned up floating face down in the Moose

River, the first time anyone had seen him since he'd been released after his "interview."

All those years, Mason thought, you turned a blind eye in the name of preserving the peace, except that wasn't really the reason — there was no use denying it now. You did it because it was just easier to say nothing than it was to face the truth.

He'd never thought much about it before but over the years it would have had to have taken thousands of police officers across the country doing the same, and worse, with everyone else turning the same blind eye as him.

All of us telling ourselves we were looking out for their best interests when all we were doing was looking out for our own. Seeing now that all we'd really accomplished was clearing a fertile breeding ground for homegrown monsters like the Kraniches and Robert Pickton and for untold serial predators — some of them cops — given free range as long as they kept their killing-ways confined to "Indians."

And then, finally, when The Truth did rear its ugly head and we could no longer deny the scope of the violence, how did we respond? By dismissing our transgressions as a mere trifle, nothing but a loose thread to be snipped when in reality it's what's woven, and continues to weave, the very fabric of who we are as a nation.

It's no wonder we're all so fucked up, Mason thought, and that was bookended by another, no less pervasive: Oh well, it's too late to do anything about that now.

Perhaps paradoxically, that had him turning back to the boathouse with newly inflamed resolve. A light flared in the window on its second floor and a moment later Kranich's security chief appeared in its glow, pulling the blinds down. All of a sudden Mason saw a clear image in his mind of Emma Dupuis, tied up on a bed, wriggling against her restraints, screaming through the gag over her mouth, and the elder Kranich, drooling like some slobbering beast, running his gnarled old fingers over her naked flesh.

It was crystal clearyin his mind what he had to do.

All he'd need was some sort of a . . . distraction.

Deacon reading to the end of that line and then backtracking to the one before.

It was crystal clearyin his mind what he had to do, he reread and then sat staring at it for a moment more. Sure enough, the y between the r and the i was slightly off-kilter. It must have been added later. So here was the message he'd been waiting for all along, but what did it mean? His eyes ever-narrowing on the passage, zeroing in on crystal cleary.

She must have been involved somehow in whatever Dylan had planned . . .

But he was unable to think his way past what Dylan had already done to her. Glaring at the extra y and that seeming to mirror his thoughts, posing a question of its own. Tracking then down to a . . . distraction.

A distraction, he thought. *Is that why Dylan gave me the pages now? To serve as some kind of a distraction. Or was it Crystal who was supposed to be the distraction?*

He didn't have enough to go on and scanned down to the next paragraph.

No sooner had Mason thought that when he heard a sudden and cataclysmic Boom! The air itself seemed to quiver against its wrath as a ball of fire flared from behind the boathouse, shredding the night sky in its furor.

Startled then from the page by his phone buzzing on the table.

Likely, he told himself, recovering from the fright, it was just another update about the flood — he had already received a half-dozen more since that morning. Still, he stared at it with morbid dread, worried that it wasn't. Finally, he couldn't stand the not-knowing any longer and picked up the phone. He swiped at the screen and saw the last message from the *Flood Watch!* stream was an hour ago, then hit the back button. The top message was from *Unknown Caller*, and simply read one word:

Boo!

Boo!? Was that supposed to be some kind of a joke? Seemed a little juvenile, even by Dylan's standards, and Deacon didn't have more than a breath to ponder on that before his phone buzzed again.

Sorry, the next text read. *Clumsy thumbs. That's: Boom!*

Boom!? Deacon thought, equally confused, and then looked again down at the page, seeing it written there too.

"Oh shit!" he muttered, but it was the sudden and cataclysmic that had him lunging to his feet and scurrying away from the reading chair as if at any moment he expected it to explode into a ball of fire meant just for him.

16

His panicked flight had taken him as far as the bunkie's door. The pounding rain outside had deterred him from fleeing the barn altogether and his fright over Dylan's forecasted *Boom!* had quickly been consumed by the more pressing matter of crystal cleary.

The first time Dylan had given Deacon pages from George's *No Quarter*, they forecast a climax! during which Dylan butchered the entire Wane family and set half of Mesaquakee on fire. It was only logical to assume then that Dylan had given him the rest of the book in advance of a similar end, and the idea that the Swansons were maybe his target this time had Deacon thumbing Crystal's name on his phone's contact list. When he put the phone to his ear he was transferred immediately to voice mail and while he listened to her message — "You have failed to reach Crystal Cleary. You know what to do." — he tried to think of what he might say to suitably warn her without it degenerating into some lunatic rant about her brother. When he couldn't, he tapped *End Call* and then the envelope icon, knowing she always responded quicker to text messages anyway. Their last few appeared onscreen and scanning down those hardly eased the dread winding a knot into his stomach.

Hey Deacon, she'd written on March 19, three days ago, *I'm hosting a script reading for* A Precious Few *this weekend. You feel like hanging out with some real live movie stars?*

Worried that maybe Grace would be there, he'd texted back, *Sorry, promised Tawyne I'd join him at a sweat lodge this weekend.*

That was a lie but he'd found that using Tawyne as an excuse had served him well in the past, and all the better if they were doing something "Indigenous."

If you change your mind, the last text read, *we'll be up at the cottage all weekend. Drop by anytime.*

That she and Ward and "some real live movie stars" were currently holed up at the Swansons' isolated wilderness retreat left little doubt in his mind that Dylan would be staging his next climax! there.

If history had taught Deacon anything, it was that he was probably too late already to do anything about that but still he wrote, *The sweat lodge was called off on account of rain. Thinking I might drop by after all. That still okay?*

Pressing send, he stared at the screen, waiting for a response. When none had come after a minute or two, he let his gaze wander back to the manuscript sitting on the table beside George's reading chair, not thinking so much of an explosion anymore but of a camera.

Several years earlier, he'd been changing a lightbulb in the loft's ceiling fan and had come across a small device, what a Google search would later tell him was a pinhole camera with a fisheye lens. It wasn't hidden very well and Deacon suspected Dylan had wanted him to find it. Such rage and shame he'd felt, seeing it was pointed directly at his bed, thinking how he and Laney must have fucked a dozen times there over the past six months, not to mention how many times he'd jerked off in between, his inflated manhood no doubt sufficiently illuminated in the glow from the porn playing out on his laptop.

He'd thrown the camera to the ground and stomped it to bits, then mounted an exhaustive search of the premises. He hadn't unearthed any other cameras then, and while he'd mounted several more searches at regular intervals since, he hadn't done so for months. In the meantime, Dylan could have installed another, or maybe a dozen. Could have been he'd wired the whole damned property and his Jeep and the *Chronicle*'s office too, and spent his off hours like the Games Master in the *Beast* trilogy, following Deacon's every move on a bank of screens in his own personal lair. How he must have laughed just moments ago after sending him the *Boom!* and seeing him scurrying towards the door, where he now stood immobilized by the sensation that he was helpless to do anything except provide Dylan with further cause for amusement.

His phone was buzzing again. It was still in his hand and he was overwhelmed by the sudden urge to throw it against the wall.

Fuck Dylan and fuck his fucking games!

But he was feeling all of a sudden dizzy and weak and barely had the energy to simply stand there. He hadn't eaten a thing all day except the shake and hadn't drunk anything either except that and two travel mugs full of coffee, the second of which was spiked with a healthy dose of rye. He felt a little like throwing up and took a deep breath, trying to ease his nausea, but was thwarted in this by a sudden knock on the door behind him.

Spinning, he saw Gabe peering anxiously through the window. "Are you reading this?" Gabe asked after he'd let him in.

He was holding up his phone and onscreen a text read:

Extreme Flood Alert! All Residents Along The North Branch Of The Mesaquakee River Must Seek Higher Ground Immediately! Take Nothing! Repeat: Seek Higher Ground Immediately! Do Not Delay!

"What do you think it means?"

Deacon answered that by shaking his head even as a vague idea was forming in his mind, the . . . distraction and all those exclamation marks and the *Boom!* and the *Extreme Flood Alert!* congealing together with a headline he'd written not six months previous. "Mesaquakee Watershed Authority Complete Work on Two Reservoirs," is what it had read. The accompanying article had detailed how the MWA had received funding from both the provincial and federal governments to do just that as part of their combined mandates to double the country's renewable energy supplies by 2030 in an effort to avert further climate-related catastrophes.

The end result was that there were some five hundred million cubic metres of water currently being stored between the reservoirs at Wilsons Falls and the one just south of the Lake of Bays, where the river's north branch originated.

If Dylan's *Boom!* had anything to do with that . . .

A thought cut in half by the sharp *bring bring* of the phone ringing in his hand.

Grover, the caller ID read and he swiped at the receiver's icon, planting the phone at his ear.

"Deacon," Grover said, "you looking at your phone right now?"

"I was just about to call Frank Darling," Deacon answered, "to see what's up."

"Don't bother. I already called. It's going straight to voice mail."

"Hey," Gabe was then saying, "did you just hear that?"

Deacon had — a slight concussive thud, rattling the window glass. He could still feel it reverberating in his bones.

"It sounded almost like a —"

"Boom!"

"Yeah. Like when they were blasting up at —"

"Wilsons Falls!"

The exclamation's vigour seemed to catch Gabe off guard and it took him a moment to recover.

"Right," he said. "When they were building the new reservoir."

But Deacon wasn't listening to him anymore. If Dylan's texted *Boom!* had signalled he'd blown the reservoir at Lake of Bays, it would have taken the wave of water unleashed . . . what? Five, maybe six minutes before it got to Wilsons Falls, which was about how long it had been before Deacon had heard the concussive thud. Wilsons Falls was only two klicks from downtown and if he'd blown the reservoir there too . . .

"Tawyne!" he gasped.

Grover was saying something through the phone, Deacon couldn't hear what, nor did he care as he stabbed *End Call* and punched 2, the number he'd assigned to speed-dial Tawyne. He was already pushing past Gabe and running across the lawn, listening to it ring, twice, three times and then four. The lights in the house flickered briefly and then faded and the streetlight beyond the cedars had gone out too, casting him into an utter dark enlivened only by the screen in his hand.

"Hey, Chief," Tawyne answered just as Deacon was breaching the treeline separating the yard from his Jeep. "Did your power just —"

"Where are you?" Deacon cut him off.

"Home. Why?"

"You need to get out of there! Now!"

"What's —"

"Don't talk. Just run. Get to higher ground. You're dead if you don't. Go!"

Hearing then Tawyne's muffled voice saying, "We got to get out of here!" and another voice, faint, answering him something, Deacon couldn't hear what. Listening then and hearing what might have been a door slamming open and then feet thumping down stairs. And he could hear something else too: a distant tremor no more profound than what a snowplough might make rumbling by on the street but increasing in volume and tenor with each passing tick, growing towards a thunderous roar.

"Are you going to tell me what's going on?" Tawyne was yelling at him through the phone. He sounded a little out of breath, which Deacon took to be a good sign.

"Where are you now?" Deacon answered him as he wrenched open the Jeep's door and slid inside, jamming the key into the ignition.

"Just passing Chancery Lane," Tawyne answered, referring to the cobblestoned walkway that led from the back alley's summit into the downtown.

"Keep going. When you hit Dominion, head towards Main. I'll meet you there. Hurry!"

He had the phone wedged between his jaw and his shoulder and was hammering the Jeep's stick into reverse. The Jeep's wheels spun a half-rotation on the wet asphalt before catching and then thrust the vehicle backwards towards Hiram Street.

"Holy fuck! What the —"

This from his phone — an exclamation that didn't sound like Tawyne's voice, but the next one sure did.

"Go!" he was screaming, "Go! Go!"

"What's happening?" Deacon yelled into the phone, slamming on the brakes as he shot onto Hiram and spinning the wheel, pointing the Jeep towards downtown. There was no answer from the phone and when he pried it from his ear the message onscreen read, *Call Ended*. Hammering his foot on the gas, he hit speed-dial

2 again but it didn't even ring before the call was transferred to voice mail.

Anne Street was fast approaching. He tossed the phone onto the passenger seat, searching through the rain lashing at the windshield for any reason not to just blow through the stop sign. Seeing nothing ahead, he chanced a harried glance both ways, catching a splash of something on his left. Backwash from what couldn't have been anything but a tidal wave had channelled up the ravine leading down to the river. There was an eight-foot culvert that funnelled the stream under Anne Street but that wasn't even remotely big enough to contain the backwash's volume. The wave was slamming against the embankment, spraying upwards with the force of a train wreck and wrenching the culvert right out of the road.

Beyond the intersection there were four houses on Hiram that backed onto the ravine. All were dark and water was gushing between them at the height of maybe five feet, washing over the street and dashing up against the back of the arena. He could see a spot of white thrashing amongst the fray, a dog of some sort — a Pomeranian, maybe — tied up in the front yard and mad-paddling its paws against the surge, fighting a losing battle to keep its head above the water.

No time to worry about that.

Jerking the wheel hard right, he swerved onto Anne. A geyser spray of water erupted from the storm drain at the corner, pummelling the Jeep's undercarriage. The vehicle bucked and it seemed for a moment the geyser would lift him right off the ground but then the Jeep's wheels were spinning on the asphalt again, not that it did them much good. They were hydroplaning through a puddle, fishtailing out of control. The driver's frontside tire struck the curb with a grinding *clank!* and bounced him back into the middle of the road. The impact must have bent the axle, because when he tried to straighten himself out, the wheel was turned at a forty-five-degree angle from where it should have been.

No time to worry about that either.

Up ahead he saw a flash of blue and red as a police cruiser — sirens blaring — screamed along Main, heading for downtown. A train of vehicles were pulled over to let it pass, blocking the intersection. James Street was fast approaching and he made a calculated guess that it'd be quicker if he took that. He tapped the brakes and spun the wheel left and as the vehicle careened around the corner there was a voice screaming in his head, *Oh shit! The Timbits!*

He'd printed an announcement in that week's paper about how the Timbits hockey league was running a tournament at the arena that weekend. The power had gone out in the arena too and a crowd of kindergarten-sized kids and their parents was streaming into the street, hurrying for the parking lot on the far side.

Jamming on the brakes didn't slow him down much on the rain-slicked asphalt and he pounded his thumb on the steering wheel's horn, trying to clear a path as the Jeep slid towards the throng. Mothers and fathers were snatching up their kids, fleeing from his path, leaving only one man still blocking his way in rabid defiance. Between his size — gargantuan — and his beard — almost as prodigious as his gut — he looked more than a little like Grizzly Adams, but from the way he was glaring at Deacon as the Jeep's bumper shimmied to a stop inches from knocking him down, he'd got to more resembling the good-natured hillbilly's ursine namesake. He slammed both hands on the hood with such vitriol that the vehicle shook. Then he was pointing at Deacon with a finger as sharp as a harpoon.

"You stay right the fuck there, asshole!" he shouted, reaching into his pocket and retrieving his phone, no doubt to call the police.

And maybe he would have too had he not become suddenly distracted. From the way he jerked his head backwards, he must have heard tell of something dire and it was only a second before Deacon could see why. A three-foot swell had turned the street on the far side of the arena into a de facto chute. A mother and her two children — one wearing a helmet and carrying a stick, the other but a toddler — must have just been crossing over from the side parking lot when the wave hit. They'd been swept off their feet in a desperate flail of arms and legs and were just then being pummelled like pieces of driftwood against the guard rails surrounding the arena's frontside parking lot.

Grizzly Adams took off like a load of buckshot to render them aid and Deacon floored the gas. Swerving into the left-hand lane, he passed the man's frantic lumber with the speedometer tilting towards forty, ten klicks over the limit on the *Community Safety Zone* sign he was just passing by, though that hardly eased his foot on the pedal.

The swell had subsided some but there was still two feet of water draining in its wake. The Jeep balked when he struck that but the automatic four-wheel drive kicked in, powering him on through. He was going sixty by the time the James Street Retirement Home was passing by on his right and eighty when he'd come to the end of the block. He foreswore Ida Street, which would take him back to Main, for heading straight. The road rose on a slight incline towards the highest point of elevation on this side of the river before dead-ending at Mary. A black minivan and a green pick-up truck were parked front to back over both of Mary Street's lanes. The drivers were talking through their open driver-side windows and a spiral of flashing reds and blues alerted him to the police cruiser parked lengthwise across Main just this side of the movie theatre.

He hit the brakes and the moment the Jeep had skidded to a halt he shifted into park and threw open the door. The noise that greeted him was beyond all reckoning — a thunderous rumble that sounded more like mountains crumbling than a deluge. It drew him to the top of the cement steps leading down into the parking lot behind the old feed store. Five feet below where he stood, the stairs' handrail had been snapped clean off by the raging current sweeping along the rim of the bowl-shaped concavity upon which the downtown had been built.

Scanning over the water's dark tumult he could make out the backsides of the Pantheon Greek Restaurant and the Feathered Friends Pet Shop beside it but precious little else below where Main dipped steeply towards its intersection with Entrance Drive, except for the river's seething breadth. It was like the hand of some great and vengeful god had simply swept the town away. Knowing it was Dylan's hand that had done it — and Dylan was only a man and not a god at all — seemed a paltry sort of comfort.

A flare on his left swivelled Deacon's head towards the valley's far slope.

Several sprouts of flame, chimeric, had erupted from within the moil, rising almost to the top of the ridge, and whorls of them were dancing over the surface of the flood waters with the zeal of mischievous nymphs. A strange and wondrous sight added gravity by the pungent waft of diesel fuel. Peering through the rain, spotting a large black cylinder pinwheeling like a giant cork caught in a whirlpool and thinking, *The train!*

How many cars full of crude and natural gas had it been carrying? Dozens at least, and likely a whole lot more. Looking then back at the whirling nymphs, which were really just pockets of fuel set alight. So far it seemed none of the containers had blown but if even one of them did . . .

The ground under his feet suddenly lurched downwards and Deacon leapt backwards as a crack like a lightning bolt quartered the cement where he'd been standing. Backing away, expecting the earth to drop out from beneath his feet at any moment and finding himself caught within the scalding glare of headlights as the minivan swerved around him, its wheels jumping onto the sidewalk to avoid the Jeep with a grating crunch as it careened around the corner.

The green pick-up was accelerating the other way and Deacon ran after it.

When he came onto Main, the darkened movie theatre was just releasing a restless throng onto the sidewalk. Most were dashing straight away into the downpour, though a few remained cowering from the rain under the theatre's marquee, peering with tremulous eyes towards the downtown.

The truck had stopped beside the police cruiser. Its driver was screaming something at Officer Rhimes, who was standing in front of his open driver's side door. Deacon couldn't quite hear what over the thunderous roar but as he skirted past the cruiser's front bumper he did manage to catch at least a few words, "Lac-Mégantic," and "evacuate," and "now!" most prominent among them.

Lac-Mégantic was the name of a town in Quebec that had been levelled by an explosion caused by a runaway train carrying crude petroleum fuel in 2013. Forty-seven people had died and its mere mention brought back clear into his mind the black cylinder — one amongst dozens — Deacon had seen bobbing in the sway.

Scanning past the post office and the library — both still intact — he searched out any evidence of Tawyne and found only ruin.

"Holy fuck! What the —"

What the stranger had screamed in the background while Deacon had been on the phone with Tawyne. An exclamation that must have signalled the moment the wave had crested, smashing into downtown. Tawyne had said he was just passing

Chancery Lane at the time, which would have placed them behind the old Smellies stationery building. Deacon couldn't see anything at all left of its three storeys, and whatever there might have been was drowning under the angry gnash of the river funnelling down Dominion Street. Its current was lashing in violent surges at the courthouse on one side and the fire station on the other, its reach high enough to shatter the windows on both buildings' second floors.

"Go! Go! Go!"

The last words he heard Tawyne speak before they were cut off and maybe the last he'd ever hear. Imagining the boy swept under and his body bashed and battered at mercy to the torrent. Seeing his eyes gaped wide in mortal fear and his mouth open in a silent scream as the water gushed in, never feeling more like a father than he did just then and that feeling just like he was drowning right alongside Tawyne.

Banishing that thought with another, less grim.

If he survived, it would have been by way of Quebec Street. And if he fled down there he'd have looped onto Kimberley Avenue, which would take him to the backside of Memorial Park. Maybe he's walking down the lane between that and the Norwood right now.

Spinning, Deacon started off at a run, his eyes trained on the dark beyond the far corner of the theatre and catching only parcelled glimpses of the park through the dispersing crowd. Peering through them, trying to catch any hint of Tawyne's familiar lank on the far side. Spying a jostle of hair that could have been his and losing it amongst the crowd, pushing his way through and calling out, "Tawyne!"

Forgetting that the boy only ever answered to Keef or Kiefer and calling again the name his real father had given him as he came into the laneway. Scanning down it, past the row of vehicles parked there, and seeing a dozen or so people scurrying out of the theatre's back doors, hunkering down against the rain and fleeing towards their cars, but no sign of Tawyne. Reaching into his pocket, he felt for his phone before he remembered he'd left it in the Jeep. He detected then a sudden movement on his periphery and tracked it to the bandstand in the middle of the park.

Even in the dark he could see it was clearly Tawyne standing at its near rail. He was waving both hands over his head and Deacon was so happy to see him he could have wept.

Tawyne was shouting something too but Deacon couldn't make out what and set off at a hard run. Tawyne was coming down the steps to meet him as he approached. Standing behind him there was another boy, almost as skinny as Tawyne, and taller still. He was wearing a black Toronto Raptors jersey and his rain-greased skin, illuminated by the phone he was texting into in his hand, bore the hue of oiled coffee beans. Deacon recognized him right away. His name was Ethan Parnell and he'd appeared front and centre in every one of the photos Tawyne had submitted along with his coverage of the high school basketball team's last four home games. From the way the teenager shied nervously from Deacon's gaze when he'd caught him looking, it seemed that maybe that wasn't much of a coincidence.

Ethan had been with Tawyne in his apartment when he'd called him moments ago and could have been he was also the reason Tawyne wouldn't open his door more than a crack when Deacon had picked him up on the way to Algonquin Road. He'd heard the shower starting then and if it had been Ethan who'd been in the bathroom that'd mean —

No time to think about that now though.

"What the fuck is going on?" Tawyne was shouting and Deacon responded by grabbing at his arm.

"We've got to get the hell outta here!" he shouted back, dragging Tawyne on a hard diagonal towards where Kimberly Avenue intersected with Nelson Street at the northwestern corner of the park. Nelson would take them to John Street and John to Willis, which would lead them back to Main, and from there it was two short blocks to the house on Baker.

Even if one of those canisters does explode, he was telling himself as they came to the span of cars parked along the edge of the park, *we oughta be safe there*.

A thought given exclamation and also rendered inconsequential by a genuinely sudden and cataclysmic *boom!*

All three jerked towards it as a fireball shredded the charcoal-grey sky beyond the theatre's roof. The air itself did seem to quiver against its wrath, and the rain lashing Deacon's head and shoulders in its vertical assault whooshed on a dire lateral, driven by a gust of wind from the explosion and feeling like needle points prickling against his face.

Firming his grip on Tawyne's arm, he spun on his heels with the anguished fury of a mama bear protecting her cub from a hunter's peril.

"Run!" he screamed. "Goddammit, run!"

CRYSTAL

"**F**ade Out."

The hair was hackling on Crystal's arms and the back of her neck as she spoke the final two words in a gleeful whisper, hardly able to contain her enthusiasm over how well the reading had gone. And she needn't listen further for proof of that than the quiet that had settled over the table as she closed the script, delaying the inevitable moment when she'd be forced to look up by smoothing out a fold in the title page's top right-hand corner.

When no one had said anything after a couple of seconds, she snuck an apprehensive peek at the seven others seated before her. Aside from Grace, every one of them had played a castaway in the original *Beast* and every one of the actors also now wore the same stunned expression, as if none of them had expected her to be capable of writing something like that.

The moment was broken by Alicia pronouncing, "Wow!"

It wasn't much more than a whisper but emphatic nonetheless and the actor who'd played Helen, the med school student strapped for tuition in *Beast*, and had just read for Polly, opened her mouth again as if feeling the undeniable urge to say something more meaningful. But when she spoke again all she could muster was, "I mean, Wow!"

The only two at the table who weren't nodding when she said it were Grace, who was still hidden behind the tangled fray of the black witch's wig concealing her face, and Aleesha. Aleesha Mendes had parlayed her role as a tough-as-nails army cadet in *Beast* into a starring turn in the hit TV series 24/7, where she'd played a tough-as-nails secret service agent. If Crystal had learned anything while mounting her second draft, it was that it was always best to keep an open mind, and that's what she was telling herself as she appraised the uncertainty knit into Aleesha's deeply furrowed brow.

"Is there something you'd like to add, Aleesha?" she asked when it seemed the actress might keep whatever reservations she had to herself.

"No," Aleesha answered. "I mean —" Shaking her head and looking down at the script, seeking some sort of guidance. When she looked up again she was wearing an expression veering towards genuine confusion — a rare moment of befuddlement for Aleesha, who was about the most decisive person Crystal had ever met.

"So," she finally asked, "we were the bad guys all along?"

Crystal had taken the utmost care not to more than imply that anywhere in the script but it was in fact the Core Concept always in the forefront of her mind while she was writing and Aleesha speaking it out loud now felt like high praise indeed.

"That's the general idea, yeah," she replied, trying to keep her tone on the mild side of diffident.

Aleesha didn't seem to know how to respond to that and glanced back down at the script again.

"But Chandra —" she said. "I mean Chandra, she's based on me, isn't she?"

In fact, all the principal characters were based on the actors who Crystal had chosen to play them, aside from Polly, who was based on Crystal herself, and Cassandra, who was, of course, inspired by Grace. It was obvious from the way she was biting the corner of her lip that Aleesha was having a hard time reconciling herself to the idea that Crystal had written a character based on her as one of the bad guys and Crystal scanned over those seated at the table, looking for similar signs of discontent from the other actors.

Finding none, she settled her gaze on Vincent Yi. He'd be playing Doug — a rich kid from North Vancouver who'd mined his culture and affluence for laughs as a stand-up comic and who'd just signed with Netflix for his first comedy special — and was rarely, if ever, at a loss for words.

His eyebrows were scrunched and his hand rested on his chin, his forefinger tapping against his lips as if he was deep in thought. He caught Crystal looking and that was all it took for him to offer: "It's just like in *Joker*. You go in thinking he's the villain and then it turns out he's actually the hero."

This produced another burst of glee in Crystal, for *Joker* had been one of the movies ever present in her mind while she'd been writing.

Gordon Lang, who'd be playing Spencer — a Golden Globe–winning actor with a law degree from Harvard who bore a startling resemblance to Cary Grant — chimed in with "It's more like *Parasite* meets *Deliverance*, if you ask me. The way it blurs the lines until you aren't quite exactly sure *who* the villains are."

"Wait a minute." This from Malcolm Campbell, the youngest of the actors by seven years, who'd just read the part of Marlon, a rising hip-hop star who bore a striking resemblance to a young Bob Marley. "Joker was the hero?"

Vincent was opening his mouth about to respond to that but was interrupted by Alicia, who never seemed satisfied unless she got in the final word, even if it was quite often rather pedantic. "Well, I just loved it!" she blurted. "Really. And the ending — So touching. Great job, Crystal. I mean, really — Wow! It's just — Wow!"

Crystal had since spied Alicia flicking her thumb's red-tinged fingernail against her index finger, which she only did when she was aching for a cigarette. That suggested her all-abiding enthusiasm might have been in service of ending the conversation as quick as possible so she could get outside and have a smoke. Still, such an effusive proclamation certainly didn't do much to dampen Crystal's mood.

The last "Wow!" had been emphatic enough to silence any and all further discussion and Ward, on Crystal's right, used that as good enough a cue to drum his fingers in a rimshot's *baddum tss* on the table. "All righty then," he added, doing a fair impression of Ace Ventura as he pushed himself to his feet. "Dinner will be served in fifteen minutes. So if anyone wants to freshen up . . ."

The allusion to what the Host had said near the end of *Beast* elicited several groans and as many bemused grins as the troupe rose from the table. Crystal watched after them as they shuffled off towards the elevator, murmuring in hushed exultations, and Vincent responding to something Malcom had said by draping his arm over the other's shoulder, teasing, "I see you still have much to learn, young Padawan."

Malcom shrugged him off but it was a playful shrug and immediately inspired in Crystal memories of how Vincent had taken the younger actor, then only fourteen, under his wing while they'd filmed *Beast*, treating him like a long-lost younger brother rather than some stranger he'd just met.

Alicia and Gord had also bonded during the production, though hardly in such a wholesome fashion. In the meanwhile they'd both been married and divorced and in Alicia's case married again but as they waited for the elevator to arrive, that didn't much deter her from clutching at Gord's arm and whispering something, no doubt racy, into his ear. Vincent responded to that by holding up his phone behind them and exclaiming, "Say cheese!" which was also how he'd interrupted them one night, after they'd snuck off to fuck on one of the island's secluded beaches, by means of the speaker on the drone he and Malcolm had commandeered to surveil them.

An "edited for TV" version of the footage they'd shot had figured prominently in the "production diary" Ward had assembled for the wrap party, as had the footage Gord and Alicia had later captured after they'd enlisted the production's prodigious inventory of exotic snakes to seek their revenge. While Vincent was showering several mornings later, they'd fed a dozen or so of them through an open bathroom window in his cabana, saving an adolescent boa constrictor for last and feeding that through the shower's ceiling vent. The ensuing hilarity of Vincent's panicked clamber to get away from it only to find the floor a seething wriggle and the bathroom door wedged shut with a chair had apparently struck a chord when Alicia had shown it to the rest of the cast. The production diary would include a montage of not less than twelve separate incidents where the cast and crew sprang all manner of creepy-crawlies on an unsuspecting Vincent, and the mini-movie he'd posted on his YouTube channel of his escalating paranoia had gone a good way to securing his fame.

In the intervening years, Gord must have been harbouring fond memories of his part in the stunt, for even as he responded to Vincent's "Say cheese!" with a chastising frown, he was reaching into his blazer pocket and pulling out what appeared to be a black adder, coiled and ready to strike.

"I don't think you've met my new friend," Gord said, and no sooner had he spoken than the snake did in fact strike, leaping from his hand, Vincent dodging backwards in mock alarm as the snake bounced harmlessly off his chest. And though by then it was obvious to everyone that it was of the spring-loaded and rubber variety, Vincent played up the gag with his characteristic histrionics, shrieking like a little girl and clambering onto Malcom's back in a deft display of comedic acrobatics under feint of trying to get his feet out of reach of the snake's fangs.

Watching their good-natured if slightly juvenile antics, Crystal was thinking approvingly, *It's like the last eight years never happened at all, the way they're carrying on.*

It struck her as vaguely ironic, in that the notion to recast them came to her while she was thinking about how far she herself had come since they'd filmed *Beast*. She'd intended the reunion, in part, as a means of gauging her progress thus far and the decision had paid dividends almost immediately: it was after she got the idea of bringing them back together in *A Precious Few* as the cast of a post-apocalyptic thriller flying back to Toronto from a location in the wilds of Northern Ontario that the script had really sprung to life.

When she'd told Ward her idea, he'd had his doubts, warning, "Don't expect them to be the same group of actors we worked with before. They were all unknowns then, and now Alicia and Aleesha have both been on hit TV shows and Gord's won a Golden Globe and Vincent just did that Netflix special —"

"I know, his stand-up career is really taking off."

"And Malcolm's about to release his second album and will probably be on tour for the next year, maybe two."

"You forgot about Dieter," she'd said and the look of utter dismay curdling Ward's face told her he had not.

"Dieter's a total fucking write-off, you know that. And besides, you yourself said we'd have to hire a private detective if we wanted to track him to whatever hole he's crawled into."

"Well, I guess that's what we'll have to do, because we simply can't make it without him."

She'd started making phone calls that very day.

Every one of those had played out pretty much the same, with each of the actors all answering with variations of, "How could I possibly say no?"

To which she'd replied, "You couldn't," and each of them knew it just as well as she did.

If it wasn't for her, none of them would be where they were now, and not only because it was Crystal who'd had a hand in giving them their big break by casting them in *Beast*. Filming that had seemed like the adventure of a lifetime, made even more precious in that it was an adventure she'd never in her wildest dreams have imagined she'd get to have. Deeply moved by the camaraderie on display in the production diary when it was screened at the wrap party, and further buoyed by a few too many Mai Tais and a couple or three lines of coke with Dieter, she'd even got a little weepy when she'd expressed her gratitude to the assembled cast and crew.

She'd ended her toast by promising, "Anything you need — and I mean anything! — just give me a call. I'm here for you. All of you! Because we're family. We are! And family helps each other. That's what families do!"

And while nobody present would have begrudged her for reneging on a drunken promise, she'd go on to prove to each and every last one of them that she'd meant exactly what she'd said. Over the next five years, she'd spent almost as much time helping out her "new family" as she had producing the two *Beast* sequels — making phone calls on their behalf, connecting them with Hollywood agents, paying for them to attend the most exclusive workshops, getting them interviews on *Entertainment Tonight* and *etalk* and securing them auditions, then offering an ear to vent when they got passed over for a part (or, in Dieter's case, when a court order had forced him back into rehab), sending them bottles of Dom Pérignon whenever they landed a choice role or signed a lucrative contract.

Her unwavering commitment to the members of her newly extended family had ensured that not a single one of them dared say no when she called to recruit them for *A Precious Few*.

"So when can I see a script?" was the oft-repeated question they asked her after they'd agreed and to that she'd replied, "That's the hitch. You can't."

"You don't have a script?"

"Oh, we've got a script all right."

"So when *do* I get to see it?"

"Not until the reading."

"And when's that?"

She named the date she'd chosen — the third Saturday in March — and finished the call by advising them that she'd send a limo to pick them up at the appointed hour. What she didn't tell them was that the limo would drive them to one of four airfields — one in Los Angeles for Alicia and Aleesha; another for Malcolm and Vincent in New York; Gord's in Dallas (where he was filming a buddy cop movie); and Dieter's in Ajax, Ontario (where, the PI they'd hired had informed them, he'd been living in his parents' basement for the past three months). Four private jets then flew them to the airport in North Bay, where one of the Swansons' three helicopters was waiting to ferry them to the wilderness retreat.

"Christ," was Ward's reaction when she first told him of her plans, "the reading alone is going cost as much to produce as *Beast* did!"

That earned him a smirk as she'd chided, "You're exaggerating."

"Not by much."

"I just want to set the right mood, is all."

"The script sets the right mood all by itself," Ward had assured her. "You ought to just let it stand on its own."

But Ward knew better than anyone that when she got an idea in her head it was about as easy to dislodge as an impacted wisdom tooth. And after what he'd spent on the party, Crystal was only too happy to remind him, he wasn't in much of a position to argue anyway. In the end he'd given her his blessing to indulge in whatever her heart might so desire. As an additional show of support, just before he'd gone up to fetch the cast in the elevator so he could bring them down to the bunker, he'd donned his "lucky" *Beast* ballcap, which he only ever wore when he was on set. Then, when he'd returned a short while later, he'd proclaimed "Showtime!" as he stepped out of the elevator, which was what he always said by way of christening a film on his way to declaring the first "And . . . action!"

She'd decided to hold the reading in the Swanson family's underground bunker for the obvious reason that it figured prominently in her script and also because holding it down there would go a good way to setting the mood she was after. Regardless of how Ward had described it in *his* script, the provisions in the real bunker were all kept in a sub-bunker. Its main floor didn't so much resemble a Walmart as it did the Swansons' New York penthouse suite on West 57th, an impression furthered the first time Crystal had stepped into it by the window-sized screens implanted in the far wall, broadcasting — in real time — a view over Central Park. Ward's excuse for making the change had been that the sort of opulence on display in the real bunker didn't exactly set the requisite mood for an apocalyptic horror movie but Crystal couldn't have disagreed more.

Given that the bunker beneath the Swansons' cottage had played such a pivotal role in bringing her and Ward together, it was only natural that they'd want to consummate their wedding vows there. It had been the first time Ward had brought her down, and when she'd stepped out of the elevator that had just transported them through fifty feet of Canadian Shield, her initial reaction had been to quip, "The apocalypse is looking better all the time, at least for us Swansons, anyway" — the very thing Tom Willis had said upon coming into the Parsons' bunker in her grandfather's *A Precious Few*.

But while Crystal's jocularity had been enhanced by the preceding ceremony and reception, and even more so by the half-bottle of champagne she'd drunk in the helicopter, Tom's had been tempered only by a growing unease.

> Stepping out of the elevator, it seemed that it hadn't descended fifty feet through solid granite but had somehow transported them some four hundred kilometres all the way back to the Parsons family's Toronto penthouse suite on Lakeshore Drive, an impression furthered by how the wall of glass across the room from him did indeed seem to be looking out over the city's harbourfront. It only took him a moment to realize the view was painted on but in that moment he was immediately reminded of the one New Year's Eve party his father-in-law had invited him to there.
>
> He'd felt plenty uneasy then, circulating amongst the country's most privileged few. All of whom, as far as he could tell, had made their fortunes carving up the

world until it was falling to pieces around us and now
seemed to have nothing better to do than stand around
sipping champagne and eating canapés with the fervour
of lemmings upon the precipice, all the while bragging
about the role they'd played in shepherding humankind
towards the brink of extinction.

It was Tom's startling sense of disconnect as his sister-in-law berated a maid for the crime of serving her a salad topped with tinned salmon rather than her preferred smoked that Crystal had mined for tension in her script. Thus, she couldn't have been more pleased with the suitably ebullient expressions of wonder and awe on the faces of *her* precious few as the group of actors stepped out of the elevator and got *their* first glimpse of the bunker.

For dramatic purposes, she'd added to its decor a few flourishes of her own, primarily a rack on the wall on one side of the elevator strung with six haz-mat suits and one on the other side sporting five replica AR-15 assault rifles. At the last minute, she'd added to those the very real twelve-gauge shotgun Ward's grandfather had given him when he was twelve so they could shoot skeet together when he came up to the cottage, and had then lined up a row of shotgun shells on the rack's top ledge, for authenticity's sake.

Her final touch had been to broadcast footage she'd previously captured on the cottage's exterior surveillance cameras on the faux-window's twelve-by-six-foot screen.

It was divided into quadrants and in each of its four boxes stood a figure of varying sizes, from the husky six-foot-seven of the Swanson family's groundskeeper, Jared, to the diminutive five-foot-three of their chef, Inez. All were wearing overalls and plaid shirts and, over their heads, burlap potato sacks with ragged holes cut for eyes — the costume she'd chosen for her legion of "villainous" townsfolk.

When Ward had first read that he'd commented, "I see you're paying homage to Jason Voorhees after all."

And so she had, though really it was meant more as a subtle nod to the throng of horror movie icons Ward himself had used as the villains in his script.

Wyatt, their chauffeur and bodyguard, was the masked figure in the faux-window's bottom left-hand quadrant and he was also clutching the replica of Dieter's severed head they'd made for *Beast*. But by the time he was holding it up and walking towards the camera, the six actors, to a one, had become fixated upon the no-less-menacing figure of Grace. She was seated at the foot of the table, not so much looking like Carrie White as she did the ghost of that Japanese girl in *Ringu*. She was wearing a black dress and her head was downturned and her face concealed behind the mad tangle of the witch's wig Crystal had given her to try on after Grace had agreed "to help out" so that the others would have someone "to play off of."

Cassandra didn't have any lines and the only direction Crystal had given Grace was "to sit there and look suitably menacing." She'd certainly managed that in spades and as per Crystal's instructions she'd remained as still as humanly possible through-out the reading until the climactic moment when

INT. BUNKER NIGHT

```
Tears streak down Polly's cheeks as
Wilt draws her close, holding her in
a tight embrace. Polly sobs in great
heaves and pounds at his chest, crying
out in despair:
```

                    POLLY
        Why? Why are they doing this?

The elevator dings and as the doors
swish shut the ribbon of light cast
from within ever narrows along with
it, plunging them into an abyss out of
which it seems they might never again
emerge.

The only sound we hear is that of
Polly's gasping sobs. An interminable
moment broken by the sudden and
not-too-distant scuttle of footsteps.

                    WILT
        Shh!

                    POLLY
        What?

                    WILT
        There's someone else here.

                    POLLY
        What! Who?

                    WILT
        Shh!

A moment listening. All is quiet save
for Polly's ragged breaths. A beacon of

light then flares: the torch on Wilt's
phone.

He casts the beam in a widening arc,
tracing over the room and finding
nothing but the furniture casting
deepening shadows against the walls.
Footsteps scutter again and the light
jerks back towards the dining area.

There's nothing there.

The light then turns to Polly. She's
sniffling and wiping at her nose with
the back of a blood-soaked hand,
smearing red over her face.

                    WILT
        Take the phone.

She gapes back at him as if not
understanding.

                    WILT
        Take it!

Pressing it into her hand, he steps
past her, angling the shotgun ahead of
him.

                    WILT
        Give me some light.

With shaky hands, Polly shines the
light after him and he ventures a
tentative step forward, then another
and another, with Polly inching slowly
after him.

A pained moaning erupts from somewhere
offscreen and Polly jerks the light
towards whence it came as a potato-sack-
masked figure lurches into view from
within the dining area, moaning and
madly dashing headlong towards them.

Polly screams and Wilt jerks the
shotgun up, barely taking aim and firing
at the masked man. The load of birdshot
hits him in the chest and at first only
seems to stun him, stopping him in his
tracks. In the torch's harsh glare we
now see that the gunshot is only one of
three wounds oozing blood. There's a
blotch of it too on the mask where his
mouth would be and another down below,
soaking the groin of what we now see
are a pair of boxer briefs.

These all add to Wilt's confusion
as the masked figure takes one more
tottering step forward and then
crumples to the floor, Polly tracking
after him with the light as Wilt moves
to take a closer look.

                    WILT

        Jesus Christ! Oh fuck! Oh
        shit!

                    POLLY

        What?!

                    WILT

        Oh fuck, oh fuck!

                    POLLY

        What is it?

                    WILT

        His hand. Look.

The beam searches out his hand and
glints off the ruby-studded ring on its
pinky.

                    WILT

        It's Howard!

                    POLLY

        Howard? Your grandfather?

A sudden scuttling of footsteps arises
from nearby, closing in with startling
celerity. Polly jerks the phone towards
the footsteps and its beam captures
Cassandra, in all her fearsome glory,
charging towards Wilt.

```
Within the mad tangle of hair her eyes
shine with a hate like Carrie White's
after they dropped the bucket of pig's
blood on her and Wilt barely has time
to gasp, much less raise the shotgun,
before the butcher knife reared over her
head is slashing downwards at his chest.
```

It was at this point that Crystal had instructed Grace to stab the butcher knife she was concealing within her dress viciously into the table in front of her. She did so with such force that it rattled the ice in the three pitchers of water dispersed evenly among the performers and also caused Alicia to let out the high-pitched squeak of a mouse as a trap snapped down upon its neck, which was more than Crystal could possibly have hoped for.

T he knife had remained imbedded in the table's oak for the rest of the reading and was still there as Crystal let the cast jostle good-naturedly through the just-opened elevator doors and turned back to Grace. She was still sitting in her chair with her head downturned and her face hidden behind the brackish wig.

Though Crystal had never seriously considered casting her in the role for the film, as she set eyes on her again she was thinking, *Maybe she'd make a good Cassandra after all. She sure is taking the role seriously enough.*

But that was a decision that could wait for another day.

Right then the only thing on her mind was the script. She already had a few ideas on how to tighten it and was eager for a little alone-time so she could go over the three or four dozen *s she made in its margins — mostly annotating lines of dialogue in need of tweaking.

Ward had since retreated to his den. Other than Grace, the only people still lingering were Brad and his brother Mark, who were collecting the webcams stationed on the table where each of the actors had sat, and Dieter. He'd read Wilt — the youngest son of the richest man in the country who had used his trust fund to finance his aspirations as film director only to let drugs derail a once promising career and was now getting his life back on track thanks to Polly hiring him to direct her latest movie. Dieter was now holding his hands clasped in front of him as in prayer and bending with the reverent bow of a Buddhist monk, his way of offering her his deepest thanks for giving him another chance, though in that moment it struck Crystal as more of a blessing. She reciprocated the gesture and Dieter hurried off to catch up with the others, leaving Crystal alone with Grace.

She still hadn't moved so much as a twitch and Crystal's earlier goodwill towards her began to degrade under her mounting impatience to get back to the script.

Maybe she's taking her role a trifle too seriously, she thought, tapping her pen against the bound sheaf of papers trying to get Grace's attention.

But Grace kept up her ghastly-spectre routine, refusing to move an inch — or, it would appear, even breathe. Ward reappeared a few seconds later, pocketing his phone as he passed behind his sister, ignoring her altogether as he approached Crystal.

"I told you there was nothing to worry about," he said, bending down to give Crystal a kiss on the forehead.

She replied with a benevolent smile and he responded to that by asking, "You heading up for dinner?"

Crystal shook her head.

"I want to run through it one more time, while it's still fresh."

"Figured you might. I set up the recording in the den, if you want to use that."

"Maybe I will."

"All you have to do is press enter."

"Thanks."

"Is there anything I can get you?"

"A pot of coffee?"

"With some Baileys in it?" It was how she usually took hers in the evening.

"If you don't mind."

"Nothing would please me more. Anything else?"

"I think that's everything."

Ward kissed her on the forehead again by way of a goodbye and as he backed away from the table he cast a skittish glance at his sister, pointing a finger at the back of her head and mouthing to Crystal, "What a freak!"

Crystal mouthed, "I know," and was startled a second later, when she looked back to the table, to find Grace was staring right at her. She'd since exchanged her ghastly-spectre routine for her Carrie White glare and that gave Crystal all the incentive she needed to snatch up her script and make haste towards Ward's den, suddenly eager for the welcome sanctuary awaiting her therein.

Ward called it his den but really it was just the smallest of the bunker's four bedrooms, a little warren to call his own where he could hide away — often for weeks — while he was hashing out a new project.

Its only adornments were a queen-sized bed and a dresser, an expansive oak desk and a cushy office chair, both of the latter set dead centre in front of the three fifty-five-inch TV screens Ward had suspended from its southernmost wall for the purpose of assembling a preliminary rough cut of *Beasts*.

They'd been in the middle of filming that when they'd heard the first reports, in late 2019, of a novel coronavirus arising in China and threatening to turn into a global pandemic. Given that they were in relative seclusion on the Swansons' tropical island and that they'd already shot the movie's interiors at their studio in Toronto, it hadn't affected the production much. The pandemic was in full swing by the time they'd wrapped and when they'd returned to Toronto they'd taken one of the Swansons' helicopters from Pearson International Airport to the their wilderness retreat, where they planned to sequester themselves for their mandatory fourteen days of self-isolation.

That had turned into a nine-month stay — how long it had taken Ward to edit the film and then for both of them to write *Beast Planet* together — and it was the surreality of that time that would later inspire Crystal to change the calamity that sent her precious few seeking refuge at the Parsons' cottage from a nuclear war to a deadly virus. But it was a conversation that she'd had with Ward while the two of them were soaking in the Jacuzzi tub in the ensuite of the bunker's master bedroom on the first night of their quarantine that would most definitively shape the course of her life over the next five years.

"Nothing's ever going to be the same again," she'd moaned, submerged under a three-inch froth of bubbles. A tear was trickling down her cheek as she spoke, her sudden despondency not so much because of the pandemic as because she'd just learned that her mother had started another round of chemo, her third and what she'd announced would be her last. Given the precariousness of her health, the doctors were advising her to maintain a strict quarantine of her own and it was the thought that she might never again get to hug her mom that had got Crystal to weeping.

"Maybe," Ward had replied, "but maybe it's also a blessing in disguise."

It had struck her as a deeply insensitive thing to say, what with the world on virtual lockdown and the memory so clear in her mind of how frail her mother had looked while they were Zooming earlier that evening. Ward must have gleaned that from the way she'd pursed her lips and he'd hastily added, "I mean, you did say you could use a break."

That much was true.

In contrast to *Beast*, shooting its sequel had been a debilitating ordeal for Crystal. Given its budget — ten times the original's — and the demands placed on the production by its ensemble cast of Hollywood movie stars, she was but one producer amongst a legion, and the most junior of any of them. She'd often felt like a third or fourth or even a tenth wheel, consigned mostly to smiling and nodding and keeping her mouth shut, telling herself all the while that it was a valuable learning experience but feeling a little more deflated every day. It hadn't helped either that all three of the more veteran producers to whom she'd given her original draft of *A Precious Few* had responded with variations of "The premise is sound but it'll need major rewrites. You may want to think about hiring a *professional* for those."

But most troubling for her was that Ward had never seemed more in his element and, as the production ground on, it had become increasingly clear that his patience was wearing thin with all of her "petty quibbles." So when he'd said that bit about her needing a break it had seemed he was once again trivializing her very real concerns and she shot back at him with a rather caustic, "This is hardly the kind of break I was talking about!"

Undeterred, Ward had then offered, "Well, there's nothing we can do about that now. The only thing we *can* do is to try to make the best out of a bad situation."

Good advice, perhaps, but it had only further degraded her mood.

"Make the best out of a bad situation?" she'd spat. "Out of my mother dying and me maybe never seeing her again?"

"No, I mean — The pandemic. I mean —"

He stopped there, maybe not altogether certain what he had meant. He'd then taken a deep breath, trying to regain a measure of composure.

"Do you remember what Brad said his dad's theory was about Covid-19?" he'd finally asked after exhaling.

She did. Brad had mentioned it during what was supposed to be *Beasts'* wrap party but ended up being just her and Ward and Brad and a few members of the crew drinking at the mostly empty bar in the resort on Turks and Caicos, the entire cast having fled earlier that day so they could get back to their loved ones as quickly as possible. She'd spent a few too many moments ruminating on what a grim affair that had been and Ward had prompted her again, "Do you remember or not?"

"What does that have to do with anything?" she spat back.

"Just humour me."

It seemed to take a mountain of will for Crystal to keep her voice on an even keel when she'd answered, "He said it was just a trial run."

"Right, a trial run, in advance of what?"

"Another, more deadly virus."

"One designed to wipe out half the people on the planet," Ward added. "The ultimate means of population control."

"Seemed a little far-fetched to me," Crystal countered. "And besides, how in the hell are we supposed to make the best out of *that?*"

"What if *Beast* and *Beasts* were just the Games Master conducting his own trial runs too?"

There was a trace of the wolf-sizing-up-his-prey glint in his eyes, like he was challenging her to play along. It was the first time he'd used it on her since the morning they'd met and that did give her pause to consider.

"Maybe —" Ward started when she'd been thinking a moment too long but by then Crystal had already picked up on the thread.

"Maybe," she interrupted, "he's planning to unleash his beasts on the world."

"And so where would he start?"

"With the poorest people on the planet, I'd guess. Probably in some third-world slum."

"But a slum where?"

"I don't know. There's plenty to go around. Rio, maybe?"

"How about . . . Wuhan?"

"Wuhan?"

"Sure, why not?"

Crystal didn't have an answer for that, except maybe that it would seem in poor taste to exploit the ongoing tragedy for their own selfish ends. But by then her creative juices had begun to flow and she sidelined any concerns she had by responding with a question of her own.

"So how would *we* begin?" she asked.

"I don't know. Where would *you* begin?"

It had been a great disappointment to her that Elliot Page hadn't been available to play the investigative journalist in *Beasts.* They'd ended up cutting out that character altogether, thinking maybe they could use him if they made a *Beast 3,* and so that had

305

seemed, to Crystal, as good a place to start as any. They'd spent the next few hours hashing out a plausible scenario, moving from the Jacuzzi to Ward's laptop in the den and finishing the night in bed, consummating the rush they'd felt drafting their first outline together, passing out an hour later sweaty and tangled up in each other's arms.

She counted that night as the moment she'd truly been birthed as a writer. Bolstered by that thought, her mood was veering towards transcendence as she now approached the desk where she and Ward had truly come together as one, if only on the page.

Ward had fed footage from the webcams through his laptop and from there to the three screens above the desk. The one in the middle was split into six, each box showing one of the actors sitting at the table in freeze frame, while the one on the left was all Crystal and the one on the right all Grace.

Nice touch, she thought as she sat down at the desk and set the script in front of her.

Opening it to the first page, she took a deep breath to centre herself, exhaling in a long, steady stream before reaching over to the laptop's keyboard and finally pressing enter.

She'd watched through the footage of the reading without so much as looking down at the script until she'd reached its climax.

Her intention to mount a few corrections had been swept away almost immediately by the exhilaration of hearing her words spoken aloud again, her elation in no small way aided and abetted by the two Percs she'd fished from the mint tin secreted in her blazer's pocket immediately after pressing enter, so that they might provide her with an "enhanced" perspective.

At first she'd only cast fleeting glimpses at Grace, trying to detect a crack in her ghastly-spectre routine. When, after a half-hour or so, she'd been unable to, her gaze had begun to wander to Grace's screen more and more until finally, approaching the climax, it had settled on her permanently. So absorbed had she become in Grace's unwavering malevolence that she'd entered into an almost meditative state — the voices emanating from the speakers relegated to a background drone, as irrelevant as the gurgles from her stomach reminding her of the untouched fruit plate Inez had brought down along with the pot of coffee — and she was only jarred from this by the sudden jerk of Grace's arm as she jammed the knife into the tabletop.

The corresponding *bang!* and the rattle of the ice in the pitchers amplified through all seven microphones startled her as much as it had Alicia, making her jump, and her fright was given perfect expression by the corresponding, and no less sudden, squirt she felt spraying into her underwear.

Her doctor had advised her that one of the side effects she could expect from such a late-term miscarriage was a weakened bladder. She'd had a few minor spills since leaving the hospital and always made sure to wear a pad to guard against those. She was wearing one now, so really it wasn't much of a bother, but that hardly lessened the shame of wetting herself, even if it was only a squirt.

Onscreen, Grace had again assumed her Carrie White glare and was seemingly staring right at Crystal. The corners of her lips were slightly upraised and while it would be a stretch to suggest she was smiling, it struck Crystal that she was, and she couldn't shake the feeling that Grace was taking no small amount of pleasure in having made her — a grown woman — pee her pants. A rather dubious bit of reasoning, perhaps, since the Grace staring back at her now was a recording made some two hours previous.

Her own voice was then ringing out from the speakers: "As Wilt pitches backwards, a spray of blood spackles Cassandra's face, beaming now with devious glee as she turns her sights on Polly."

At that, Grace seemed to smile a fraction wider still even as she lowered her head. The way her face disappeared behind the mad fray of her witch's wig — like it was gradually sinking beneath the surface of a pool of black water and not behind a wig at all — struck Crystal as rehearsed. It reinforced the idea that Grace's performance had been orchestrated for Crystal's benefit alone, as if Grace knew she would be watching it later, stoned on Percocet. Crystal thus couldn't help but be unnerved by the subtlety of how Grace transformed herself back into a faceless and ghastly spectre at the very moment her fictional counterpart was about to have at Crystal's.

Crystal's own voice was saying through the speakers, "Polly is backing away, shaking her head and pleading . . ."

This was followed by an awkward silence of a variety likely to arise whenever an actor — in this case, Alicia — had missed a cue. At the time, Crystal had searched her out at the table and shot her a mildly admonishing frown. She did so again now, going so far as to even prompt along with her onscreen otherself: "Pleading . . ."

This had the effect of drawing Crystal right back into the drama of the thing, watching Gord's elbow appear onscreen, nudging Alicia in the arm and causing her to startle yet again, realizing she'd just missed a line.

Frantically, she looked down at the page on the table in front of her. "No! No!" she pleads. "Please! Just leave me alone!"

"Tears are streaming down her face," Crystal read, "as she bumps against the closed elevator doors, and though she's still shaking her head, the fight has clearly gone out of her. Her legs buckle beneath her and she slumps downwards to the floor, sobbing helplessly.

"Wilt's phone sits a few feet away, inches from its owner's still-twitching hand, but its torchlight doesn't so much resemble a beacon anymore as it does a silent witness to Polly's impending doom. As Cassandra steps into the field of its bright, the light casts her shadow into that of a giant looming over Polly from the ceiling and glints off the bloodied knife, gripped at her side.

"Please just let me go," Alicia begged through sniffles. "I won't tell anyone, I promise. Please just let me go!"

"Cassandra's expression softens and for a moment it looks like maybe she will. But only for a moment. In a flash, Cassandra rears the knife over her head and strides forward, out of the light and into a dark so complete it seems to swallow the both of them whole.

"Polly gasps, cringing and turning her head away, holding her breath and waiting for Cassandra to strike. A second passes, then another and yet another. Releasing a stuttered exhale, she finally looks back up but it is not towards Cassandra that her gaze wanders; it's to the young girl standing beside her and clutching at Cassandra's hand, apparently holding her at bay. She has red hair and freckles like caramel sprinkles on either cheek and is wearing a pink princess outfit replete with frills and a tiara. At the sight, Polly's eyes grow wide with the realization that she's seen her before.

"Exterior, Beach, Lakeside, Day (Flashback). Polly stares down at the photograph of the same girl wearing the same costume that the Raggedy-Looking Woman has just handed her and then glances back at the Raggedy-Looking Woman fleeing back through the cover of trees whence she came."

"What was that all about?" Dieter asked.

"Wilt's coming down the stairs carrying his shotgun slung over his shoulder and while it seems hardly coincidental that the Raggedy-Looking Woman has fled with such haste at his approach, Polly doesn't seem to have made the connection."

"I don't know," Alicia answered. "Just some crazy woman, I think."

"Well, it is the end of the world after all," Dieter said. "Bound to be a few of those around. Did she say what she wanted?"

"Her daughter. She said she'd been abducted."

"Abducted? By who?"

Alicia shook her head.

"She didn't say."

"Polly then looks back at the photograph, at the smiling, beaming face staring up at her from under a tiara. Interior Bunker Night. The same smiling, beaming face is gazing down at her now, beatific and angelic — the face of her would-be savior. After a moment the girl looks up at Cassandra beseechingly.

"It's okay, Cassie," Crystal continued, reading the part of the girl. "She won't hurt us. I know she won't. (Looking then back at Polly.) You won't hurt us, will you?"

During the reading, that bit of dialogue had struck her as extraneous. As her onscreen otherself continued — "Sniffling, Polly shakes her head" — she flipped through the script until she'd come to the second-to-last page, using her pen to scratch out the offending lines, obliterating all traces of them as the reading wound itself towards denouement.

Cassandra had indeed spared Polly's life and the script ended with Polly and the young girl holding hands in the elevator transporting them back up to the cottage's main floor. The door opens to the sight of a legion of the villainous townsfolk crowding in front of it and "Polly gasps at the sight of the hulking man standing at its fore.

"He's holding a machete, doused with what she knows to be Chandra's blood, and his shirt and potato-sack mask are speckled with the same. Polly startles, backing away, and the young girl clenches her hand a little tighter, signalling it'll be okay, though that hardly diminishes the figure's menace.

"As if seeking to provide some reassurance of his own, the man lifts off his mask and we see that, far from a monster, he is a rather simple-looking, dowdy-faced middle-aged man, someone you might expect to be stocking shelves at the local hardware store rather than participating in a killing spree.

"His expression bears traces of shame in the way he can't meet Polly's panicked gaze and he wipes a handkerchief over the sweat plastered on his brow with a fevered hand, as if what he's really trying to wipe away is the guilt of what he's done. No time to reflect on that, though, as the Raggedy-Looking Woman is even then jostling through the crowd of now-unmasked townsfolk, the look of abject longing on her face eclipsed suddenly by one of utter relief.

"The young girl's face lights up too. Releasing Polly's hand, she hurries towards her mom and Polly is reduced to a mere bystander, the hapless despair in her eyes a trifle compared to the joy beaming from those of the woman, now wrapping her arms around the girl with the desperate clutch of a mother who thought she'd never be able hug her daughter ever again.

"Fade Out."

The recording ended a moment before Alicia's "Wow!" and thus Crystal was deprived of its emphatic affirmation but the hair again hackling over her arms and the back of her neck felt almost as good.

The faces onscreen had freeze-framed and that only served all the better to highlight their stunned expressions, excepting, of course, Grace, whose face was downturned and hidden behind the mad tangle of hair so Crystal couldn't tell of her expression. The squirt in her underwear had come to reside as a spot of cool and damp, and as she turned back to Grace's screen it served as an ever-present reminder of just how effective Grace had been as the "villain."

Appraising her again now, Crystal was at the point of conceding that, in the very least, they could arrange a screen test for her but was distracted from that thought by a small greyish rectangle she'd just spotted suspended beneath Grace's breasts. Its outline was about the size of a postcard and there was a blurred image inside its border, she couldn't tell of what. It was comprised of a curved bank of striations of blurred grey against a black background and seemed vaguely familiar, almost like that fossilized fish she'd once found on a family trip to the Bay of Fundy.

But, leaning forward to get a better view, she saw it didn't really look like that at all.

It looked almost like a —

Cutting herself off because, no, surely it couldn't have been that.

Standing then and craning her head forward further still, peering into the depths of the pixelated image and seeing that it appeared to be — it did! — a picture of an ultrasound just like the one she and Ward had sent out to friends and family as a way of announcing they were pregnant.

But it couldn't be that. It just couldn't —

Her mounting consternation was interrupted by the gentle rap of a knuckle *knock knock knock*ing at the door. Such was her alarm at seeing what she just had on the heels of listening to what she just had, she halfway expected to find Grace standing there, brandishing the knife, ready to have at her. Spinning, she found it was Ward instead. He was standing just beyond the door's threshold, as if he was reluctant to disturb her any more than he had to.

"Hey," he said jovially, "just checking in."

All Crystal could muster in reply was an open-mouthed gape. He must have read something dire in it, because his brow was furrowing in response — an expression of mild admonishment he generally reserved for when the glaze to her eyes told him she was stoned again, and she was feeling plenty stoned now. Her tongue suddenly felt like it was encased in plaster and her head cement and she glanced back at Grace's screen, trying to find a way out of her muddle.

But the photo of the ultrasound staring back at her only added to it.

"You okay?" Ward asked.

He'd taken a step into the room and Crystal lashed her head back towards him on a pivot hard enough to whip her hair against her cheeks.

"I —" she started but the words still weren't there. The only one she was able to conjure at all was, "Grace!"

The panic in her voice didn't do much to ease the concern creeping into Ward's eyes.

"Grace?" he asked. "What about her?"

"Have you seen her?"

His brow was crinkling even more as he answered, "Not since the reading. Why?"

"It's —"

"Is something wrong?"

"No. I mean — I just — I was thinking maybe we could arrange a screen test for her?"

Ward's eyebrows raised a notch as he considered that.

"Say, that's not a bad idea," he finally said. "I can track her down for you if you want."

"No!"

It came out sounding a little extreme for a response to an offer of help and its virulence took Ward further aback. His expression of mild admonishment was rapidly deteriorating into one of genuine concern — could have been over the current state of her mental health — and that only served to make her clamp her mouth shut, worried that anything she might say would only make her seem like she'd truly gone off the rails.

"You sure you're okay?" Ward asked with the stilted caution of someone who wasn't really sure he wanted an answer.

Crystal nodded, mumbling an affirmative "Mm hm" through sutured lips.

"Have you eaten anything today?" Ward asked.

Finally a question she could answer with a degree of confidence.

"Uh huh," she offered and then added, "Inez brought down a fruit plate with the coffee."

Ward was even then craning his head slightly, appraising the plate beside the laptop. It was so layered with honeydew melon, passion fruit, strawberries, grapes and pineapple that it was hard to conceive how it could have been stacked any higher without the aid of, say, a dozen toothpicks — an inconvenient truth he sidestepped by urging, "There's still half a prime rib and some smoked salmon left from dinner if you want something a little more . . . solid."

"I'm good. For now. I'll have something. When I come up."

"Any idea when that'll be? Your guests are waiting."

"I'll only be a . . . couple of minutes. Ten, at most."

"I guess I'll leave you to it, then."

"I won't be long."

"Luv ya."

"Luv ya more."

Their standard goodbye came out strained on her part but it got her something vaguely resembling a smile and Ward turned away again, this time without looking back.

She waited until she heard his footsteps receding towards the end of the hall then scurried over and shut the door. On second thought, she locked it as well and, as she returned to the desk, she felt a slight stitch in her belly. Her doctor had advised her that phantom pain, like that experienced by people who'd lost a limb, was another of the expected side effects from a late-term miscarriage. They'd arise without any rhyme or reason, as if they were her body's way of never letting her forget what she'd lost. And she'd rarely felt that loss more than she did as her eyes again zeroed in on the photo Grace was holding up against her dress.

They had, of course, sent the birth announcement to Grace and so it could very well have been the same image. The thought that Grace had kept it after they'd lost Baby Rose was disturbing enough in itself but that she'd then gone through the trouble of concealing it beneath her dress — along with a butcher knife, no less! — waiting for the reading to end and then holding it in front of her . . .

The thought trailing off, replaced immediately by another.

But why? Why would she do such a thing? It doesn't make any goddamned sense!

Unless — Unless . . .

"It was goddamned murder!"

What she'd screamed at Ward after she'd awoken following the "extraction." The memory of the pain she'd felt then — like it was tearing her apart from the inside out — incited another phantom stab in her gut. It also had her eyes locked in what felt like a death grip on Grace's screen, staring at it with a facsimile of the unbridled and piercing hate Grace had stared at her through the crowd of partygoers on New Year's Eve.

At the time, Crystal had cursed "Little freak!" as she stormed up the stairs. But if Grace really had done what Crystal suspected she had —

But she couldn't have, she told herself. *She'd have to be more than just a little freak to do something like that. She'd have to be a fucking psychopath!*

The ghastly image of Grace on the screen didn't do much to allay her fears and she stared at it a moment longer, biting her lip and thinking of how she might prove or disprove her suspicions, one way or another.

How someone had managed to slip her a near-lethal dose of misoprostol had never really been much of a mystery. Crystal's assistant, Janine, had always parcelled the weekly regimen of pregnancy supplements into a pill container divided into seven rows of three, the top boxes labelled *Morning*, the middle *Noon* and the bottom *Night*. Her nightly allotment was six tablets and on New Year's Eve she'd downed those as she always did, popping them into her mouth all at once and washing them down with a gulp of water. Later, in the hospital, she'd had plenty of time to reflect on who might have had cause to switch out her pills but she hadn't come to any definite conclusions.

But if it had been Grace . . .

The footage from the party!

Crystal was standing pretty much in the exact same spot as she had been on New Year's Eve when she'd discovered the real reason why Ward had thrown such an elaborate celebration instead of the conservative gathering of select friends and business associates they'd agreed upon.

During the hour they'd spent talking over tea in the bunker's living room, her anger had drained out of her until it was but a mere remnant — no more substantial than the smattering of camomile leaves clinging to the bottom of her cup — and afterwards she'd gone to take a long, hot soak in the master bedroom's Jacuzzi tub. She'd fallen asleep and was awoken by her phone giggling with a baby's laugh, the ring tone Janine had used for the thrice-daily alarms she'd programmed reminding Crystal to take her supplements. They were in her bag, which, last she knew, was still in the Range Rover, and after she'd slipped into her bathrobe she'd texted Wyatt to see if he might bring it down.

She'd then texted Ward to see where he'd got to.

I'm in the den, he'd replied and when she'd sought him out there, he was sitting in his chair, wearing a pair of headphones, his eyes roving over the three television screens, deeply entranced.

Each screen was divided into eight separate boxes and every one of those appeared to contain footage being broadcast, in real time, from twenty-four separate locations around the cottage and the surrounding property. Hard then not to feel a sudden resurgence of her doubt, seeing no small similarity between his surveillance activities and those of his fictional villain, the Games Master. She'd stood at the door, apprehensive, and after a few seconds Ward had glanced back, maybe wondering what was taking her so long.

"What's going on?" she'd asked after he'd slipped off the headphones.

Her uncertainty must have been written all over her face and there was a clipped sort of urgency in his voice when he'd hastily explained, "It's research. For the Gatsby reboot."

The way he averted his eyes when he said it didn't make that seem entirely true. But doubting Ward's intentions had already caused her enough grief over the past few hours and she'd banished her unease by adopting her characteristically sardonic tone as she offered, "Well, at least the party should be tax-deductible then."

That had got her a gracious smile.

"I want it to be as true to life as possible," Ward had then enthused. "A real peek inside the lives of the rich and famous during the, quote, 'New Normal.'"

But Crystal wasn't really listening anymore. Something in one of the squares had just caught her attention. The scene was from inside one of the trailers they used on location, six of which Ward had driven up to the property in preparation, he'd said, for filming *A Precious Few*. She saw now though that he hadn't been entirely truthful about that either, which would explain why he'd have them brought up before she even had a serviceable script. And while that omission itself had seemed just shy of a betrayal, she'd since become far too distracted by what was happening onscreen to mount much of a protest.

A man was bent over the trailer's bed and a woman was standing behind him. She was wearing a giant purple strap-on dildo and pounding him up the ass with such ferocious thrusts that it seemed she was on the verge of splitting him in two.

"Isn't that —" she started, taking a step closer, her feeling of indiscretion choking Gordon Lang's name in her throat.

"It is," Ward assured her, "and that's Alicia Simmonds."

"But she just got married a month ago!"

"Uh huh," Ward said. "Her husband's there too. You can just make him out between Gord's legs."

Bending closer, she could indeed see another man kneeling in front of Gord, apparently sucking him off.

Right then she'd felt the baby kicking up a storm, as she often did after a hot bath, and she was feeling tired and weak and a little nauseous. The scene playing out onscreen was about the last thing she'd have wanted to see and it added a tinge of disgust to her voice when she asked, "You are going to delete that, right?"

"Of course," Ward shot back at her. "No, of course, of course. I'll be deleting all of it . . . when I'm done."

It was at that moment that Wyatt had texted her to say he was waiting in the elevator with her bag. Summoning a little more goodwill, she'd kissed Ward on the cheek, telling him she was going to turn in. Two hours later she'd awoken screaming in the master bedroom's king-sized bed, feeling like Baby Rose had grown talons and was trying to claw her way out.

During her time in the hospital, Crystal had become convinced that it had been Janine who'd switched her pills as, just before Christmas, Janine's boyfriend had ghosted her. Crystal had already begun to suspect that Janine blamed the break-up on being at Crystal's beck and call 24/7 and while she could never really conceive that "mousy little Janine" was capable of poisoning her and her unborn child, creeping doubts had created a rift, in her mind, between them. She fired Janine the day she'd returned to work.

It wasn't one of her proudest moments, for sure, and one that now seemed like another stab in the gut, thinking of how much she'd missed Janine's steadying influence in the meanwhile, when it must have been Grace who'd switched out her pills.

If she had, she'd have had to have done so on New Year's Eve and so it stood to reason there might be some evidence of her crime in Ward's surveillance footage. But, of course, Ward had promised he'd delete it and that thought had her staring down at his laptop, worried that maybe he had.

Finally telling herself, *Well, there's only one way to find out*, she sat at the desk. Clicking on File Explorer then the folder marked *GBreboot 2025*, the NYEP file appeared where it had always been. One click later the footage popped up on the twenty-four squares over the three screens. The time index in the bottom said it was 18:04 and the only person other than staff on any of the screens was Ward, whose face was filling one of the upper boxes in the middle one. He had his finger over his mouth and was whispering, "Shhhh!" — no doubt an in-joke to be chuckled over by his later self. Keeping an eye on the screen fed by the camera pointed towards the driveway, she scrolled the footage forward until she saw a flicker of red — her Range Rover pulling into view.

Watching herself storming out of the driver's side door towards the stairs as the cottage's front door opened of its own volition and then searching out the boxes for the cottage's main floor. Her heavily pregnant otherself was already threading her way through the crowd of revellers and then suddenly stopped, catching sight of Grace. Grace was little more than a pinkish blur amid the throng and after the server had passed, taking Grace with her, Crystal scanned the screens, waiting for her to reappear. A few moments later she located her talking with Deacon on the back patio. She was passing him something, it looked like a cigarillo. He responded by taking it up and drawing on it with such relish that she knew it must have been a joint.

After a couple of puffs he tried to give it back but Grace demurred and they went on talking while he smoked it pretty much down to its nub. Grace had since wrangled them a couple of martinis. Deacon was just finishing off his when he suddenly lurched off balance. It looked like his legs had turned to rubber. Grace slipped herself under his arm, helping him to stay on his feet as she led him back into the main room.

Crystal turned to that screen but it wasn't Grace and Deacon that she sighted on first, it was Wyatt. He was walking up the stairs carrying what was quite obviously her travel bag. He must have spotted it in the Range Rover and brought it inside as a courtesy. Chances were he was taking it to her and Ward's room on the second floor, and the second floor was also where Grace was taking Deacon. She watched them stepping into the elevator and then watched through its camera as Grace thumbed the DNA scanner to gain access to the living quarters, which were always out of bounds to everyone except family during gatherings such as these.

Deacon, meanwhile, was clinging to the rail wrapped around the elevator's back wall with the desperate clutch of someone worried that the ground was about to give out from beneath him at any moment. His lips were moving, muttering something, and Crystal clicked on the microphone icon on the corresponding grid on the laptop's screen so she could hear what he might be saying.

His voice, not muttering at all, blared out of the speakers.

"—andpaper!" he was screaming. "They're wiping his ass with sandpaper! God, man, what kind of parents would do such a thing? They must be fucking monsters!"

It sounded enough like gibberish that between it and his frenzied clutch, Crystal realized that Grace must have dosed him with something too. Her suspicion was added no little veracity by the way Grace was then looking up full-faced into the camera, assuming her Carrie White glare, but only for a moment. As the elevator doors opened at the second floor, her expression relented into a mischievous grin. She topped that off by putting her finger over her lips and whispering "Shhh," a strange enough coincidence after what Ward had done earlier that it had Crystal thinking that Grace must have known he was watching and was, what, signalling to him her nefarious intent?

Could it have been they were somehow . . . in league?

Ward did, after all, suggest you use the recording of the reading when you'd have been just as happy to go through the script itself. And didn't he also appear the moment after you'd discovered Grace holding

321

the picture of her ultrasound? Except it was his idea to have a baby in the first place.

Thinking back to New Year's Eve. At the time Grace and Deacon were in the elevator, Ward was making her a cup of tea in the bunker's kitchen and so he couldn't have been watching.

No, she reassured herself as Grace led Deacon out of the elevator, *you're just being paranoid. Probably she was just sending a message to her future self — a little giggle for later on — just like Ward had likely intended with his.*

There was no footage from the second floor and Crystal pressed fast-forward, waiting for Grace to reappear in the elevator. She did, twenty minutes later. She was still leading Deacon by the hand but he seemed to have evened out a bit. He wasn't screaming gibberish, anyway, and though his legs did seem a little loose in their stride, he was able to maintain an upright position merely by leaning against the rail as Grace pressed the button for the rooftop patio. All in all, he actually looked pretty cool-headed, which had as much to do with his casual slouch as it did with how he was dressed. He was wearing the white linen suit and pink shirt Ward had worn when he and Brad had dressed up as Crockett and Tubbs for the eighties-themed party they'd hosted at the cottage to celebrate being double-vaxxed against Covid, and his eyes were concealed behind the pair of mauve-tinted tortoiseshell sunglasses — Carrera's, if she remembered correctly — Ward had special-ordered to accessorize. The outfit had hung in the closet in her and Ward's second-floor bedroom ever since and that left no doubt in Crystal's mind that that's where Grace and Deacon were coming from.

That took care of the matter of how Grace had switched out her vitamins but hardly put a dent in the matter of *why* she'd do such a thing. Tracing back through her memory, looking for something she might have done or said to Grace that would have incited the requisite malice. Coming up blank, her thoughts circled back to the photo she'd held up at the end of the reading. That posed another question, no less sinister.

If she really killed Baby Rose, why would she confess to it now?

Reminded then of a bit of insight Ward had imparted while they were writing *Beast Planet*.

"A horror film," he'd said, "is a lot like a good joke: it's all in the set-up. Getting the audience to 'buy in,' that's the key. And the most successful writers and directors all know that the best way to do that is to tap into the audience's natural powers of imagination and let it do most of the work."

Grace had certainly let hers do the lion's share of the work in that regard, Crystal seeing now how Grace had used her minimalist performance to pique her curiosity then had used the picture of the ultrasound to twist that into a mounting horror which sent her back to the footage of the party, seeking a clue to confirm her suspicions. Under different circumstances, Crystal might have been impressed. But as things stood, the thought that Grace had merely been setting her up for something worse yet to come had her staring mind-numbed at the footage of the now-empty elevator, the anger at what Grace had done eclipsed by a mounting dread, wondering what she might have planned next.

Onscreen, two young men dressed in ski suits were stumbling into view. The first pressed the floor-one button and that had Crystal thinking she ought to be getting her ass up there, too, so she could warn Ward and the others —

But warn them of what, exactly?

That Grace was a fucking psycho and she . . . what? She was, what? Planning on, what?

Biting her lip, unable to really, truly fathom what that could possibly be and telling herself, *Well, whatever it is, the fact that she*

323

just confessed to killing Baby Rose makes it a good bet it's already well in the offing.

In the elevator onscreen, one of the young men was heaving over, puking on the floor.

"Oh, dude," the other said, dodging out of range of its splatter. "Not cool, man. Not fucking cool at all. This is the last time I fucking invite you anywhere."

The one who'd puked responded by wiping his mouth and grinning up at the other like the goose who'd just laid a golden egg. The elevator door was then reopening and the other guy was storming out, with his friend trying to keep up in his drunken stumble.

Just this morning, Crystal had discovered that the elevator's camera was still where Ward had hidden it for the party. She had been expecting her guests at any moment and was heading down to the bunker to see how Ward was doing. She was feeling a little nervous and to take the edge off she'd fished from her blazer's inside pocket the Altoids breath mint tin containing her Percs. She was popping two when she'd been overcome with the feeling that she was being watched. That wasn't so odd in itself, as she often got the same feeling when she was sneaking one of her little "pick-me-ups."

Two weeks previous, the feeling had been so intense that she'd practically torn her bathroom apart, certain that the careful scrutiny with which Ward had appraised her at breakfast meant he'd planted a camera in there to catch her in the act. She hadn't found any surveillance devices then but with that feeling overwhelming her again in the elevator, she scanned its ceiling and was shocked to discover what appeared to be a small camera staring down at her from on top of the emergency light's battery pack.

Ward had given her no indication that he'd caught her little indiscretion and Crystal had chalked that up as yet another reminder that she'd have to be more discreet in the future. Now, though, the idea that he hadn't removed that camera suggested that maybe he hadn't removed any of the other cameras either. That had her looking down at the laptop, searching along the task bar at the screen's bottom edge for an icon to indicate how she might pull that footage up now. The graphic of a video camera seemed her best bet and she clicked on that. Sure enough, the footage from the party disappeared and was replaced at once by a live stream in all twenty-four boxes.

The exterior ones were clouded by dark and all she could make out on the six of those were vague shadows, mostly the trunks of trees. She searched the others for any signs of Grace and only found any sort of activity in two. In one, Vincent, Malcolm, Aleesha and Dieter were sitting in the hot tub on the back deck. Aleesha was sipping what looked to be a Caesar but was probably a Virgin, since she rarely drank alcohol, and a dozen or so empty bottles of beer littered the hot tub's rim. The three men also had bottles in hand and were passing a joint between them. From the way they were laughing and carrying on, it seemed they were having the time of their lives.

The other feed was from inside one of the trailers, where she could see Alicia and Gord up to their old tricks on its bed. Alicia was straddled on top of him with her hair lashing in time to her violently thrusting hips.

That didn't help her with Grace but all of her guests, anyway, were present and accounted for, which left only Ward, Brad, Mark, Jared, Inez and Wyatt. Jared lived in one of the guest cottages and could very well have been there, while Wyatt spent most of his off hours at the cottage in the garage, tinkering with the snowmobiles and quads. Ward hadn't put any cameras on the second floor, so it was possible that was where the others were.

Crystal had intentionally left her phone upstairs during the reading and so the only way to make sure the latter six people were okay would be to go upstairs herself. She was rising to do just that when she caught hint of a sudden flicker from the top left-hand box on the right-side screen, one of those that had been blanked by the dark. She now saw on it a figure standing there, holding up a road flare in front of a bench that had once sat next to the ice-skating path.

Clicking on its grid on the laptop, she brought the footage to full screen and gave out a little gasp, seeing that the figure was a rather hulking man wearing a potato-sack mask over his head. It struck her that it must have been Wyatt. He was about the same height and relative build and was also wearing the same black pants and black sweater with the Swanson insignia on his breast that he always wore at the cottage. She barely had half a breath to consider that before he started walking forward, lifting his free hand into the air. It had been down beneath the field of vision before and as it slowly came into view she could see it was holding something . . . something by the hair . . . a severed head . . . he was holding Jared's severed head!

The rain that had been coming down in torrents had since relented to a light drizzle that wetted Jared's cheeks, beading in his bushman's beard and dripping off the bullring pierced through his nose. His face was otherwise paled and bore a suitably pained expression. As the masked figure raised the head towards the camera, filling the screen, the horror of it had Crystal lunging from her chair, dodging backwards and bumping against the bed, her hand clamped to her mouth and yet her eyes fastened, as if by tethers, to the screen.

She was telling herself, *This can't be real. It just can't —*

But there was no denying that the severed head looked real enough, plenty more real anyway than the one they'd made of Dieter's for *Beast*.

Then the head was gone, tossed off to the side. The masked figure — Wyatt! — was gone too. In his stead, Grace was standing on the far side of the bench, plying her ghastly spectre routine within the smoky red haze of another road flare on the ground at her feet. Crystal had been staring at her for only a second or two before she caught hint of movement from one of the other screens and turned towards it.

It was from the camera that had been positioned over by the hockey rink, though the only evidence remaining of that was a flattened rectangle of graded dirt. The masked figure was lit by the road flare upraised in his hand like a torch and he was traversing the field with a deliberate stride that immediately called to mind Jason Voorhees, as did the sight of him drawing from the sheath on his back what appeared to be a machete.

On the far side of the rink was a copse of cedar trees and on the other side of those the maintenance shed. The trailers were parked in the clearing in front of that and, as the masked figure strode out of view, Crystal turned towards the footage from inside Alicia and Gord's trailer. They were both now lying naked on top of the bed, breathing hard, and Gord was lighting a cigarette, taking only the briefest of drags before passing it to Alicia.

You've got to warn them!

A sharp and definitive exhalation but how Crystal might be able do that wasn't so abundantly clear. It'd take, at best, a full minute before she'd even be able to get to the main floor and then what? A frantic text? A mad dash across the yard? Neither'd do them or her a lick of good as, right then, the trailer's door was crashing inwards. Gord and Alicia gave a sudden start and Crystal could well imagine the latter uttering a no-less-sudden squeak, like she had during the reading. The masked figure was then storming into the trailer, the machete at his side, and Gord and Alicia were scrambling to cover themselves up.

Both were hurling angry invectives at the masked figure, the same way they had at the drone when Vincent and Malcolm had caught them in the act while filming *Beast*. The sound was muted but it was clear to Crystal that whatever they were saying, they thought this was merely some kind of ruse. They'd recovered from their original fright and, as the masked figure approached the bed, Alicia flicked her cigarette at him. It struck him in the chest with a smattering of sparks and the masked figure responded by raising the machete over his head. Crystal still wasn't entirely certain, herself, that this wasn't some kind of ruse and was caught almost as off guard as the two on the bed were when the machete slashed downwards, imbedding itself in Alicia's skull.

The way her arms suddenly lashed out from her sides in a palsied twitch and her body slumped listlessly to the floor as the masked figure wrenched the blade from her head eradicated any and all doubts in Crystal's mind that what was happening was real, and it had eradicated all of Gord's doubts as well. He was scrambling off the bed in a frenzy to get out of the masked figure's reach and that's where Crystal left him, hurtling towards the den's door in her own mad scramble to get upstairs, knowing that it'd be a damned miracle if she got there in time to save the others.

Riding up to the main floor had given her a few interminable moments to think and what she was thinking was:

Please, let Ward be all right. Whatever happens, please let him be okay. Please, please, please!

Who she was praying to she couldn't exactly say. Not to God, that was for sure. To the *numinous* perhaps, then. It was a term

Ward often used when events conspired in such a fashion to make him — also a devout atheist — seriously question whether, maybe, there wasn't a higher power at work somewhere after all. The first time she'd heard him use it was at the end of the toast he'd made during their wedding reception.

"To the great and powerful numinous," he'd exulted, raising his glass, "which brought us together."

She hadn't heard the word before and had discreetly googled it while Deacon, the next in line to speak, was stepping to the podium.

This is what Wikipedia told her it meant: "arousing spiritual or religious emotion; mysterious or awe-inspiring."

As his toast, Deacon had told a slightly redacted version of her and Ward's Origin Story. While that certainly was suitably *mysterious and awe-inspiring*, hearing Deacon recount it had compelled Crystal to lean over to Ward and whisper into his ear, "*Numinous*, that's a good word. Except it wasn't the numinous which brought us together, honey. It was George."

So it could have been she was really praying to her grandfather, a dim proposition at best, since his books rarely, if ever, had a happy end.

But whoever she was praying to, it seemed to have worked. She'd barely lunged out through the elevator's opening doors before Ward was calling to her from the stairs, "Oh, hey there, sweets. What's with the, uh, shotgun?"

By that he'd meant his own. Crystal was clutching it in both hands, having grabbed it from the rack and loaded it with six shells after she'd pressed the elevator's call button.

Ward was wearing a pair of blue swim shorts and had a towel slung over his shoulder. He must have been heading out to join the others in the hot tub and the relief she felt at seeing her husband alive and well was consumed at once by thoughts of the four actors already out there. She was cocking the gun the way Ward had taught her as she angled towards the sliding doors. If that wasn't enough to tell Ward something dire was afoot, the virulence in her voice as she yelled "Stay there!" most surely was.

As the doors slid open, she heard a peal of laughter from the far-right side of the deck, which could only have come from Malcolm, who had about the most riotous laugh she'd ever heard.

"Everybody out!" she screamed, storming towards them. "Get out! Everybody! Get out of the goddamned water!"

They all reacted to the initial outburst with quizzical looks, like a bunch of siblings whose mom, in a drunken fit, had just kicked over the Lego set they'd spent the entire afternoon building.

"What's going on, Crystal?"

This from Ward, who'd trailed after her. He was gaping at her, mystified, with an anxious my-wife's-finally-gone-off-the-deep-end-and-what-do-I-do-now expression and Crystal ignored him as she spun back to the hot tub.

"Get! Out! Of! The! Fucking! Water!"

When that produced plenty of alarm in the actors' eyes but failed to incite the necessary action, she pointed the shotgun in the air and squeezed the trigger.

The resulting *boom!* stunned them pretty much the same and, assuming the tone that commanded her the utmost respect on set, she added a definitive "Now!"

That, finally, got them moving. Malcolm was the first to react and Aleesha the last and each clambered out, grabbing their towels and phones from the deck's railing as they scurried past, Crystal hastening after them with a propulsive "Go! Go! Go! Go!"

"Jesus Crystal, what the fuck?"

Ward was blocking the doorway as he spoke and she darted past him without answering. A quick jog right brought her to the nearest of the cottage's security panels. She punched in her personalized code and immediately heard the lock click on the sliding door. This was followed by the whirr from the motor lowering the cottage's shutters, encasing its windows in reinforced steel.

"Sweets," Ward was then saying, adopting a conciliatory tone as he stepped up beside her, "you want to tell us what's going on?"

She opened her mouth, trying to think of what she might say, but the words were sucked right out of her by the image of the machete's downward slash and the way it almost split Alicia's head in two. Closing her eyes against the memory and seeing Jared's disembodied head staring back at her from the dark. Startled from this by a resounding *clank!* — the shutters sealing them in — her eyes jarred open again even as she felt the weight of what she'd seen pressing down on her, suffocating the breath right out of her lungs.

Taking a deep breath, trying to regain her composure but still hardly able to breathe.

"They're dead," she finally choked out.

"Dead?" This from Aleesha, standing at the fore of the group of actors. "Who's dead?"

"Gord and Alicia. And Jared. They're all dead."

A stunned silence followed, the actors all looking from one to another and Ward.

"What do you mean?" Ward finally asked.

"Dead! They're fucking dead! She — She killed them."

"Who killed them?"

"Grace."

"Grace?"

"She's a fucking psycho."

"Who's Grace?"

It was Vincent who'd asked and all eyes turned to him.

331

"My sister," Ward answered, dismissively. "And she didn't kill anyone." Then turning back to Crystal and firming his tone. "Grace didn't kill anyone."

"Oh, yes she did. She killed Alicia and Gord and Jared. Or at least she had Wyatt kill them."

"Wyatt?"

"And she killed Rose too."

"Rose?" Aleesha asked. "Baby Rose?"

"She's the one who switched out my pills."

"Okay, honey, that's enough."

"She did!"

Ward responded by grabbing her by the arm, hard enough to rattle her bones, something he'd been doing with ever-increasing frequency of late.

"Enough!" he said. "Grace didn't kill anyone. And she certainly didn't kill —"

"Call them then," Crystal said cutting him off. "If you don't believe me, fucking call them!"

All four of the actors were holding their phones in their hands but all the entreaty got Crystal was another round of blank stares.

"Why isn't anyone calling them?!"

"Uh," Ward answered, "it's because the phones are down."

"The phones are down?"

"They went out sometime during the reading. Jared, he thought maybe the cell tower got damaged in last night's storm. I, uh, sent him to check on it. I'm sure it's nothing to worry about."

That elicited a nervous titter from Crystal.

"Tell that to Jared," she said.

She was veering towards hysteria and she could see that well reflected in the five sets of eyes, all staring right at her.

"You just need to calm down, okay?" Ward said. "I'm sure there's a reasonable — Hey, where are you going?"

For she was striding away from him, on a direct line for the elevator.

"The helicopter," she answered. "We have to get the fuck out of here!"

She hammered at the button and the doors opened right away. She hurried inside, hitting the button for the third floor and looking back at the others. None of them had moved an inch except Ward, who was walking towards her like the floor was all thin ice ahead.

"Honey," he said, "the helicopter's gone."

"Gone?!"

"Brad and Mark and Inez had to be back in T.O. tonight. We talked about this."

She had a vague memory of him telling her something about that, though it hardly diminished the feeling that the universe was conspiring against any of them ever leaving the place alive. The elevator doors were closing and Ward stuck his arm in the way, forcing them open again.

"How many pills have you taken today?" he asked sharply and that struck Crystal like a slap in the face.

"What does that have to do with anything?!"

Her vitriol seemed only to deflate Ward further and he averted his eyes, maybe trying to think of what he might say to get her to listen to reason. The four actors had since assembled behind him. All were wearing expressions of tender mercy. The way they were crowding around her in a semi-circle, so emphatically empathetic, recalled to her the intervention she herself had organized after the first time Dieter had overdosed.

Stunned then beyond all recourse.

Is that what they all really thought of her? That she was some pill-popping junkie on a downward spiral and the way she was acting now was just — What? Proof of a complete psychotic break?

They were all looking at her like they were certain that's what was happening and she knew, right then, that Ward had spoken to them all beforehand, warned them of her fragile state, asked them for their help because there wasn't anyone she trusted more, knowing now with perfect clarity that she could hardly blame him for that. She had gone a little off the rails after losing the baby and she had, perhaps, come to rely a little too heavily on the pills — a couple to get her up and a couple more to put her down, a handful more to get her through her waking hours, popping them on some days like they really were breath mints. Telling herself all the while that it was just her way of coping with her loss, that the pills were helping her while everyone around must have known the truth — she could see that in the deep-seated concern, the love, imprinted on every one of the faces crowding around her now.

On any other day, she might have responded with an unequivocal love of her own. But then on any other day she wouldn't have witnessed what she just had — Alicia and Gord butchered right before her eyes and Jared dead too, her trusted chauffeur and bodyguard conspiring along with that psychotic little freak Grace, and the lives of almost everyone in the world she loved hinged on her being able to convince them that what she'd seen wasn't part of some drug-induced psychosis.

"I know things seem pretty bleak right now," Dieter was saying with the smooth assurance of a therapist. "But trust me, it'll get better. Whatever you think's happening, it's not. It's just the pills talking. Your family's here now and we all love you. We do. We'll help you get through this together."

"It's not the fucking pills!" she screamed and that sounding exactly like what a drug addict would say.

"Crystal," Ward said. "You're just tired, is all. You need a break. A little rest. After all you've been through . . ."

Gritting her teeth, summoning whatever resolve she had left.

"What I need is for you to listen to me. Alicia and Gord and Jared are dead. They're fucking dead! And whoever killed them must have disabled the cell tower, which means they'll be coming for us next."

Ward opened his mouth about to say she could only guess what but she beat him to the punch.

"And I can prove it!"

Her glare brokered no argument from Ward even as it wilted his expression. He averted his eyes and then sought her out again under cover of a sideways glance.

"Go ahead then," he said with a beleaguered, almost terminal, resign, "prove away."

"There," she said. "They were murdered right there!"

She'd led them into the bunker's den, charging right in and pointing to the grid with the live stream from inside the trailer. But when she looked back at the door, Ward was barring the way, guarding against the others coming in.

"Excuse us for a second," he said by way of an explanation as he closed the door, sealing them out.

"What the hell, Crystal?" he whispered as he approached her at the desk. "You know no one else is allowed in here!"

But concealing her husband's "research" activities was the least of her concerns. She'd since brought the live stream from inside the trailer up to full screen. While there was no sign of Alicia or Gord, the bed and the sheets were soaked with enough blood to account for both of their murders, and Jared's too.

"Will you just look," she said.

Craning forward, Ward gave the screen a hard stare but if he saw in the gore any definitive proof his expression gave off not even a whiff of it.

"That certainly is a lot of blood," he said. "Or at least something red." Then looking up at Crystal. "It must be a put-on. Gord's idea of a joke? He always did have a twisted sense of —"

"Tell me if you think this is a joke too."

Crystal was even then cueing the cursor on the laptop, bringing it to bear on where the video progress bar should have been but no matter how many times she swiped the cursor over it, the bar refused to appear.

"Come on," she urged.

"What's wrong?" Ward asked, bending beside her.

"I can't get it to play back."

"That's odd." Thinking a moment then. "You did click record, right?"

"Record? I —"

"You have to click on record if you want it to play back later."

"But —"

Gaping dumbfounded at the screen, feeling like an idiot, her gaze then searching out the bench beside what had been the ice-skating track.

"Look here," she said, bringing that up full screen.

Grace was still standing in front of the bench, her figure given extra menace in the hazy, now sputtering glow from the road flare at her feet. She hadn't moved an inch — which did seem a little odd — but there was something moving about her head. Craning forward, Crystal saw it was a small black bird with white highlights on its wings — a magpie, it looked like. It was foraging in her hair, pecking at her scalp. After a second or two it flittered away, carrying a few strands of hair in its beak.

"I don't —" Crystal started and was interrupted by Ward placing his hand on her shoulder.

"It's just a dummy," he said. "A mannequin made to look like Grace."

"But —"

Looking back to the Grace dummy, wondering, *Why in the hell?* And then it came to her. *It wasn't a dummy at all, it was a —*

A thought sliced in two by Ward saying, "Hey look, there's Wyatt now."

He was pointing at a box on the left-side screen, its camera peering down from the front door. Sure enough it was Wyatt, dressed exactly as she'd seen him before, except he wasn't wearing a mask. He was walking across the driveway's cobbled-stones, wiping his hands on a rag, like he really had been in the garage and had only just now noticed someone had activated the cottage's defensive shield. He was peering up at the camera as he approached the stairs and Ward clicked on his grid, bringing it to full screen.

Wyatt had just mounted the first step when something to his right caught his attention and he turned into the bright of an approaching vehicle's headlights driving into frame. It was a green SUV — a Forester — and its driver's side door was even then opening. The man who stepped out was heavily bearded and wearing camo gear and Crystal's first thought was that maybe he was just some hunter who'd come down the wrong road. It had happened before.

Wyatt, though, was then striding forward, offering his hand in greeting, and if it really had been a hunter he'd have shooed him away right quick. Crystal pondering on that and staring, rapt, as the hunter chucked him on the arm. Wyatt was smiling when he did so and it occurred to Crystal that they must have known each other. And then it began to seem to her that she knew him too.

"Isn't that your brother?" Ward asked.

"Dylan?"

Looking closer and seeing it was. It was the beard that had confused her, since she'd never known him to be anything but clean-shaven.

"What's he doing here?"

Crystal shook her head. It was a mystery, all right.

The impression that Wyatt was in league with Grace had never really departed her and while it seemed starkly out of place with how congenially he'd welcomed Dylan — exactly like an old army buddy he hadn't seen in years — it still had her hurrying for the door.

"Where are you going now?" Ward asked, trailing after her.

"Someone's got to warn him!"

"Now, honey —"

But she was already opening the door and pushing past the actors still crowded in the hall, her haste in no small way chastened by what she'd thought just a second ago, pondering on the matter of why someone would have made up a mannequin to look like Grace.

Her first thought was that Grace was using it as a decoy and why she'd have done that was equally clear: Grace had wanted Crystal to think she was somewhere other than where she really was. That meant she could have been hiding anywhere, could have been she'd never left the bunker at all.

She came to the end of the hallway and into the dining room, pivoting the shotgun left then right.

"Are you going to tell us what the fuck's going on?" Aleesha asked, sidling up to Crystal, who shushed her with a perfunctory "Shhh!"

It was maybe ten strides from there to the main room and another ten from there to the elevator. They could all be there in a matter of seconds but that would mean a panicked dash. Thinking that, Crystal was reminded of a line from her own script.

"In situations like this," Wilt had told Polly, trying to reassure her after it had become readily clear that the end of the world was upon them, "panic will kill you quicker than any virus. If we can keep our heads, stay calm, we'll get through this. Okay?"

"Crystal," Ward was imploring but she ignored him.

"We need to keep together," she said. "Stay close and whatever happens, follow my lead."

"But Crystal," Ward again implored, grabbing her arm, holding her at bay.

She shrugged him off and moved forward with a deliberate stride, her head swivelling back and forth, trying to take in the whole room at once as she skirted past the table. The lights were still on and their bright left Grace with nowhere to hide, a comforting thought that carried Crystal into the living room. Seeing she'd have had no place to hide there either and starting across it, her eyes locked on the elevator, worried that Grace, or Wyatt, might have tampered with it in an effort to trap them down below.

But when she'd reached it and pressed its call button, the doors indeed opened. Her relief at that was washed away at once by the bunker's lights fizzling out. Spinning back to the room and seeing Ward standing within the column of light cast from within the elevator. He'd caught the look of panic in her eyes and was moving towards her, assuring, "It's nothing to worry about. Probably just a break —"

But Crystal knew otherwise and cut him off, screaming, "Hurry! Get in. Everyone, get into the elevator. Move, goddammit, move!"

In the dark, all she could see of the actors were four beacons of light from the torches they'd activated on their phones. All of them were moving towards her at a fair clip and then the light in the rear gave out a sudden wobble. Its owner was toppling to the ground and the phone wrenched loose from his or her grip and skittering along the floor, alighting on Marlon as he wheeled around, bringing his light to bear. He was probing his beam over the floor, searching out Vincent's form, struggling on all fours to get up. There was a deep gash oozing blood running the length of his bare back and he could hardly muster the strength to raise himself even a few inches from the floor before he collapsed.

"Vinnie!" Malcolm cried out and then his phone was jerking up, illuminating the no less ghastly image of Grace. She wasn't more than a few feet in front of him, the deft rapidity with which she moved catching Malcolm off guard as she slashed the butcher knife on a quick horizontal, at level with his throat. The blade must have struck its mark, for he lurched backwards, dropping his phone and toppling after it, crumpling to the floor.

Aleesha gave out a scream and Crystal raised the shotgun but Grace had since disappeared back into the dark and all she could make out in it were two spots of light from the phones swinging in Aleesha and Dieter's hands as they charged headlong towards the elevator. It was Dieter who reached the square of light cast from within its doors first. No sooner had Crystal caught the look of utter panic on his face when a flash of light and a sharp *bang!* erupted from behind. The shot had hit him between the shoulder blades and exploded out through his chest, the force of it knocking his feet out from under him and sending him sprawling.

Then there was another flash and a *bang!* and Aleesha came reeling into the light. Her hands were hanging listlessly at her side and the phone was slipping from the one as the other clutched at her side, blood oozing through her fingers from a hole just above her navel. She was stumbling onwards, about to fall, and Crystal yelled back at Ward, "Grab her!" as she strode past, raising the shotgun.

Pressing the trigger and feeling the recoil of the blast knocking her back then pumping and firing again, aiming both shots into the pitch at about where she'd seen Grace's last muzzle flare.

She felt Ward then clutching at her arm. He was yelling, "Crystal, goddammit, get in here!" and she released one last blast as he dragged her backwards into the elevator. Aleesha was sitting propped against its far wall. A strand of bloody spittle was draining from the corner of her mouth and her eyes were staring up, wide and vacant. She was already as good as dead.

The doors were closing and Crystal turned back to them, seeing Grace striding into the ever-narrowing column of light, raising her head, and her face again appearing as from within a pool of black water. She was beaming with brazen and gleeful delight at the violence she'd wrought, and the malice beading in her eyes told Crystal she was all too eager for more.

"Dylan!"

Crystal was hustling down the front steps and Dylan spun her way, smiling as brightly as he always did whenever they met.

"Hey, sis," he said. "I was just in the neighbourhood, thought I'd drop — Whoa now, watch where you're pointing that thing!"

She was swinging the shotgun's barrel past him and sighting on Wyatt as she came onto the driveway.

"You stay right the fuck there!" she ordered and Wyatt looked back at her like she'd just commanded him to drink a cupful of angry hornets.

"Uh, what's going on, sis?"

"Get in the truck!" she ordered.

"But —"

"Just do it!"

Glancing back then at Ward.

He was only a few steps behind her and wearing the same expression he had ever since they'd escaped from the bunker, like he'd been hit in the back of the head with a brick and was one misstep away from falling down.

"What are you waiting for?" she yelled. "Move!"

The tenor in her voice seemed to bring him back to life and he was already hurrying for Dylan's Forester.

The same couldn't be said for her brother.

"Now hold on there, sis," he was saying, approaching her from the side. "There's something I think you really ought to know."

It was a line that immediately caught her off guard.

It was what he'd always said when they were growing up and he'd had some bad news to impart. His tone would be filled with the same casual aloof that imprinted it now, like whatever he had to say was of no undue importance so the surprise of informing her, say, that their dad had taken their poodle, Muffin, to the vet to be put down, or, when she was sixteen, that her then-boyfriend, Corey Vance, had been charged with drugging and raping a fourteen-year-old girl, would strike her double or treble, and Dylan seemingly taking untold pleasure in that.

The last time he'd sidelined her this way was when she was seventeen — it was how Crystal found out her mom had cancer. She'd never really forgiven him for that. Hearing him say it again after all these years had her twitching with the memory and she turned towards him with the utmost reluctance, to find he was holding what appeared to be a tranquilizer gun pointed directly at her.

342

It gave out a *pop!* and she felt a sudden stab in her neck.

"What the fuck!" she gasped as she snatched at the dart imbedded just above her collar.

She'd barely got it out when her head began to feel like it was filling with helium and her hands like two balloons floating away, her legs like straw. They were buckling beneath her. She heard the clatter of the shotgun hitting the cobblestones as it fell, and then she was falling too. As she tilted sideways, Dylan swept forward, grabbing her around the waist, holding her up. But it wasn't her well-being he was so much concerned about.

Whisking her around, he turned her to face Wyatt. Wyatt had his Glock raised in front of him, trying to catch a bead on Dylan's head as he ducked behind Crystal and scowling with the hateful gaze of an unwitting soldier who'd just let an enemy combatant get the drop on him.

"Let her go, Dylan!" Wyatt commanded and Crystal felt the scratch of Dylan's beard on the back of her neck as he peered out from behind the cover of her head.

"I'm afraid that's not how this is going to play out, Lieutenant."

No sooner had Dylan spoken than a red dot appeared dead centre on Wyatt's forehead. That halted his approach but he stood there with his finger still twitching on the trigger like he was considering even then taking the shot. Another red dot appeared on his breast and then one on his cheek and then three more winked on at once, roving over his chest, all of them telling Crystal there were at least five other men hidden somewhere in the dark, could have been all ex-soldiers like Dylan and Wyatt. Hell, it could have been their whole damn unit out there.

"You know the drill, soldier," Dylan said and Wyatt raised his hands over his head even as he knelt. He set the gun on the ground and then stood again, his eyes like two laser beams trying to drill holes right through the man standing in front of him.

"Don't you worry," Dylan was then saying, "I aim to give you a sporting chance. I owe you at least that. There's just one other matter —" His face then lighting up with something akin to unbridled joy as he cut himself off and exclaimed, "There she is now!"

Crystal turning with a bobble-headed thrust of her neck and seeing Grace coming down the stairs. She'd exchanged her black dress and wig for her pink jumpsuit. Her hair was dyed a vibrant orangish-red and styled into what looked like shoots of flame flourishing three inches above her head. She was carrying the bloodied butcher knife in one hand and in the other a side-arm of a military grade, painted pink. She didn't look so much like she'd just stepped out of a horror movie as out of a comic book, though from the sheen of brazen satisfaction on her face as she swaggered down the stairs, she could very well have been the heroine of a coming-of-age story who'd just transformed herself into the woman she'd always wanted to be.

She was raising the gun in her hand and Dylan spun with Crystal gripped like a life-sized Raggedy Ann doll so she could see Grace was sighting on Ward. He was standing in front of the Forester's open passenger side door, his eyes growing wide as his sister strode towards him.

"Grace, no," Ward gasped. "Please. Wait!"

A desperate plea at once answered and further punctuated by the sharp retort of the gun going off. The bullet struck him right between the eyes, splattering his blood and brains out the back of his head and shattering the vehicle's passenger side window. The impact had thrown him up against its door and Crystal was thrashing feebly against Dylan's hold, screaming, "Ward!" as he slid slowly towards the ground.

Grace was then approaching her, beaming with untold delight at what she'd just done — to her own brother! — and seemingly more so at the way Crystal was unleashing her wanton despair in staccato sobs, crying out, "No! No! No!"

She was still struggling against Dylan's hold but the fight had clearly gone out of her. She was sagging in his arms, helpless to do anything but peer down at Grace, who beamed up at her with Cassandra's gleeful malevolence while preening:

"Who's the poor little thing now?"

It was something Crystal herself had said once, or maybe thrice, talking about Grace, not meaning anything by it, but there it was nonetheless — the clue she was looking for to explain Grace's malicious intent, that seeming a trifle compared to what Grace and Dylan had just done.

Dylan had since procured a splitting axe from somewhere and was using its blade's blunt end to scratch at his back, playing a right old hick as he enthused in an exaggerated southern drawl, "Ain't she a peach!"

His voice carried within it the jubilation of a man who'd just found his one true love after a lifetime of searching and that feeling to Crystal like salt being poured into an open wound, since the one and only time she'd ever seen them together was at her wedding reception.

She'd gone out to grab a smoke on the country club's back terrace. She'd promised Ward she'd quit and so was hiding behind one of its potted cedar trees when she'd heard Dylan exclaim, "Nineteen?! I'm afraid I'm going to have to see your driver's licence before I believe that."

Peeking out through the cedars' boughs, she'd found Dylan and Grace standing at the terrace's rail. Dylan's back was to her so she couldn't make out his expression but she could see Grace was looking up at him with a coquettish come-hither look.

"So," she said, reaching out to the cuff of his shirt, rubbing it between a thumb and forefinger, "tell me about George."

"My grandfather?"

"You know," she'd said leaning closer and lowering her voice, "I've never told anyone this but . . . I'm his biggest fan."

The memory tunnelling through her haze and Crystal trying to fit that piece of the puzzle into the rest as if there was any sort of coherent picture that could possibly explain any of this. Dylan was lowering her into a lawn chair that had appeared out of nowhere and she flailed out at him with hands like two dead fish.

"You bastard!" she cried. "How could you? How could you?!"

"Shh!" Dylan said putting a finger over her lips. "Hush now. It'll all be over soon."

Her body felt all of a sudden hot like fresh taffy and it was as if she was looking through taffy too. The world was reduced to vague shadows growing dimmer and she felt her eyes drifting towards sleep. Snapped then into wakefulness by Grace grabbing her by the hair, forcing her head upwards with a vicious jerk.

"Wakey, wakey," she said and the sudden shock poked a hole through the caramelized blur so she could see again. Crystal's hands had since been attached to the chair with zip ties and all she could see in the entire world was her brother glowering down at her.

"We're here today to talk about pain," he was declaring with the reverent bluster of a soapbox minister, "we're here to talk about deprivation, we're here to talk about fucking sacrifice!"

As he spoke he was removing his jacket and then his T-shirt, both in the service of revealing the tattoo emblazoned on his chest. It was of *a green and leafy tree cast against a diffusion of oranges and reds as would colour a sky approaching dusk* — a line from one of her grandfather's books, she couldn't remember exactly which, though probably it was *The Sons of Adam* since it was a carbon copy of the tattoo worn by the titular biker-gang-cum-doomsday-cult.

That seeming like a cold splash of water, since Dylan had always told her he'd never even read a single one of their grandfather's fictions. It was clear now that if he'd been lying to her about that all these years, he must have been lying to her about a lot of other things too.

"I don't know why you're looking so surprised, sis," he was then saying, bending almost close enough to Crystal for their noses to touch. "What'dya think was gonna happen? Hiding out all these years with your head in the clouds, building your little castles in the sky, frittering away all that privilege while the world goes to shit around you. Oblivious to everything and everyone . . ." — shaking his head and *tsk tsk tsk*ing — "even your own mother . . . dying."

Crystal opening her mouth, trying to speak, to defend herself, to tell him he had it all wrong, that she was a good person who cared about those around her — she really did! — sometimes even a little too much. But her tongue might as well have been made out of cement and her jaw a rusted-over spring from the squeak that came out — all she could mount in her drugged state by way of a protest.

"I expected more from you, sis, I really did," Dylan was saying as he stood back up, taking the axe again and using its blunt end this time to scratch at the scar on his cheek. "Oh well, nothing we can do about that now."

Crystal hearing a sudden roar and Dylan arching his head, watching a helicopter swooping in low just over the tree line, kicking up a torrent of dust and wind as it angled towards the landing platform on the cottage's roof.

"Shoot," he said, "there's my ride. I guess we ought to dispense with the rest of the preamble and just get at her."

Turning away from Crystal, he gave the splitting axe a lackadaisical swing as he approached Wyatt. Wyatt had since come to be holding an identical axe suspended between both hands, though the red sights dotted about his face and chest had precluded all thoughts of using it. Dylan knocked the head of his axe on the cobblestones, twice, and the dots all disappeared at once and then there was only ten feet of cobblestones between him and Wyatt. The look of open and tremulous hate in her chauffeur's eyes was telling Crystal he'd a score to settle with Dylan long before then and also that he didn't think it likely he'd live long enough to settle it now.

Dylan was goading him with "I toldya you should have joined The Sons when you had the chance," and Wyatt charged forward, swinging the axe only to have Dylan dodge lithely out of the way.

"That's the spirit!" he exulted, coming back at the other with a swing of his own.

But all of a sudden it seemed so far away to Crystal — a flickering of lights — vague and inconsequential — projected onto some faraway screen that was even then receding into the distance.

She could hardly breathe.

17

It was Chief Marchand who'd given Deacon the news.

The day after the flood, he'd dropped by the barn to tell him in person that Crystal was dead, apparently poisoned, and so was Ward — shot in the head — as were eight others who'd been at the Swansons' wilderness retreat. Six of those had been actors and one the groundskeeper, the last Crystal and Ward's bodyguard and chauffeur, Wyatt. The latter still had what would later be determined to be Kylie Farmer's splitting axe planted in his head when the RCMP had arrived, too late to get their man this time.

Deacon spent the next two days and nights lying on his couch, blaming himself and suckling at his grief, as moribund as if he'd drunk himself into oblivion, though he hadn't taken even a sip from what was left in the bottle of Canadian Club. It was also Marchand who'd finally wrench him back towards life. He'd shown up on the third morning after the flood, banging on the door and threatening to kick it in unless Deacon opened up. When Deacon finally had, Marchand informed him in no uncertain terms that he was to be at the station at one the next afternoon to have "a little sit down" with Detective Grieves, the lead investigator on the case, who considered him "a person of interest" for reasons never specified. Deacon arrived at the scheduled time only to be told that Grieves was running late, though Deacon would shortly be given some cause to suspect that Marchand had called him early for reasons entirely of his own.

As Deacon settled into his chair, the Chief was fixing him with a rueful glare and tugging on his moustache.

"You going to tell me where he is, *Deke?*" he said, getting right to the point.

Only Dylan ever called him "Deke," and Marchand using that to punctuate what he said made it seem like more of an accusation than a question. It already had Deacon squirming in his seat, thinking maybe Marchand knew more than he was letting on.

"I- I don't know," he answered.

That much was the truth, though from the way he'd faltered, it came out sounding even to himself like a lie, and he quickly added, "You might want to ask Grace about that."

When he'd learned Grace had been the lone survivor he knew she must have somehow been involved, and from the way she'd acted on New Year's Eve — the night Baby Rose was murdered — he was equally certain she must have been in on it right from the start. The Swanson family's lawyer had released a statement asking the media to respect her privacy while she recovered from such a traumatic experience and, as far as Deacon knew, she hadn't spoken to anyone since. Without any evidence to back up his own suspicions, he'd kept those to himself, and from the castigating frown with which Marchand was glowering at him, he wished he hadn't said anything about her now either.

"Are you talking about Grace *Swanson?*" Marchand asked, though the implication should have been plenty clear.

It was too late to do anything but barge onwards and so Deacon said, "She must have been in on it right from the start. There's no two ways about it. And if she conspired along with Dylan, that means she's probably as psychotic as he is."

Marchand took a moment to digest that before tugging at his moustache and asking, "So you're saying she helped Dylan kill the Wane family too?"

That's not what he'd meant at all but Marchand saying that gave Deacon every indication he'd drawn a few conclusions of his own. Could have been he was baiting Deacon, that he thought Deacon had somehow been involved in Dylan's plot and was hoping to catch him up in a lie. This thought doing little to loosen Deacon's tongue.

"Well?" Marchand prompted when it was obvious Deacon wasn't going to say anything else.

"No," Deacon said, completely unsure as to what he might say next. "I mean — As far as I know, the first time they met was at Crystal's wedding."

He'd seen them talking on the Rosedale Country Club's back patio when he'd gone out to have a smoke.

"And that was what, two years after the Wanes were killed?"

"Roundabouts."

Marchand jotting that down in his notebook and then tapping the pen against the page a couple of times before looking up again.

"So she couldn't have been in on it from the start, then."

He had him there and Deacon sidestepped any considerations of that, thinking about when he could logically deduce she'd become involved.

"New Year's Eve," he said, not really meaning to speak it aloud, but there it was nevertheless. When that only served to raise Marchand's eyebrows, he continued, "It must have been Grace who murdered Baby Rose."

"Baby Rose?"

"Crystal and Ward's daughter."

"I wasn't aware they had a daughter."

"Well, no. I mean. She was still a fetus at the time. They poisoned her and Crystal spent a week in the hospital up in North Bay afterwards."

Marchand was writing in his notebook again and when he'd finished he asked, "So let me get this straight. You're saying that on New Year's Eve, Grace Swanson, in collusion with Dylan Cleary, poisoned Crystal, resulting in the death of her unborn baby, and then two and a half months later they brutally murdered ten people together."

"That's right."

"You have any evidence to back that up?"

The only real evidence he had was a niggling doubt in the back of his mind, thinking of how Grace had acted on New Year's Eve, but how to formulate that night into any semblance of coherency seemed well beyond him.

"So that's a no," Marchand said, intuiting that.

"But she was involved. I know she was!"

There was enough urgency in his voice that Marchand at least seemed willing to consider what he said. He was back to tapping his pen against the pad and he added to this a rather abrupt tug at his moustache so that it seemed to Deacon he was about to finally say something.

Instead, though, he opened the file folder sitting in front of him. Putting on his bifocals, he leafed through the hundred or so pages contained within until he'd found what he was looking for.

"When Miss Swanson," he read, "was asked by this investigator why she thought the alleged perpetrator of these crimes had spared her, she answered —" Clearing his throat and taking a sip from his travel mug, squinting at the page as if he couldn't quite yet believe what it said, before continuing. "She answered (through tears) that Dylan Cleary told her he didn't want to, quote, 'deprive Deke of his little fuck doll.'"

Deacon flushing red and it feeling like the chair beneath him was turning to quicksand as Marchand peered at him over the rims of his glasses, not so much in silent reproach but with the stern countenance of an elder cop warning a rookie it'd be best for everyone involved — himself in particular — if he kept such accusations to himself.

As to what the consequences of disregarding his warning might be, all Marchand said was, "This is the picture Miss Swanson provided to investigators when they asked who this 'Deke' fella was." Pulling out a sheet from the file and holding up a copy of a picture Grace must have taken on New Year's Eve, though Deacon had no memory if it. They were lying in her bed, Deacon on his back, naked and drenched in sweat, grinning at the camera like God's own fool. Grace was naked too and snuggled up beside him, her arm wriggled under his head so she could snap the post-coital selfie and otherwise looking as much like a thirteen-year-old girl as she ever had.

The chair beneath Deacon was beginning to feel more like lava than quicksand as he watched Marchand, his meaning made clear, slip the photo back into the file.

"I hate to think of how Becca would feel, seeing something like that," Marchand said by way of drawing another conclusion of his own, though the truth of the matter was that it was Laney who'd sprung immediately to Deacon's mind. It came as quite a surprise to him that he'd think of her since he hadn't thought of Officer Myers for some time but Marchand didn't give him even a moment to linger on her.

"Is there anything else you'd like to add?" he asked, closing the file.

Deacon shook his head and Marchand looked at his watch.

"Well, I guess I better go and see what's keeping Detective Grieves," he said, standing and heading for the door.

Whether Marchand believed what he'd said about Grace, Deacon couldn't tell. He was equally unsure as to whether he'd intended Grace's quote and the photo as a warning or a threat as to what might be in store for Deacon if he felt inclined to spread such spurious rumours about the only surviving child of the richest man in the country. Either way, it was clear to him why he'd become "a person of interest" in the RCMP's investigation and though he'd spend the next four hours talking with Detective Grieves about his relationship with Dylan Cleary, he'd never, not once, felt inclined to utter the name "Grace Swanson" to her.

18

I t was the following Sunday that the town council had set
aside for the memorial service to pay tribute to the victims of
the flood and the ensuing fireball.

One hundred and fifty-seven were confirmed dead, with
twelve people still unaccounted for. While Tildon's residents
had only been allowed back into their homes on the Friday after
the evacuation, Mayor Wylde had urged the council to pass his
motion so, in his words, "the good people of Tildon could begin
the long road towards healing."

The service was held in the arena — the largest venue in town
— though even that wasn't enough to handle the multitudes
who'd come to share their grief. Closed-circuit TVs were set up
in the lobby and both conference rooms and when those were full
the organizers scrounged up a digital projector so the mourners
stranded outside could still watch the service screened on a white
sheet suspended over the arena's front doors.

Deacon had arrived late and watched from the back of the crowd, seeing little from where he was but hearing every word loud and clear. After the mayor had read the names of those whose lives had been so "unduly and prematurely ended by the tragedy," Mesaquakee's MP, Gavin Acheson, mounted the podium. He had a prepared speech but only got through the first line of that before setting it aside, overcome with emotion and telling his constituents after he regained his composure that the words of comfort that he'd originally written seemed to him false, given the tenor of the times.

"We don't need to be comforted," he declared, "what we need is justice. Justice is the only thing that can restore to me, and I'm sure to many of you, the country which that terrorist stole from us eight days ago. And Dylan Cleary is a terrorist, make no mistake. He's a terrorist because his only goal was to spread fear and chaos, to deprive us of our sense of well-being and our security — our very sense of ourselves — and I make a pledge to you now that I will not sleep a single wink until he is either behind bars or in the ground."

His speech came across to Deacon as mere electioneering but it seemed to have struck a chord with the assembled mourners. They greeted it with the reverent murmur of congregants moved towards exultation by a particularly compelling sermon. The people in front of Deacon were all nodding and the cries of "justice" were rippling throughout like swells within a stormy sea, quieted only when the mayor returned to ask every one to bow their heads for a minute of silent reflection.

The service ended with the playing of "O Canada." The crowd sang along in hushed whispers. Husbands hugged their wives and mothers their daughters, a smattering of fathers standing proud with one hand on heart, the other rested on their son's head or shoulder; Deacon could see one holding a baby slapping joyously at the tears running down his father's face like a child smacking a stick into a puddle of water.

The man was full-bearded with a belly to match and dressed in his Sunday best. He immediately looked familiar to Deacon but it was only when the crowd began to disperse and the man had turned full-face towards him that Deacon saw it was none other than the Grizzly Adams look-alike who'd slammed his hands on Deacon's Jeep the night of the flood, ordering, "You stay right the fuck there, asshole!" The man didn't seem to have recognized him and Deacon was thankful at least for that as he watched him shuffling down James Street with his infant son. A woman wearing a simple black dress and holding the hand of a school-aged girl dressed the same was walking beside him and the family halted when they came to a stuffed Snoopy dog affixed to the guardrail spanning the southernmost perimeter of the arena's parking lot.

Deacon had since learned that the toddler he'd seen pummelled against it like a stick of driftwood had succumbed to his injuries and his mother had used his favourite stuffed animal to memorialize the spot where she'd lost her son. From the way Grizzly Adams was burying his face in his prodigious hand, sobbing unconstrained, it seemed to Deacon that the boy may very well have died in his arms. His body was bucking with the force of his anguish and his wife was rubbing at his back, trying to offer him whatever comfort she could.

During the past week Deacon had felt himself sliding into an emotionless void so complete he no longer felt much of anything at all, but watching the big man weeping so brazenly opened up his own floodgates and he was powerless but to sob right along with him.

O ver the following weeks he'd be given plenty of other reasons to cry and where he'd shed most of his tears was at funerals.

Of Tildon's churches, only the Catholic and the Anglican — across from each other on McMurray Street — were wholly spared the ravages of the flood and the ensuing explosion. Both were booked solid through April with a seemingly endless slate of funerals and Deacon attended every last one of those. He was always first to arrive and the last to leave, which seemed the least he could do to pay penance for the not inconsiderable part his indecision — or rather, his outright cowardice — had played in the tragedy.

Crystal's and Ward's were held together at the same place they'd been married — the Metropolitan United Church on Queen Street East in Toronto. The date — April 1st — was chosen to coincide with what would have been their eighth anniversary, which had also been designated by a unanimous vote in the House of Commons as a national day of mourning to honour, in the prime minister's words, "some of our country's brightest lights being extinguished all at once."

Deacon's Grand Cherokee had been reduced to a charred husk by the explosion caused, he'd learned, by eight canisters of crude petroleum fuel that had become bottlenecked in the bridge spanning Tildon Falls. He'd yet to find the time to get another vehicle and had been driven down to the city in the backseat of Gabe's RAV4, spending most of those two hours shaking a baby's rattle, trying to mollify a screaming Adele, who, Cheryl had warned him when he'd asked for a ride, had been teething all week.

Any hope he had of finding a measure of solace sitting in the back of the church was stripped from him before he'd even made its front steps. Gabe and Cheryl had lingered behind so they could change Adele's diaper on the church's expansive front lawn and Deacon was standing alone taking furtive drags on a cigarette when he saw two men dressed in black suits and dark sunglasses coming down the stairs, quite obviously headed towards him. At first he thought they might be ushers come to advise him smoking wasn't allowed on the property, though they looked more like secret service agents tasked with protecting a visiting head of state.

He was disabused of the former notion the moment the first one spoke.

"Are you Deacon Riis?" the man asked.

"I am," Deacon answered.

"I'm sorry to inform you that you will not be allowed to attend the service."

Deacon, dumbstruck, blurted, "What do you mean I'm not allowed to attend the service?"

"I'm sorry, sir, but that comes straight from Mr. Swanson. We've been told to escort you off the property, if need be."

He was already grabbing for Deacon's arm and Deacon flinched, jerking backwards out of the man's reach. The security agent on the stairs was hurrying to offer his partner assistance and Deacon turned away, worried that anything he might say to either would only provide them with an excuse to make good on that threat. Cheryl was pushing Adele towards him in the stroller and Gabe was walking beside her, his expression dour and a question curdling on his lips.

"What's going on, Deacon?" he asked.

"They're not going to let me in."

"Not let you in? Why wouldn't they let you in?"

Could have been that Mr. Swanson thought Deacon was somehow involved in his son's death; or maybe he'd also seen the post-coital pic Grace snapped and simply couldn't bear the thought of someone like him being with his only daughter.

"Orders from Mr. Swanson, they say," Deacon answered, sidestepping any further consideration.

"That's strange." Glancing then over at the two security agents. "Did they say anything about us?"

Gabe was wearing the same expression as he so often had since hearing it was his cousin who'd blown the reservoirs before killing ten others, one of whom was his own sister — a stilted look of apprehension, more embarrassed than mortified, as if Dylan's real endgame had been to sully the Clearys' otherwise upstanding name.

"No," Deacon answered, "they only mentioned me."

That seemed to give Gabe a measure of comfort. He nodded anyway before turning back to Deacon.

"What are you going to do?" he asked.

"Well, I guess I'm going to wait out here."

Gabe was still staring over at the two men and, though nothing about them suggested they were the type to be easily given over to persuasion, he offered, "I could have a word with them."

"Don't bother. I'll just grab a coffee somewhere."

Gabe nodded, apparently relieved for an easy way out.

Neither security agent so much as twitched when Gabe and Cheryl hefted the stroller between them and up the church steps. After he saw them safely inside, Deacon lit another cigarette and smoked it while staring over at the two security agents, his anger mounting with every drag, though he wasn't really angry with them. He was angry about Crystal — lying in a coffin and at least partway because of him — and about Dylan and Grace, who'd put her there and were still roaming free; and he thought, at last, of Michael Swanson, the richest man in the country, who'd offered a five-million-dollar reward for any information leading to Dylan's capture but who, Crystal had once confided, treated Ward more like a nuisance than a beloved only son and who seemed more concerned about his standing on the Fortune 500 than he ever was about his own flesh and blood.

Finding there a welcome focus for his rage and that feeling like just another form of mania, which Deacon welcomed with the warm embrace of a dear old friend as he muttered, "That goddamn fucking bastard!"

19

Rain was married on June 21st and Deacon treated her wedding like it was a funeral.

He'd received the invitation hand-delivered in his mailbox only the day before and that made him suspect she hadn't planned on inviting him at all. "Please Come Celebrate the Loving Union of Barry Wylde and Rain Meadows" the card had read in gold-embossed letters and his surprise at discovering that Rain was marrying the town's mayor was only slightly greater than the fact that she would be doing so at the Tildon United Church, since she'd often remarked that she had about as much use for churches as she did for politicians.

That she'd marry one in the other came as a double blow. While Rain had found the wherewithal to move on, here was Deacon practically falling over standing still. He'd thrown the card in the garbage and sworn he'd never go and yet here he was the very next day, sitting in the back of the church before even the ushers had arrived, idling his time reading *East of Eden* as a shield against the slow trickle of well-wishers filling the pews.

He'd been spending a lot of time with Steinbeck over the past few weeks. There was a comfort in his words that Deacon derived from precious few other authors, partly because he wrote of the world as it was rather than as he merely imagined, or wished, it to be and partly because of how Deacon had been introduced to him. It was after he'd finished reading *The Stray* for the fifth time and was running his finger along the spines of George's other books on his way back to *A Bad Man's Son*.

When Deacon had come into the barn George had been napping in his reading chair, as he often did on hot summer afternoons, but he was awake by the time Deacon was turning back to the room with the book in his hand.

"What'dya got there?" the old man asked, squinting against the low light.

Deacon held the book up for him to see and if there was an expression that was the diametric opposite to the one he'd been wearing standing at the house's rear sliding door the first time he'd observed Deacon reading one of his fictions, it was the one planted on his face right then.

"I was thinking," he said rather gruffly, "maybe you ought to give mine a rest for a while."

Reading George's books had become the only connection, albeit a tenuous one, Deacon had left with his family and he was just opening his mouth to protest when George cut him off.

"Go on, put it back," he said.

There was no arguing with his tone and Deacon grudgingly obliged, slipping it back onto the shelf where it belonged.

"If you're looking for something else to read, you could do worse than Steinbeck," George had then offered.

"Steinbeck?" Deacon had asked. "Isn't he the guy you quoted at the beginning of *Nickel Down*?"

"He is, and for good reason too."

That being convincing enough for Deacon and he needn't look further than the shelf above George's fictions to see twenty or so of Steinbeck's books collected there.

"Which one was it?" he asked, scouring over the titles.

"The book I quoted?"

"Yeah."

"I wouldn't want to spoil the surprise. My advice would be to start with his first and work your way up from there."

But starting from the last had served Deacon well enough with George's books and so he'd taken *Travels with Charley* down instead. After that he'd read *Cup of Gold* and a dozen others before George had read him the quote from *Another Country* and he'd switched to James Baldwin. He'd never come across the passage George had used as *Nickel Down*'s epigraph and though he could have easily googled it, that seemed too much like cheating. He was thus gratified to see that it was staring up at him on the page right now, and he thought, *One mystery solved anyway. Maybe not the most important but at least it was something.*

To quote:

"There's more beauty in the truth even if it is dreadful beauty. The storytellers at the city gate twist life so that it looks sweet to the lazy and the stupid and the weak, and this only strengthens their infirmities and teaches nothing, cures nothing, nor does it let the heart soar."

Reading over again what Lee had told Adam Trask in *East of Eden*, Deacon's thoughts were drawn to his own proposed version of *No Quarter*. He'd been thinking about it more and more of late, telling himself that since everything was out in the open now anyway, it was maybe about time he finally got around to writing it. If there was any truth to be gleaned from what Dylan had done, it would certainly have to be of the dreadful kind and, staring down at Lee's lament, he was altogether uncertain whichever way he'd tell it, he'd be able to teach anything or cure anyone, much less find the means to let the heart soar.

It all seemed so fucking horrible.

And yet, he asked himself, *was it any worse than anything George wrote* or, thinking about what he'd written last, *what's woven, and continues to weave, the very fabric of who we are as a nation.*

The epigraph George had used in his *No Quarter* spoke of a soul left in darkness. He'd made it pretty clear throughout the book that the darkness had infected the Kraniches, Del and Emma, Big Willy and his gang and even Mason Lowry, sparing no one except Dalton Briggs — the cop who'd found Emma Dupuis after she'd killed Reinhold Kranich, a character plainly based on his grandson Dylan. Dalton had been the one who'd blown the propane tank behind the Kraniches' property to serve as a distraction while he rescued Emma, no doubt a bit of wishful thinking on George's part, for he must have at least suspected by then that his epigraph's darkness had already blackened Dylan's soul more than most.

Aside from Dalton, there was precious little light in the book at all, except . . . except that wasn't entirely true either.

There was a light, he thought, *if only the light George shone by writing it.*

The book itself was George's means of banishing the darkness, he told himself, *and so it followed that if you want to tell your own version of events, it will have to do the same.*

But how would I go about doing that?

It was a question that would have to wait for another day, though, as the opening notes of "Here Comes the Bride" were calling out from the pipe organ at the front of the church.

The service was about to begin.

The United Church had been one of the first buildings to be restored. Mainly that involved replacing its stained-glass windows and its roof, the latter of which had been sheared clean off in the explosion. Deacon had written an article in the *Chronicle*'s as of yet only online edition to commemorate the restoration and in Rain's vows she used the rebuilding, and the wedding itself, as an all-too-obvious metaphor for the hope proffered through such clearly evidenced signs of renewal and resilience.

She was wearing one of her handsewn dresses — a kaleidoscope of colours that seemed as out of place at a wedding as it would have at a memorial — and Barry a rather plain grey suit enlivened only slightly by a pink tie. But the contrast in their apparel only furthered the impression of how seemingly miraculous it was that two such obviously different people could have found each other. She ended her vows by professing that love had come to her late in life, "long after I'd given up hope that I'd ever find true love at all," and how her love for Barry, "so unexpected, has renewed my faith in the power of love itself."

Her words struck Deacon as an affront to the love for her that he'd coveted and had him sinking into his pew, feeling much like he had in Marchand's office when the chief had read him Grace's statement. But then Rain had never gazed so lovingly, and publicly, at him like she was gazing at her soon-to-be-husband and he knew he'd been wrong. He'd never loved her and she certainly had never loved him *and if you want to be completely honest with yourself*, he thought acrimoniously, *you've never really loved anyone at all.*

He was feeling worse listening to Rain speak than he ever had listening to the seemingly endless litany of eulogies. It was as if her words really were "weapons full of danger, full of death" and spoke to him not so much of *her* future-oh-so-bright but of *his* own lack thereof.

In his wallow, he barely caught a word of what Barry said, only that he finished, apparently going off-script, by taking Rain's hand in his and gazing into her eyes as he confessed, "You've not only renewed my faith in love but in life itself, and even if we live to be two hundred years old I'll never be able to repay you for the gift you've given me."

Deacon was still sitting in his pew after most of the other congregants had followed the newly wedded couple up the aisle and then down the front steps.

He'd only afforded Rain the most fleeting of glimpses as she'd passed and was startled to see that she was staring straight back at him. But only for an instant. The moment their eyes had locked she'd looked away, shying from the resident glower on his face with such abrupt disdain as if her point had been to tell him, unequivocally, that whatever shit *he* was going through right now, it wasn't *her* problem anymore.

So close on the heels of the sucker punch to the gut that hearing her vows had been, this felt like her going out of her way to kick him when he was down. He'd been sitting there stewing ever since, not so much thinking of Rain but of the walk home and the empty bunkie awaiting his return.

The only other people still left in the church were two middle-aged women who had been sitting right up front. They'd also been waiting for everyone else to leave and were now coming up the aisle. The one on the right was short and stout and wearing a simple wine-coloured pantsuit. The one on the left was only marginally taller and was wearing a summer dress with a floral design. She had an oddly misshapen face, like her real face had been torn clean off and then stitched back on by a blind surgeon, and was walking with a lopsided hobble with her one hand clamped in a desperate clutch onto the crooked arm of the other.

"She really is a marvel," the latter was saying when they'd come within earshot.

"I've been telling you that for years," the other replied, somewhat brusquely, as if they'd had this conversation many times before and she'd resigned herself to just letting it play itself out.

"But I couldn't — I couldn't have — The way the room grew so suddenly cold and then they'd found Lenny buried in the snow, not even an hour later."

The mention of the room going cold and more so of Lenny had Deacon sitting bolt upright in his pew, staring at the woman who he now knew must be Eleanor Wilson.

"I mean, how do you explain that?" she was saying and the other woman answered, "When it comes to Rain Meadows, I've found some things are best left unexplained."

No truer words had ever been spoken, though Eleanor didn't seem entirely satisfied with her friend's response.

"Maybe so," she started, "but —"

Whatever she'd meant to say, she didn't get a chance, for a husky voice was then calling to her from the end of the aisle.

"Eleanor, just the person I was looking for!"

The man was even then coming into the church, walking stoop-backed with mincing steps like every single one caused him considerable pain, and Deacon saw it was Rod Norris. He owned a boarding kennel up on Kirk Line, just outside of town, and was wearing the same grey suit and pink tie as Barry Wylde, having just served as an usher at the wedding.

"You're looking for me?" Eleanor asked with enough inflection in her voice to suggest it came as a great surprise that anyone could possibly be looking for her.

"Actually," Rod amended, as he drew near, "I was looking for your boy."

"Jody?"

"He was supposed to come by this week to clear some brush — the property's become a jungle ever since I put out my back — but he never showed. I tried calling him but he's not answering his phone."

Frustration was written clear in his voice and it wasn't much relieved when Eleanor said, "Oh, Jody's gone."

"Gone?"

"And it was the strangest darn thing too."

"How's that?"

"Well, I heard a noise — a clattering — coming from the garage in the middle of the night. It was on March 21, I remember because it was the very next day that Officer Cleary blew those two reservoirs, which I thought was an odd sort of coincidence, since him and Jody had once been so close."

"Jody knew Dylan Cleary?"

There was a taint of panic in Rod's voice, as there generally was when people spoke Dylan's name, as if he'd since become some sort of bogeyman, haunting the nightmares — waking or otherwise — of everyone in Mesaquakee.

"Since Jody was twelve," Eleanor said, "though as far as I know they haven't seen each other for years."

That came as a shock to Deacon as much as it did to Rod but while Deacon would have liked nothing better than to hear more, Rod seemed to want to change the subject as quick as he could.

"You were saying something about hearing a noise in the garage?" he prompted.

"Yes, I heard a noise — a clattering. I haven't been able to sleep much since my accident — I just can't get comfortable in bed — and so I was awake, even though it was two o'clock in the morning. At first I thought maybe I'd left the door open and a racoon had got in — it's happened before — but when I went to investigate I found it was Jody."

"Jody was in your garage at two o'clock in the morning? What was he doing?"

"He was loading his truck up with food."

"Food?"

"I always keep a shelf in the garage stocked with non-perishables, you know, for when my other kids drop by. My eldest, he has three boys, and they can eat through —"

"But why would he be taking food from your garage at two a.m.?"

"I asked him that very same thing myself. He said he was leaving."

"Leaving?"

"He said Milt — that's my eldest — had found him a job in Fort Mac. Said the offer was only good for a few days and that he'd have to leave right away."

"But why did he need all the food?"

"You know, he never did say. I guessed maybe it was because they were driving out and didn't want to waste any time stopping for groceries."

"And he took his wife and son? Sorry, I can't remember their names."

"Tina and Clyde."

"He took them with him?"

"Oh, he'd as soon leave them behind as he would chop off one of his arms. I never knew a more devoted father and husband — or son, for that matter — than my Jody."

They'd come to the doors and were moving towards the stairs.

"Fort Mac," Rod was saying as they passed from Deacon's view, "that's a helluva drive with a toddler."

"Oh, you don't have to tell me!"

Thereafter their voices were reduced to receding whispers, none of which Deacon could make out, though he'd heard plenty enough by then already.

It seemed hardly coincidental that Jody's father had turned up buried under a snowbank with a quote from one of George's fictions tacked to his steering wheel and that Jody had then fled town on the very eve of Dylan's twin climax! Thinking then again of *No Quarter* and what had happened to Reinhold Kranich, the same thing which would later happen to Ronald Crane. Deacon had always assumed that Dylan had killed Crane, his first salvo in the war he was waging to bring George's last book to life. Hearing what Eleanor Wilson had just said, it seemed to Deacon all at once that it could just as easily have been her son, Jody. Ten years ago, he'd have been about the same age as Emma Dupuis and if he had killed Ronald Crane, it stood to reason that he'd also killed his father ten years later, likely for what he'd done to his mom.

Thinking of Lenny buried in the snow led naturally back to what Eleanor had said about the room growing cold — the exact same thing Rain had told him — and that led to how many times he'd thought to himself that there was nothing about Rain that could possibly surprise him anymore. And yet here was irrefutable evidence — like she was offering him one last, final parting shot — that where she was concerned, it was never too late for *her* to prove *him* wrong.

20

"**R**ough night?"

Gabe was standing at the bunkie's open door, staring over at Deacon on the couch, who was rubbing the sleep out of his eyes and wincing against the throbbing pain turning his temples into a belfry at high noon. The bottle that had done most of the damage was still on the coffee table next to an overflowing ashtray. Gabe's eyes had wandered to those but then his gaze fastened on what was sitting beside them.

"Hey, is that Gramps's gun?" he asked, starting into the room. "I always wondered where it'd got to." He was reaching down for it and then stopped, looking to Deacon for his consent.

"Do you mind?"

"Knock yourself out."

Picking it up, Gabe's hand settled over its grip and his index finger on its trigger.

"Gramps was right," he said. "It really does seem to know how it should be held."

Striking a pose then like a gunslinger facing off against a foe on the main street of some podunk western town. Before he could quickdraw, something must have occurred to him and he turned back to Deacon.

"You still got that meeting with Frank Darling at ten?" he asked and Deacon knew that was the real reason Gabe had knocked on his door a few seconds ago, probably noticing the lights were still out and thinking Deacon must have slept in.

"Is it Monday already?" Deacon asked, reaching for the pack of smokes on the coffee table.

"It is."

"Then I guess I must. What time is it?"

"Almost nine thirty."

"I better get a move on, then," Deacon said, lighting the cigarette in his mouth and taking a long and lusty drag, clearly in no particular hurry.

Gabe was setting the gun back on the coffee table as Deacon exhaled. He spent a moment staring down at it as if there was something else on his mind but he hadn't quite summoned the courage to broach whatever it was. It was a look he'd been harbouring more and more of late but whatever was on his mind, he must have decided that it could wait for yet another day.

"Catch you at the Arc," he said, turning for the door.

The Arc was what Deacon had christened the loft over Grover's garage. Grover had been using it as a satellite office for the Canadian Association of Black Journalists, of which he served as treasurer, and had offered it up as temporary lodgings for the *Chronicle*. The first thing Gabe had done after they'd moved in was change the masthead on the paper's website from "Our Town. Our Stories." back to "How About Some Good News for a Change?" It seemed more fitting, given what they'd just been through, and boy did Grover ever make a big deal over that.

"Don't forget your shovel," Deacon answered and though he'd said it a dozen times, Gabe shot him a wry, conspiratorial grin on his way out the door.

Mercifully alone again, Deacon closed his eyes against the encroaching light and the throbbing pain in his temples. He'd been dreaming of Laney before Gabe had awoken him — though really it was more of a memory than a dream good and proper — and he sought it out again as a salve against the dour monotony of another day spent alone.

He and Laney had been coming back from the Calgary Stampede. He was in the passenger seat of her vintage Chevy C10 pick-up truck and she in the driver's. She had one hand draped over the wheel and the other out the window, her palm open to the breeze, catching the first drops of rain that were just then spattering the windshield, a welcome bit of cool in the unrelenting heat that had dogged them since they'd passed into Saskatchewan. There was a red Twizzler dangling out of the corner of her mouth and she was chewing on it with the lassitude of a farmer chewing on a stalk of grass gone to seed, like she hadn't a care in the world even though the sky behind them was black, the winds gale force, and an emergency broadcast had only moments ago interrupted an old-timey country singer who was warning a Mr. Toronto Man to stay away from his door with an equally dire warning about a tornado threatening from North Dakota.

It had always been his favourite memory of her. So bright was the light it shone that it seemed to have burnt itself into his mind's retina, for after Gabe had left, it was still there waiting for him when he closed his eyes. As he drove his new-to-him 2022 Grand Cherokee to Meeford Cove, where he'd arranged to meet Frank Darling for his weekly progress report on the Mesaquakee Lake clean-up operations, Laney was ever on his mind — funny little memories rising up like leaves swirling in a creek filled with the spring thaw, almost but not quite chasing away the spectre of her disembodied gape — a reflection of his own expression on the night they'd parted ways and his only memory of her since she'd ghosted him.

He was still thinking about her while he took the back way to Windermere, the small settlement on the outskirts of which Loretta and Grover, upon retiring, had built their dream home on two hundred acres of mostly hardwoods. It was only when he was driving down Windermere Side Road that he remembered he'd meant to nip over to the reserve so he could drop in on Tawyne. After the flood, he'd returned to living with his aunt Jean and over the past two months they hadn't seen each other all that much.

But he could already see Grover's modest two-storey brick house coming into view through the maple trees lining the driveway and, activating his left turn signal, he promised himself he'd stop in and check on Tawyne tomorrow.

After he'd posted his update of the clean-up efforts on the *Chronicle*'s website, he stepped out onto the platform atop the Arc's exterior stairs to have a smoke. To his right, Loretta was kneeling in the garden behind the garage, pulling at the weeds encroaching on her strawberries, and Grover was sitting on the bench under an apple tree in the orchard on its far side, his two border collies — Cain and Mabel — sleeping at his feet. He was reading a book and Deacon hadn't been standing there for more than a drag when he looked up from its pages. Deacon raised his arm, about to wave, and then realized Grover wasn't looking up at him but over at his wife. Neither of them had said a word, as far as Deacon could hear, but she was gazing over at her husband at the exact same moment. Though Deacon couldn't see her face, he could see a glowing reflection of it in Grover's, smiling with the beneficent expression of a Buddhist monk who'd just achieved nirvana, as if he couldn't want for anything in the world but what he had right here.

Such a minor thing — two old people smiling at each other across their yard — but in that moment it spoke to Deacon of something far more profound, of how they'd found each other, some might say against all odds, and of the life they'd made together ever since. It seemed to him if you were to distill the secret of the world into one fleeting glimpse, that would serve as well as any other, and as he started down the stairs, he knew he couldn't go another day without seeing Laney, even if it was only one last time.

21

E laine Myers lived in an old brick farmhouse on fourteen acres outside of Utterson at the end of a cul-de-sac off the 142, just before it intersected with Highway 4. It was only ten minutes later that Deacon was pulling into her driveway.

Her Chevy wasn't parked where it usually was, a few feet from her front door, and as he pulled into her spot he was thinking, *She's probably at work.*

If she was working the day shift she'd be home within the hour, unless she had other plans, of course. Shifting into park, he opened the door, pulling his smokes from his pocket and knowing he'd wait for her all night, if that's what it took to see her again.

The house was built at the top of a small hill that sloped into the five-acre field where Laney had built a barn and a paddock for her horse. Both were concealed by the span of cedars running along the bottom of the rise and the only evidence of either from where he stood was a scattering of hay lingering over the tractor path leading down from the house. Beyond where it turned towards the paddock's gate, a footpath led through a two-acre stretch of hardwoods — mostly maples and birch — which dead-ended at the creek that bordered her property. It was, in fact, the same creek that eventually wound its way past his parents' old place some twenty kilometres southwest of there on its way towards Lake Rosseau and this had seemed a marvel to him on the day, almost three years ago, when he'd first discovered that.

So the creek, more than the barn, was on Deacon's mind as he made his way down the rutted tractor path, thinking maybe he'd take a walk out there just to pass the time. He'd only made it halfway to the cedars when he heard a horse's nicker, which seemed strange since Laney never left her horse out when she was at work. It hastened his pace and sure enough, when he came past the cedars he could see her red-and-white striped pick-up truck backed halfway through the paddock's gate. It had a trailer hitched behind it and it was obvious that Laney had just released her quarter horse, Daisy, from the same. The mare was canter-ing about, kicking up her hind legs, which she always did after a long trip, and Laney's German shepherd, Sarge, was chasing after, nipping playfully at the horse's hind hooves.

Then there was Laney too, stepping out of the trailer, carry-ing a shovelful of manure.

She was wearing chaps and a cowboy hat, boots and a shirt, the latter bright red and spun with a lasso design over its breast, so Deacon knew she must have just got back from a rodeo. She was calling, "Sarge, cut it out!" and the dog took a hard turn, hurrying back towards her with its head lowered, penitent. It must have caught sight of Deacon, or maybe just smelled his smoke, for all of a sudden it stopped mid-stride with its head cocked towards him before letting out a sharp bark. That was enough to get Laney's attention and she turned, seeing Deacon too.

Deacon offered her an awkward wave and she responded by turning her back on him and continuing along towards the manure pile she kept beside the barn. But a few minutes later she was smiling at him as she parked her truck alongside his Jeep and though it was a cautious smile, it seemed to bode well for him, as did the first thing she said while she was opening the driver-side door.

"It's funny, but I was just thinking of you."

Sarge had since curled up at Deacon's feet, which was the dog's way of begging for a rub. Deacon had obliged by bending so he could scratch it behind the ears, as happy for the distraction as he was with the way Laney had greeted him.

"Me?" he asked, about all he could muster.

"Well, about something the chief said, anyway."

"How's that?"

She was looking at him with her lips smunched, like maybe she thought she'd said too much already, but then still she answered, "He said he's about had it with George Cleary."

Him and me both, Deacon was thinking but instead he asked, "Why'd he say that?"

"You got me. Must have had something to do with Byron Chance, I guess."

"Byron Chance?"

"You know him?"

Deacon did but only because he was on the revised list of eight people who were still unaccounted for after the flood. All he really knew about Byron was that he drove a truck for the town — a water truck in the summer and a snowplough in the winter — and lived alone on High Falls Road. He said as much to Laney and she replied:

"Well, he's been found now. Except it wasn't the flood that killed him. It was the claw end of a hammer."

"What?"

"That's what the coroner's report indicates, anyway. A hiker found his body up in the woods a klick from his house. Since he lives up on High Falls Road, I guess they figured he'd died when his house was washed away in the flood."

"But he didn't."

"No, it was the claw end of a hammer that killed him, like I said. They found it beside the body, though there wasn't much left of that, since Byron had been there for going onto three months."

"What does he have to do with George Cleary?"

"You got me. All I know is that I was the first on the scene, and when Marchand came to look at his remains, he got all agitated. He was muttering something under his breath about another goddamned increasingly savage, and apparently random, murder and that's when he said he'd about had it with George Cleary. I asked him what he meant and he told me —"

Pausing there again and giving Deacon a sideways glance, as if she wasn't sure if she should tell him, and then barging on anyway.

"He told me, 'You're going to have to ask your boyfriend *Deke* about that.'"

Looking up at him again, this time full faced. It was the first time she'd looked him in the eyes since she'd ghosted him and though he'd have liked nothing better than to meet her eyes with a similarly bold address, his courage suddenly failed him and he looked away.

"That mean anything to you?"

Deacon shook his head, even though it meant plenty. But what was really on his mind was how Marchand had referenced another increasingly savage, and apparently random, murder. It meant Dylan must have given Marchand a copy of *No Quarter* too and why the chief would withhold that information had Deacon wondering what else he might have kept from him.

"You want to tell me what's going on?" Laney was asking.

She'd asked him practically the same question, three years before, after she dropped by the bunkie to invite Deacon to a party at the Griffin Pub to celebrate Marchand being made chief of police. Deacon had begged off, telling her Jean had asked him to take Tawyne to his drum circle, an obvious lie and one she hadn't believed for a second.

"It's because Dylan'll be there, isn't it," she'd said, not so much a question as an accusation.

"I don't know what you're talking about," he'd blurted, a little too emphatically to fool her.

"Because I know something's going on between you two. You want to finally tell me what that is?"

It was the last thing she'd said before ghosting him and even now he could feel himself sliding towards the disembodied gape with which he'd answered her. It took a mountain of will to snap himself out of that and when he looked back up he was expecting her to have turned her back on him in a huff and be walking away, which is what she'd done then.

But she wasn't looking so much angry as she was concerned.

"You look like you could use a cup of tea," she said. "Why don't I put on a pot and then you can tell me all about it."

I t all came pouring out while Laney was sipping at her cup and Deacon was letting his grow cold on the kitchen table in front of him.

He'd started with getting the call from Dylan about Ronald Crane and proceeded from there, intending to leave out only the matter of Rain, for he had no idea how to account for her involvement without making the story sound more implausible than it already was, a ploy that lasted all of about two sentences.

"But I thought you were at Rain Meadows's house that night," she interjected with a quizzical frown the moment after he'd said Dylan left him that first message ten years ago while he was in the shower in his apartment. She was looking at him as she might at a suspected perp handcuffed in one of the station's interview rooms and Deacon knew right then and there she must have been conducting her own investigation these past few months. Could be she'd talked to Rain and if she'd talked to Rain that meant she probably knew almost as much about what had happened as Deacon. That and the look on her face were telling him that the next lie out of his mouth would also be his last, at least as far as Laney was concerned.

"That's right," he said, starting over again. "I was at Rain's house when I heard the first siren, just after midnight."

After that he kept strictly to the truth, Laney listening in quiet deliberation, biting her lip and not saying a word until Deacon came to the part where he outlined his suspicion that it had been Dylan who'd killed the Wanes and started the forest fire that had burnt down half of Mesaquakee.

"I knew it!" she exclaimed, which didn't come as much of a surprise to Deacon. She'd always had her own suspicions and it was, point of fact, her frustration over Deacon's refusal to so much as talk about them which had led to her ghosting him. Such a load of grief he'd caused himself for not telling her the truth right from the start and he was still thinking about what a fool he'd been when she prodded his arm, coaxing, "Well, don't stop now."

She wouldn't interrupt him again until Deacon was describing the photo of him and Grace in bed that Marchand had shown him.

"But I know it was Grace who killed Baby Rose," he said, his voice cracking through a lump in his throat and tears welling in his eyes, thinking about how Crystal's unborn child dying had felt to him like his mother dying all over again.

He'd already told her about how Grace had drugged him and how they'd ended up in bed, and he hadn't been able to look at Laney ever since, fearing that whatever reproachful glare she might have lying in wait for him would shatter him to bits.

"She really messed you up bad, didn't she?" Laney then said, her tone not bearing a hint of reproach, not really bearing much emotion at all.

Deacon then did look over at her and was startled to find that there was quite a lot more than a hint of reproach in her pointed glare, telling him in no uncertain terms that he'd once messed *her* up, maybe just as bad.

"Boy, do I ever know what that feels like," she added, driving the point home.

But there was a trace of a smile prodding at the corners of her lips so he knew she'd mostly forgiven him. She seemed to want him to know that too, for she was quick to change the subject.

"But," she said, "it could have just as likely been Dylan who killed Baby Rose. He was, after all, practically living at his parents' place, helping take care of his mom. You said Crystal spent Christmas there. Maybe he switched her pills then and Grace really is innocent."

Given his own feelings on the matter, that seemed rather unlikely to Deacon. But he wasn't in much of a mood to argue and managed to croak out a rather unconvincing "You might just be right about that."

"Makes sense since he left you practically the same message after he killed Ronald Crane."

"Except he didn't kill Ronald Crane," Deacon countered.

"What do you mean? Of course he did."

Shaking his head, Deacon told her, "As far as I know, a boy named Jody Stokes killed Ronald Crane, just like Emma Dupuis killed Reinhold Kranich in the book."

"You don't say," Laney said, deliberating upon that.

"You know something about Jody Stokes?" Deacon asked.

He hadn't quite figured out how to fit Jody into the story and so hadn't said a word about him until just then. Laney had gone back to biting her lip and that gave Deacon every indication that she was withholding something from him.

"No. I mean — I don't know him, per se," she finally said. "It's just something Rain told me when I talked to her."

Adding to that confession a sideways glance, as if she was embarrassed to admit she had in fact been talking to Deacon's ex behind his back.

"And what's that?" Deacon offered, letting her off the hook. It seemed the least he could do.

"She said what Dylan did, killing the Wanes and the Swansons and all the rest, and for that matter, even giving you *No Quarter*, was really just a . . . distraction."

"A distraction?" The question came out pinched, thinking about how a . . . distraction had figured so prominently in his own ruminations on the matter of Dylan's twin climaxes.

"She said that whatever endgame Dylan is playing at doesn't have anything to do with any of that, that it's really about something else entirely."

"And did she tell you what?"

"A boy with blood on his cheek."

"A boy like Jody Stokes."

"Could be. Whoever it is, Rain said the real story is all about him, and only him."

"What'd she mean by that?"

"She didn't say. Only that we'd find out soon enough."

"That so?"

"That's what she said."

"And did she, perchance, tell you how she came about this information?"

"She did."

"So?"

"She made me promise if you ever asked not to tell you. Said it'd just get you all in a . . . *tizzy* was the word she used."

She was probably right about that so Deacon let it slide.

"You don't think it might have something to do with *My Brother's Keeper?*" Laney then asked after neither had said a word for a few breaths.

It didn't come as much of a surprise to Deacon that she'd reference one of George's books, since he knew Dylan had introduced her to his grandfather's fictions right after she'd joined the force, eight years ago. She'd read them all and after she'd learned Marchand had shot a man named René Descartes, she couldn't help but notice more than a few similarities between George's books and what was happening in Tildon. It was, in fact, the reason she'd first asked Deacon out.

Why she'd reference *My Brother's Keeper* in particular wasn't so clear, though, and so Deacon asked, "Why would you say that?"

"Because of the note the RCMP found pinned to Crystal's body at the Swanson place."

"They found a note?" he asked.

"Ain't no turning back now," she said, *"for either of us."*

The blood seeming to turn to cement in Deacon's veins, hearing Laney speaking the answer William had given his younger brother when the latter had asked why he'd killed their pa instead of simply running away, like they'd planned. Knowing *My Brother's Keeper* was more a confession on George's part than a fiction, it had

385

always seemed to Deacon an even clearer declaration of George's resolve than the Whitman quote he'd used at the beginning of *The Road Ahead*.

Laney seemed to have reached the same conclusion, for she was then saying, "So I guess that means it's probably not over yet."

"I wouldn't bet on it."

She thought about that for a moment and then, snapping herself back to task, prompted, "Well, go on then."

There wasn't much else to tell. Deacon told her so and she stood up from the couch, stretching her arms and apparently catching a whiff of something foul.

"Oh god, I stink like horse," she said, though that was one of the things Deacon had always loved about her. "I'm going to go grab a shower. Why don't you roll us something in the meanwhile. It's where it always is."

By "it" she meant her weed and by "where it always is" she meant the drawer beside her bed. The only time Laney ever smoked weed was before they had sex because, she'd told him, it helped a woman relax, which had always been a problem for her, and as he followed her up the stairs Deacon couldn't help but think that things were definitely looking up. There were condoms in the drawer too — another good sign — but while he rolled the joint he wasn't so much thinking about Laney as he was about Dylan; how if it hadn't been for him, Deacon likely wouldn't be sitting here now on Laney's bed, his hopes for a better future perfectly rendered in the gentle hum of her voice coming through the wall — her singing some old-timey country jig in the shower as she so often did.

While he waited for Laney to return, he got to thinking maybe that was Dylan's plan all along, though his reasons for such seemed as unfathomable as the rest. Then he got to thinking about what Rain had said about the story really only

386

being all about a boy with blood on his cheek, could very well have been Jody Stokes, and how they'd find out how he fit into the scheme of things soon enough. If George's books were any indication, whatever the future held was bound to be just as bloody as the past, maybe even more so. That thought got Deacon thinking about Byron Chance, the latest increasingly savage, and apparently random, murder. The second of those, after Reinhold Kranich, had appeared in the fourth chapter of George's *No Quarter* and there were twelve distinct killings by the end, four of them entire families. If the Wanes were the second after Ronald Crane and Lenny the third, the Swansons the fourth and now Byron Chance the fifth — and Dylan really was hoping to bring his grandfather's last book to life — that'd mean he wasn't even halfway done yet.

And with a very real-life cold-blooded killer presently at large . . .

A thought that sent him back all over again to the text that had started it all, though it seemed to him, knowing what he did, that Dylan's warning might very well have been a trifle premature.

Maybe, he was thinking, *it's only really beginning right now.*

In Memory Of

John Hunter, Sharon Riis & Rod Norris

With Extra Special Thanks to

Emily Schultz, for playing along

David Caron, for signing the cheques

Peter Norman & David Marsh
for keeping their eyes peeled

Samantha Chin, Elham Ali, Aymen Saidane
and all the other fine folks at ECW

My sister Jennifer and her husband, Jay,
for their "Origin Story"

David Birnbaum, as always

&

Tanja, obviously